TAIWAN AND VIETNAM:
LANGUAGE, LITERACY AND NATIONALISM

Wi-vun T. CHIUNG (GS. TS. Tưởng Vi Văn)

TAIWAN AND VIETNAM:
LANGUAGE, LITERACY AND NATIONALISM

First published in July 2020

Published by Asian A-tsiu International
http://www.atsiu.com/
& Center for Vietnamese Studies, NCKU
http://cvs.twl.ncku.edu.tw/

Copyright © 2020 by Wi-vun T. CHIUNG

ISBN 978-986-98887-0-7 (hardcover)

Printed in Taiwan

CONTENTS

FOREWORD 1

Dr. NGUYỄN Văn Hiệp
Director, Institute of Linguistics
Vietnamese Academy of Social Sciences, VIETNAM

This book of professor Wi-vun CHIUNG could be regarded as a chronicle of Taiwan, the island state that has special relations with Mainland China and has suffered vicissitudes in history, as it used to happen in Korea, Japan and Vietnam.

This book provides many scientific information on Taiwanese language, literature and culture, especially the revitalization and Romanization of Taiwanese language, which is linguistically different from Mandarin Chinese.

The author has portrayed a colorful picture of the island Taiwan. He compared Taiwan with Japan, Korea and Vietnam with regard to the preservation and development of language, literature and culture.

The author has pointed out that the KMT regime considered Taiwan as a Chinese territory divided by geography, so KMT adopted wrong and cruel policy on Taiwan's languages, literature and culture to prevent Taiwanese people from being identify themselves as Taiwanese.

The author also surveyed the efforts of Taiwanese people to preserve and develop their language and literature in order to retain their national identity. For example, the efforts on Romanization movement, which is still on the half way to success. Or the successful reforms on politics and education in recent decades, which have promoted Taiwan to a modern society with its unique features in the globalization era.

The cultural and economic exchanges between Taiwan and Vietnam have significantly increased in recent decades, this book thus provides valuable references for Taiwanese and Vietnamese people to understand each other better and further to share their experiences in maintaining their own cultural characteristics.

This book also provides valuable knowledge about Taiwanese and Vietnamese from the perspectives of linguistics and orthographies. They are helpful for learning Vietnamese and Taiwanese languages.

Professor Wi-vun CHIUNG is not only a prestigious scholar, but also an enthusiastic patriot. In addition to academic research, he promotes Taiwanese language and literature in order to remain national identity of Taiwan. He also promotes academic exchange between Vietnamese and Taiwanese scholars through many practical events such as international conferences or workshops held by Center for Vietnamese Studies at National Cheng Kung University.

In short, I appreciate and admire what Professor Wi-vun CHIUNG has done so far. I sincerely introduce this book to readers, especially those in Vietnam.

FOREWORD 2

Professor NGÔ Văn Lệ
Former president
University of Social Sciences & Humanities-TPHCM, VIETNAM

Taiwan and Vietnam have had strong relationships in the field of economy and culture for more than 30 years. Taiwanese enterprises have constantly invested in Vietnam, particularly in Ho Chi Minh metropolitan areas over decades. However, mutual understanding regarding history, language, literature and culture between Vietnam and Taiwan is still very limited.

The author Wi-vun CHIUNG is a Taiwanese researcher with many in-depth research results about Vietnam in the fields of language, culture and history. With over 20 years of research on Vietnam, professor Chiung has great contributions to introducing Vietnam to Taiwanese readers. In particular, his former book entitled "Vietnamese Spirit: Language, Orthography and Anti-hegemony" published in Taiwanese and Chinese provide readers a comprehensive understanding of Vietnam.

This new book "Taiwan and Vietnam: Language, Literacy and Nationalism" in English is an overall survey of Vietnam and Taiwan from a perspective of comparative studies. In addition, this book also introduces and compares the history of language, orthography and literature in the Hanji cultural sphere, such as Vietnam, Taiwan, Korea and Japan. This book can be considered one of the rare publications introducing the history of language and literature of Taiwan to Vietnamese readers.

I sincerely introduce this book to readers as a valuable resource to learn about the historical development of language, literature and nationalism in Taiwan!

FOREWORD 3

Dr. Binh NGO
Director of the Vietnamese Language Program
Harvard University, USA

Prof. Wi-vun T. CHIUNG (Chiúⁿ Ûi-bûn / 蔣為文) is a distinguished scholar in the field of Taiwanese and Vietnamese studies. His new book Taiwan and Vietnam: language, literacy and nationalism is an insightful and original work on comparative study of Taiwan and Vietnam in many areas, including history, linguistics and sociolinguistics.

This book is divided into eleven chapters. The first chapter introduces the history of Vietnamese-Taiwanese economic and cultural ties, Vietnamese studies in Vietnam and Taiwan, and Taiwanese studies in Taiwan and Vietnam, as well as how they were established and developed. This chapter also points out the importance of the comparative studies of Vietnam and Taiwan.

Chapter two discusses the historical background of Chinese character usage in Japan, Korea, Vietnam and Taiwan and the creation of each country's own writing systems at different periods of time in the past. The passage which deals with the Mandarin Chinese used in Taiwan and the romanized Taiwanese writing system from the perspective of the Taiwanese is exceptionally informative.

The third chapter is a continuation of the second, with a focus on romanized writing systems in Vietnam and Taiwan. The author argues that romanized Taiwanese script, along with Chinese characters, should be adopted as Taiwan's national writing system.

Chapter four compares the phonetic and writing systems of Chinese, Vietnamese and Taiwanese, which is invaluable from the standpoint of both contrastive analysis and language pedagogy.

Chapter five deals with the difficulties that learners of Chinese characters encounter, and with the advantages of a romanized Vietnamese writing system.

The sixth chapter introduces the diverse ethnic and linguistic history of Taiwan, including how and when different immigrant groups arrived from mainland China, resulting in the complex ethnic relations we see in Taiwan today. The author also examines the relationship between the mother tongue and ethnic identity of different groups in Taiwan based on survey data.

Chapter seven covers the origin and the eventual romanization of Taiwan's writing system, which leads into the author's proposed plan for language learning in Taiwan.

In chapter eight, the author argues that romanized Taiwanese script should be regarded as part of the intangible cultural heritage of Taiwan based on its linguistic and sociolinguistic origins.

In chapter nine, Chiung addresses the controversy over the terms Taiwanese (language) versus Southern Min (dialect). The author proposes that the term Lán-lâng-ōe (咱人語) be used for the dialect spoken in Southeastern China, Taiwan and several Southeast Asian countries, and that a prefix indicating the region where the respective version of the dialect is spoken be added when relevant.

The tenth chapter introduces different ways of writing Taiwanese. Based on the statistical results of the survey, the author concludes that most Taiwanese people who write using Chinese characters do not consider it necessary to learn an additional writing system. However, the author believes romanized Taiwanese script should be adopted due to its being easy to learn.

The last chapter delves into which criteria should be considered for proficiency tests in Taiwanese. This is very helpful from the perspective of Taiwanese language teaching methodology.

Professor Chiung's book is well structured and covers a wide variety of topics within Vietnamese and Taiwanese studies with a focus on linguistic issues. Many chapters contain appendices that will prove extremely useful to those interested in learning about a particular aspect of Vietnamese or Taiwanese linguistic, historical and social studies. The book makes a significant contribution to the field.

PREFACE

Why Taiwan and Vietnam? Most works of my research are related to comparative studies of Taiwan and Vietnam. Someone may be curious to know why I chose Vietnam to compare with Taiwan?

I was a promoter of Taiwanese languages before I went to graduate school in the USA. I was trying to save the Taiwanese languages which were suppressed by the Chinese monolingual policy of the Chinese KMT regime in Taiwan. I did not know much about Vietnam at that time. My limited impressions about Vietnam were a war and the orthographic transformation from Han characters to Roman scripts. I did not have the chance to get to know the Vietnamese people until I started my graduate studies.

Taiwan and Vietnam share a similar historical experience: that is, both used to be invaded and colonized by the Chinese Empire. As a consequence, Han characters were adopted in Taiwan and Vietnam. Although ancient China had occupied Vietnam for a thousand years and consequently had great influence on the Vietnamese culture, Vietnam has created its own culture with distinct characteristics. How could Vietnam successfully retain their language and national identity? How could Vietnam have so amazingly replaced Han characters with Vietnamese Romanization? In contrast, Roman scripts such as Sinkang Manuscripts or Pe̍h-ōe-jī were the first writing systems that appeared in Taiwan. However, Han characters, which came after Roman scripts, have become the dominant orthography in current Taiwanese society. What are the factors driving different outcomes in Taiwan and Vietnam? Will Taiwan have the potential to revive Taiwanese languages or to replace Han characters with Roman scripts? Those questions stayed in my mind while I was doing my research.

All the papers collected in this book try to answer these questions from different perspectives. The papers were originally presented in conferences, journals or book chapters. They were appropriately revised and updated to make a more consistent and systematic book. I expect this book to provide readers a better understanding of language, literacy and nationalism in Taiwan and Vietnam.

Wi-vun Taiffalo CHIUNG
National Cheng Kung University, TAIWAN

1

Features and Prospects in Comparative Studies of Vietnam and Taiwan

1. Introduction

Marriages between persons from different countries have become more and more common in the globalization era. Taiwan is no exception to this phenomenon. The international marriages between Taiwan and foreign countries especially Southeast Asian countries generally started in the early 1990s and reached its highest tide in the early 2000s. According to the statistics of Taiwan's National Immigration Agency, Ministry of Interior, foreign spouses in Taiwan numbered 539,090 in August 2018[1]. These foreign nationals account for 2.28% of Taiwan's total population[2]. Among the foreign spouses, many were from China (356,874), followed by Vietnam (103,923), then Indonesia (29,853), Thailand (8,822), Philippines (9,484), Cambodia (4,317), Japan (4,870), Korea (1,682) and other countries together (19,265). In general, about 1/5 of marriage number is contributed by the foreign spouses in Taiwan's recent decade[3]. Among the Southeast Asian countries Vietnam is the major source country of foreign spouses. Among the Vietnamese spouses, most of them are female, and only 1.36% or 1,412 persons are male.

In addition to international marriages between Taiwanese and Vietnamese citizens, economic and educational exchanges between the two countries have also significantly increased in the two recent decades.

---

[1] Data provided by Taiwan's National Immigration Agency available at
<https://www.immigration.gov.tw/ct.asp?xItem=1353426&ctNode=29699&mp=1>

[2] By September of year 2018, the amount of Taiwan's total population is 23,577,488 according to Taiwan's recent updated statistics of the Department of Household Registration of MOI, available at < https://www.ris.gov.tw/app/portal/346 >

[3] Data available at <http://www.immigration.gov.tw/public/Attachment/212016212134.xls>

In December 1986, the Communist Party of Vietnam approved the Economic Renovation Policy (Đổi mới), which was followed by a series of attractive economic open policies for foreign investors. Taiwanese businessmen were some of the earliest foreign investors to come right after Vietnam's economic renovation policy (Shiu 2003:124-127). A few years later, the Taipei Economic and Cultural Office (TECO) was established in Hanoi, Vietnam, in November 1992 to promote mutual cooperation between the two countries. Thereafter, economic activities between Taiwan and Vietnam have flourished tremendously. Soon Taiwan became one of the top three investors in Vietnam.

According to the statistics of Taiwan's Ministry of Education, there are a total of 22,366 international students in Taiwan by 2010 (Oo and Tan 2010). The number reached 106,680 by 2018. They are either studying for accredited degrees or enrolled in non-credited language courses. Among the international students studying for undergraduate degrees, the top three countries in numbers are Malaysia, Vietnam, and Korea (South), respectively. As for master's programs, the top three countries are Vietnam, Indonesia, and Malaysia. In doctoral programs, the top three are India, Vietnam, and Indonesia. Overall, students from Vietnam are among the top three countries to study in Taiwan.[4]

In addition to the relations mentioned above, Taiwan and Vietnam share a similar historical experience, that is, as former colonies. Vietnam used to be colonized by Japan, France, and China. However, Vietnam eventually established a culturally and politically independent country in 1945. Although China had occupied Vietnam for a thousand years and consequently had great influence on the Vietnamese culture, Vietnam has created its own culture with distinct characteristics. Taiwan used to be colonized by Japan and China too. Although Taiwan is currently politically independent from China, "national identity" is still a controversial issue in Taiwan. To some extent, Vietnam is probably a good model for Taiwan with regard to nation-building.

Since both Taiwan and Vietnam have a lot to learn from each other with respect to economy, culture, education, and anti-colonialism, it is inevitable to form comparative studies of Taiwan and Vietnam. The purpose of this paper is to survey current development of comparative studies of Vietnam and Taiwan, and provide further perspective on this area of study's future development.

---

[4] There are a total of 2,592 Vietnamese students in Taiwan in the year 2009-2010. The number increased to 14,051 Vietnamese students in 2018.

2. Vietnam studies in Vietnam and Taiwan

2.1. Vietnam studies in Vietnam

To some extent, initial area studies were connected to colonialism. Colonizers have always investigated their colonies in order to gain the maximum profits from them. This was no exception in the cases of Vietnam and Taiwan. In the case of Vietnam, investigation on Vietnam from a Western perspective started during the period of French occupation of Vietnam (Vũ 2004:633-634). The well-known 7 (Trường Viễn Đông Bác cổ Pháp; EFEO, thereafter) was established by French colonizers in Hanoi in 1900. Vietnam, as part of French Indochina, was considered as a subject for colonial research.

Vietnam studies from Vietnam's perspective were not well planned until Vietnam's independence after World War II. Tổ Việt ngữ, the earliest Vietnamese language program established by the Đại học Tổng hợp Hà Nội [5] (Hanoi Comprehensive University, HCU) in 1956 could be considered the beginning of Vietnam studies. A decade later, Khoa Tiếng Việt, the Department of Vietnamese Language, was officially established by HCU in 1968. The main purpose of this department was to teach Vietnamese language and culture to foreigners. Many instructors in this department were sent overseas to teach Vietnamese in foreign countries. This department is currently renamed as Khoa Việt Nam Học và Tiếng Việt[6] or Department of Vietnam Studies and Vietnamese Language, which is part of the University of Social Sciences and Humanities [7], Vietnam National University-Hanoi. It offers BA degree in Vietnamese studies to both Vietnamese and foreign students. It also provides non-credit language courses to foreign students.

In addition, Graduate Institute of Vietnam Studies and Scientific Development [8], which was directly established by the Vietnam National University-Hanoi in 2004, offers Master's degree in Vietnam studies. This institute was formerly known as Center for Vietnam Studies and Cultural

---

[5] Nowadays, it was renamed as Đại học Quốc gia Hà Nội, Vietnam National University-Hanoi.

[6] It is located at Nhà B7 Bis, phố Trần Đại Nghĩa, phường Bách Hoa. For details, refer to the official guide to the department at <http://ussh.edu.vn/faculty-vietnamese-studies-and-language /1754>

[7] Trường Đại học Khoa học Xã hội và Nhân văn Hà Nội. Official website at <http://ussh.edu.vn/>

[8] Viện Việt Nam học và Khoa học phát triển in Vietnamese. It is located at Nhà A, Tầng 2, 336 Nguyễn Trãi, Thanh Xuân. Readers may refer to its official website at <http://ivides.vnu.edu.vn/ >

Exchange[9], which was established in 1989 by HCU.

Accompanied with the economic renovation of 1986, the demand for learning Vietnamese language and studying its society by foreigners has increased since then. Consequently, more and more universities established centers or departments related to Vietnamese language and Vietnam studies. Currently, the major schools providing Vietnamese studies programs or departments and their descriptions are as follows:

Department of Vietnam Studies[10], Hanoi University was officially established in 2004 in order to recruit international students. Students are trained in Vietnamese and subjects regarding Vietnam studies. It offers BA degree in Vietnam studies. The students in this department are mainly from China, Japan and Korea. Prior to 2004, the department was known as Center for Teaching Vietnamese to Foreigners, which provides non-credit Vietnamese classes for foreigners.

Department of Linguistics[11] is another unit related to Vietnam studies at the University of Social Sciences and Humanities, Vietnam National University, Hanoi. The department specializes in linguistic studies, including Vietnamese and many other domestic and foreign languages. It offers BA, MA and PhD degree for both domestic and foreign languages. The major foreign students are from China and Japan.

In addition to Vietnam National University and Hanoi University, Vietnam Academy of Social Sciences[12] (VASS) plays an important role in Vietnam studies too. All researchers at VASS are Vietnamese. Most institutes at VASS are highly related to Vietnamese studies, such as Institute of Linguistics[13], Institute of Lexicography and Vietnamese Encyclopaedia[14], Institute of Han-Nom Studies[15], Institute of Literature[16], Institute of Cultural Studies[17], etc.

All the institutes and universities mentioned above are located in Hanoi,

---

[9] Trung tâm Nghiên cứu Việt Nam và Giao lưu Văn hoá.
[10] Khoa Việt Nam Học in Vietnamese. It is located at Km 9, đường Nguyễn Trãi, quận Thanh Xuân. Readers may refer to its offical website at <http://web.hanu.vn/vnh>
[11] Ngôn ngữ học in Vietnamese. Readers may refer to its offical website at <http://ussh.edu.vn/faculty-linguistics/1742>
[12] Viện Khoa học xã hội Việt Nam in Vietnamese. Official website at <http://www.vass.gov.vn>
[13] Viện Ngôn ngữ học in Vietnamese. Official website at <http://www.vienngonnguhoc.gov.vn/>
[14] Viện Từ điển học và Bách khoa thư Việt Nam in Vietnamese. Official website at <http://bachkhoatoanthu.vass.gov.vn/>
[15] Viện Hán Nôm in Vietnamese. Official website at <http://www.hannom.org.vn>
[16] Viện Văn học in Vietnamese. Official website at < http://www.vienvanhoc.vass.gov.vn/ >
[17] Viện Nghiên cứu văn hoá in Vietnamese. official website at <http://www.ncvanhoa.org.vn>

which is in northern Vietnam. In southern Vietnam, the University of Social Sciences and Humanities[18], Vietnam National University-Ho Chi Minh City plays an important role in Vietnamese studies. There are departments related to Vietnam studies, such as Department of Vietnamese Studies [19] and Department of Literature and Language[20], etc. The Department of Vietnamese Studies offers both BA and MA degrees to both Vietnamese and foreign students.

2.2. Vietnam studies in Taiwan

Vietnam studies in Taiwan was initiated in the late 1980s and developed in 1990s under the Go-South policy (南進政策) of Taiwan's former president Lee Teng-hui (Lee 2003; Shiu 2003). The so-called Go-South policy is mainly an economic policy promoting economic cooperation among Taiwan and Southeast Asian countries. In 2016, a new policy called "the New Southbound Policy" (新南向政策) was adopted by the President Tsai Ing-wen to enhance cooperation and exchanges between Taiwan and 18 countries in Southeast Asia, South Asia and Australasia.

In the 1990s, the economy in China was rapidly flourishing. It attracted more and more Taiwanese businessmen to invest in China. To avoid potential political and economic risks caused by overwhelming investment in China, Taiwan's Go-South was developed in the 1990s.

In 1994, the Center for Southeast Asian Studies (1994-2001) was established by Taiwan's Academia Sinica. It was the first center to promote area studies focusing on Southeast Asia. Vietnam, as a member of Southeast Asian countries, was therefore considered a research subject for the center. The center was later expanded as Center for Asia-Pacific Area Studies[21] (CAPAS). At present, CAPAS is still the major center carrying out research on Vietnam and other Southeast Asian countries.

In addition to Academia Sinica, there are some major universities conducting research or teaching project relating to Vietnam studies, as follows:

In 1996, the Graduate Institute of Southeast Asia Studies was established by Tamkang University in Taipei. It offered MA degree and was the first institute to promote Southeast Asian studies on campus. The institute was later combined

---

[18] Trường Đại học Khoa học Xã hội và Nhân văn TP. Hồ Chí Minh. Official website at <http://www.hcmussh.edu.vn>

[19] Khoa Việt Nam Học in Vietnamese. Official website at <http://www.vns.edu.vn/>

[20] Khoa Văn học và Ngôn ngữ in Vietnamese. Official website at <http://khoavanhoc-ngonngu.edu.vn>

[21] 亞太區域研究專題中心 Official website at <http://www.rchss.sinica.edu.tw/capas/>

with Graduate Institute of Japanese Studies and renamed Graduate Institute of Asian Studies[22] in 2009.

Another university to promote Southeast Asian studies is National Chi Nan University in central Taiwan. Center for Southeast Asian Studies and Graduate Institute of Southeast Asian Studies[23] were established in 1995 and 1997, respectively. It was further reorganized as Department of Southeast Asian Studies in 2015. It currently offers BA, MA and PhD degrees.

In addition to Tamkang University and Chi Nan University, National Kaohsiung University of Applied Sciences (KUAS[24]), National Cheng Kung University (NCKU[25]), and National University of Kaohsiung (NUK) in southern Taiwan, also carry out research projects on Vietnam. In 2003, Vietnam Economic Research Center[26] was established by the National Kaohsiung University of Applied Sciences to conduct research projects on Vietnam's economy. In 2008, Department of East Asian Languages and Literature[27] was founded by the National University of Kaohsiung.

As for NCKU, Center for Vietnamese Studies[28] was officially founded in 2013. Prior to the establishment of the Center, research projects were mainly carried out by researchers in different departments, such as Department of Taiwanese Literature[29], Department of Chinese Literature, Department of History, and Graduate Institute of Political Economics.

In recent years, some courses on Vietnam are regularly offered at NCKU, such as "Vietnamese Language[30]," "Vietnamese Society and Culture[31]," "Language and Literature: A Comparative Study of Taiwan and Vietnam[32]," and "Han Literature in Vietnam," etc. NCKU is the first university that regularly offers accredited Vietnamese classes to college students in Taiwan. In addition, with financial supports from Taiwan's Ministry of Education, a project to collect

---

[22] 淡江大學亞洲研究所 <http://www.tiix.tku.edu.tw/>
[23] 國立暨南大學東南亞學系 <http://www.dseas_anth.ncnu.edu.tw/main.php>
[24] 國立高雄應用科技大學 <https://www.nkust.edu.tw/>
[25] 國立成功大學 <http://www.ncku.edu.tw/>
[26] 越南經濟研究中心 <http://www.kuas.edu.tw/files/11-1000-59.php>
[27] 高雄大學東亞語文學系 <https://deal.nuk.edu.tw/>
[28] CVS at <http://cvs.twl.ncku.edu.tw/>
[29] 台灣文學系<http:///www.twl.ncku.edu.tw>
[30] Conversational Vietnamese is offered in two semesters, two credit hours in each semester. The course has been offered every one or two years since 2007. It is taught by Wi-vun Chiung with Vietnamese assistants.
[31] It is a course of two credit hours offered by Wi-vun Chiung every one or two years since 2004.
[32] It is a graduate course of three credit hours offered by Wi-vun Chiung every 2 years since 2008.

Vietnamese books was carried out in 2009. So far, around two thousand books written in Vietnamese have been collected. Although the quantity is not large, it is currently the largest collection in Taiwan. In addition, International Vietnamese Proficiency Test[33] was designed and organized by Center for Vietnamese Studies at NCKU twice every year since 2016.

In 2006, the Vietnamese students at NCKU organized the Vietnamese Students Association [34] (VSA), the first Vietnamese student organization in Taiwan. Since 2007, VSA has hosted Vietnam Cultural Week every year.

Regarding Vietnamese teaching, some other schools also offer non-credit or accredited Vietnamese classes in recent years. They are: Wenzao Ursuline College of Languages in Kaohsiung, National University of Kaohsiung, National Chengchi University in Taipei, National Taiwan University in Taipei, and Chung Yuan Christian University in Taichung, etc. Some private or NGO organizations also offer Vietnamese classes from time to time, such as Taiwanese Romanization Association[35], Association for Taiwanese and Vietnamese Cultural Exchange[36], and Pearl S. Buck Foundation[37], etc. To date, all except NCKU all Vietnamese classes have been taught by part-time teachers. The teachers are mainly Vietnamese immigrants or Vietnamese students in Taiwan. This fact shows that Taiwan is short of qualified Vietnamese teachers.

As time goes on, more and more researchers and graduate students have joined the academic circle of Southeast Asian studies. Annual Conference of Taiwan's Southeast Asia Studies[38] initiated by Academia Sinica in 1999 has become the most important of such annual conferences in Taiwan. In addition, Taiwan Association of Southeast Asian Studies[39], the first academic organization on Southeast Asian studies, was officially established in April 2005. Currently, there are around 100 members in the association. Furthermore, the Association for Taiwanese and Vietnamese Cultural Exchange, the first Vietnam-specific academic association, was established in December 2009.

Because economic and cultural exchange between Taiwan and Vietnam has rapidly increased, Vietnam is gradually becoming the major subject in Taiwan's

---

[33] For details, please refer to its website at <http://cvs.twl.ncku.edu.tw/ivpt/>

[34] 國立成功大學越南學生會 <https://duhocsinhdailoan.com/vi/>

[35] 台灣羅馬字協會 It was established in August 2001. Official website at <http://www.tlh.org.tw/>

[36] 台越文化協會 It was established in December 2009. Official website at <http://taioat.de-han.org/>

[37] 賽珍珠基金會 <http://www.psbf.org.tw>

[38] 台灣東南亞區域研究年度研討會

[39] 台灣東南亞學會 <https://www.taseas.org/>

Southeast Asian studies. For example, there were 17 research papers directly on Vietnam among the total of 88 papers presented in the 2010 Annual Conference of Taiwan's Southeast Asia Studies. They account for 19.3% of the presented papers.

To get a better picture of the development of Southeast Asian studies, we may take a look at the number of MA and PhD theses on Southeast Asian countries offered in recent years. The data is based on information found in the National Digital Library of Theses and Dissertations in Taiwan[40] as of September 30, 2010. Thesis/dissertation title and keyword were chosen as the search range. Names of Southeast Asian countries in Chinese characters were inputted for search. The statistics of MA and PhD theses are listed in Table 1. It shows that Vietnam is the country with the highest number of MA and PhD theses, accounting for 30.7% of all theses. As for their research topics, most theses/dissertations are related to Vietnamese immigrants and economic relations.

Table 1. Statistics of MA and PhD theses
on Southeast Asian countries (2010)

Countries	Quantity
Vietnam	442
Singapore	301
Thailand	174
Malaysia	161
Philippines	144
Indonesia	141
Myanmar	39
Cambodia	20
Lao	9
Timor-Leste	7
Brunei	0

Although more researchers and graduate students have joined the circle of Vietnam studies, there are still some difficulties to overcome. The first is probably researchers' Vietnamese language ability. Almost all Taiwanese researchers do not possess Vietnamese language ability. They always have to rely on interpreters or literatures in English. The major causes could be 1) Vietnamese language education is not well-planned in colleges, and 2) the researchers were not required

---

[40] 台灣博碩士論文知識加值系統 <http://ndltd.ncl.edu.tw>

to possess Vietnamese ability while they were graduate students. In my opinion, establishment of undergraduate level of department or program in Vietnamese language is necessary for solving this problem.

3. Taiwan studies in Taiwan and Vietnam

3.1. Taiwan studies in Taiwan

In the same way that Vietnam used to be a colony, Taiwan had also been colonized by several foreign colonial regimes. The first foreign regime was established by the Dutch people in the seventeenth century. It was followed by the Koxinga (鄭成功) regime and the Chinese Ch'ing (清) regime. Two centuries later, the sovereignty of Taiwan was transferred from the Chinese Ch'ing to Japan in 1895 as a consequence of the Sino-Japanese War (Chiung 2004). During the Japanese period, a great number of surveys and investigations about Taiwan's geography, census, ethnicity, languages and customs were carried out by the Japanese. Those investigations are still useful references and have been studied by researchers, even though they were originally for colonization purposes. Such reports include Japanese-Taiwanese Dictionary (日臺大辭典 1907), Taiwanese-Japanese Dictionary (臺日大辭典 1931), and Taiwanese Ethnography (台灣文化志 1928).

At the end of the World War II, Japanese forces surrendered to the Allied Forces. Chiang Kai-shek[41], the leader of the Chinese Nationalists (KMT[42] or *Kuomintang*) took over Taiwan and northern Vietnam on behalf of the Allied Powers under General Order No.1 of September 2, 1945 (Peng 1995:60-61; Chiung 2010). At the time, Chiang Kai-shek was fighting the Chinese Communist Party in Mainland China. In 1949, Chiang's troops were completely defeated and pursued by the Chinese Communists. At that time, Taiwan's national status was supposed to be dealt with by a peace treaty among the warring nations. However, because of his defeat in China, Chiang decided to occupy Taiwan under the excuse that "Taiwan was traditionally part of China." He planned to make use of Taiwan as a base from which he would fight back and retake Mainland China (Kerr 1992; Ong 1993; Peng 1995; Su 1980). Consequently, Chiang's political regime the

---

[41] 蔣介石 in Chinese. Tưởng Giới Thạch in Vietnamese.

[42] KMT (中國國民黨 Trung Quốc Quốc Dân Đảng) was the ruling party in Taiwan since 1945 until 2000, in which year *Chen Shui-bian*, the presidential candidate of opposition party Democratic Progressive Party was elected the new president. Thereafter, the KMT won the presidential election again in 2008, and has become the ruling party again since 2008.

Republic of China (R.O.C) was relocated and resurrected in Taiwan and has remained there since 1949.

After People's Republic of China (P.R.C.) was established in Mainland China, Chiang still asserted that R.O.C. was the only legitimate government of China. Because Taiwan was regarded as a base and a part of China in the viewpoint of Chiang, the Taiwanese people were not allowed to identify themselves as Taiwanese but only as Chinese (Ong 1993). To convert the Taiwanese people's identity into a Chinese identity, martial law was carried out from 1949 to 1987. Under the 38-year-long martial law, the Taiwanese were not allowed to organize any opposition party[43] or hold any national-level elections such as presidential or legislative elections. Besides these, the Taiwanese people did not have freedom of the press or mass media. The National Language Policy, or Mandarin Chinese-only policy, was adopted. Under the policy, the Taiwanese people were not allowed to speak their vernaculars in school and in public. Moreover, they were forced to learn Mandarin Chinese, Chinese history, Chinese geography and to identify themselves as Chinese through the national education system (Cheng 1996; Tiuⁿ 1996). Research on Taiwan was definitely forbidden in this period.

Taiwan studies were not allowed until the lifting of martial law. The call for Taiwan studies came with the movement of Taiwanization, which was initiated along with the rise of native political activities against Chinese KMT regime in the middle of 1980s. After a decade's efforts, the first college department on Taiwan studies eventually appeared in 1997, in which year the Department of Taiwan Literature[44] at Aletheia University, a private university, as well as the Graduate Institute of Taiwan Languages and Language Education[45] at National Hsinchu University of Education were established.

In 2000, the Department of Taiwanese Literature[46] at National Cheng Kung University was established. At present, the Department of Taiwanese Literature at NCKU is the only department offering BA, MA, PhD degrees in Taiwanese literature in Taiwan. Although the department was named Taiwanese literature, faculty research and teaching are not limited to literature, but also language, culture, and history.

During the ruling period (2000-2008) of former president Chen Shui-bian,

---

[43] Democratic Progressive Party (民主進步黨) was the first Taiwanese party during KMT era, which was not organized until September 28, 1986.

[44] 真理大學台灣文學系 <http://hl006.epage.au.edu.tw/bin/home.php>

[45] 新竹教育大學台灣語言與語文教育研究所 <http://www.nhcue.edu.tw/~gitll/>

[46] 國立成功大學台灣文學系 <http://www.twl.ncku.edu.tw>

many schools were urged and approved to found departments or graduate institutes relevant to Taiwanese studies. Currently, there are around 20 universities with this kind of department or institute. In general, their research fields are mainly in literature, languages, history, culture, anthropology, ethnicity, and geography.

Because Taiwan studies were regarded as political taboo, most researchers in Taiwan did not dare do it. Once the political restrictions were officially lifted in the 1990s, it soon attracted many of the new generation of Taiwanese students to join the circle. Consequently, Taiwan studies curriculum in most schools is usually planned for domestic students rather than for international students. This is the difference of Taiwanese studies in Taiwan from Vietnamese studies in Vietnam. In addition, because Mandarin Chinese has been adopted as the official language in Taiwan's schools for over sixty years, many of the younger generation of Taiwanese cannot speak or write fluently in languages other than Mandarin Chinese. As a result, most curricula are taught in Chinese rather than in Taiwanese. Moreover, many schools do not require that students who major in Taiwan studies learn Taiwanese language(s) (Chiung 2007:354-377). This is quite ironic!

3.2. Taiwan studies in Vietnam

In Vietnam, Taiwan studies came along with China studies in the early 1990s. In September 1993, the Center for Chinese Studies (CCS) at Vietnam Academy of Social Sciences was approved by the Vietnamese government. It reveals that the unfriendly relations between Vietnam and China after the 1979 border conflicts had improved. In addition, the rising economy in Taiwan and China is another factor effecting the establishment of CCS.

Taiwan, Hongkong, and Macao were considered as subjects for area studies under the framework of China studies in CCS. Therefore, a research branch called Studio for Taiwan, Hongkong and Macao Studies was established under CCS. The studio was later renamed as Studio for Taiwan Studies in 2001. Further, it was promoted to Center for Taiwan Studies (CTS) when CCS was promoted to Institute of Chinese Studies[47] in 2005. Currently, CTS is the only official center conducting research projects on Taiwan. Members in the center number less ten. Major concerns are issues on Taiwan's economy, transformation from rural to industrialized society, Vietnamese laborers and brides, and education.

In addition, Taiwan Education Center[48] was established at University of

---

[47] Viện Nghiên cứu Trung Quốc <http://vnics.org.vn/Default.aspx>
[48] 台灣教育中心 <https://www.fichet.org.tw/基金會活動/臺灣教育中心/>

Social Sciences and Humanities, Vietnam National University-Ho Chi Minh city, and at University of Foreign Languages, Vietnam National University-Hanoi, in 2008 and 2010, resepectively. The center was sponsored by Taiwan's Ministry of Education and run by the school's Department of Oriental Studies. The center mainly provides students information regarding studying abroad in Taiwan.

In addition to the centers mentioned above, some research projects related to Taiwan may be carried out by individual researchers in different schools or institutions. For example, the Institute of Northeast Asian Studies, Institute of Han Nom Studies, and Institute of Linguistics at Vietnam Academy of Social Sciences. and relevant departments in Vietnam National University and Hanoi University.

4. Comparative studies of Vietnam and Taiwan

Why are comparative studies of Vietnam and Taiwan important? The major reason is that it can benefit and strengthen both Vietnam studies and Taiwan studies themselves. It can help researchers and the general public in Vietnam and Taiwan to understand their motherland more clearly. Some concrete examples are provided in this section.

For example, in the case of Chiang Kai-shek's occupation of Taiwan and northern Vietnam in 1945 after the Japanese surrendered, readers may not have a clear picture of this issue without comparing Vietnam to Taiwan. In Taiwan, all history textbooks for schools only describes that "Taiwan was returned to Chiang's Republic of China in 1945 according to the Cairo Declaration." The textbooks never mention the fact that Chiang took over both Taiwan and northern Vietnam on behalf of the Allied Powers under General McArthur's order. Why was Vietnam missing in Taiwan's textbooks? What happened when Chiang's military troops took over northern Vietnam? Why did Chiang's troops eventually leave Vietnam, but remained in Taiwan? What would have happened if Chiang's troops remained in Vietnam? Why was the great Vietnamese leader Ho Chi Minh regarded as a liar and traitor by Chiang? All the questions can not be well answered without mutual comparisons.

The second example is the issue on orthographic Romanization in Vietnam and Taiwan. Both Vietnam and Taiwan used to be colonized by China. Consequently, Han characters were adopted as the official writing for a long time. In Vietnam, it finally replaced Han characters with the Romanized chữ Quốc ngữ right after Ho Chi Minh proclaimed the Democratic Republic of Vietnam. In contrast, Han characters are still the dominant orthography in current Taiwanese society even though Roman scripts has been introduced since the 17th century.

Why is Vietnam so successful in replacing Chinese characters? Why did Ho Chi Minh choose Romanization rather than Nom or Ham characters? Is there any possibility for Taiwan to become Romanized in the future?

5. Concluding remarks

As economic, cultural, and educational exchanges flourish, Taiwan and Vietnam are getting closer than ever before. To gain better understanding and mutual benefits, it is important to promote comparative studies of Vietnam and Taiwan.

In Taiwan, departments of Vietnamese language or Vietnam Studies should be organized on campus in order to provide better training courses in Vietnamese language and Vietnam studies. It should be the same in Vietnam, departments of Taiwanese language and Taiwan studies should be planned. In addition, Taiwan studies should be conducted from a Vietnamese perspective rather than from the Chinese perspective.

Acknowledgements

This is an updated revision of the article with same title originally published in 2011 *Journal of Taiwanese Vernacular*, 3(2), pp.122-141.

References

Cheng, Robert L. 1996. 民主化政治目標 kap 語言政策 [Democracy and language policy]. In C.H. Si, pp.21-50.

Chiung, Wi-vun. 2004. *Lịch Sử và Ngôn Ngữ Đài Loan [Oceanic Taiwan: History and Languages]*. Tainan: National Cheng Kung University.

Chiung, Wi-vun. 2005. *Language, Identity and Decolonization*. Tainan: National Cheng Kung University.

Chiung, Wi-vun. 2007. *Language, Literature, and Reimagined Taiwanese Nation*. Tainan: National Cheng Kung University.

Chiung, Wi-vun. 2010. 留 Tiàm tī 越南 ê 農技人員吳連義 ê 案例研究 [A case study of Ngo lien Nghia: the Last Taiwanese solider remained in Vietnam after 1945]. 《台灣風物》 [*The Taiwan Folkways*], 60(2), pp.63-86.

Kerr, George H. 1992. 被出賣的台灣 [*Formosa Betrayed*]. Taipei: Chian-ui Press.

Lee, Wen-Chih. 2003. The construction of Taiwan's "Go-South" worldview: the vantage point of struggle between sea power and land power in Asia-Pacific. In Hsiao, Hsin-Huang. (ed.). *Taiwan and Southeast Asia: Go-South Policy and Vietnamese Brides*, pp.1-41. Taipei: Center for Asia-Pacific Area Studies, Academia Sinica.

Nguyen, H. T. and C. Y. Shih. 越南的中國研究──中國研究中心／院的概況 [Chinese

Studies in Vietnam: Current development of the Institute of Chinese Studies].

Ong, Iok-tek. 1993. 台灣苦悶的歷史 [*Taiwan: a depressed history*]. Taipei: Independence Press.

Oo, Chheng-hui and Gi-cheng Tan. 2010. 大學招生缺額，外籍生補足 [Foreign students may supplement the vacancy].《自由時報》[*Liberty Times*], August 15.

Peng, Ming M. and Ng, Yuzin C. 1995. 台灣在國際法上的地位 [*The legal status of Taiwan*]. Taipei: Taiwan Interminds Publishing Inc.

Shiu, Wen-tang. 2003. A decade of development in Taiwan-Vietnam relations. In Hsiao, Hsin-Huang. (ed.). *Taiwan and Southeast Asia: Go-South Policy and Vietnamese Brides*, pp.117-161. Taipei: Center for Asia-Pacific Area Studies, Academia Sinica.

Si, Cheng-hong. (ed.) 1996. 語言政治與政策 [*Linguistic politics and policy*]. Taipei: Chian-ui.

Su, Beng. 1980. 台灣四百年史 [*Taiwan's 400 year history*]. San Jose: Paradise Culture Associates.

Tiuⁿ, Juhong. 1996. 台灣現行語言政策動機 ê 分析 [An analysis on the Taiwan's current language policy]. In Cheng-hong Si, pp.85-106.

Vũ, Minh Giang. 2004. Tình hình nghiên cứu Việt Nam ở một số nước trên thế giới [Current status of Vietnam studies in some countries of the world]. *Conference proceedings of the 2004 International Conference on Vietnamese Studies*, pp.633-661. Hanoi: Vietnam National University.

2

Language, Literacy, and Nationalism: Taiwan's Orthographic transition from the perspective of Han Sphere

1. Introduction

The Han sphere, including Vietnam, Korea, Japan, Taiwan and China, adopted *Hàn-jī* (Han characters) and classical Han writing as the official written language before the 20th century. However, the advent of the 20th century brought along great changes. In Vietnam, Han characters and their domestic derivative characters, *chữ Nôm*, which had been adopted as writing systems for more than a thousand years, were officially replaced by the romanized *chữ Quốc ngữ* in 1945, the year of the establishment of the Democratic Republic of Viet Nam. Han characters in Korea were finally replaced by phonemic system *Hangul* after World War II. In Japan, the syllabary *Kana* system was gradually developed after Japan's adoption of Han characters; the number of Han characters used by Japanese decreased from thousands to 1,945 frequently used characters by 1981 (Hannas 1997).

In Taiwan, although romanized systems such as *Sin-káng Bûn-su* and Pėh-ōe-jī were developed centuries ago, Han characters remain the dominant orthography today. In China, simplification of Han characters seems the only harvest after China's efforts at reforming characters for over a century.

This paper examines Taiwan's orthographic transition from the perspective of Han Sphere. Both internal and external factors have contributed to the different outcomes of orthographic reform in Taiwan, Vietnam, Korea, and Japan. Internal factors include the general public's demand for literacy and anti-feudal hierarchy; external factors include the political relationships between these countries and the origin of Han characters (i.e. China).

2. Historical background within the Han sphere

The Chinese attitude towards their neighbors and foreigners can be exactly expressed by an old Chinese philosophy, the Five Clothes System (*Wufuzhi*). The Chinese empire set up a world outlook: the capital is great, civilized, and the central point of the world. Further, the empire used the capital as the center of a circle, to draw five circles per 500 kilometers of radius. The farther barbarians are from the central capital, the more barbaric they are.

Following the thought of the Five Clothes System, the Chinese empire always tried to conquer the "barbarians" and brought them under the domination of China in order to "civilize" them. As a consequence, the "barbarians" were either under China's direct domination or were demanded to pay tributes every certain number of years to recognize the empire's suzerainty (i.e., become a vassal state under China).

In this pattern, Vietnam, Korea and Taiwan had been directly occupied by China for long periods. Although later on they were no longer under direct domination, they became China's vassal states until modern times. For example, Vietnam was brought under China's direct domination in 111 BC by *Han Wu Di*, the Chinese emperor of *Han* dynasty. Vietnam could not liberate itself from China until AD 939, during the fall of the powerful Chinese *Tang* dynasty (Hodgkin 1981). Thereafter, although the Vietnamese established their own independent monarchy, they had to recognize the suzerainty of imperial China in exchange for a millennium of freedom until the late 19th century (SarDesai 1992:19).

Although Japan was not under China's direct domination, due to China's powerful regimes during the times of Han and Tang dynasties, China was the model of imitation for Japan until the 19th century. For example, Japan's *Taika* Reform in the seventh century "marked the first step in the direction of the formation of a Chinese-style centralized state" (Seeley 1991:40).

In general, China's main influences on these countries include: 1) The adoption of Han characters and classical Han writing (*wenyan*) to write Vietnamese, Korean, Japanese, and Taiwanese, and 2) The importation of Buddhism, Confucianism, the civil service examination and the government official system.

According to the civil service examination system, the books of Confucius and Mencius, which were written in classical Han Chinese, were accorded the status of classics among scholars and mandarins who assisted the emperor or king in governing his people (Taylor and Taylor 1995:144-152). Everyone who desired to become a scholar or mandarin had to learn to use Hanji and read these classics and pass the imperial examination, unless he had a close relationship with the emperor. Consequently, as Coulmas (2000:52) has pointed out that such literacy skills functioned "as a crucial means of social control," and "the Mandarin scholar-bureaucrat embodied this tradition, which perpetuated itself above all through the civil service examination system." Han characters and their classical Han writing thus became the orthodoxy of written language in the Han sphere for over a thousand years.

From the perspective of literacy, the classics were not only difficult to read (i.e., Hanji), but also hard to understand (i.e., the texts), because the texts were written in classical literary style instead of colloquial style (*baihua*). In other words, because most of the people were farmers who spent their days laboring in the fields, they were not highly interested in learning Hanji and classical writing. As a consequence, a literate noble class and an illiterate peasant class were formed and this class division reinforced the feudal system.

In short, as Chen (1994:367) has pointed out, since high illiteracy and low efficiency caused by the use of Han characters became impediments to national modernization, the demand for widespread literacy was one of the advising factors pushing orthographic reform in the Han sphere.

3. Vietnam's orthographic tradition and transition

In Vietnam, Han characters were employed since 207 BC during the *Nam Viet* period (Nguyen 1999:2). Thereafter, Han characters retained their orthodoxy status during the millennium of Chinese occupation. Not until the tenth century when Vietnam achieved liberation could the domestic scripts Chu Nom have been prominently developed (DeFrancis 1977:21). Chu Nom, or Nom scripts, means southern writing or southern orthography in contrast to Chu Han, Han writing or Han characters. Chu Nom in the early period was used as an auxiliary tool of classical Han to record personal or geographical names and local specialties (Nguyen, 1999:2). Literary works in Chu Nom achieved popularity from the 16th to the 18th century, and reached their peak at the end of the 18th century (DeFrancis 1977:44). For example, *Truyen Kieu*, a novel in Chu Nom considered the masterpiece of Vietnamese literature, was published at the end of the 18th century.

Although the domestic Nom scripts have been around since the 10th century, they neither reached the same prestige as Han characters, nor replaced the classical Han writing. In contrast, Chu Nom was generally regarded as a vulgar writing, which indicates the low language in digraphia. Moreover, Nom scripts were eventually forced to yield themselves to the *Chu Quoc Ngu*, a romanized writing system originally devised in the early 17th century, which finally became the only official orthography of Vietnam in 1945. The factors that contributed to the fate of Chu Nom are as follows:

First, the Vietnamese were deeply influenced by Chinese values with regard to Han characters. Since Hanji was regarded highly as the only official orthography in China, which was the suzerain of Vietnam, the Vietnamese people had no choice but to follow this traditional value assignment. As a consequence, the Vietnamese rulers in all dynasties, except a few short-lived strongly anti-Chinese rulers, such as *Ho Quy Ly* (1400-1407) and *Quang Trung* (1788-1792), had to recognize Han characters as the institutional writing criteria.

Second, writing in Nom scripts was restricted by the civil service examination. Because the examination system was based exclusively on the contents of Chinese classics written in Hanji, all the literati that wished to pass the exam had to study the classics. Once they passed the exam and became bureaucrats, they had to maintain the examination system to ensure their monopoly of power and knowledge in the Chinese-style feudal hierarchy (DeFrancis 1977:47).

Third, the development of Nom scripts was highly restricted by the nature of their orthographic structure. Because Chu Nom comprises one or two Han characters to form a new Nom character, it inherited all the defects of Han characters (DeFrancis 1977:25). The much more complicated structure caused Nom scripts even more problems in areas of efficiency, accuracy, and consistency. Normally, one has to learn Han characters first before s/he could fully master Nom scripts. Consequently, learning to read and write in Nom scripts is more laborious than in Han characters.

In the late 16th and early 17th century, European missionaries from countries including Portugal, Italy, and France gradually came to preach in Vietnam. To get their ideas across to the local people, the missionaries recognized that knowledge of spoken Vietnamese was essential. The romanized writing system was thus devised to assist missionaries to acquire the Vietnamese language (Do 1972).

The development of romanized writing in Vietnam can be divided into four periods: 1) Church period, from the early 17th century to the first half of the 19th century. During this time, Roman scripts were mainly used in church and among religious followers. 2) French promotion period during the second half of the 19th century after the French invaded Vietnam in 1858 (Vien Van Hoc 1961:21-23). In this period, romanized Vietnamese were intentionally promoted by the French aiming to replace the classical Chinese with French ultimately (DeFrancis 1977:129-134). 3) Nationalist promotion period during the first half of the 20th century. In this period, Vietnamese romanization was promoted by anti-colonialism organizations, such as the *Đông Kinh Nghĩa Thục* or Dong Kinh Free School and *Hội truyền bá quốc ngữ* or Association for Promoting Chu Quoc Ngu (Vien Van Hoc 1961:24). Because roman scripts were no longer associated with the French colonialists, but were considered as an efficient literacy tool, romanization thus received much more recognition by the Vietnamese people than in the period of French promotion (DeFrancis 1977:159). 4) National status period after 1945, when Ho Chi Minh declared the exclusive use of Chữ Quốc ngữ (Ho Chi Minh, 1994:64-65). The number of people who acquired literacy in Quoc Ngu after the achievement of independence was reported by Le Thanh Khoi (quoted in DeFrancis 1977:240) to have risen from 20 percent in the year 1945 to 70 percent in 1953.

How was Vietnam able to successfully replace Han characters and Chu Nom with romanized Chữ Quốc ngữ? I would attribute this success to two crucial factors: 1) internal factors of social demand for literacy and anti-feudal hierarchy, and 2) external factors of political interaction between Vietnam and China in the international sphere during the first half of the 20th century. These two crucial points also apply to other cases of language and orthographic reform in the Han sphere.

Internal factors of social demand for literacy and anti-feudal hierarchy are understandable. Recall that China was the only major threat to the traditional feudal society of Vietnam prior to the 19th century. Under such conditions, although the adoption of Han characters could cause the majority of Vietnamese to be illiterate, it could, on the other hand, minimize the potential invasion from China, and more importantly, preserve the vested interests of the Vietnamese bureaucrats in the Chinese-style feudal hierarchy. However, with the advent of the 20th century, Vietnam faced a train of international colonialism. Since Ho Chi Minh claimed that 95 percent of Vietnam's total population was illiterate, it was important to equip the people with primary education, which was considered essential to modernization in order to fight against imperialisms (Ho Chi Minh 1994:64-65). Although the domestic-made Nom scripts, to some extent, represented the Vietnamese spirit, their fatal weakness in literacy had withdrawn themselves from the candidates of being a national writing system in the modern time. Thus, the efficient and easily learned romanization was the best choice for literacy in contrast to the complexity of Han characters and Nom scripts. Since the majority of Vietnamese were illiterates, and only a few elites were skilled in Han writing or French during the promotion of Quoc Ngu, it was clear that romanized Vietnamese would be favored by the majority, and thus win the literacy campaign.

External factors involve the complexity of the international situation in the 1940s. As Hodgkin (1981:288) stated, the Vietnamese were "faced with a varying combination of partly competing, partly collaborating imperialisms, French, Japanese, British and American, with *Kuomintang* China." At that time, Vietnam was considered an important base from which to attack southern China when Japan's invasion of China became more apparent and aggressive since the 1930s (Hodgkin 1981:288). The Japanese military eventually entered Vietnam and shared with the French the control of Vietnam in the early 1940s. From the perspective of China, suppression against Japan's military activities in Vietnam was desired. However, the French were afraid that China would take over Vietnam again if Chinese troops entered Vietnam under the excuse of suppression of the Japanese forces (Jiang 1971:181). For the Vietnamese people, maintaining their national identity and achieving national independence from the imperialisms were considered priority by their leaders such as Ho Chi Minh. Ho's Chinese strategy was to keep Chinese forces away from Vietnam, and minimize the possibility of a Chinese comeback in Indochina. Politically speaking, Ho opposed Chinese army entering Vietnam (Jiang 1971:107) as well as instigated anti-Chinese movement (Jiang 1971:228-240). Culturally, romanized Vietnamese was considered a distinctive feature of the cultural boundary between Vietnam and China. These considerations impelled Ho in favor of romanization rather than Han characters which are used in China.

4. Korea's orthographic tradition and transition

Han characters became institutionalized after Han Wu Di brought northern Korea under direct Chinese domination in 108 BC (Ledyard 1966:23). China's control of northern Korea lasted until the fourth century when the Koreans built their own kingdom.

Once the Koreans adopted Han characters, they encountered difficulties in understanding the classical Han writing. They gradually developed their own remedial measures to make the writing in Han characters more accessible to the Korean-speaking people. Beginning in the late sixth and early seventh centuries, two major remedies were developed, later known as *Hyangch'al* and *Idu*, which were designed based on Han characters (Ledyard 1966:34).

Although the Korean elites had developed Hyangch'al and Idu, the demand for a more accessible writing system grew stronger as the 15th century progressed (Ledyard 1966:70). In the 15th century, the Korean King *Sejong* and his scholars undertook a project of new scripts for writing the Korean vernacular. The project was carried out in 1443, and was officially proclaimed in the title of *Hun Min Jong Um* or Correct Sounds to Instruct People in 1446 (Ledyard 1966:91-99). The scripts of the Hun Min Jong Um were known in the 20th century as Hangul, the Korean alphabets, consisting of 28 letters to write Korean in a phonemic way (Shin et al. 1990).

Although the new system of Hangul was very efficient, thus possible as a tool for widespread literacy, it soon faced opposition from the privileged bureaucrat and literate classes. The best-known anti-Sejong faction was led by *Malli Choi*, the highest purely academic rank in the College of Assembled Worthies (Ledyard 1966:99-114). In 1444, Choi presented Sejong with a petition against the new orthographic invention "it is a violation of the principle of maintaining friendly relations with China, to invent and use letters, which do not exist in China... Those who seek position in the government will not seek to learn Chinese characters with patience" (Lee 1957:30-31).

The opposition to the new scripts lasted decades even after the death of Sejong. Moreover, writing in Hangul was banned by the regent *Yonsan'gun* after the literati purge of 1504 (Ledyard 1966:322). Consequently, Hangul was suppressed and used in very limited circles and domains. For centuries after its creation, Hangul was variously called "*onmun*" (vulgar script), "women's letters," "monks' letters," or "children's letters" (Taylor and Taylor 1995:212).

The inferior development of Hangul reached a turning point at the beginning of the 20th century. During Japanese occupation of Korea (1910-1945), Japan's harsh policy to restrict the use of the Korean language had enhanced the Korean identity of Hangul (Coulmas 2000:56). Moreover, the user-friendly characteristic of Hangul made it favorable to the Korean nationalists in the consideration of literacy. In other words, Hangul, similarly to Chữ Quốc ngữ in Vietnam, was chosen as the tool to eliminate illiteracy in order to fight against the Japanese imperialism. As Hangul gained more recognition and had become more widespread than ever before, it was further promoted to the status of the official national script when the Korean people began to build their modern nation-state(s) after the World War II.

5. Japan's orthographic tradition and transition

It is estimated that around the fifth century, Han characters were brought over to Japan by Korean scholars (Seeley 1991:6). Once the Japanese embraced the classical Han writing, they encountered similar difficulties in reading the Chinese classics as were seen in the cases of Vietnam and Korea. To solve this problem, several syllabic writing systems were gradually developed. Among the various simplified syllabaries, *Katakana* and *Hiragana*, currently in use after modern standardization, were well developed and widely used at least by the 10th century (Habein 1984:22-35; Seeley, 1991:69-75).

The issue of script reform was raised again as the public became highly concerned with the opening of Japan to the West from the later part of the 19th century onwards. After the imperial regime was restored in 1868, Emperor Meiji opened his door to foreign countries, which resulted in enormous changes in daily life. Among the changes was the increase of new words coined for the overwhelming number of unfamiliar concepts and objects from the West. In this situation, the intellectuals raised the issues of language reform in the consideration of better literacy and education.

After the successful political reform of Emperor Meiji, which was manifested in two victorious wars, i.e. the Sino-Japanese war of 1894-95 and the Russo-Japanese war of 1904-05, the Japanese stimulated by the victories embarked on the idea that the nation could be mobilized through more effective education, to which script reform was considered important (Gottlieb 1995:25). This belief eventually brought language reform into practical trials in the early part of the 20th century. Because using Kana-only or romanization was considered too radical, the orthographic reform was thus, in fact, centered on restricting the number of commonly used Han characters and the standardization of the Kana usage (Seeley 1991:142).

As time went on, Japan's language policy was driven by imperatives from modernization to imperialism in the first half of the 20th century (Gottlieb 1995:21). The influence of the military and the ultranationalists became more and more powerful when Japan became more aggressive in preparation for conquering China. The influence was substantial especially after the Manchuria Incident of 1931, in which three northeast provinces of China were under Japan's occupation. From the perspective of the military and ultranationalists, Han characters and historical Kana usage were *kotodama*, the "spirit of the Japanese language," which constitutes the essence of the Japanese national spirit. Therefore, reform proposals, such as abolition of Han characters, romanization, or new Kana usage, were considered to be attempts at tampering Japan's spirit, culture, and history (Gottlieb 1995:75-88; Seeley 1991:147-148).

Although many efforts were brought to the script reform, wider adoption of reform proposals could not become reality until the end of World War II, when the Japanese army surrendered to the Allied Forces (Seeley 1991:151; Hannas

1997:43). After the defeat of 1945, the military and ultranationalist voices were suppressed. As Eastman (1983:23) has pointed out, without any social, cultural, or political changes, orthography reform is not likely to succeed. Japan's dramatic changes after the war thus created the atmosphere and conditions necessary to carry out script reform. In 1946, under the supervision of the Supreme Command for the Allied Powers (SCAP), Japan's cabinet promulgated *Toyo kanjihyo*, the list of 1850 characters for daily use, and *Gendai kanazukai*, the new modern Kana usage, as the first step of script reform after the war (Unger 1996:58; Seeley 1991:152).

At present, Han characters and Kana syllabary all serve as the official scripts in the hybrid Japanese writing system. This fact makes Japan the only case, among examples analyzed in this paper, where Han characters were not officially abolished after domestic scripts were promoted to national status. Why were Han characters not abolished in Japan? Both internal and external factors have contributed to the outcome. From the perspective of literacy and anti-feudal hierarchy, by the early 20th century, Japan had reached a much higher degree of literacy and modernization in comparison with other Asian countries (Unger 1996:35; Okano and Tsuchiya 1999:19). This achievement gave the conservatives the impression that Han characters need not be abolished as long as Kana syllabary was in actual use. Furthermore, although Han characters were originally imported from China, they were converted from a pure foreign invention to an indigenized writing system over more than a thousand years of adoption use. In other words, Hanji was regarded by the Japanese as part of their language, which was totally different from the case of the Vietnamese, who considered Han characters as Chinese script and Chu Nom as their own. Why did Japan and Vietnam have reverse perceptions of Han characters? Recall that historically, Japan was never under the direct control of China. On the contrary, Japan's imperialism and militarism became a fateful threat to China in the modern period. However, battles against China frequently occurred in the history of Vietnam. That is to say, the Japanese did not associate the use of Han characters with the potential invader (i.e., China). As a matter of fact, the use of Han characters was even considered necessary once Japan launched invasion of China. For example, the Interim Committee's proposal, Toyo kanjihyo of 1931, was strongly opposed by the military because of the practical need to write a large number of Chinese personal and place names of the newly occupied Chinese territories (Seeley 1991:147).

6. Taiwan's orthographic tradition and transition

Although Taiwan is currently a Hanji-dominated society, romanization was once the first and the only writing system used in Taiwan (Chiung 2001c). Sinkang Bunsu, the first system of romanization was introduced by the Dutch missionaries in the first half of the 17th century. Thereafter, Han characters were imposed in Taiwan by the sinitic Koxinga regime in the second half of the 17th century. As the number of Han immigrants from China dramatically increased, Han characters gradually became the dominant writing system in Taiwan. Until 2001, only Han characters and modern standard Chinese (Mandarin) are taught in Taiwan's national education system. Starting fall semester 2001, a 40-minutes mother tongue elective course is added to the curriculum of elementary schools. Teachers may choose to teach romanization or other scripts for written Taiwanese.

Taiwan is a multilingual and multiethnic island country. Generally speaking, Taiwan's population can be divided into four primary ethnic groups: indigenous (1.7%), Hakka (12%), Tâi-gí (73.3%), and Mainlanders (13%) (Huang 1993:21). Hakka and Tâi-gí are the so-called Han people. In fact, many of them are descendants of intermarriage between sinitic immigrants and local Taiwanese aboriginals during the *Koxinga* and *Qing* periods (Brown 2004:149). Mainlanders, or *Bîn-hiong-jîn* (民鄉人) who came to Taiwan with the Chiang Kai-shek's KMT regime in the late 1940s, are the latest immigrants from China. Although Hakka, Tâi-gí, and Mainlanders are all immigrants originally from China, they have different national identities. For example, most of the Tâi-gí and Hakka people identify themselves as Taiwanese. However, according to Ong's investigation, 54% of the surveyed Mainlanders still identified themselves as Chinese. Only 7.3% identified themselves as Taiwanese, and the rest were neutral (Ong 1993: 87). A survey conducted in 1997 by Corcuff (2004:104) revealed that only 10% of the surveyed Mainlanders, who were born in China, identified themselves as Taiwanese. As for the surveyed Mainlanders who were born in Taiwan after 1968, only 43% of them identified themselves as Taiwanese. Mainlanders' divergent identity of Taiwan is also a factor influencing the promotion of Taiwanese language(s).

In addition to being a multiethnic society, Taiwan has been colonized by several foreign regimes since the seventeenth century. Prior to foreign occupation, Taiwan was a collection of many different indigenous tribes, which did not belong to any countries, such as China or Japan. In 1624, the Dutch occupied Taiwan and established the first alien regime in Taiwan. Roman scripts were then introduced to Taiwan by the Dutch. The first romanization was used to write the indigenous

Siraya language, which has since become extinct. In 1661, Koxinga, a remnant force of the former Chinese *Ming* Dynasty, failed to restore the Ming Dynasty against the new Qing Dynasty and subsequently retreated to Taiwan. Koxinga expelled the Dutch and established a sinitic regime in Taiwan as a base for retaking the Mainland. Confucianism and civil service examination were thus imposed in Taiwan during Koxinga's regime and maintained under the Qing Dynasty. The Koxinga regime was later annexed by the Chinese Qing Dynasty in 1683. During the late Qing period (in the second half of the 19th century), *Peh-oe-ji* or Scripts of Vernacular Speech, the second romanization in Taiwan, was introduced by western missionaries (Tiu[n] 2001; Chiung 2001b). Peh-oe-ji is mainly used for Tâi-gí Taiwanese, who constitutes the majority of Taiwan's current population. *Tâi-oân-hú-siâ[n] Kàu-hōe-pò* or Taiwan Prefectural City Church News, the first public newspaper in Taiwan was published in Peh-oe-ji since 1885 until 1970. Two centuries after the Qing's occupation, the sovereignty of Taiwan was transferred from China to Japan as a consequence of the Sino-Japanese war in 1895. At the end of World War II, Japanese forces surrendered to the Allied Forces. *Chiang Kai-shek*, the leader of the Chinese Nationalist Party (KMT or *Kuomintang*), took over Taiwan and a part of French Indo-China (Nowadays, Vietnam, Lao, and Cambodia) on behalf of the Allied Powers under General Order No.1 of September 2, 1945 (Peng and Ng 1995:60-61). Simultaneously, Chiang Kai-shek was fighting against the Chinese Communist Party in Mainland China. In 1949, Chiang's troops were completely defeated and then pursued by the Chinese Communists. At that time, Taiwan's national status was supposed to be dealt with by a peace treaty among the fighting nations. However, because of his defeat in China, Chiang decided to occupy Taiwan as a base from which he would fight to recover the Mainland (Kerr 1992; Ong 1993; Peng and Ng 1995; Su 1980). Consequently, Chiang's political regime called the Republic of China (R.O.C), which was formerly the official name of the Chinese government (1912-1949) in China, was renewed in Taiwan and has remained there since 1949. Once the R.O.C was renewed in Taiwan, the ruling party KMT claimed that R.O.C has sovereignty over Mainland China and was the only legal government, which represented all of China. This extravagant claim was not changed until 2000, when the opposition party Democratic Progressive Party (DPP) won the presidential election.

National Language Policy or monolingual policy was adopted both during the Japanese and KMT occupations of Taiwan (Huang 1993; Tsao 1999; Png 1965; Tiu[n] 1974; Heylen 2005). In the case of KMT's monolingual policy, the Taiwanese people were not allowed to speak their vernaculars in public. Moreover, they were forced to learn Mandarin Chinese and to identify themselves as Chinese through the national education system (Cheng 1996; Tiuⁿ 1996). As Hsiau (1997:307) has pointed out, "the usage of Mandarin as a national language becomes a testimony of the Chineseness of the KMT state," in other words, the Chinese KMT regime tried to convert the Taiwanese into "becoming" Chinese through Mandarin monolingualism.

In response to KMT's National Language Policy, the promoters of Taiwanese have protested against the monolingual policy and have demanded bilingual education in schools. This is the so-called *Tâi-bûn Ūn-tōng* "Taiwanese language movement" that has substantially grown since the second half of the 1980s (Hsiau 1997; Erbaugh 1995; Huang 1993; Li 1999; Lim 1996; Heylen 2005).

Under the pressure of the Taiwanese language movement, the ruling KMT regime had no choice but to open up some possibilities for vernacular education. Eventually, the president Lee Teng-hui approved the compromised proposal that elementary schools be allowed to have vernacular education starting in fall semester 2001. Prior to implementation of the vernacular education proposal, KMT lost its regime during the 2000 presidential election for the first time in Taiwan. Chen Shui-bian, who is a native of Taiwan was elected president. Consequently, the Democratic Progressive Party (DPP) became the ruling party until 2008 when the KMT retrieved regime again. This vernacular education proposal was thus conducted by the ruling DPP starting in fall 2001. A class called 'pún-thó͘ gí-giân' (native languages), with a period of 40 minutes per week, is required in all elementary schools. Schools may choose the vernacular languages to teach in accordance with the demands of their students.

There are two core issues for the Taiwanese language movement. First, the movement wishes to promote spoken Taiwanese in order to maintain people's vernacular speech. Second, the movement aims to promote and standardize written Taiwanese in order to develop Taiwanese (vernacular) literature[1]. Because written Taiwanese is not well standardized and not taught through the national education system, most Taiwanese speakers have to write in Modern Written Chinese (MWC) instead of Written Taiwanese (WT). Although more than a hundred orthographies have been proposed by different persons enthusiastic for the standardization of written Taiwanese, most of the designs have most likely been accepted and used only by their own designers. Moreover, many of the

---

[1] Although the issues of written Taiwanese include Hakka and indigenous languages, most literary works are written in the Tâi-gí language. This fact makes the Tâi-gí language the focus of the written Taiwanese. Therefore, the term "written Taiwanese" in this paper refers only to the written form of the Tâi-gí language, if not specified.

designs were never applied to practical writing after they were devised. Because of the wide use of the personal computer and electronic networks in Taiwan since the 1990s, most orthographic designs, which require extra technical support other than regular Mandarin software, are unable to survive. Therefore, the majority of recent Taiwanese writing systems are either in Han characters, Roman alphabet or a mixed system combining Roman and Han, as Cheng (1990) and Tiu[n] (1998) have documented.

The orthographic situation in Taiwan is as complicated as Taiwan's political status and people's national identity. Linguistically, people in Taiwan have to face the issue of whether to use MWC or WT as their written language. Furthermore, people who choose WT have to decide which scripts will be adopted while they are writing in Taiwanese. Politically, Taiwan is currently in an ambiguous political status, i.e., neither nominally an independent Republic of Taiwan nor substantially a province of the People's Republic of China (Peng and Ng 1995). This political ambiguity mirrors people's divergent national identity, which is usually categorized as 1) Taiwanese-only, 2) Chinese-only, and 3) both Taiwanese and Chinese. Consequently, the diversity of the public's national identity has led to different political claims, i.e., independence, unification with China, or maintaining the status quo.[2]

The contemporary Taiwanese language movement since the 1980s reflects Taiwan's socio-political complexity and its colonial background. In terms of Fishman's (1968) nationalism and nationism, it reveals the controversial relationship among Chinese nationalism-nationism[3] Taiwanese nationalism and Taiwanese nationism.

In the dimension of nationalism and nationism, it reveals the political tensions between Chinese and Taiwanese. Chinese nationalism can be inherited internally from Chinese KMT and as well as externally from the People's Republic of China. The strong conflicts between KMT's Chinese nationalism and Taiwanese nationalism were overt in the anti-KMT movement during the second half of the 1980s and the entire 1990s. The conflicts between PRC Chinese

---

[2] Their proportion of supporters may vary slightly from poll to poll, but in general, less than 20% of Taiwan's populations in recent years are in favor of unification with China (Huang 2000; Tse 2000).

[3] At the beginning of Chinese KMT's occupation of Taiwan, Chinese nationists may have held different opinions from Chinese nationalists. However, later on when the use of Mandarin by people in Taiwan dramatically increased, the objects of Chinese nationalism and Chinese nationism became the same. That is, to keep using Mandarin since it has dominated educational and governmental functions in Taiwan. Therefore, I do not distinguish Chinese nationalism from Chinese nationism here.

nationalism and Taiwanese nationalism started in the late 1980s and reached the climax in 1999 when the former president Teng-hui Lee claimed that Taiwan and China hold "special state to state" relationship.

In the dimension of Taiwanese, the chart shows the expanding tension between Taiwanese nationalism and Taiwanese nationism. Some Taiwanese politicians and intellectuals who lead socio-political movement, such as *Sui-kim Phenn* do not view the Taiwanese language movement as a necessary step even though they identify themselves as Taiwanese rather than Chinese. In their ideology, they disapprove of the KMT's strict national language policy; however, they have come to the stage to accept the results of the national language policy. In other words, they recognize the legitimate status of the colonial language, i.e., Mandarin Chinese as the official language since it has been widespread in Taiwan after more than sixty years of promotion. However, they are criticized by Taiwanese nationalists who claim that they have ignored the threat of Chinese nationalism from China. From the perspective of Taiwanese nationalism, Taiwanese language is not only a medium for communication, but also a part of history and spirit of Taiwan. Moreover, it is considered a national defense against Chinese nationalism of the PRC and the ROC (Chiu[n] 1996; Lim 1996, 1997, 1998; Li 1999).

The complexity of the socio-political background has prevented Taiwan's domestic scripts from being promoted to a national status. Therefore, in contrast to Vietnam, Korea, and Japan, Taiwan is the unique case where the vernacular writing is still under development. Both internal and external factors, as I proposed, have contributed to the inferior development of Taiwanese orthography.

In terms of internal demands for literacy and anti-feudal hierarchy, written Taiwanese was not effectively promoted at the right time when the public met their literacy demands in the early 20th century during the Japanese occupation[4]. Nowadays, Taiwan has shifted from a traditional feudal society to a modern one, in which the requirement of a minimum of 9 years of compulsory education has been in place since 1968. It is claimed that Taiwan's current population has reached a literacy rate of 94% based on the statistical data of Taiwan's Minister of Interior. That is, the majority of people in Taiwan have acquired some literacy skills in Han characters and Modern Written Chinese. This fact has reduced the need to promote a new orthography on the bases of public's literacy.

---

[4] The causes are complicated. On one hand, it was because of the opposition from the Japanese colonialist; on the other hand, the elites' preference for Han characters was caused by their internalized socialization and misunderstanding of the nature and function of Han characters (Chiung 2001a).

From the perspective of external factors, because of the complexity and ambiguity of the political relationship between Taiwan and China, Han characters are not substantially regarded as a foreign script by the people in Taiwan. In contrast, roman scripts are generally considered as a foreign invention, even though romanized writing has existed in Taiwan for hundreds years (Chiung 2001a). As Gelb (1952:196) has pointed out, "in all cases it was the foreigners who were not afraid to break away from sacred traditions and were thus able to introduce reforms which led to new and revolutionary developments." The weak distinction between Taiwanese and Chinese people in terms national identity has thus undermined the promotion of roman scripts and written Taiwanese.

7. Conclusion

In addition to linguistic factors, nationalism is another driving force in East Asia's orthographic transition. Although nationalism may or may not consist of a linguistic component as Edwards (1985:37) noted, it is definitely the case in the Han sphere that language and scripts play a substantial role in nation-building. For more than a millennium, Han characters and classical Han writing have served as the hallmark and tie between China and the sinitic countries in the Han sphere. From the nationalistic viewpoint, abolition of Han characters was thus considered an important step to the construction of a newly independent nation-state. On the contrary, nationalism has prevented China from success in orthographic reform. For example, Latinization, known as *latinhua* in China, was finally aborted in the consideration of China's cultural and political unity (Barnes 1974; DeFrancis 1950:221-236; Norman 1988:257-264).

In the case of Taiwan, it is apparent that external factors remain variable and will play a crucial role in the current development of the Taiwanese language movement. Chiung's survey of 244 college students reveals that Taiwanese identity and assertion of Taiwanese independence are two significant factors that effect students' attitudes towards written Taiwanese (Chiung 2001a). Although writing in Taiwanese is still far removed from the main-stream Taiwanese society, it is not surprising that as conflicts between Taiwan and China increase, people's enthusiasm about written Taiwanese will be mobilized. For example, the Association of Taiwanese Romanization (ATR), established in 2001, is the first non-religious organization aiming to promote writing in romanized Taiwanese. The establishment of ATR can be considered Taiwan's reflection of the increased military threat from China in recent years.

Acknowledgements

This is an updated revision of the article with same title originally published in 2007 *Journal of Multilingual and Multicultural Development*, 28(2), pp.102-116.

References

Barnes, D. 1974. Language planning in Mainland China: standardization. In J. A. Fishman (ed.) *Advances in Language Planning*, pp.457-477. The Hague.

Brown, M. J. 2004. *Is Taiwan Chinese? The Impact of Culture, Power, and Migration on Changing Identities*. Berkeley: University of California Press.

Chen, P. 1994. Four projected functions of new writing systems for Chinese. *Anthropological Linguistics* 36(3), pp.366-381.

Cheng, R. L. 1990. *Ianpian-tiong e Taioan Siahoe Gibun* [*Essays on Taiwan's Sociolinguistic Problems*]. Taipei: Chu-lip.

Cheng, R. L. 1996. Bin-chu-hoa cheng-ti bok-phiau kap gi-gian cheng-chhek [Democracy and language policy]. In C.H. Si, pp.21-50.

Chiuⁿ, U. B. 1996. Hui Han-ji chiah u chai-tiau tok-lip [We could not achieve independence unless we abolish Han characters]. In U. Chiuⁿ (ed.) *Haiang* (pp.176-208). Taipei: Tai-leh.

Chiung, W. T. 2001a. Language attitudes towards written Taiwanese. *Journal of Multilingual & Multicultural Development* 22(6), pp.502-523.

Chiung, W. T. 2001b. Peh-oe-ji, gin-a-lang the iong e bun-ji? Tai-oan kau-hoe Peh-oe-ji e sia-hoe gi-gian-hak hun-sek [Missionary scripts: a case study of Taiwanese Peh-oe-ji]. *The Taiwan Folkway* 51(4), pp.15-52.

Chiung, W.T. 2001c. Romanization and language planning in Taiwan. *The Linguistic Association of Korea Journal* 9(1), pp.15-43.

Corcuff, S. 2004. *Fong He Rih Ruan: Taiwan Wayshenren yu Guojia Rentong de Jhuanbian* [*Changing Identities of the Mainlanders in Taiwan*]. Taipei: Unsin.

Coulmas, F. 2000. The nationalization of writing. *Studies in the Linguistic Sciences* 30(1), pp.47-59.

DeFrancis, J. 1950. *Nationalism and Language Reform in China*. Princeton: Princeton University Press.

DeFrancis, J. 1977. *Colonialism and Language Policy in Viet Nam*. The Hague.

Do, Q. C. 1972. *Lich Su Chu Quoc Ngu: 1620-1659* [*History of the Quoc Ngu Script: 1620-1659*]. Saigon: Ra Khoi.

Eastman, C. M. 1983. *Language Planning*. San Francisco: Chandler & Sharp Publishers, Inc.

Edwards, J. 1985. *Language, Society, and Identity*. New York: Basil Blackwell.

Erbaugh, M. 1995. Southern Chinese dialects as a medium for reconciliation within Greater China. *Language in Society* 24, pp.79-94.

Fishman, J. A. 1968. Nationality-nationalism and nation-nationism. In J. Fishman, et al. (eds) *Language Problems of Developing Nations*, pp.39-51. New York: John Wiley & Sons.

Gelb, I. J. 1952. *A Study of Writing.* London: Routledge and Kegan Paul.

Gottlieb, N. 1995. *Kanji Politics: Language Policy and Japanese Script.* London: Kegan Paul International.

Habein, Y. S. 1984. *The History of The Japanese Written Language.* Tokyo: University of Tokyo Press.

Hannas, W. C. 1997. *Asia's Orthographic Dilemma.* Hawaii: University of Hawaii.

Heylen, A. 2005. The legacy of literacy practices in colonial Taiwan. Japanese-Taiwanese-Chinese: language interaction and identity formation. *Journal of Multilingual & Multicultural Development* 26(6), pp.496-511.

Ho, C. M. 1994. *Ho Chi Minh: Selected Writings 1920-1969.* Hanoi: The Gioi.

Hodgkin, T. 1981. *Vietnam: The Revolutionary Path.* London: The Macmillan Press Ltd.

Hsiau, A. C. 1997. Language ideology in Taiwan: the KMT's language policy, the Tai-yu language movement, and ethnic politics. *Journal of Multilingual and Multicultural Development* 18(4), pp.302-315.

Huang, S. F. 1993. *Gi-gian Sia-hoe kap Chok-kun I-sek* [*Language, Society, and Ethnic Identity*]. Taipei: Crane.

Huang, S. F. 2000. Language, identity, and conflict: a Taiwanese study. *International Journal of the Sociology of Language* 143, pp.139-149.

Jiang, Y. J. 1971. *Ho Chi Minh ti Tiong-kok* [*Ho Chi Minh in China*]. Taipei.

Kerr, G. H. 1992. *Hong Chhut-be e Tai-oan* [*Formosa Betrayed*]. Taipei: Chian-ui Press.

Ledyard, G. K. 1966. *The Korean Language Reform of 1446: the Origin, Background, and Early History of the Korean Alphabet.* PhD thesis, University of California, Berkeley.

Lee, S. L. D. 1957. *The Origin of Korean Alphabet Hangul: According to New Historical Evidence.* Seoul: Tong-Mun Kwan.

Li, H. C. (ed.). 1999. *Tai-gi Bun-hak Un-tong Lun-bun-chip* [*Collection of Essays on Taigi Literature Movement*]. Taipei: Chian-ui.

Lim, I. B. 1996. *Tai-gi Bun-hak Un-tong-su-lun* [*Essays on the Tai-gi Literature Movement*]. Taipei: Chian-ui.

Lim, I. B. 1997. *Tai-gi Bun-hoa Teng-kin-su* [*Essays on Taiwanese Language and Culture*]. Taipei: Chian-ui.

Lim, I. B. 1998. *Gi-gian Bun-hoa kap Bin-chok Kok-ka* [*Language, Culture, and Nation-States*] Taipei: Chian-ui.

Nguyen, Q. H. 1999. Chu Han va chu Nom voi van hien co dien Viet Nam [Han characters, Nom characters, and Vietnam's historical references], *Ngon Ngu & Doi Song* 6(5), pp.2-7.

Norman, J. 1988. *Chinese.* Cambridge: Cambridge University Press.

Okano, K. and Tsuchiya M. 1999. *Education in Contemporary Japan.* Cambridge: Cambridge University Press.

Ong, H.C. 1993. Seng-chek iong-hap e pun-chit [The nature of assimilation between Taiwanese and Mainlanders]. In M.K. Chang (ed.) *Chok-kun koan-he kap kok-ka gin-tong* [*Ethnic Relations and National Identity*], pp.53-100. Taipei: Iap-kiong.

Ong, I. T. 1993. *Tai-oan: Khou-bun e Lek-su* [*Taiwan: A Depressed History*]. Taipei: Independence Press.

Peng, M. M. and Ng, Y. C. 1995. *Tai-oan ti Kok-che-hoat-siong e Te-ui* [*The Legal Status of Taiwan*]. Taipei: Taiwan Interminds Publishing Inc.

Png, S. T. 1965. *Gou Chap Ni Lai Tiong-kok Kok-gi Un-tong-su* [*History of the National Language Movement in China in the Past 50 years*]. Taipei: Mandarin Daily News Press.

SarDesai, D. R. 1992. *Vietnam: The Struggle for National Identity*. (2nd ed.). Colorado: Westview Press.

Seeley, C. 1991. *A History of Writing in Japan*. Netherlands: E. J. Brill.

Si, C. H. (ed.). 1996. *Gi-gian Cheng-ti kap Cheng-chhek* [*Linguistic Politics and Policy*]. Taipei: Chian-ui.

Su, B. 1980. *Tai-oan-lang Si Pah Ni Su* [*Taiwan's 400 Year History*]. San Jose: Paradise Culture Associates.

Taylor, I. and Taylor, M. M. 1995. *Writing and Literacy in Chinese, Korean and Japanese*. PA: John Benjamins.

Tiun, J. H. 1996. Tai-oan hian-heng gi-gian cheng-chhek tong-ki e hun-sek [An analysis on the Taiwan's current language policy]. In C.H. Si, pp.85-106.

Tiun, H. K. 1998. Writing in two scripts: a case study of digraphia in Taiwanese. *Written Language and Literacy* 1(2), pp.225-247.

Tiun, J. H. 2001. *Peh-oe-ji Ki-pun-lun* [*Principles of POJ or the Taiwanese Orthography: An Introduction to Its Sound-Symbol Correspondences and Related Issues*]. Taipei: Crane.

Tiun, P. U. 1974. *Tai-oan Te-khu Kok-gi Un-tong Su-liau* [*Historical Materials for the Promotion of Mandarin in Taiwan*]. Taipei: Taiwan Business.

Tsao, F. F. 1999. The language planning situation in Taiwan. *Journal of Multilingual and Multicultural Development* 20(4&5), pp.328-375.

Tse, K. P. J. 2000. Language and a rising new identity in Taiwan. *International Journal of the Society of Language* 143, pp.151-164.

Unger, M. J. 1996. *Literacy and Script Reform in Occupation Japan*. NY: Oxford University Press.

Vien Van Hoc. 1961. *Van De Cai Tien Chu Quoc Ngu* [*Aspects of Reforming Chu Quoc Ngu*]. Hanoi: Nha Xuat Ban Van Hoa.

3

Road to Orthographic Romanization:
Vietnam and Taiwan

1. Introduction

Hanji (Han character) cultural areas, including Vietnam, Taiwan, Korea, Japan, and China, used Han characters and the classical Han writing[1] (*wenyan* 文言文) before the twentieth century. However, there were great changes before the advent of the twentieth century. In Vietnam, Han characters (chữ Hán) and its derivative characters, *Chu Nom* (*chữ Nôm* 字字喃), which had been adopted as writing systems for more than a thousand years in Vietnam, were officially replaced by the Romanized *Chu Quoc Ngu* (*chữ Quốc ngữ*) in 1945, the year of the establishment of the Democratic Republic of Viet Nam. The Chu Quoc Ngu was developed on the basis of Romanized Vietnamese writing, which was originally developed by missionaries in the seventeenth century. In Korea, Han characters were finally replaced by *Hangul* (한글 諺文) after World War II. Hangul, the Korean phonemic writing system, was originally designed and promulgated by King *Sejong* in 1446. In Japan, the syllabary *Kana* (かな) system was gradually developed after Japan's adoption of Han characters; although Han characters are not completely replaced by Kana, the number of Han characters used by Japanese decreased from thousands to 1,945 frequently used characters in 1981 (cf. Hannas 1997).

In Taiwan, there are currently three types of Taiwanese writing schemes: 1) using only Han characters, 2) using Han characters and Roman scripts, and 3) using only Roman scripts (Cheng 1990; Tiu[N] 1997; Chiung 2001a). The chaotic situation of writing Taiwanese reflects the complex of political claims and relation

---

[1] For details about the Han characters and classical Han writing, see DeFrancis 1990; Norman 1988.

between Taiwan and China. That is, unification with China, maintaining current political status, or independence. In Hong Kong, people keep using Han characters with minor revision of Han characters to write Cantonese. It reflects their fate that Hong Kong had to return to China in 1997. As for China, although writing reform has been in progressing since the late period of the nineteenth century, Han characters are still widely used and taught in the national education system. It seems that Han characters will still be the dominant orthography, at least for the present (cf. DeFrancis 1950, 1990; Hannas 1997).

Among these countries, Vietnam and Taiwan were both introduced to Romanized writings by Western missionaries in the seventeenth century. However, they have different consequences today. That is, Chu Quoc Ngu eventually became the official written language of Vietnam, but Romanization is still excluded from the national education system of Taiwan. What are the factors that led to the different consequences of Vietnam and Taiwan? Is Taiwan going to adopt Romanization in the future? This paper examines the developments and influences of Romanization in the traditional Hanji dominant Vietnamese and Taiwanese societies. Both internal and external factors have contributed to the different outcomes of Romanization in these two countries. Internal factors include the general public's demands for literacy and anti-feudal hierarchy; external factors include the political relationships between these countries and the origin of Hanji (i.e. China).

2. Socio-cultural background in the Hanji Sphere

The Chinese attitude toward their neighbors and foreigners can exactly be expressed by an old Chinese philosophy, the Five Clothes System (五服制). The Chinese emperor set up a world outlook: the capital is great, civilized, and the central point of the world. Further, the emperor used the capital as the center of a circle, to draw five circles per 500 kilometers of radius. The farther barbarians are from the central capital, the more barbaric they are. Chinese people call the barbarians from the east as '*Dong-yi*'(東夷), barbarians from the south as '*Nan-man*' (南蠻), barbarians from west as '*Xi-rong*'(西戎), and barbarians from the north as '*Bei-di*'(北狄). All the words are different animal names. In such thought of Five Clothes System, the Chinese empire always tried to conquer the "barbarians" and brought them under the domination of China in order to "civilize" them. In this pattern, Vietnam, Korea and Taiwan had been directly occupied by China for long periods. Although later on they were no longer under direct domination, they became China's vassal states until modern times. Although

Japan was not under China's direct domination, due to China's powerful regimes during the times of Han and Tang dynasties, China was the model of learning for Japan.

China's major influences on these countries include: 1) The adoption of Han characters and classical Han writing to write Vietnamese, Korean, Japanese, and Taiwanese[2]. 2) Imported Buddhism, Confucianism, the civil service examination (or imperial examination system (科舉制度) and the government official system. According to the Han characters and the imperial examination system, the books of Confucius and Mencius were accorded the status of classics among scholars and mandarins who assisted the emperor or king in governing his people. Everyone who desired to become a scholar or mandarin had to learn to use Hanji and read these classics and pass the imperial examination, unless he had a close relationship with the emperor. However, the classics were not only difficult to read (i.e., Hanji), but also hard to understand (i.e., the texts), because the texts were written in classical Han writing instead of colloquial speech (*Baihua* 白話). In other words, because most of the people were farmers who labored in the fields all day long, they had little interest in learning Hanji and classical writing. As a consequence, a noble class and a peasant class were formed and the classes strengthened the feudal society. This complication of Hanji could be well expressed with the old Taiwanese saying, "*Hàn-jī nā thàk ē-bat, chhùi-chhiu tō phah sí-kat.*" It means that you cannot understand all the Han characters even if you studied until you could tie your beard into a knot. In short, the demand for widespread literacy was the advising factor pushing reform of writing systems.

Writing in Hanji was considered morphosyllabic writing (DeFrancis 1990:88). The primary problem of the morphosyllabic writing is a higher number of characters inventory and its inefficiency[3] for writing. Consequently, writing in Han character become a burden of its learner, and may cause some further problems as Chen pointed out "to a large responsible for the country's high illiteracy and low efficiency, and hence an impediment to the process of modernization" (Chen 1994:367).

In contrast to the internal factor of social demand of literacy, the external factor was the political interaction between China and those countries.

---

[2] The influence of Han characters on China's neighbors was reflected on the early historical books, which were the first annals written and compiled in classical Han by their governments to record their early history. They are "古事記" (712 A. D.) and "日本書紀" (720 A. D.) in Japan, "三國史記" (1145 A. D.) in Korea, and "大越史記" (1253 A. D.) in Vietnam.

[3] For detailed discussion about the efficiency of Han characters and classical Han writing, see DeFrancis 1990, 1996, Norman 1991, and Chen 1999.

Historically, the Chinese people had the dominant status in Han sphere prior to the twentieth century. Consequently, the reform of written language against classical Han writing would be considered a violation of the Chinese Empire. In the second half of the nineteenth century, Western colonialism came to the Han cultural areas. As a result, China was no longer able to dominate these areas. She was even unable to defend herself from the Western invasions. On the other hand, the rise of modern nationalism against the Western colonialism in these areas, forced those people to consider their national transitions from a feudal society to a modern society. To achieve this purpose, considering a writing reform to reduce the population of illiterate people became an important job. In addition, the nationalism against colonialism also caused Vietnam, Korea, Japan, and Taiwan to reconsider their relationships with China. That is to say, they had to maintain the vassal relationship with China or become a politically and culturally independent country. Under the consideration of literacy and independence, Vietnam, Korea, and Japan were successful in the great changes from Han character to *Chu Quoc Ngu*, *Hangul*, and *Kana*. However, in China, although there were many proposed orthographic designs since the late period of the nineteenth century, such as *Qie-yin-zi* (切音字), *Quan-hua Zi-mu* (官話字母), and Latinization, Han characters have been only successfully simplified so far. The pattern of writing reforms in Asia is the same as Gelb mentioned in his famous book about the world's writing reforms, "in all cases it was the foreigners who were not afraid to break away from sacred traditions and were thus able to introduce reforms which led to new and revolutionary developments" (Gelb 1952: 196).

3. Language, literacy, and nationalism in Vietnam

3.1. History of domination by foreign powers in Vietnam

After the first Chinese emperor *Shih Huang Ti* (秦始皇), who built the Great Wall, annexed six countries (221 B.C.), Shih Huang Ti continued to suppress South of Mountain (嶺南, present southern China). In 207 B.C., Trieu Da (趙佗), a Chinese general who commanded the *Kwantung* and *Kwangsi* provinces of present China, brought the Red River Delta[4] under his jurisdiction and built up an autonomous state called *Nam Viet* (南越). In 111 B.C., the Chinese emperor of the *Han* dynasty, *Han Wu Ti* (漢武帝), sent his forces against Nam Viet and annexed

---

[4] Currently northern Vietnam.

Nam Viet under the direct domination of China until 938. In 939, Nam Viet[5] separated from China at the moment of the fall of the powerful *Tang* dynasty (唐朝), and then became an independent monarchy, which refers to the present Vietnam (Chavan 1987; Hodgkin 1981; Holmgren 19??; SarDesai 1992; Tran 1992).

Although the Vietnamese established their own independent monarchy, Vietnamese had to recognize the suzerainty of Chinese empire to exchange a later millennium of freedom until the late nineteenth century (SarDesai 1992:19). As SarDesai (1992:21) describes, "despite strong political hostility toward the Chinese, the Vietnamese rulers deliberately set their nation on a course of sinicization." China's influence on Vietnam was never dismissed even though Vietnam had achieved a monarchical status. For example, during the early feudal period of Vietnam, *Ly* and *Tran* dynasties (1010 A.D.-1428 A.D.), the Vietnamese government established a Confucian Temple of Literature and the Han-Lin Academy for study in Confucianism[6], and imported many systems including civil service examination and hierarchical bureaucracy from China (SarDesai 1992:21). Consequently, Chinese classics such as *Four Classical Books* (四書) and *Five Canonical Books* (五經) became the textbooks and orthodoxy for the Vietnamese scholars and officials (Nguyen 19??:2; cf. Pham 1980). In short, although Vietnam was not under China's direct domination in the second millennium, there was also great influence on Vietnam from China, as the late Vietnamese historian, Tran Trong Kim (1882-1953) described (Tran 1992:2):

> No matter adult or child, the Vietnamese only learned Chinese history instead of Vietnamese history when they went to school. They had to obtain materials from Chinese literature when they wrote poems or articles and they never mentioned their own country, Vietnam. Besides, Vietnamese always looked down on their own history and thought that it's not useful to know Vietnamese history. This was because the Vietnamese did not have their own Vietnamese language, the Vietnamese had to learn knowledge by other people's language and other people's characters.

Beyond Chinese domination, Vietnamese faced the French imperial power

---

[5] I keep using the term *Nam Viet* for readers' convenience, although its name changed over different periods. See Hodgkin (1981:349) for names given to Vietnam at different periods of history.
[6] For details of Confucianism in Vietnam, see Nguyen 1979.

since 1862, in which year Vietnam ceded three provinces of Cochin China to France, until the end of First Indochina War in 1954 (Hodgkin 1981; SarDesai 1992; McLeod 1991).

In the end of the fifteenth century, due to new technology, which made west European traveling by sea easier, and the discovery and control of new sea routes, the European such as the Portuguese, the Dutch and the Spanish, gradually appeared in South China Sea for trading, religious mission, or colonization. Before French imperial power entered Vietnam, there had been some missionary activities there. For example, in 1624 a French missionary named *Alexandre de Rhodes*, who was usually referred to as the inventor of *Chu Quoc Ngu*, a method of writing the Vietnamese language in Roman scripts instead of the traditional Han characters, arrived in Vietnam beginning his mission there for about four decades. In many colonized countries, missionary activities resulted in some conflicts between missionaries and local people, and there was no exception in Vietnam. Due to religious conflicts, there was a marked increase in hostility toward the Catholics and foreign influences. Consequently, large scale persecution of converters and missionaries began in the 1820s under Emperor *Minh Mang* (SarDesai 1992:32). Religious conflicts became an excuse of the French to invade Vietnam and finally won the conquest of Vietnam.

3.2. Modern nationalist movement in Vietnam

In many colonies, intellectuals usually have different thoughts on the relationship between locals and immigrants, i.e. they may choose to collaborate, to resist, or to retreat. It was no exception in the case of Vietnam. The Vietnamese mandarin class in the transition of nineteenth century to the twentieth century was divided by SarDesai (1992:44) into three groups: 1) those who had collaborated with the French, 2) those who retreated to the villages in a kind of passive noncooperation, and 3) those who battled to bring new meaning and ethnic salvation to their country. Prior to the twentieth century, many Vietnamese mandarins were under the illusion that Vietnamese would maintain cultural and spiritual independence even thought they had lost their land and political control to French. But a new generation of mandarins was aware of the pervasive educational and cultural impact of colonial rule, thus they devoted themselves to nationalist movement.

In the second decade of the twentieth century, the Vietnamese nationalist movement gradually flourished. SarDesai (1992:46-47) attributes the result to two primary reasons. First, the result of French education. Although it was a colonial education, it provided Vietnamese a chance to gain knowledge and ideas such as nationalism, democracy and nation-state. Second, the early twentieth century was the rise of nationalism. More than 100,000 Vietnamese soldiers and workers in France had experienced nationalism during World War I (1914-1918). Besides, the pronouncement of right of self-determination of nations (1918) by the U.S. President Woodrow Wilson, had inspired the nationalist movement.

On September 2, 1945, the Vietnamese communist leader, Ho Chi Minh, declared the birth of Democratic Republic of Viet Nam. However, the new Republic was not soon recognized by any country, and it caused the First Indochina War (1946-1954), in which the French power attempted to suppress the independence of Vietnam. Finally, the French power failed to maintain control of Vietnam, but Vietnam was divided into two zones until the end of the Second Indochina War (1964-1975), which expelled all alien forces. Consequently, the Vietnamese eventually established their own reunited independent country, the Socialist Republic of Viet Nam (Chavan 1987; Hodgkin 1981; SarDesai 1992).

3.3. Linguistic tradition and modern language movement in Vietnam

Hanji was first employed in the writing system of Vietnam. Later on Chu Nom occurred in the tenth century, and Romanized Vietnamese in the seventeenth century. The relation between languages and political status since 111 B.C. in Vietnam is shown in Table 1:

Table 1. Relation between languages and political status in Vietnam

Period	Political Status	Spoken Languages	Writing Systems
111B.C.-939A.D.	Chinese colonialism	Vietnamese/Chinese	Chinese (Han characters)
939-1651	Monarchical independence	Vietnamese/Chinese	Chinese/Nom
1651-1861	Monarchical independence	Vietnamese/Chinese	Chinese/Nom/ pre-Quoc Ngu
1861-1945	French colonialism	Vietnamese/Chinese /French	Chinese/Nom/ Quoc Ngu/French
1945-	National independence	Vietnamese	Quoc Ngu

*Based on John DeFrancis 1977.

Nom, also called *Chu Nom* (字字 字喃 or 字喃), means southern writing or southern orthography in contrast to Han characters, or *Chu Nho* (字儒), the writing of Confucian scholars (DeFrancis 1977:26-28). Chu Nom was created gradually after the classical Han writing was introduced to Vietnam. The Vietnamese found that it was not easy to use Hanji to express their colloquial speech. Therefore, they modified Hanji to develop Nom characters. It is estimated that the full development of Chu Nom came after the Vietnamese achieved independence from China in the tenth century (DeFrancis 1977:21). Although the Vietnamese created their own Chu Nom, it was generally regarded as a vulgar writing, which refers to the low language in digraphia[7]. Consequently, it neither achieved the same prestige as Han characters, nor replaced the classical Han writing. There are three major factors that contributed to the fate of Chu Nom. First, the Vietnamese were deeply influenced by the Chinese value with regard to Han characters. Since Hanji was highly regarded as the only official orthography in China, which was the suzerain of Vietnam, the Vietnamese people had no choice but to follow this traditional value. As a consequence, the Vietnamese rulers in all dynasties, except a few short-lived strongly anti-Chinese rulers, such as *HO Quy Ly* (1400-1407) and *NGUYEN Quang Trung* (1788-1792), had to recognize Han characters as the institutional writing criteria. Second, writing in Nom scripts was restricted by the civil service examination. Because the examination system was held exclusively with the contests of Chinese classics written in Hanji, all the literati that wished to pass the exam had to study the classics. Once they passed the exam and became bureaucrats, they had to maintain the examination system to ensure their monopoly of power and knowledge in the Chinese style feudal hierarchy (DeFrancis 1977:47). Third, from the perspective of orthography, Chu Nom was still difficult for the masses to learn to read and write. Chu Nom was even more difficult and complicated than Han characters because Chu Nom often combined two Han characters, one which expressed the meaning and another which expressed the pronunciation, to form a new Nom character. For example, they combined "字" with "字" to form a new Nom character "字字," and combined "字" with "南" to form "字南." The complication of Chu Nom reflects the consequence that Chu Nom was not widespread even under the promotion of Vietnamese rulers such as Ho Quy Ly (DeFrancis 1977:20-48; Nguyen 1984).

In the early part of the seventeenth century, Portuguese, Italian, Spanish, and French missionaries gradually came to preach in Vietnam. To get their ideas

---

[7] For the idea of digraphia, refer to Dale 1980 or DeFrancis 1984.

across to the local people, it was recognized by missionaries that knowledge of the spoken Vietnamese was essential. Romanized writing was thus devised to assist missionaries to acquire the Vietnamese language. It is apparent that the Vietnamese Romanization resulted from collective efforts, with the influences of diverse backgrounds of missionaries (Thompson 1987:54-55). Among the variants of Vietnamese Romanization, Alexandre de Rhodes is usually referred to as the person who provided the first systematic work of Vietnamese Romanization (DeFrancis 1977:54). In 1624, the French Jesuit Alexandre de Rhodes arrived in central Vietnam. He used Roman scripts as a writing system to describe the Vietnamese language and then he published the first Vietnamese-Portuguese-Latin dictionary, *Dictionarivm Annamiticvm, Lusitanvm et Latinvm,* and a Vietnamese catechism *Cathechismus* in 1651. De Rhodes' Romanized system with some later changes became the foundation of present Quoc Ngu, the national writing system of Vietnam (Do 1972; DeFrancis 1977:48-66; Thompson 1987:52-77).

The development of Romanized writing in Vietnam can be divided into four periods in terms of its spread (Chiung 2003): 1) Church period, from the early seventeenth century to the first half of the nineteenth century. Roman scripts were mainly used in church and among religious followers. 2) French promotion period during the second half of the nineteenth century after the French invaded Vietnam in 1858 (Vien Van Hoc 1961:21-23). In this period, Romanized Vietnamese was intentionally promoted by the French aiming to replace the classical Chinese ultimately with French (DeFrancis 1977:129-134). 3) Nationalist promotion period during the first half of the twentieth century. Vietnamese Romanization was promoted by anti-colonialism organizations, such as the *Đông Kinh Nghĩa Thục* (東京義塾) or 'Dong Kinh Free School' and *Hoi Truyen Ba Quoc Ngu* 'Association for Promoting Chu Quoc Ngu' (Vien Van Hoc 1961:24; Hoang 1994:94; Nguyen, Pham, and Tran 1998:44-54). Because Roman scripts were no longer closely associated with the French colonialist, but considered as an efficient literacy tool, Romanization thus received much greater recognition by the Vietnamese people than in the period of French promotion (DeFrancis 1977: 159). 4) National status period after 1945, when Ho Chi Minh declared the exclusive use of Chu Quoc Ngu (Ho Chi Minh 1994:64-65).

During the French colonial period, the French regime allowed TRUONG Vinh Ky (Trương Vĩnh Ký 1837-1898) to publish the first Romanized Vietnamese newspaper *Gia Dinh Bao* (*Gia Định Báo*) in Saigon since 1865 until his death. Truong served as the editor-in-chief of Gia Dinh Bao. The role of Gia Dinh Bao for Vietnamese is somewhat similar to *Tâi-oân Hú-siân Kàu-hōe-pò* (the first

Romanized newspaper in Taiwan since 1885) for Taiwanese in Taiwan (Chiung 2016).

From the perspective of literacy, roman script was much easier to acquire than Han character or Chu Nom. However, Vietnamese Romanization was not widespread until the early twentieth century. There are two primary reasons. First, the use of Romanized Vietnamese was primarily limited to the Catholic community prior to the twentieth century. DeFrancis (1977:64) has pointed out that most missionaries "looked upon it [Romanization] chiefly as a tool in working with the Vietnamese language and were not greatly concerned with urging its use in other areas." Moreover, even if people outside the Catholic community wanted to learn the Romanization, they were afraid of being treated as Catholic or collaborators with foreign missionaries since there were conflicts between local people and foreign missionaries. Consequently, there was no wide usage outside the Catholic community (DeFrancis 1977:61). Second, it was the reflection of people's psychological preference of the Han character since Han character has reached the orthodox status since the Ly dynasty. This phenomenon of preference is especially true to the traditional scholars and officials. For example, it was reported that Confucian schools, which are essential access to acquisition of Han writing and Chinese classics, continued to exist and attract students as late as the first decade or two of the twentieth century (DeFrancis 1977:124).

Since French colonization was involved in the colonial history of Vietnam, what role have the French (1861-1945) played in the orthographic transition of the Vietnamese language?

First of all, the French had weakened or even replaced the role played by the Chinese in Vietnam. In the nineteenth century, China was losing her dominance of Asia since the Opium war in 1842. In addition, Japan's successful Westernization, shown in such wars as her victories over China in 1895 and over Tsarist Russia in 1904-1905, had impressed the Vietnamese. The appearance of the French power in Indochina[8] enforced the Vietnamese people to experience the new political power from Western society, and further reconsidering their relationship with the traditional feudal China.

Second, French's antagonism toward Chinese had strengthened the promotion of the Romanized system. Their hostile attitudes toward Chinese was summed up in a letter of 15 January 1866 by a French administrator, Paulin Vial, who held the position of *Directeur du Cabinet du Gouverneur de la Cochinchine,*

---

[8] Indochina includes present Vietnam, Laos, and Cambodia.

"from the first days it was recognized that the Chinese language was a barrier between us and the natives…; it is the only one which can bring close to us the Annamites of the colony by inculcating in them the principles of European civilization and isolating them from the hostile influence of our neighbors" (quoted in DeFrancis 1977:77). Thus, the actions taken by the French colonialists included termination of the traditional civil service examination, and promotion of the Romanized Vietnamese, which was regarded as a closer connection to French since both French and Romanized Vietnamese were using Roman scripts. Nevertheless, the eventual goal of the colonialists was to replace Vietnamese with French after the Vietnamese acquired the Romanized system (DeFrancis 1977:131).

In contrast to the French ruler in Vietnam, the Japanese ruler in Taiwan played different role in terms of orthography (Chiung 2017b:152). In the case Taiwan, the Japanese rule did not felt a strong antagonism toward Han characters until 1937 when the Japanese overwhelmingly invaded China. Moreover, the Japanese rule utilized Han characters to reduce Taiwanese people's hostile attitude towards Japanese. Recall that Japanese writing consists of both Han characters and Kana syllabary. In the early period of Japanese occupation, the Japanese governors in Taiwan occasionally organized literary events for Taiwan's traditional mandarins to make them feel that Japanese and Taiwanese were in the same family of Han writing. As for Roman scripts which was favored by the French ruler in Vietnam, was not favored by the Japanese ruler since the Japanese prefer using Kana to Roman scripts. As a consequence, Roman scripts were not widely spread during the Japanese period (1895~1945) in Taiwan.

Although the French colonialists and collaborationists had promoted Romanized Vietnamese for decades by the twentieth century, it received only a slow growth (DeFrancis 1977:69). In contrast, Romanized system reached a rapid growth under the promotion of the Vietnamese nationalists when they lunched their modern nationalist movement in the early twentieth century (DeFrancis 1977:159). Romanized *Quoc Ngu* or the National Language was promoted by nationalists in the example of *Dong Kinh Nghia Thuc*[9]. In 1907 Vietnamese nationalists established Dong Kinh Nghia Thuc, Tokin Free School, a private school to teach students Western ideas, science, and to train students as well-promoters of Vietnamese nationalist movement. One of the significant features of Tokin Free School was promotion of Quoc Ngu. As Marr (1971:167) stated, the teachers at Tokin Free School showed "a new willingness to employ quoc-ngu

---

[9] For details, see Marr (1971:156-184) and Chuong (1982).

when introducing outside ideas or techniques, and they urged each student to use the Romanized script subsequently as a device for passing on modern knowledge to hundreds of their less literate countrymen."

Although Quoc Ngu had spread out rapidly in the early part of the twentieth century, it does not mean that Quoc Ngu had replaced Chinese or French. Spoken Vietnamese and Quoc Ngu were still subordinated to French and Chinese until the establishment of Democratic Republic of Viet Nam in 1945. The contemptuous attitudes of the Vietnamese language could be well shown by a Vietnamese politician, *HO Duy Kien*, who referred to the Vietnamese language as a "patois" similar to those found in Gascogne, Brittany, Normandy, or Provence, during an otherwise routine Cochinchina Colonial Council discussion on primary education in 1931. Furthermore, Ho even concluded that it is going to take Vietnamese more than five hundred years to improve their "patois" to the level of French and Chinese (Marr 1981:136).

A few days after Ho Chi Minh declared the establishment of Democratic Republic of Viet Nam on September 2, 1945, Ho soon issued a decree to promote Quoc Ngu and Vietnamese on September 8 (DeFrancis 1977:239). Meanwhile, Ho Chi Minh launched an "Appeal to Fight Illiteracy" in October as follows (Ho, 1994:64-65):

> Citizens of Viet Nam!
>
> Formerly, when they ruled over our country, the French colonialists carried out a policy of obscurantism. They limited the number of schools; they did not want us to get an education so that they could deceive and exploit us all the more easily.
>
> Ninety-five percent of the total population received no schooling, which means that nearly all Vietnamese were illiterate. How could we have progressed in such conditions?
>
> Now that we have won back independence, one of the most urgent tasks at present is to raise the people's cultural level.
>
> The Government has decided that before a year has passed, every Vietnamese will have learnt Quoc Ngu, the national Romanized script. A Popular Education Department has been set up to that effect.
>
> People of Viet Nam!
>
> If you want to safeguard national independence, if you want our nation to grow strong and our country prosperous, every one of you must know his rights and duties. He must possess knowledge so as to be able to

participate in the building of the country. First of all he must learn to read and write Quoc Ngu.

Let the literates teach the illiterates; let them take part in mass education. Let the illiterates study hard. The husband will teach his wife, the elder brother his junior, the children their parents, the master his servants; the rich will open classes for illiterates in their own houses.

The women should study even harder for up to now many obstacles have stood in their way. It is high time now for them to catch up with the men and be worthy of their status of citizens with full electoral rights. I hope that young people of both sexes will eagerly participate in this work.

The number of people who acquired to read and write Quoc Ngu after the achievement of independence was reported by LE Thanh Khoi (quoted in DeFrancis 1977:240) to have risen from 20 percent in the year 1945 to 70 percent in 1953. Similar statistics were reported by Huang as follows:

Table 2. Numbers of literate in Vietnam

Year	Numbers of Literate	Percentage of Total Population
1945	2,520,678	14%
1946	4,680,000	27%
1947	6,880,000	39%
1948	9,680,000	55%
1949	11,580,000	66%
1950	12,000,000	68%
1953	14,000,000	79%

*Percentage was calculated based on the data of Huang (1953:20).

How could Vietnam successfully replace Han characters and Chu Nom with Romanized Quoc Ngu? Hannas (1997:88-92) stated twelve factors, and concluded that "the compelling factor behind this success is that Vietnam never had a top-down, coordinated, state-backed movement to effect the reform" (1997:84). Although it is true that bottom-up grass root movement played an important role in Vietnam's orthographic transition, I would attribute the consequence to two crucial factors: 1) external factor of political interaction between Vietnam and China in the international situation of the first half of the twentieth century, and 2) internal factor of social demand for literacy and anti-feudal hierarchy. These two crucial points can apply to the case of Taiwanese Romanization, and explain why Romanized system has not achieved popular and official status in Taiwan (Chiung 2003).

The external factor involves the complexity of international situation in the 1940s, as Hodgkin (1981:288) stated that the Vietnamese "faced with a varying combination of partly competing, partly collaborating imperialisms, French, Japanese, British and American, with *Kuomintang* China." At that time, Vietnam was considered an important base to attack southern China[10] when Japan's invasion of China became more apparent and aggressive since the 1930s (Hodgkin 1981:288). The Japanese military eventually entered Vietnam and sharing with French the control of Vietnam in the early 1940s. From the perspective of China, suppression against Japan's military activities in Vietnam was desired. However, in the viewpoint of the French, they were afraid that China would take over Vietnam again if Chinese troops entered Vietnam on the excuse of suppression against Japanese forces (Jiang 1971:181). For the Vietnamese people, how to maintain their national identity and achieve national independence from the imperialisms were considered priority by their leaders such as Ho Chi Minh. Ho's Chinese strategy was to keep Chinese forces away from Vietnam, and minimize the possibility of Chinese comeback in the Indochina. Politically speaking, Ho refused Chinese army entering Vietnam (Jiang 1971:107) as well as instigating anti-Chinese movement (Jiang 1971:228-240). Culturally, Romanized Vietnamese was considered a distinctive feature of cultural boundary between Vietnam and China. These considerations have impelled Ho in favor of Romanization rather than Han characters which are used in China (Chiung 2013, 2017).

The internal factor of social demand for literacy is understandable. Recall that China was the only major threat to the traditional feudal society of Vietnam prior to the nineteenth century. In that situation, although the adoption of Han characters could cause the majority of Vietnamese to be illiterated, it could, on the other hand, minimize the potential invasion from China, and more importantly, preserve the vested interests of the Vietnamese bureaucrats in the Chinese style feudal hierarchy. However, with the advent of the twentieth century, Vietnam has faced a train of international colonialism. Since Ho Chi Minh claimed that 95 percent of Vietnam's total population were illiterates, it was important to equip

---

[10] In the view point of Japan, domination of Vietnam and its northern trade-route was essential for effective control of southern China since the *Tonkin* Railway from *Haiphong* to *Yunnan* was vital source of supplies for Kuomintang China (Hodgkin 1981:288).

the people with primary education, which was considered essential to modernization in order to fight against imperialisms. Thus, the efficient and easily learned Romanization was the best choice for literacy in contrast to the complexity of Han characters. In addition, it is more aggressive for illiterates to accept a new writing system than literates to shift their literacy to a different orthography. For example, in the case of English, Stubbs (1980:72) points out that "conservatism and the inertia of habits and tradition" played an important role in explaining why English spelling reform is not successful. Since the majority of Vietnamese were illiterates, and only a few elites were skilled in Han writing or French during the promotion of Quoc Ngu, it was clear that Romanized Vietnamese would be favored by the majority, and thus won the literacy campaign.

4. Language, literacy, and nationalism in Taiwan

4.1. History of domination by foreign powers in Taiwan

In 1624 the Dutch occupied Taiwan and established the first alien regime in Taiwan. Roman scripts were then introduced to Taiwan by the Dutch. In 1661 *Koxinga* (國姓爺 or 鄭成功), a remnant force of the former Chinese *Ming* Empire, failed to fight against the new *Qing* Empire, and therefore he retreated to Taiwan. Koxinga expelled the Dutch and established a sinitic regime in Taiwan as a base to fight back to Mainland China. Confucianism and civil service examination were thus imposed to Taiwan since Koxinga's regime until the early twentieth century. The Koxinga regime was later annexed by the Qing Empire in 1683. Two centuries later, the sovereignty of Taiwan was transferred from Qing to Japan because of the Sino-Japan war in 1895. At the end of World War II, Japanese forces surrendered to the Allied Forces. *CHIANG Kai-shek*, the leader of the Chinese Nationalist (KMT or Kuomintang) took over Taiwan and Northern Vietnam on behalf of the Allied Powers under General Order No.1 of September 2, 1945 (Peng 1995:60-61). Meanwhile, Chiang Kai-shek was fighting against the Chinese Communist Party in Mainland China. In 1949, Chiang's troops were completely defeated and then pursued by the Chinese Communists. At that time, Taiwan's national status was supposed to be dealt with by a peace treaty among the fighting nations. However, because of Chiang's defeat in China, Chiang decided to occupy Taiwan as a base under the excuse that, "Taiwan was traditionally part of China," and from there fight back to Mainland China (Kerr 1992; Peng 1995; Su 1980; Ong 1993). Consequently, Chiang's political regime

Republic of China[11] (ROC) was renewed in Taiwan and has remained there since 1949.

In comparison of Taiwanese and Vietnamese histories, although both of them were dominated by alien forces, there were distinctive differences which explain why the Taiwanese did not establish an independent country at the end of World War II as Vietnamese did. First of all, the Taiwanese have never established their own independent state. In fact, the idea of establishing a modern nation-state did not come to mind of the Taiwanese people until 1947[12], when the February 28 Massacre happened (Ng 1994:202). The concept of nation, as Anderson defines, is an "imagined political community" (Anderson 1983:6). It indicates that nations are invented rather than naturally born. Thus, having collective historical experience is quite important for the members of a group to restore their collective memory and thus take further actions to achieve their collective objects. For example, many revolts during Qing's occupation of Taiwan had to gather masses by restoring their historical experience of "Anti-Qing and restore the Ming dynasty" (反清復明). By the end of the nineteenth century, the memory that the Taiwanese had was the proposed renaissance of the Ming, which refers to an alien historic Chinese dynasty rather than a localized modern Taiwanese nation-state. In other words, the creation of Taiwanese nation is not long enough to become mature. Second, the re-occupation of Taiwan since 1945 by the Chinese is the crucial point explaining why Taiwanese do not form their own nation-state so far. Would Vietnam become independent if it was under the control of China at the end of World War II? During the occupation of Taiwan, the Chinese ROC regime reconstructed the Chinese identity of the Taiwanese people in the way, which will be detailed in the following sections.

4.2. Modern nationalist movement in Taiwan

Generally speaking, Taiwan was an indigenous society before the Dutch occupation in the early seventeenth century. There was only tribal awareness and no consciousness of being "Taiwanese."

After vast Han immigration, Taiwan became an immigrant society. In the early period of immigration, most of those immigrants just proposed to live in

---

[11] Republic of China was formerly the official name of the Chinese government (1912-1949) in China, but was replaced by the People's Republic of China (P.R.C) in 1949.

[12] The exact date for the origin of Taiwanese independence movement may vary from scholar to scholar. But, the February 28 Massacre of 1947, in which over twenty thousand of Taiwanese people were killed by Chiang's troops (Kerr 1992:303), is usually considered the origin of current Taiwanese independence movement (Ng 1994).

Taiwan provisionally, and they identified themselves with their original clans in southeast China (Tan 1994:140-141). However, during the course of the Qing Dynasty, Taiwan moved from an immigrant society to a native society through the process of indigenization (Tan 1994:92). That means that the immigrants to Taiwan began to settle down and to distinguish themselves from people who lived in China. Therefore, there is an old Taiwanese saying that *"Tngsoann-kheh[13], tui-poann soeh[14]."* It means that you should not believe Chinese too much while you are doing business with them. In short, the late of Qing dynasty era was the origin of a pro-Taiwanese nation in terms of Su (Su 1992:196-200).

Owing to modernization and capitalization during the Japanese occupation, the earlier pro-Taiwanese identity has advanced to Taiwanese nationhood (Su 1992:220). Those immigrant identities, once attached to the place of their ancestors such as *"Chiang-chiu* people," and *"Choan-chiu* people," have been replaced by a developing sense of being a *"Taioan-lang"* (literally Taiwanese people, in contrast to the Japanese). Thereafter, "Taioan-lang" was widely used by the people all over Taiwan.

The strong Taiwanese identity[15] during the Japanese era could be well illustrated by the following organizations, which made the Taiwanese nationalist movement flourished in the 1920s. For example, the guidelines of *Sin-Bin Hoe* (新民會 New People Association), which was established in 1920, mentioned: "To push the political reform in Taiwan in order to improve the happiness of Taiwanese.[16]" (Ong 1988:44-49).

Moreover, the declarations (1925) of the Association of Taiwanese Academic Studies (東京台灣學術研究會), which was also organized by some overseas Taiwanese students in Tokyo included (Ong 1988:91-92):

"To support the liberation of Taiwan!"

"To obtain the freedom to speak Taiwanese!"

"Taiwan independence forever and ever!"

After the identification as a Taiwanese[17] nation during the era of the Japanese

---

[13] The Han people who already settled down on Taiwan called themselves *"Pun-te-lang"* (本地人 local people), in contrast to *"Tngsoann-lang"* (唐山人 Mainland China people) who lived in China (Su 1992:196-200). *"kheh"* means a guest or a traveler. *"Tngsoann-kheh"* means travelers from Mainland China.

[14] 唐山客, 對半說 You should discount the words of the Chinese people.

[15] The Taiwanese identity in the Japanese era is much more on the ground of Taiwanese vs. Japanese, rather than Taiwanese vs. Chinese.

[16] "為增進台灣人的幸福, 進行台灣統治的改革運動" (Ong 1988:44-49).

[17] Even though some people might identify themselves as Japanese during the *Hong-bin-hoa* movement (皇民化運動 movement of being the glorious people of the Japanese Empire),

occupation, came an era of confused identity (i.e., Taiwanese consciousness versus Chinese consciousness). This was mainly caused by the new immigrants[18] who came into Taiwan along with Chiang around 1949. Nowadays, most new immigrants still identify themselves as Chinese (Ong 1993:87). In addition, the KMT's sinicization of Taiwan also played an important role in the construction of Chinese national identity.

Since the awareness of being a Taiwanese was a threat to the Chinese KMT regime, the KMT regime proposed to "brain wash" Taiwanese through the national education system and the mass media (Ong 1993:70-71). Taiwanese people were forced to learn Chinese language, literature and history. As a result, some Taiwanese, especially those taught in Chinese education, were more likely to identify themselves as Chinese.[19]

In short, the people of Taiwan today remain divided in the view of themselves and where they should go politically. Their diversity of national identity has affected not only political issues regarding Taiwan's national status, but also cultural issues, such as Taiwanese writing and Taiwanese literature, which are the main concerns of the contemporary Taiwanese language movement.

4.3. Linguistic tradition and modern language movement in Taiwan

The first written language in Taiwan was the so-called *Sinkang* Manuscripts, a Romanized system to write the vernacular of indigenous Siraya tribes during Dutch occupation of Taiwan in the seventeenth century. Thereafter, the classical Han writing was adopted as an official language by government, and *Koa-a-chheh* was treated as the popular writing for the public during the Koxinga and the Qing occupations. In addition to those two written forms, other Romanized systems have been developed to write Taiwanese[20] and Hakka languages since the

---

most people still regarded Taiwanese as a different nation from Japanese. For example, the Japanese awarded so-called "National Language Family" (國語家庭) to selected Taiwanese who were qualified to be Japanese. The qualified people were only 0.9% of total population of Taiwan in 1942 (Huang 1993:94).

[18] More than one million (Huang 1993:25) soldiers and refugees, who currently make up 13% of Taiwan's population, came to Taiwan along with the KMT regime around 1949, while the Mainland China was under the control of Chinese Communist Party. They were called "*Goa-seng-lang*" (外省人 Mainlanders or people from other provinces) by native Taiwanese. According to Hu-chhing Ong (1993), 54% of Mainlanders identified themselves as Chinese, only 7.3% identified themselves as Taiwanese, the rest are neutral. In other words, most of those Mainlanders still identify themselves as Chinese nowadays.

[19] For updated information on the identity issues, readers may refer to Chiung (2017a).

[20] Taiwanese is usually called Taigi in Taiwan. It is occasionally called Holooe, Southern Min, or

nineteenth century (Chiung 2016). After Taiwan became a part of Japan (1895-1945), Japanese writing became the official written language in Taiwan. After World War II, Mandarin Chinese became the orthodoxy of writing under Chiang Kai-shek's occupation of Taiwan. The relation between language and political status in Taiwan was shown in Table 3.

Table 3. Relation between language and political status in Taiwan

Period	Political status	Spoken Languages	Writing Systems**
-1624	Tribal society	Aboriginal	Tribal totem
1624-1661	Dutch colonialism	Aboriginal/Taiwanese*	Sinkang Classical Han (文言文)
1661-1683	Koxinga colonialism	Aboriginal/Taiwanese	Classical Han Sinkang
1683-1895	Qing colonialism	Aboriginal/Taiwanese	Classical Han Koa-a-chheh (歌仔冊) Peh-oe-ji Sinkang
1895-1945	Japanese colonialism	Aboriginal/Taiwanese/Japanese	Japanese Classical Han Colloquial Han (in Taiwanese) Colloquial Han (in Mandarin) Peh-oe-ji Kana-Taiwanese (臺式假名)
1945-	KMT/ROC colonialism	Aboriginal/Taiwanese/Mandarin	Chinese (Mandarin) Taiwanese Aboriginal

* Taiwanese means Taigi and Hakka languages here.

** The order of listed writing systems in each cell of this column do not indicate the year of occurrences. The first listed orthography refers to the official written language adopted by its relevant governor.

Min-nan. Taigi speakers account for 73.3% of Taiwan's population, Hakfa 12%, indigenous 1.7%, and Mandarin speakers who came to Taiwan with KMT account 13% (Huang 1993:21).

Romanization was first introduced to Taiwan by the Dutch missionary in the seventeenth century. As Campbell (1903) described, "they [i.e., Dutch] not only carried on a profitable trade, but made successful efforts in educating and Christianising the natives." The natives around Sinkang[21] were first taught Christianity through the learning of the Romanization[22] of Sinkang dialect, which are extinct today. The were some textbooks and testaments written in Romanized Sinkang, such as the The Gospel of St. Matthew in Formosan Sinkang Dialect and Dutch (*Het Heylige Euangelium Matthei en Jonannis Ofte Hagnau Ka D'llig Matiktik, Ka na Sasoulat ti Mattheus, ti Johannes appa. Overgefet inde Formosaansche tale, voor de Inwoonders van Soulang, Mattau, Sinckan, Bacloan, Tavokan, en Tevorang.*), which was translated by Daniel Gravius in 1661 (Campbell 1888; Lai 1990:121-123).

After Koxinga drove out the Dutch, classical Han writing was adopted as the official writing, and it was succeed by the following Qing dynasty. Although classical Han writing was adopted as official writing, the Koa-a-chheh[23] (literally, song books) was the popular writing among the common people. I refer this popular writing to Koa-a-chheh or *Koa-a-ji* (literally, the characters of song book) because many traditional song books were written in this system.

In Koa-a-chheh writing, each sentence was composed of either five or seven characters. These characters were derived from Han characters. In general, people chose characters from an available inventory of characters or created new characters[24]. The choice of characters could vary from writer to writer. In other words, different writers could choose different characters to express the same word. There are three main principles while choosing from available characters:

First, the same etymon is written with the same Han characters. For example "想" (*siunn*: think) in the Koa-a-chheh sentence "蚊仔想著足怨切" (*bang-a siunn tioh chiok oan-chheh*: the mosquito was very sad while he thought about that). Second, the meaning of a character was ignored; only the sound was attended to. For example, "足" (pronounced as *chiok*) was supposed to be the meaning of "foot" in classical Han writing, however, it means "very" (*chiok*) in

---

[21] Sinkang (新港), also spelled in Sinkan, was the place opposited to the Tayouan where the Dutch had settled in 1624. The present location is Sin-chhi district of Tainan city (新市區, 台南市).

[22] After Koxinga drove the Dutch out from Taiwan, that Roman scripts were still used by those plain tribes for a period. It is said that those aborigines continued to use the romanization for over a century-and-a-half after the Dutch had left Taiwan (Naojiro Murakami 1933).

[23] For more details regarding koa-a-chheh, see Ong (1993:169-215).

[24] For instance, "勿," which means "no," was combined with "會," which means "able," to represent the new character "勿會," which means "unable" in Taiwanese.

the Koa-a-chheh sentence above. Third, the pronunciation of a character was ignored, and its meaning borrowed to express the same meaning in different languages. For example, the meaning of "蚊" was borrowed to express "mosquito" (*bang*) in Taiwanese.

Modern language movement in Taiwan can be divided into three periods. The first period refers to the Romanized Pėh-ōe-jī movement in the late nineteenth century and early twentieth century. In this period, Romanization was mainly limited to church activities. The second period refers to the movement of colloquial writing (白話文運動) in 1920s and 1930s. In this period, the literates especially those who were taught in traditional Han characters or Japanese language were highly involved in the debates. The third one refers to the contemporary Taibun movement (Tâi-bûn 台文運動) since the 1980s. Taibun literally means Written Taiwanese. The contemporary Taibun promoters attempt to promote the standardized/modernized Taiwanese to a national status in Taiwan.

In 1865, the first religious mission after the Dutch, was settled in present *Tailam* city, by missionary James L. Maxwell and his assistants (Hsu 1995:6-8; Lai 1990). Before missionaries arrived in Taiwan, there were already several missionary activities in Southeast Asia. They had started developing Romanization of Hokkien[25] and Hakka. For instance, Walter H. Medhurst's *A Dictionary of the Hok-këèn Dialect of the Chinese Language,* which was considered the earliest existing dictionary for Hokkien was published in 1837. The role of Medhurst's dictionary for Hokkien is somewhat similar to Alexandre de Rhodes's dictionary for Vietnamese.

George L. Mackay's *Chinese Romanized Dictionary of the Formosan Vernacular*, which was considered the first dictionary to focus on the Taiwanese vernacular spoken in Taiwan, was completed in 1874. *Chinese-English Dictionary of the Vernacular or Spoken Language of Amoy, with the Principal Variations of the Chang-chew and Chin-chew Dialects*[26] was published by Rev. Carstairs Douglas in 1873. The currently most popular Romanized dictionary in Taiwan, *E-mng-im Sin Ji-tian*[27] edited by Rev. William Campbell, was first published in Taiwan by Taiwan Church Press in 1913 (Lai 1990). The first *New*

---

[25] Hokkien (Southern Min) is usually referred to as the origin of modern Taiwanese language Taigi (現代台語).

[26] 《廈英大辭典》; See "Introduction to Douglas' Amoy-English dictionary," by ANG Ui-jin 1993.

[27] *A Dictionary of the Amoy Vernacular Spoken throughout the Prefectures of Chin-chiu, Chiang-chiu and Formosa* 《廈門音新字典》 There have been fourteen editions by 1987. This dictionary has been reprinted and renamed as *William Campbell's Taiwanese Dictionary* since 2009.

Testament[28] in Romanized Amoy was published in 1873, and the first *Old Testament*[29] in 1884.

That Romanization was called *Pėh-ōe-jī* (白話字) in Taiwan (Chiung 2001b, 2016). It means the script of vernacular speech in contrast to the complicated Han characters of *wenyan*. If Sinkang writing represents the first foreign missionary activities in Taiwan, then the development of *Peh-oe-ji* reveals the comeback of missionary influences after the Dutch withdrawal from Taiwan (Chiung 2001c). The wide use of Poe-oe-ji in Taiwan was promoted by the missionary Reverend Thomas Barclay while he published monthly *Tai-oan-hu-sia*[n] *Kau-hoe-po* [30] (Taiwan Prefectural aCity Church News) in July 1885. In addition to publications related to Christianity, there were some other publications written in Peh-oe-ji, such as *Pit Soan e Chho· Hak* (Fundamental Mathematics) by GE Ui-lim in 1897, *Lai Goa Kho Khan-ho·-hak*[31] (The Principles and Practice of Nursing) by G. Gushue-Taylor in 1917, and the novel *Chhut Si-Soa*[n] [32] (Line between Life and Death) by TE[n] Khe-phoan (鄭溪泮) in 1926. Besides, recently there were a series of novels translated from world literatures into Peh-oe-ji by the members of "*5% Tai-ek Ke-oe*[33]" (5% Project of Translation in Taiwanese) since 1996.

In short, the Peh-oe-ji was the ground of Romanization of modern Taiwanese colloquial writing. Even though currently there are several different Romanizations for writing Taiwanese, many of them were derived from Peh-oe-ji. Besides, the use of Peh-oe-ji and its derivations were more popular than other systems of Romanization in contemporary Taiwanese literature.

Prior to the twentieth century, the classical Han writing was the dominant writing accepted by feudal mandarins in Taiwan. Most traditional literary works were then written in this system. However, about two decades later under the

---

[28] *Lan e Kiu-chu Ia-so· Ki-tok e Sin-iok* 《咱的救主耶穌基督的新約》

[29] *Ku-iok e Seng Keng* 《舊約的聖經》

[30] 《台灣府城教會報》 Taiwan Prefectural City Church News has changed its title several times, and the recent title (1988) is Taioan Kau-hoe Kong-po (台灣教會公報 Taiwan Church News). It was published in Peh-oe-ji until 1970, and then switched to Mandarin Chinese (Lai 1990:17-19).

[31] 《內外科看護學》

[32] 《出死線》

[33] Five Percent 台譯計劃. In November of 1995, some Taiwanese youths who were concerned about the writing of Taiwanese decided to deal with the Taiwanese modernization and loanwords through translation from foreign language into Taiwanese. The organization 5% Project of Translation in Taiwanese was then established on February 24, 1996. Its members have to contribute 5% of their income every month to the 5% fund. The first volume includes 7 books. They are Lear Ong, Kui-a Be-chhia, Mi-hun-chhiu[n] e Kui-a, Hoa-hak-phin e Hian-ki, Thi[n]-kng Cheng e Loan-ai Ko·-su, Pu-ho·-lang e Lek-su, and Opera Lai e Mo·-sin-a, were published by Tai-leh (台笠) press in November 1996.

Japanese rule, Taiwanese intellectuals started the issue of reforming classical Han writing. They published and argued against the traditional Han writing. Some examples are *NG Teng-chhong*'s (黃呈聰 1922) "Essay on the mission of vernacular writing,[34]" and *NG Tiau-khim*'s (黃朝琴 1922) "Issue of reforming the classical Han writing.[35]" In general, the movement of colloquial writing from the 1920s to the 1930s centered on two points. First, they intended to reform the complicated classical Han writing and then develop a new writing form, which was based on the colloquial speech. Second, they attempted to create a new literature, which was based on the new colloquial writing, instead of the old literature, which was based on the classical Han writing. (Ou 1985, Iap 1993; Phenn 1992; Lim 1993; Lim 1996; Tiunn 1993).

Regarding the claim of reforming classical Han writing, it quickly and successfully aroused a sympathetic echo from the public. However, it raised another controversy. What language should be the base of colloquial writing? Japanese, Mandarin, or Taiwanese? At that time, Taiwan was under the control of Japan, and the modern Japanese writing was taught through the national education system. It seemed that Japanese writing was the best choice, if considering the economic factors. However, Japanese was not the vernacular of the Taiwanese people. Most of the people still used Taiwan languages in their daily life. Therefore, people such as *NG Chioh-hui* (黃石輝 1930) and *KOEH Chhiu-seng* (郭秋生 1931), published "Why don't we promote homeland literature?,[36]" and "A proposal for constructing the Taiwanese language.[37]" They advocated that Taiwanese people should use colloquial Taiwanese to write poems, fiction, and so on. In other words, they asserted that the new literature should be written in Taiwanese. In addition to Taiwanese, Mandarin was also proposed by a few people such as *TIUNN Ngou-kun* (張我軍), who had studied in China. Because Tiunn thought that Taiwanese vernacular was too vulgar to become a literate language, he advocated using Mandarin[38] as the literate language to create this

---

[34] <論普及白話文的新使命>, 發表 ti《台灣》第 4 年第 1 號

[35] <漢文改革論> 發表 ti《台灣》

[36] <怎樣不提倡鄉土文學> 發表 ti《伍人報》

[37] <建設台灣話文一提案> 發表 ti《台灣新聞》

[38] Under the Japanese occupation, most of the Taiwanese spoke either Taiwanese or Japanese. Only a few who had studied abroad in China were able to speak in Mandarin. The key point that someone proposed to promote Mandarin writing as the new writing system was because Mandarin was written in Han characters. People would be able to guess the meanings from Han characters, even though Mandarin was not the vernacular of the Taiwanese people. Besides, modern colloquial writing of Mandarin had been promoted since the movement of May 4, 1919 (五四運動) in China. Those promoters asserted that it would be better for Taiwan to follow China's writing reform.

new literature.

As a consequence, the so-called New Literature developed in the 1920s was generally written in the colloquial speech of Japanese, Taiwanese, and Mandarin. Although Japanese writing was the only official written language, writings in colloquial Taiwanese or Mandarin, which primarily used Hanji (these were so-called *Hanbun* 漢文) were still allowed in some particular newspapers and magazines until 1937, the year the Japanese started to attack China. In order to win the war against China, Japan promoted the *Hong-bin-hoa*[39] movement in Taiwan, which strongly forced Taiwanese to identify themselves as Japanese, and then fight for the Japanese against the Chinese. During the Hong-bin-hoa movement, Han writing, which was the symbol of a connection between Taiwanese and Chinese, was then prohibited by Japan. The movement of colloquial writing since 1920s was therefore ended in 1937.

Although the colloquial writing movement successfully converted the traditional classical Han writing to modern colloquial writing, Hanji still was the dominant orthography. There were only a few colloquial writing promoters such as *CHHOA Poe-hoe* (蔡培火), who pointed out that colloquial writing in Hanji was still a heavy burden for most Taiwanese (Chiung 2017b:141). The role of CHHOA Poe-hoe for Taiwanese Romanization is somewhat similar to PHAM Quynh or NGUYEN Van Vinh for Vietnamese Romanization (Chiung 2017b). Chhoa advocated using Taiwanese Romanization to liberate illiterates. He pointed out the relationship between new Taiwan and Roman scripts as follows (Chhoa 1925:14-15):

Pún-tó lâng lóng-kiōng ū saⁿ-pah lȧk-chȧp-bān lâng, kin-kin chiah chha-put-to jī-chȧp-bān lâng ū hȧk-būn, kiám m̄-sī chin chió mah? Che sī sím-mih goân-in neh? Chit hāng, sī lán ka-tī bē-hiáu khoàⁿ hȧk-būn tāng; chit hāng, sī siat-hoat ê lâng bô ū chȧp-hun ê sêng-sim. Iáu koh chit hāng, chiū-sī beh ȯh hȧk-būn ê bûn-jī giân-gú thài kan-kè hui-siông oh-tit ȯh.

We Taiwanese have 3.6 millions of population, but only two hundred thousand of them are literate. Is not it too few? What are the reasons? One is that we think little of literacy; another reason is that the ruler is not sincere to promote education; and the third

---

[39] 皇民化運動: Movement of being the glorious people of the Japanese Empire.

is that the orthography [i.e., Hanji] and language are too difficult
to learn literacy.

However, although Romanization is much more efficient than Hanji,
Romanized Taiwanese is not widely accepted by people in Taiwan. Writing in
roman script is regarded as the low language in digraphia. There are three crucial
points for this phenomenon (Chiung 2001a, 2001b, 2001c).

First, people's preference for Han characters is caused by their internalized
socialization. Because Han characters have been adopted as the official
orthography for two thousand years, being able to master Han characters well is
a symbol of scholarship in the Han cultural areas. Writing in scripts other than
Han characters may be regarded as childish writing. For example, when *Tai-oan-
hu-sia^n Kau-hoe-po*, the first Taiwanese newspaper in Romanization, was
published in 1885, Rev. Thomas Barclay exhorted readers of the newspaper not
to "look down at Peh-pe-ji; do not regard it as a childish writing" (Barclay 1885).
In general, it is difficult to change people's preference unless the ruling class is
strongly in favor of Romanization as it was in Vietnam during the French colonial
period.

Second, misunderstanding of the nature and function of Han characters has
enforced people's preference for Hanji. Many people believe that Hanji are ideally
suited for the Han language family, which includes the Taiwanese language; they
believe that Taiwanese cannot be expressed well without Hanji because Hanji are
logographs and each character expresses a distinctive semantic function. In
addition, many people believe LIAN Heng's (1987) claim that "there are no
Taiwanese words which do not have corresponding characters." However,
scholars such as Cheng (1989) have pointed out that not all Taiwanese words have
corresponding Han characters. According to Cheng (1989:332), approximately
5% of the Taiwanese morphemes have no appropriate Han characters, and they
account for as much as 15% of the total number of characters in a written
Taiwanese text. Regarding the structure of Hanji, DeFrancis (1996:40) has
pointed out that Han characters are "primarily sound-based and only secondarily
semantically oriented." In DeFrancis' opinion, it is a myth to regard Han
characters as logographic. He even concludes that "the inefficiency of the system
stems precisely from its clumsy method of sound representation and the added
complication of an even more clumsy system of semantic determinatives"
(DeFrancis 1996:40). If Han characters are logographs, the process involved in
reading them should be different from phonological or phonetic writings.

However, research conducted by Tzeng et al. has pointed out that "the phonological effect in the reading of the Chinese characters is real and its nature seems to be similar to that generated in an alphabetic script" (Tzeng et al. 1992:128). Their research reveals that the reading process of Han characters is similar to that for phonetic writing. In short, there is no evidence to support the view that the Han characters are logographs. Moreover, the case of Vietnamese Romanization has proven that there was no difficulty to convert Han characters into Romanization from the perspective of linguistics and orthography.

The third reason that Peh-oe-ji is not widespread in Taiwan is because of political factors. Japan and Chinese KMT were two foreign regimes ruling Taiwan in the twentieth century. Both Japan and China are the countries in favor of Han characters. In the case of Japan, they attempted to reduce Taiwanese people's hostile attitude towards Japanese colonialism as I mentioned in previous section. As for China, symbolically, Han characters are regarded as a symbol of Chinese culture by the Chinese ROC regime. Writing in scripts other than Han characters is forbidden because it is perceived as a challenge to Chinese culture and Chinese nationalism. For example, the Romanized New Testament "*Sin Iok*" was once seized in 1975 because the Romanized Peh-oe-ji was regarded as a challenge to the orthodox status of Han characters (Chiung 2016:153).

The third period of Taiwanese language movement refers to the "*Taibun* movement" from the mid-1980s to the present day. It reveals the upsurge in promoting standardization for Taiwanese languages, and the promotion of *Taigi* literature[40]. Taibun, on the grounds of its characters, means modern Taiwanese writing or Taigi writing. It was created in contrast to *Zhongwen* (中文), which means modern Mandarin Chinese writing.

As the colloquial writing movement became allied with the political movement in the 1920s, the Taibun movement also occurred along with the rise of the native political activities against the foreign KMT regime in the middle of 1980s. Generally speaking, the Taibun movement consists of two dimensions: the linguistic and the literature dimensions. From the linguistic dimension, vernacular education and standardization of written Taiwanese are the two primary goals of Taibun promoters. From the perspective of literature, the Taibun movement attempts to link to the issue of Taiwanese writing, which occurred during the colloquial writing movement in the early period of the twentieth century, and then

---

[40] The term "Taigi literature" (台語文學) is to specify the literature in Taiwanese language(s). It refers to literature works written in native languages such as Taigi and Hakfa. Occasionally, it refers to works in Taigi only.

establish Taigi literature. For example, Yam Poetry Society[41] was established by some Taiwanese writers in May 1991. They claimed that their objectives were "to create the Taiwanese literature in the native Taiwanese languages[42]," and "to achieve the standardization and literaturization of Taigi[43]" (Lim 1996:97-99).

Under the colonial rule of KMT, not only was vernacular writing suppressed[44], but even literary works about the Taiwan society, which were written in Mandarin Chinese by native Taiwanese writers were not recognized as Taiwan Literature[45]. They were belittled as so-called "Literature of Home Villages[46]." In other words, literature in Taiwan was treated as a branch of China Literature[47], i.e., it was regarded as the frontier literature within the larger frame of China Literature. Thereafter, in the 1980s, as soon as the rise of the native political movement and the debates on Taiwanese consciousness versus Chinese consciousness were becoming more common, more and more Taiwanese people started to recognize the national status of Taiwan Literature. In other words, the derogatory term "Literature of Home Villages" was replaced by glorious Taiwan Literature, which exhibits equality with China Literature. Consequently, Taiwan Literature acquired the national status it deserved in the 1980s (Phenn 1992; Iap 1993; Tiunn 1993).

After Taiwan Literature achieved national status, people paid more attention to the relationship between Taigi literature and Taiwan Literature. Taibun writers, such as *LIM Chong-goan,* claimed that Taiwan Literature must be written in Taiwanese. Lim mentioned, as follows (Lim 1984:18-21):

今仔日台灣文壇為何猶未寫出不朽的精采的作品，除了一寡因素之外，就是作家忽視母語，輕視母語，… 一個無自信的人，怎有才調寫出不朽的精采的作品，結果也只好乖

---

[41] *Han-chi Si-sia* 蕃薯詩社.

[42] 用台灣本土語言創造正統的台灣文學.

[43] 追求台語文字化與文學化.

[44] Vernacular writing was denounced as "Dialect Literature" (方言文學) and then rebelled by the majority of Mandarin Chinese writers before 1980s. Only a few writers such as *Chong-goan Lim* (林宗源) and *Hiong-iong* (向陽) dared to take the risk of writing in vernacular (Lim 1996:16-21).

[45] The term "Taiwan Literature" is used to translate the term "台灣文學." It occurred in the so-called Debates on Literature of Home Village in the late 1970s. "Taiwan Literature" indicates the national status instead of regional literature under the national frame of China. "Taiwan Literature" was adopted here instead of Taiwanese literature, because "Taiwanese literature" may refer to "literature in Taiwanese languages."

[46] This term is from the so-called Debates on Literature of Home Villages (鄉土文學論戰) in the second half of 1970s. For details, see Phenn 1992, and Iap 1993.

[47] China Literature was adopted instead of Chinese literature is in contrast to Taiwan Literature.

乖做文化的屬民，文學的奴隸。所以今仔日的作家，著愛
重新整合創新台語，按呢，才有才調寫出現時現地醞釀佇
心靈中的世界。

Why does immortal work still not occur in the literature of Taiwan? There are some factors, one is that our writers ignored and looked down our own mother tongue because they were not confident of their vernacular. How could a writer without any confidence create an immortal work? Consequently, they had to subordinate themselves to Chinese culture and become the slaves of Chinese literature. So, today, we Taiwanese writers have to devote ourselves to literary works in Taigi. Then, we will be able to describe our world in our mind.

台灣文學就是愛用台語來寫…台灣文學就是台灣人用台灣
人的母語寫的文學…台語文學就是台灣文學。(Lim 1990)

Taiwan Literature must be written in Taigi…Taiwan Literature is the literature written in the mother tongue of Taiwanese people…Taiwan Literature is Taigi literature.

We could say that Taiwanese languages are regarded as important components of Taiwan Literature by Taibun writers. Therefore, they asserted that Taiwan Literature must be based on Taiwanese languages. Moreover, some writers, such as *Chong-goan Lim* and *Iong-bin Lim,* claimed that Taigi literature is the essence of Taiwan Literature; only Taigi literature can well represent the literature of Taiwan. Indeed, in normal cases, the fact that national literatures were written in their vernacular languages is not at all surprising. For instance, the Japanese language is the main literary language in Japan, and Japanese writing represents the essence of Japan literature. The situation is the same as Vietnamese in Vietnam, Korean in Korea, English in Britain, American English in the United States, and French in France. However, it seems that the vernacular writings in Taiwan do not have such fortune as they have in Vietnam and other independent nations. While "Taigi literature represents Taiwan Literature" was the claim, some Mandarin writers, such as *LI Kiau*[48] (李喬 1991) and *PHENN Sui-kim*[49] (彭瑞金

---

[48] See "A wide road of language: some thought on Taiwanese languages," (寬廣的語言大道--對台灣語文的思考) 9/29/1991, Independence Evening Post (自立晚報).
[49] See "Please don't kindle the language bomb," (請勿點燃語言炸彈) 10/07/1991, and

1991) argued that language is not an important component of literature. They asserted that literary works in any language could be Taiwan Literature. In other words, both Li and Phenn recognized the legitimate status of Mandarin writing for the literature of Taiwan.

In short, the contemporary Taibun movement since the 1980s reflects Taiwan's socio-political complexity and its colonial background. In terms of nationalism[50] and nationism[51], it reveals the controversial relationship among Chinese nationalism- nationism [52] , Taiwanese nationalism and Taiwanese nationism as illustrated in Figure 1.

"Language, writing, and literature," (語、文、文學) 10/27/1991, Independence Evening Post (自立晚報).

[50] Fishman (1968:41) defines nationalism as the "process of transformation from fragmentary and tradition-bound ethnicity to unifying and ideologized nationality." The role of language in nationalism is that it serves as link with the glorious past and with authenticity. A language is not only a vehicle for the history of a nationality, but a part of history itself (Fasold 1984:3).

[51] Fishman (1968:42) describes nationism as "wherever politico-geographic momentum and consideration are in advance of sociocultural momentum and consideration." The role of language in nationism is that whatever language does the job best is the best choice (Fasold 1984:3). In other words, language in nationism plays a more instrumental role. For example, considering government administration and education, a language or languages which do the job best must be chosen.

[52] At the beginning of Chinese KMT's occupation of Taiwan, Chinese nationists could have different opinions from Chinese nationalists. However, later on when the use of Mandarin by people in Taiwan had dramatically increased, the objects of Chinese nationalism and Chinese nationism have become the same. That is to keep using Mandarin since it has dominated educational and governmental functions in Taiwan. Therefore, I do not distinguish Chinese nationalism from Chinese nationism here.

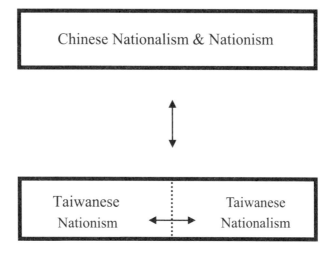

Figure 1. Relationship among Chinese nationalism-nationism,
Taiwanese nationalism, and Taiwanese nationism.

In the dimension of nationalism and nationism, it reveals the political tensions between Chinese and Taiwanese. Chinese nationalism can be inherited from the internal Chinese KMT and as well as external People's Republic of China. The strong conflicts between KMT's Chinese nationalism and Taiwanese nationalism were overt in the anti-KMT movement[53] in the second half of the 1980s and the entire 1990s. The conflicts between PRC Chinese nationalism and Taiwanese nationalism started in the late 1980s[54] and reached the climax in 1999 when the former president Teng-hui Lee claimed that Taiwan and China hold "special state to state" relationship. In the dimension of Taiwanese, it shows the expanding tension between Taiwanese nationalism and Taiwanese nationism. Many politicians and intellectuals who lead socio-political movement, such as *TAN Hong-Beng* (陳芳明) and *PHENN Sui-kim* (彭瑞金) do not value Taibun movement as a necessary step even though they identify themselves as Taiwanese rather than Chinese. In their ideology, they disapprove with KMT's strict national language policy; however, they have come to the stage to accept the results of the national language policy. In other words, they recognize the legitimate status of

---

[53] In this paper, I consider 1986, when the first native opposition party Democratic Progressive Party was born, the beginning of anti-KMT movement though its origin can be traced back to the 1970s. KMT lost its ruling status in the 2000 presidential election; therefore, 2000 was considered the end of the anti-KMT movement.

[54] For example, Iu-choan Chhoa (蔡有全), Cho-tek Khou (許曹德), and Lam-iong Tenn (鄭南榕) claimed the independence of Taiwan to the public in 1987.

the colonial language, i.e. Mandarin Chinese as the official language since it has been widespread in Taiwan after more than seventy years of promotion. However, it is criticized by Taiwanese nationalists that the Taiwanese nationists have ignored the threat of Chinese nationalism from China. From the perspective of Taiwanese nationalism, Taiwanese language is not only a communication medium, but also a part of history and spirit of Taiwan. Moreover, it is considered a national defense against Chinese nationalism of the PRC and the ROC (Lim 1996, 1997, 1998; Li 1999; Chiu[n] 1996).

In short, whether or not Taiwanese people are willing to accept or shift to Taibun deeply depends on people's national identity and their attitudes torward a new orthography.

5. Conclusion

This paper has examined the developments and influences of Romanization in the traditional Hanji dominant Vietnamese and Taiwanese societies. The different outcomes of Romanization in Vietnam and Taiwan reveal two important aspects regarding their orthographic transitions. They are 1) internal factors, which include the general public's demands for literacy and anti-feudal hierarchy, and 2) external factors, which include the political relationships between Vietnam, Taiwan and China.

In the case of Vietnam, Romanized system was promoted when the Vietnamese reached the climax of demand of anti-illiterate and anti-feudal society in the early twentieth century. In addition, the contradictory relationship among Vietnam, China, France, and Japan in the early 1940s have enforced Vietnamese leaders to choose Romanization as a distinctive cultural boundary between Vietnam and China. These two crucial points have contributed to Vietnam's successful transition from Han characters to Roman scripts. In contrast to Vietnam, Romanized Taiwanese was not widely promoted to the general public while they reached the demand of literacy and anti-feudalism in the early twentieth century. Moreover, Taiwan was directly under the military occupation of the Chinese KMT at the end of World War II. Thereafter, the Chinese ROC regime was renewed in Taiwan since 1949. Consequently, Romanization in Taiwan has a reverse outcome from Vietnam.

How can Taiwan reverse the language and orthographic situation? At least, the Taiwanese have to solve two crucial problems. First, most people in present Taiwan have acquired Modern Written Chinese and Han characters to some degree. Thus, how to persuade people to approach a new orthography is important.

Second, the current ambiguous national status and diversity of national identity in Taiwan reflect people's uncertain determinations on the issue of written Taiwanese. On the other hand, people's uncertain determinations on the Taibun issue also reflect the political controversy on national status. Chiung's (2001a) research on the attitudes of Taiwanese college students toward written Taiwanese reveals that national identity is one of the significant factors to affect students' attitudes toward Taiwanese writing. Hence, the promotion of Taiwanese identity and nationalism against Chinese nationalism are considered important.

Acknowledgements

This is a revision of the article originally presented at 3rd International Conference on Linguistics, Literature, and Culture, Universiti Sains Malaysia, Penang, Malaysia, Nov 26-28, 2014.

References

Anderson, Benedict. 1983. *Imagined Communities.* New York: Verso.

Ang, Ui-jin. 1993. Introduction to Douglas' Amoy-English dictionary [杜嘉德《廈英大辭典》簡介]. In *A Collection of Southern Min Classic Dictionaries* [閩南語經典辭書彙編 no.4], Vol.4, pp.1-9. Taipei: Woolin Press.

Barclat, Thomas. 1885. *Taiwan Prefectural City Church News* [Tai-oan-hu-sian Kau-hoe-po].

Campbell, William. 1888. *The Gospel of St. Matthem in Formosan (Sinkang Dialect) With Corresponding Versions in Dutch and English Edited From Gravius's Edition of 1661.* (republished in 1996) Taipei: SMC Publishing Inc.

Campbell, William. 1903. *Formosa Under the Dutch.* (republished in 1992) Taipei: SMC Publishing Inc.

Chavan, R. S. 1987. *Vietnam: Trial and Triumph.* India: Pariot Publishers.

Chen, Ping. 1994. Four projected functions of new writing systems for Chinese. *Anthropological Linguistics*, 36(3), pp.366-381.

Chen, Ping. 1999. *Modern Chinese: History and Sociolinguistics.* Cambridge: Cambridge University Press.

Cheng, Robert. L. 1989. *Essays on Written Taiwanese* [走向標準化的台灣語文]. Taipei: Chu-lip.

Cheng, Robert. L. 1990. *Essays on Taiwan's Sociolinguistic Problems* [演變中的台灣社會語文]. Taipei: Chu-lip.

Chhoa, Poe-hoe. 1925. *Opinions on Ten Issues* [Chap-Hang Koan-Kian].

Chiung, Wi-vun T. 2001a. Language attitudes towards written Taiwanese. *Journal of Multilingual & Multicultural Development* 22(6), pp.502-523.

Chiung, Wi-vun T. 2001b. Missionary scripts: a case study of Taiwanese Peh-oe-ji [Peh-oe-ji, gin-a-lang the iong e bun-ji? Tai-oan kau-hoe Peh-oe-ji e sia-hoe gi-gian-hak hun-sek]. *The Taiwan Folkway* 51(4), pp.15-52.

Chiung, Wi-vun T. 2001c. Romanization and language planning in Taiwan. *The Linguistic Association of Korea Journal* 9(1), pp.15-43.

Chiung, Wi-vun T. 2003. *Learning Efficiencies for Different Orthographies: A Comparative Study of Han Characters and Vietnamese Romanization*. PhD dissertation: University of Texas at Arlington.

Chiung, Wi-vun T. 2017a. Language under colonization: the Taiwanese language movement. in Jacobs J. Bruce and Peter Kang (eds.). *Changing Taiwanese Identities,* pp.39-63. NY: Routledge.

Chiung, Wi-vun T. 2017b. *Vietnamese Spirit: Language, Orthography and Anti-hegemony*. Tainan: Asian Atsiu International.

Chiung, Wi-vun; Chiu Teng-pang; Iunn Hui-ju. 2016. *The Odyssey of Taiwanese Scripts*. Tainan: Taiwanese Romanization Association & National Museum of Taiwan Literature.

Chương, Thâu. 1982. *Dong Kinh Nghia Thuc and Cultural Reform in the Early Twentieth Century [Đông Kinh Nghĩa Thục và Phong Trào Cải Cách Văn Hóa Đầu Thế Kỷ XX]*. Hà Nội: NXB Hà Nội.

Dale, Ian R. H. 1980. Digraphia. *International Journal of the Sociology of Language* 26, pp.5-13.

DeFrancis, John. 1950. *Nationalism and Language Reform in China*. Princeton: Princeton University Press.

DeFrancis, John. 1977. *Colonialism and Language Policy in Viet Nam*. New York: Mouton.

DeFrancis, John. 1984. Digraphia. *Word* 35(1), pp.59-66.

DeFrancis, John. 1990. *The Chinese Language: Fact and Fantasy*. (Taiwan edition) Honolulu: University of Hawaii Press.

DeFrancis, John. 1996. How efficient is the Chinese writing system? *Visible Language* 30(1), pp.6-44.

Do, Quang Chinh. 1972. *History of the Quoc Ngu Script: 1620-1659 [Lich Su Chu Quoc Ngu: 1620-1659]*. Saigon: Ra Khoi.

Fasold, Ralph. 1984. *The Sociolinguistics of Society*. Oxford: Blackwell.

Fishman, Joshua. 1968. Nationality-nationalism and nation-nationism. In Fishman, Joshua. et al. (eds). *Language Problems of Developing Nations* pp.39-51. New York: John Wiley & Sons.

Gelb, I. J. 1952. *A Study of Writing*. London: Routledge and Kegan Paul.

Hannas, William. C. 1997. *Asia's Orthographic Dilemma*. Hawaii: University of Hawaii.

Ho, Chi Minh. 1994. *Ho Chi Minh: Selected Writings 1920-1969*. Hanoi: The Gioi.

Hodgkin, Thomas. 1981. *Vietnam: The Revolutionary Path*. London: The Macmillan Press Ltd.

Holmgren, Jennifer. 19??. *Chinese Colonisation of Northern Vietnam*. Canberra: Australian National Univ.

Hsu, C. H. 1995. (eds). *A Centennial History of the Presbyterian Church of Formosa* [台灣基督長老教會百年史]. (3rd edition) Tailam: Presbyterian Church of Formosa Centenary

Publications Committee.

Huang, Chuen-Min. 1997. *Language Education Policies and Practices in Taiwan: From Nationism to Nationalism.* PhD dissertation: University of Washington.

Huang, Diancheng. 1953. Vietnamese experience of phonetic writing [越南採用拼音文字的經驗]. *Journal of Chinese Language* [中國語文], No.16, pp.17-22. Beijing: People's Education.

Huang, Shuanfan. 1993. *Language, Society, and Ethnic Identity* [語言社會與族群意識]. Taipei: Crane.

Iap, Chioh-tho. 1993. *A History of Taiwanese Literature* [台灣文學史綱]. Kaoshiung: Literature.

Jiang, Yiongjing. 1971. *Ho Chi Minh in China* [胡志明在中國]. Taipei.

Kerr, George H. 1992. *Formosa Betrayed* [被出賣的台灣]. (Taiwan edition). Taipei: Chian-ui Press.

Lai, Yung-hsiang. 1990. *Topics on Taiwan Church History* [教會史話 no.1]. No.1. Tailam: Jinkong Press.

Li, Heng-chhiong (ed.) 1999. *Collection of Essays on Taigi Literature Movement* [台語文學運動論文集]. Taipei: Chian-ui.

Li, Khin-hoann. 1996. Language policy and Taiwan independence [語言政策及台灣獨立]. In Si, Cheng-hong. (eds). *Linguistic Politics and Policy* [語言政治與政策], pp.113-134. Taipei: Chian-ui.

Lim, Chong-goan. 1984. Dialects and poetry [方言與詩]. In *Leh Poetry* [笠詩刊], No.123, pp.18-21.

Lim, Chong-goan. 1990. My opinions on Tagi literature [我對台語文學的追求及看法]. In Cheng, Robert. (eds). *A Collection of Taigi Poems from Six Writers* [台語詩六家選]. Taipei: Chian-ui.

Lim, Iong-bin. 1996. *Essay on the Taigi Literature Movement* [台語文學運動史論]. Taipei: Chian-ui.

Lim, Iong-bin. 1997. *Essays on Taiwanese Language and Culture* [台語文化釘根書]. Taipei: Chian-ui.

Lim, Iong-bin. 1998. *Language, Culture, and Nation-States* [語言文化與民族國家]. Taipei: Chian-ui.

Lim, Sui-beng. 1993. *Taiwanese Literature and Its Spirit* [台灣文學與時代精神]. Taipei: Un-sin.

Marr, David G. 1971. *Vietnamese Anticolonialism. 1885-1925.* California: Univ. of California Press.

Marr, David G. 1981. *Vietnamese Tradition On Trial, 1920-1945.* California: University of California Press.

McLeod, Mark. 1991. *The Vietnamese Response to French Intervention, 1864-1874.* NY: Praeger.

Naojiro Murakami, B. 1933. *Sinkan Manuscripts* [新港文書]. Taipei: Taihoku Imperial University.

Ng, Yuzin Chiautong. 1994. The development of Taiwanese nationalism and Taiwanese independence movement after Word Word II [戰後台灣獨立運動與台灣民族主義的發展]. In C. H. Si 1994, pp.195-227.

Nguyen, Dinh Hoa. 19??. Higher education in Vietnam from the early French conquest to the Japanese occupation. A report to School of Education, New York University.

Nguyen, Dinh Hoa. 1975. Nationalism in early Vietnamese literature. Working papers in South East Asian Studies, first series, No.1. School of Oriental and African Studies, University of London.

Nguyen, Khac V. 1979. *The Confucian Scholars in Vietnamese History.* Hanoi: Xunhasab.

Nguyen, Ngoc Bich. 1984. The state of Chu Nom studies: the domestic script of Vietnam. In Vietnamese Studies Papers, The Indochina Institute, George Mason University.

Norman, Jerry. 1988. *Chinese.* Cambridge: Cambridge University Press.

Ong, Hu-chhiong. 1993. The nature of assimilation between Taiwanese and Mainlanders [省籍融合的本質]. In Tiunn, Bou-kui. et al. (eds). *Ethnic Relations and National Identity* [族群關係與國家認同], pp.53-100. Taipei: Iap-kiong.

Ong, Iok-tek. 1993. *Taiwan: A Depressed History* [台灣:苦悶的歷史]. Taipei: Independence Press.

Ong, Si-long. 1988. *A History of Taiwanese Social Movement* [台灣社會運動史]. Taipei: Tiu-hiong Press.

Peng, Ming-min. and Ng, Yuzin Chiautong. 1995. *The Legal Status of Taiwan* [台灣在國際法上的地位]. Taipei: Taiwan Interminds.

Pham, Van Hai. 1980. *The Influence of T'ang Poetry on Vietnamese Poetry Written in Nom characters and in the Quoc-ngu Writing System.* PhD dissertation: Georgetown University.

Phenn, Sui-kim. 1992. *Forty years of New Literature Movement in Taiwan* [台灣新文學運動 40 年]. Taipei: Independence Press.

SarDesai D. R. 1992. *Vietnam: The Struggle for National Identity.* (2nd ed.). Colorado: Westview Press.

Si, Cheng Hong. 1994. *Taiwanese Nationalism* [台灣民族主義]. Taipei: Chian-ui.

Stubbs, Michael. 1980. *Language and Literacy: the Sociolinguistics of Reading and Writing.* Boston: Routledge & Kegan Paul plc.

Su, Beng. 1980. *Four Hundred Years of Taiwanese History* [台灣人四百年史]. California: Paradise Culture Associates.

Su, Beng. 1992. *Formation of a Nation and the Taiwanese Nation* [民族形成與台灣民族]. Taipei: Tok-tai-hoe.

Su, Beng. 1993. *Socialism and the Revolution of the Taiwanese Nation* [台灣民族革命與社會主義]. Taipei: Tok-tai-hoe.

Tan, Ki-lam. 1994. *The Traditional Chinese Society of Taiwan* [台灣的傳統中國社會]. (2nd edition) Taipei: Un-sin Press.

Thompson, Laurence. 1987. *A Vietnamese Reference Grammar.* Hawaii: University of Hawaii.

TiuN Hak-khiam. 1998. Writing in two scripts: a case study of digraphia in Taiwanese. *Written Language and Literacy* 1(2), pp.225-47.

Tiunn, Bun-ti. 1993. *The Taiwanese Conscious in the Contemporary Literature* [當代文學的台灣意識]. Taipei: Independence Press.

Tran, Trong-Kim. 1992. *Vietnamese History* [*Viet Nam Su Luoc* 越南通史]. Chinese version, by Dai Kelai. Beijing: The Commercial Press.

4

Sound and Writing Systems in
Taiwanese, Chinese and Vietnamese

In this chapter, specific writing systems, which are deeply involved in this book, are examined in detail so readers will have a better understanding of their correspondence between orthographic symbols and speech sounds. These systems are Taiwanese Romanization Peh-oe-ji, Chinese Romanization Hanyu Pinyin, Chinese Bopomo, and Vietnamese Romanization Chu Quoc Ngu.

1. Taiwanese

1.1. Sound system

The Taiwanese language is also called Taigi by its speakers in Taiwan.

The syllabic structure in Taiwanese is similar to those in Vietnamese and Mandarin Chinese, as shown in Figure 1, in which glide, nucleus and coda together are called "rhyme."

Tone			
onset	rhyme		
	glide	nucleus	coda

Figure 1. Syllabic structure in Taiwanese, Vietnamese and Chinese.

The most accepted phonological system for Taiwanese is as shown in Table 1, Table 2, and Table 3. In general, there are seventeen consonants, six vowels, and seven tones, though may vary from variety to variety. Among the consonants, the phoneme /l/ is in fact pronounced as [d] or [ɾ] in most circumstances (Tiu^n

2001:31-32). Nevertheless, we follow the traditional description of listing /l/ as a phoneme.

Table 1. Taiwanese consonants in IPA

		bi-labial -asp/+asp	alveolar -asp/+asp	velar -asp/+asp	glottal -asp/+asp
voiceless	stop	p / pʰ	t / tʰ	k / kʰ	
voiced	stop	b		g	
voiceless	fricative		s		h
voiceless	affricate		ts / tsʰ		
voiced	affricate		dz		
voiced	lateral		l		
voiced	nasal	m	n	ŋ	

Table 2. Taiwanese vowels in IPA

	front	central	back
high	i		u
mid	e	ə	o
low		a	

Table 3. Tonal categories in Taiwanese (Cheng 1997)

Categories	君 [kun˥] gentle	滾 [kunˊ] boil	棍 [kunˋ] stick	骨 [kut˩] bone	裙 [kun˨] skirt	-	近 [kun˧] near	滑 [kut˙] glide
Numerical categories	1	2	3	4	5	6	7	8
Tone marks in Peh-oe-ji	unmarked	´	`	unmarked	^		-	˙
Peh-oe-ji samples	kun	kún	kùn	kut	kûn		kūn	ku̍t
Numerical tone values	44	53	31	3	12 or 212		22	8
IPA tone values	˧	˥˩	˩˩	˙	˨˩˨		˧˧	˙

There are currently seven tonal categories in the Taiwanese language. They are traditionally called tones 1, 2, 3, 4, 5, 7, and 8. The missing element, tone 6, has merged with tone 2 or tone 7 (Ang 1985:2-3), therefore, nowadays there are only seven tones, as listed in Table 3.

Tone 5 is traditionally described as a low rising tone (12); tone 4 and tone 8 are abrupt tones (jip-siann 入聲) with low and high contrasts, respectively (Cheng 1977, 1997; Ang 1985; Weingartner 1970). However, Ong (1993) has shown that tone 5 is a low falling and then rising tone based on acoustic measurement of his own pronunciation in 1945. Chiung's (2001b) acoustic measurement of 22 Taiwanese speakers reveals that young generation is more likely to possess falling-rising feature. Tseng (1995: 32) points out that the tone shape of tone 5 can be a rising contour (∕) if the starting point is low; or a dipping contour (∨) if the starting point is slightly higher. Both contours share the low-rising pattern. As for tone 4 and tone 8, it is said that distinctions between tone 4 and tone 8 are not apparent in some areas such as in Tai-tiong city of central Taiwan (Cheng 1977:97; Khou 1990:89).

There is a Tone Sandhi Rule which has the effect of converting all but the last full tone within a tone group into their corresponding sandhi tones (Chen 1987).

Tone Sandhi Rule (TSR)

T → T' / __T within a tone group

Key: T= base tone, T'= sandhi tone

For example, consider 土地 *thó-tē* 'land', a compound word of two monosyllabic words *thó* 'soil' and *tē* 'ground.'

   Thó-tē

Base tones→ 2 - 7

After TSR→ 1 - 7

If we add 公 kong 'grandpa' to thó-tē, it becomes thó-tē-kong or 'God of Land.'

   Thó-tē-kong

Base tones→ 2 - 7 - 1

After TSR→ 1 - 3 - 1

How sandhi tones occur can be described by the Tone Circle or Tone Square[1]. In the Tone square, we assume sandhi tones and base tones share the same seven tone categories.

---

[1] This square is based on Robert Cheng (1977:123) with some modification. Taiwanese Tone Square is a little bit different from Xiamen Tone Circle.

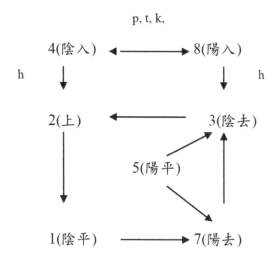

Figure 2. Tone Square in Taiwanese.

1ˢᵗ tone   陰平 → 7ᵗʰ tone 陽去 e.g. hoe-hoe 'confused' 1-1→7-1

2ⁿᵈ tone   上聲 → 1ˢᵗ tone 陰平 e.g. té-té 'short' 2-2→1-2

3ʳᵈ tone   陰去 → 2ⁿᵈ tone 上聲 e.g. chò-chò 'make' 3-3→2-3

4ᵗʰ tone   陰入 → 2ⁿᵈ tone 上聲 if with h 'glottal stop' in the final

               e.g. tah-tah 'attach' 4-4→2-4

               → 8ᵗʰ tone 陽入   elsewhere

               e.g. tap-tap 'answer' 4-4→8-4

5ᵗʰ tone   陽平 → 7ᵗʰ tone 陽去 in Southern Taiwan

               e.g. Tâi-pak 'Taipei' 5-4→7-4

               → 3ʳᵈ tone 陰去 in Northern Taiwan

               e.g. Tâi-pak 'Taipei' 5-4→3-4

7ᵗʰ tone 陽去→ 3ʳᵈ tone 陰去 e.g. chāi-chāi (steady) 7-7→3-7

8ᵗʰ tone 陽入 → 3ʳᵈ tone 陰去 if with h 'glottal stop' in the final

               e.g. pėh-pėh 'white' 8-8→3-8

               → 4ᵗʰ tone 陰入 elsewhere

               e.g. pȧk-pȧk 'tie' 8-8→4-8

In addition to following the Tone Square, there are some other special tonal sandhi rules such as Three Syllables Tonal Sandhi 三連音變調, Tone Sandhi

Preceding /a/ 仔前變調, and Tone Sandhi Based on Preceding Tone 隨前變調. Since tone sandhi is not the major concern in this study, further elaboration must be left for another time.

1.2. Written form in Romanized Peh-oe-ji

Adoption of the Roman alphabet for writing Southern Min dates back to the sixteenth century when the Spanish Dominicans worked together with their translators among the Chinese community in Manila (Van der Loon 1966, 1967; Kloter 2002). Their systems differ in many aspects from Romanization developed in the nineteenth century (Kloter 2002).

Missionary linguistic efforts on the Romanization are reflected in various Romanized dictionaries. Medhurst's *A Dictionary of the Hok-keen Dialect of the Chinese Language* 福建方言字典 published in 1837 is considered the first existing Romanized dictionary of Southern Min compiled by western missionary (Ang 1996:197-259; Heylen 2001:146). Douglas' *Chinese-English Dictionary of the Vernacular or Spoken Language of Amoy* 廈英大辭典 of 1873 is regarded as a dictionary of significant influence on the orthography of Peh-oe-ji (Ang 1993a, 1993b:1-9). After Douglas' dictionary, most Romanized dictionaries and publications followed his orthography with only minor changes. Generally speaking, the missionary linguistic efforts on Southern Min and Peh-oe-ji (POJ) have made considerable progress since Douglas's dictionary (Ang 1993b:5). William Campbell's dictionary *E-mng-im Sin Ji-tian* or *A Dictionary of the Amoy Vernacular* (1913), which was the first Peh-oe-ji dictionary published in Taiwan, is the most widespread Romanized dictionary in Taiwan and had been published in fourteen editions by 1987 (Chiung 2016).

The following list consists of some examples of the variations of spelling among these three dictionaries.

Table 4. Examples of spelling variations among Medhurst, Douglas, and Campbell

Medhurst	Douglas	Campbell	Hanji	IPA
ee^{ng}	i^n	i^n	嬰	[ĩ]
ëen	ien	ian	煙	[en]
wa	oa	oa	蛙	[wa]
oe	o͘	o·	烏	[o]

Since E-mng-im Sin Ji-tian is the most widespread Romanized dictionary in Taiwan, it will be briefly demonstrated how Peh-oe-ji works in the E-mng-im Sin

Ji-tian. For more details on how the Roman alphabet is employed in Peh-oe-ji, readers may refer to Tiuⁿ (2001) and Cheng and Cheng (1977).

Table 5. Symbols for Taiwanese consonants in the spelling of Peh-oe-ji

Consonants	Peh-oe-ji	Conditions	Examples
/p/	p		pí 'compare'
/pʰ/	ph	initial only	phoe 'letter'
/t/	t		tê 'tea'
/tʰ/	th	initial only	thâi 'to kill'
/k/	k		ka 'add'
/kʰ/	kh	initial only	kha 'foot'
/b/	b	initial only	bûn 'literature'
/g/	g	initial only	gí 'language'
/h/	h		hí 'glad'
/s/	s	initial only	sì 'four'
/ts/	ch	before i, e	chi 'of'
	ts	eleswhere	tsa 'investigate'
/tsʰ/	chh	initial only	chha 'differ'
/dz/	j	initial only	jit 'sun'
/l/	l	initial only	lí 'you'
/m/	m		mī 'noodle'
/n/	n		ni 'milk'
/ŋ/	ng		âng 'red'

Table 6. Symbols for Taiwanese vowels in the spelling of Peh-oe-ji

Vowels	Peh-oe-ji	Conditions	*Examples*
/i/	i		ti 'pig'
/e/	e	Elsewhere	tê 'tea'
	ia	Followed by **n or t**	tiān 'electric' kiat 'to form'
/a/	a		ta 'dry'
/u/	u		tú 'meet'
/ə/	o		to 'knife'
/o/	o·	Elsewhere	o· 'black'
	o	Followed by finals, except /ʔ/	tong 'east' kok 'state'

The spelling rules of Peh-oe-ji are easier than those for Vietnamese Chu Quoc Ngu. In general, there is a one-to-one relationship between orthographic symbols and phonemes as shown in Table 5 and Table 6. The only exception is the pair of <ch> and <ts> that both refer to the phoneme /ts/ (nowadays, ts has been replaced by ch). The different usages between ts and ch are based on vowel position. That is, ts precedes back vowels such as 'tso,' and ch precedes front vowels such as 'chi.' This rule was influenced by the phenomenon of palatalization of /ts/, where [ts] become palatalized [tɕ] when followed by front vowels. In other words, the missionary devisors treated [ts] and [tɕ] as two different sounds in terms of phonetics instead of phonemics, though most spelling rules in POJ are made from the viewpoint of phonemics.

After phonemes are represented, tone marks are superimposed on the nuclei of syllables and a hyphen '-' is added between syllables, such as in thó͘-tē-kong, 'the God of Land.' Because Taiwanese is a tone language with rich tone sandhi, there can be several ways to represent tones. In the design of POJ, the base tone or underlying tone of each syllable is chosen and represented by its tone mark. For example, 'the God of Land' must be represented by its underlying form thó͘-tē-kong rather than surface form tho-tè-kong (this is the form of actual pronunciation). Why is underlying form instead of surface form chosen to represent tones in POJ? This is an issue often challenged point by POJ reformers. Indeed, in some cases, especially polysyllabic loanwords, such as o͘-tó-bái 'motorcycle,' it seems ridiculous to represent motorcycle by the underlying from o͘-tó-bái rather than the actual pronunciation ō͘-tó-bái. The major reason for the missionaries to choose underlying tone is probably the influence of the monosyllabic feature of Han Characters.

We may examine the invention of POJ in terms of Smalley's criteria for a new orthography as mentioned in chapter three. All the strengths and weaknesses of Peh-oe-ji come from its nature as phonemic writing. In terms of efficiency, the relative ease of learning reading and writing in POJ over Hanji gives higher motivation to its learners. In a former agricultural society, most people were peasants who labored in the fields all day long, and they had little interest in learning complicated Han characters. In contrast to Han characters, the ease of learning POJ provided those farmers a good opportunity to acquire literacy. This is one of the reasons why there are a number of people who have no command of Han characters, only POJ. [2] Although Peh-oe-ji might provide maximum

---

[2] Huang (quoted in Xu 1992:70) estimated that by 1955 a total of 115,500 people in all Lan-lang-oe speaking areas such as Hokkian, Malaysia, and Taiwan could use Peh-oe-ji. 32,000 of

motivation to individual learners, it may not have the same motivation in a Hanji dominated society and government. Chiung (2001a) studied empirically 244 college students' attitudes toward various contemporary Taiwanese writing schemes. That study revealed that college students educated in Hanji and Mandarin tend to favor Han characters over Roman scripts. As for the attitudes of the Chinese KMT government (1945-2000), POJ was not only excluded from the national education system but was also restricted in its daily use. For instance, the Romanized *Sin Iok* (New Testament) was once seized by KMT in 1975 because Hanji was considered the only national orthography, while Romanization was regarded as a challenge to KMT's Chinese nationalism.

To have maximum representation of speech usually requires a good linguistic analysis of the language before devising an orthography. Campbell's (1913) E-mng-im Sin Ji-tian demonstrated the achievement of missionary knowledge about Amoy and Taiwanese. Campbell's choices of symbols for representing Taiwanese consonants and vowels are listed in Table 5 and Table 6. In Campbell's dictionary, 24 symbols are used to represent 23 Taiwanese phonemes (i.e., 17 consonants and 6 vowels), and those symbols consist of only 17 Roman letters. Campbell's linguistic analysis and choice of symbols are quite accurate and efficient and agree with modern linguistic treatments. For example, he primarily assigns one grapheme/grapheme set (except /ts/) to each phoneme. The letters he assigns to sound segments are very close to the IPA system (International Phonetic Alphabet), which is adopted by many contemporary linguists for transcribing linguistic data. If two letters for a phoneme are inevitable, he tries to make the symbols easy and rule based. For example, <h> indicates 'aspiration' when it is attached to *p*, *t*, *k*, or *ch*; and it represent glottal stop when it occurs in the final position of a syllable. Other than these situations, <h> refers to a glottal fricative.

Overall, Campbell's choice of phonemic symbols is fairly standard. The only controversial point is the alveolar voiceless affricate sounds. While Campbell does distinguish between *ch* and *ts*, this difference is actually 'phonetic' rather than 'phonemic.' That is to say, he could choose either *ch* or *ts* to represent the seqmental contrast.

In addition to the choice of phonemic symbols, the spelling in Campbell's dictionary is also pretty straightforward. His fundamental principle of spelling is to do phonemic transcriptions of spoken language. That is, write down phonemically what you hear. His second principle is to treat POJ as an independent orthography once the spelling of words is confirmed, rather than a

---

them were Peh-oe-ji users in Taiwan.

supplementary phonetic tool to the learning of Han characters. In Campbell's opinion, the spelling of the Romanized Bible (1873) was considered the official orthography of POJ. Therefore, as Campbell described in the preface of his dictionary, "none of the current words whose spelling differs from that standard were taken in." He made efforts to maintain the existing POJ orthography. The issue of spelling of POJ is still controversial among some of its users today. For example, people have tried to replace the forms *ian*, *oa*, and *eng*, with *en*, *ua*, and *ing*, respectively.

Although Romanized Peh-oe-ji has the strengths of maximum representation and efficiency, many people doubt its capacity for Romanizing the members of the Han language family because they think that the Roman alphabet is too inadequate to differentiate homophones. As I have demonstrated in chapter three, this doubt is not well founded. If Romanization were incapable of serving as an adequate orthography, how could it have survived for more than a hundred years in Taiwan and four hundred years in Vietnam?

Maximum of transfer is another virtue of POJ. Since POJ consists of Roman letters, and Roman script is the most widespread orthography among the world's writing systems, its users will have a better starting point to the orthographies of other Romanized languages such as English.

From the perspective of the reproduction of orthography, reproducing Romanized POJ is even easier and more efficient than Han characters (recalling that there are a total of 47,035 characters in the *Kangxi* Dictionary). Compared to the small amount of Roman letters and diacritic marks in the POJ writing, Han characters are much more difficult to reproduce in typographic composition (DeFrancis 1996:19-21). In the information age, although personal computers can easily reproduce Han characters, dealing with Han characters still involves more trouble than dealing with Roman scripts, such challenge as compatibility, OCR, and machine translation.

2. Chinese

2.1. Sound system

Mandarin Chinese is the official language in China and Taiwan. Its consonants, vowels, and tones are listed in Table 7, Table 8 and Table 9. Taiwan Mandarin[3] is slightly different phonetically from Beijing Mandarin in some of its

---

[3] Taiwan Mandarin in this study is defined as the language acquired by Taiwanese speakers

details. In generally, the retroflex feature in Taiwan Mandarin is not as prominent as it is in Beijing Mandarin; [x] and [ɤ] of Beijing Mandarin are more likely to be pronounced by Taiwanese speakers as [h] and [ə], respectively. Tone values of Taiwan Mandarin (TM) also differ from Beijing Mandarin (BM).

Table 7. Mandarin Chinese consonants in IPA

		bi-labial	labio-dental	alveolar	retroflex	palatal	velar
		-asp/+asp		-asp/+asp	-asp/+asp	-asp/+asp	-asp/+asp
voiceless	stop	p / pʰ		t / tʰ			k / kʰ
voiceless	fricative		f	s	ʂ	ɕ	x
voiced	fricative				ʐ		
voiceless	affricate			ts / tsʰ	tʂ / tʂʰ	tɕ / tɕʰ	
voiced	lateral			l			
voiced	nasal	m		n			

Table 8. Mandarin Chinese vowels

	apical		laminal		
	front	back	front	central	back
			-rd/+rd		-rd/+rd
high	ɨ	ʅ	i / y		u
mid		ɚ	e	ə	ɤ / o
low				a	

There are four base tones and one neutral tone in Mandarin Chinese. Neutral tone in Chinese only occurs in grammatical particle such as 嗎 and 的. Four base tones in Mandarin are usually described as 55, 35, 214, and 51, based on Chao's (1968) five-point scale. However, Fon and Chiang (1999) have pointed out that the four tones in TM should be considered 44, 323, 312, and 42, respectively, based on their acoustical study of a bilingual subject of Taiwanese and Mandarin. Chu's (1998) measurements of 24 Mandarin speakers from Taipei reveal that TM tone 2 falls before rising, and TM tone 3 is a low level or low falling. Chiung's

---

through KMT's promotion of Mandarin in Taiwan.

(1999) measurements of 22 bilinguals of Mandarin and Taiwanese also indicate that TM tone is a falling-rising tone, and TM tone is a low falling one. Based on these findings, I would suggest a modification of the four tones in TM as 44, 212, 31, and 53, as shown in Table 9.

Table 9. Tonal categories in Mandarin Chinese

Categories	媽 [ma] mother	麻 [má] sesame	馬 [mǎ] horse	罵 [mà] blame	嗎 [ma] particle
Traditional categories	陰平	陽平	上聲	去聲	輕聲 neutral t.
Numerical categories	1	2	3	4	
Tone marks in Pinyin	-	´	ˇ	`	unmarked
Numerical tone values (Beijin Mandarin)	55	35	214	51	
IPA tone values (Beijin Mandarin)	˥	˧˥	˨˩˦	˥˩	
Tone marks in Bopomo	unmarked	╱	ˇ	`	•
Numerical tone values **(Taiwan Mandarin)**	44	212	31	53	
IPA tone values **(Taiwan Mandarin)**	˦	˨˩˨	˧˩	˥˧	

2.2. Written form in Romanization

Although there are several schemes for Chinese Romanization, none of them except Hanyu Pinyin, which was promulgated by the People's Republic of China in 1958, is taught through national education system either in Taiwan or in China. Since Hanyu Pinyin is the only Romanization included in current schooling of China, how it works is examined in this section.[4]

The correspondences between orthographic symbols and speech sounds in Pinyin are demonstrated in Table 10 and Table 11. Diacritic marks for tones are listed in Table 9. In general, there is a one-to-one correspondence between symbols and consonants. As for the vowels, seven out of the eleven vowels are represented by more than a symbol, which should be regulated by spelling rules. In either consonants or vowels, orthographic symbols consist of a graph, such as

---

[4] For more information about Pinyin, readers may refer to Wenzi (1983), Ingulsrud and Allen (1999), and Killingley (1998).

<b>, or a digraph, such as <sh>. After phonemes are represented by their symbols, a graph <'> is added between syllables if necessary. For example, <'> is added to show that *pi'ao* 'leather' is a disyllabic word rather than a monosyllabic word *piao* 'float.'

Although Pinyin could be considered an independent writing system, it is not recognized as an orthography but as a supplementary tool for learning the standard pronunciation of Mandarin and Chinese characters. As former Chinese premier Zhou Enlai addressed, "we should be clear that Hanyu Pinyin is to indicate the pronunciation of Chinese characters and to spread the use of standard Mandarin; it is not to substitute a phonetic writing system for the Chinese characters" (Wenzi 1983:6; Ingulsrud and Allen 1999:38).

Table 10. Symbols for Mandarin consonants in the spelling of Pinyin

Consonants	Pinyin	Conditions	Examples
/p/	b		bā 八 'eight'
/p^h/	p		pī 披 'to wear'
/t/	d		dà 大 'big'
/t^h/	t		tī 踢 'kick'
/k/	g		guó 國 'state'
/k^h/	k		kāfēi 咖啡 'coffee'
/f/	f		fēi 飛 'fly'
/s/	s		sān 三 'three'
/ʂ/	sh		shān 山 'mountain'
/ɕ/	x		xī 西 'west'
/x/	h		hào 號 'number'
/ʐ/	r		rào 繞 'to circle'
/ts/	z		zá 雜 'complex'
/ts^h/	c		cā 擦 'wipe'
/tʂ/	zh		zhà 炸 'to bomb'
/tʂ^h/	ch		chá 茶 'tea'
/tɕ/	j		jí 及 'and'
/tɕ^h/	q		qī 七 'seven'
/l/	l		lā 拉 'to pull'
/m/	m		mā 媽 'mother'
/n/	n		ná 拿 'to hold'

Table 11. Symbols for Mandarin vowels in the spelling of Pinyin

Vowels	Pinyin	Conditions	Examples
/i/	i	elsewhere	bīn 賓 'guest'
	y	without initials, followed by vowels other than /i/	yā 鴨 'duck'
	yi	without initials	yīng 鷹 'eagle'
/y/	ü	elsewhere	nǚ 女 'female'
	u	preceded by j, q, x	qū 區 'area' xūn 薰 'smoke'
	yu	without initials	yuē 約 'to date'
/ɿ/	i		zì 字 'characters'
/ʅ/	i		zhī 之 'of'
/u/	u	elsewhere	lù 路 'road'
	w	without initials, followed by vowels other than /u/	wān 灣 'bay'
	wu	without initials	wū 烏 'dark'
	o	before [ŋ] or after [a]	dōng 東 'east' bāo 包 'to warp'
/ɚ/	er	elsewhere	èr 二 'two'
	r	final only	huār 花兒 'flower'
/e/	e	elsewhere	tiē 貼 'to post'
	ê	in isolation	ê 世 '/e/ vowel'
	unmarked	after [Cu]	gūi 規 'a rule'
/ə/	e	elsewhere	bēn 奔 'running' mēng 矇 'blind'
	unmarked	after [Cu]	dūn 蹲 'squat'
/ɤ/	e		é 鵝 'goose' hē 喝 'to drink'
/o/	o	elsewhere	bó 博 'knowledgeably' duō 多 'many'
	unmarked	after [Ci]	niú 牛 'cow'
/a/	a		dà 大 'big'

2.3. Written form in Bopomo

Bopomo ㄅㄆㄇ注音符號 or Phonetic Symbols for Mandarin was originally devised in China in the early twentieth century. It was brought to Taiwan in 1945 by the Chinese KMT and has been serving ever since as a supplementary tool for students' learning of Mandarin and Chinese characters. In contrast, Bopomo in China was replaced with Hanyu Pinyin in 1958.

Bopomo is an advanced invention based on the concept of Shouwen's Thirty Basic Characters, which was mentioned in chapter three. Bopomo divides syllables into three parts, i.e., initials, medials, and finals (Zhou 1987:88). Their symbols and equivalent Pinyin and IPA are listed in Table 12, and tone marks are listed in Table 9. Because Bopomo represents not only phonemes, but also syllables, it is a hybrid system of phonemic and syllabic writing.

Table 12. Bopomo with equivalent Pinyin and IPA

Types	Bopomo	Pinyin	IPA
Initials	ㄅ	b	[p]
	ㄆ	p	[pʰ]
	ㄇ	m	[m]
	ㄈ	f	[f]
	ㄉ	d	[t]
	ㄊ	t	[tʰ]
	ㄋ	n	[n]
	ㄌ	l	[l]
	ㄍ	g	[k]
	ㄎ	k	[kʰ]
	ㄏ	h	[x]
	ㄐ	j	[tɕ]
	ㄑ	q	[tɕʰ]
	ㄒ	x	[ɕ]
	ㄓ	zh	[tʂ]
		zhi	[tʂɭ]
	ㄔ	ch	[tʂʰ]
		chi	[tʂʰɭ]
	ㄕ	sh	[ʂ]
		shi	[ʂɭ]
	ㄖ	r	[ʐ]
		ri	[ʐɭ]
	ㄗ	z	[ts]
		zi	[ts1]
		c	[tsʰ]

Types	Bopomo	Pinyin	IPA
	ㄘ	ci	[tsʰ1]
	ㄙ	s	[s]
		si	[s1]
Medials	ㄧ	i	[i], [1]
	ㄨ	u	[u]
	ㄩ	ü	[y]
Finals	ㄚ	a	[a]
	ㄛ	o	[o]
	ㄜ	e	[ɤ]
	ㄝ	ê	[e]
	ㄦ	er	[ɚ]
	ㄞ	ai	[aj]
	ㄟ	ei	[ej]
	ㄠ	ao	[aw]
	ㄡ	ou	[ow]
	ㄢ	an	[an]
	ㄣ	en	[ən]
	ㄤ	ang	[aŋ]
	ㄥ	eng	[əŋ]

In Taiwan, textbooks for elementary school students are mostly written in Han characters with Bopomo, arranging text from top to bottom and from right to left. Figure 3 shows an example of how Han characters and Bopomo are arranged.

音符號的樣本

這個句子是注

。

Figure 3. Samples of Han characters with Bopomo.

3. Vietnamese

Vietnam is a country with a rich diversity of ethnicities, including such language groups as Mon-Khmer (94% of total population), Kadai (3.7%; also called Daic or Tai-Kadai), Miao-Yao (1.1%), Austronesian (0.8%), Tibeto-Burman, and Han (Grimes 2000). It is reported that there are 54 official ethnic groups, 86 living languages, and 1 extinct language (Grimes 2000). Recently, *Nung Ven* and *Xapho* (or *Laghuu*), two languages in North Vietnam were discovered and reported by Edmondson's research team. Among the ethnic groups, *Viet* or *Kinh* is the majority, and it accounts for 87% of Vietnam's total population (Dang 2000:1). The mother tongue of Viet is called the Vietnamese language. The Vietnamese language is known to its native speakers as *tiếng Việt*, and formerly known as Annamese or Annamite. Vietnamese is currently the official language of Vietnam, and its speakers account for 87% of Vietnam's population (Grimes 2000).

3.1. Sound system

The classification of the Vietnamese language has been disputed for a long time. However, at present it is widely believed that Vietnamese belongs to the Mon-Khmer language family, which is spoken throughout much of Southeast Asia, primarily in Laos, Vietnam, and Cambodia, but also in Thailand, Burma, the

Malay Peninsula, and the Nicobar Islands in the An-daman Sea (Ruhlen 1987:148). At present, there are about 156 Mon-Khmer languages (Grimes 2000). Among the Mon-Khmer languages, Vietnamese is the most well-known, largest, and most widely spoken.

Vietnamese is an isolating language, that is, one in which the words are mostly monosyllables, there is no overt morphological alternation, and syntactic relationships are shown by word order, just as in the cases of Taiwanese and Chinese. Traditionally, Vietnamese was regarded as monosyllabic because most of Vietnamese words consist of single syllables. However, recent statistical studies have shown that there is a clear tendency toward poly-syllabicity in modern Vietnamese (Nguyen 1997:35). In addition, Vietnamese is a tonal language. Modern Vietnamese possesses six tones, which distinguish different lexical meanings of words. Tone sandhi in Vietnamese is neither as substantial nor as rich as in Taiwanese.

Various foreign influences have influenced the development of the Vietnamese language because of the contacts in the past between the Vietnamese and other peoples. Among them, Chinese is probably the strongest and most lasting one donor language (Nguyen 1971:153).

The modern Vietnamese language is based on the varieties spoken in Vietnam's capital city of Hanoi and surround Red River basin. Traditionally, Vietnamese vernacular types were proposed by Henri Maspero (1912) dividing the language into two main groups: 1) the Haut-Annam group, which comprehended numerous local speech types of the small villages stretching from the north of Nghe-An province to the south of Thua-Thien province, and 2) Tonkinese-Cochinchinese, which covers all the remaining territory (Thompson 1987:78). Generally speaking, Vietnamese variation form a continuum from north to south, each pattern somewhat different from a neighboring one on either side. Hanoi, Hue, and Saigon, located respectively in north, central, and south parts, represent three major remarkable dialects in Vietnam (Nguyen 1997:10). In this book, Vietnamese refers to the standard Hanoi dialect unless otherwise specified.

3.1.1. Consonants

The identification of Vietnamese phonemes may vary from scholar to scholar[5]. According to Doan (1999:166), there are 19 consonants in the Hanoi

---

[5] For example, /ʔ/ was not recognized as a phoneme by Nguyen (1997: 20), rather, he recognized /p/ as a phoneme because /p/ nowadays can also occur at the beginning of several loanwords from French, such as *pin* 'battery,' and *po-ke* 'poker.' However, according to

variety of Vietnamese. These consonants were listed in IPA format in Table 13. In addition to the 19 consonants, other forms may contain retroflex consonants /tʂ/, /ʂ/, and /ʐ/ (Nguyen 1997:20).

Table 13. Vietnamese consonants in IPA

	bi-labial	labial-dental	alveolar	palatal	velar	glottal
			-asp/+asp			
voiceless stop			t / tʰ	c	k	ʔ
voiced stop	b		d			
voiceless fricative		f	s		x	h
voiced fricative		v	z		ɣ	
voiced lateral			l			
voiced nasal	m		n	ɲ	ŋ	

3.1.2. Vowels

Compared to Taiwanese, Vietnamese vowels are much more complex and difficult. The identification of the vowels varies from scholar to scholar. The Vietnamese vocalic system was divided into upper and lower vocalics (Thompson 1987: 19). The upper vocalics include six vowels, /i ɯ u e ɤ o/. They are formed relatively high in the mouth and characterized by a three-way position (front, back unrounded, and back rounded). Lower vocalics include five vowels, /ɛ ɔ ɐ a ɑ/. They are formed relatively low and characterized by a two-way position distinction (front, back). However, according to Doan (1999), Vietnamese vowels may be categorized into nine simple vowels, four short vowels, and three diphthongs. The vowel /ɐ/ identified by Thompson is considered /ɤ̆/ by Doan. Dispite different opinions on the Vietnamese vowel system, the vowels based on Doan (1999) are listed in Table 14, Table 15 and Table 16.

Thompson (1987: 21), the glottal stop could be recognized as a phoneme. The voicing of [b] and [d] are predictable allophones of /p/ and /t/ respectively, following initial /ʔ/ (Thompson 1987: 21). For example, [b] occurs in initial only, and [p] in final only.

Table 14. Vietnamese simple vowels in IPA

		front	central	back (-rd)	back (+rd)
upper	high	i		ɯ	u
	upper mid	e		ɤ	o
lower	lower mid	ɛ			ɔ
	low			a	

Table 15. Vietnamese short vowels in IPA

		front	central	back (-rd)	back (+rd)
upper	high				
	upper mid			ɤ̆	
lower	lower mid	ɛ̆			ɔ̆
	low			ă	

Table 16. Vietnamese diphthongs in IPA

	front	central	back (-rd)	back (+rd)
upper	i‿e		ɯ‿ɤ	u‿o
lower				

3.1.3. Tones

Mon-Khmer languages have usually been noteworthy for the linguistic category of register, which most prominently includes voice quality as a contrastive feature. Although Vietnamese is not a classic register language, voice quality as well as pitch phenomena are both important in the tone system of Vietnamese (Nguyen and Edmondson 1997:1).

Although the modern Vietnamese language is usually described as having six tones, the number of Vietnamese tones could be two, four, six, or eight, based on different criteria of classification (Doan Thien Thuat, p.c.). For example, eight tones were identified in traditional Vietnamese phonology, as listed in Table 17.

In Taiwanese, tones of Entering category are still preserved. The major reason that modern Vietnamese is recognized as six tones is mainly because the misleading of current Chu Quoc Ngu writing system. The missionaries were not aware of the differences between Falling and Entering categories while they were devising the system (Doan Thien Thuat, p.c.). The major different feature between these two categories is the length of duration: Entering tones have a slightly shorter duration than Falling tones. For example, nát 'broken' and nạt 'scold' are pronounced relatively shorter than nán 'linger' and nạn 'disaster,' respectively. Entering tones in Vietnamese always require a final *p t c* or *ch*. They are similar to tones 4 and 8 in Taiwanese.

Table 17. Traditional categories of Vietnamese tones

Traditional Categories	平(Level)		上(Uprising)		去(Falling)		入(Entering)	
Traditional categories[6]	浮(F)	沉(S)	浮(F)	沉(S)	浮(F)	沉(S)	浮(F)	沉(S)
Modern categories	ngang	huyền	hỏi	ngã	sắc	nặng	sắc	nặng
Numerical tone values	33	21	313	435	35	3	5	3
Tone values in IPA	˧	˨˩	˧˩˧	˧˥	˧˥	˧	˥	˧
Conditions							With finals p t c ch	With finals p t c ch

Tones in modern northern Vietnamese are categorized as *sac, nga, ngang, huyen, hoi,* and *nang*. They are composed of contours of pitch combined with certain other features of voice production as given by Thompson (1987:20) in Table 18.

---

6 浮 literally means 'float' or 'up'; 沉 literally means 'sink' or 'down.' 浮 and 沉 were devised by Vietnamese scholars to refer to the same categories 陰(Yin) and 陽(Yang) of traditional Chinese phonology.

Table 18. Vietnamese tone system (Thompson 1987)

TONE NAME	SYMBOL	PITCH LEVEL	CONTOUR	OTHER FEATURES
sắc	´	High	Rising	Tenseness
ngã	~	High	Rising	Glottalization
ngang	(unmarked)	High-Mid	Trailing-Falling	Laxness
huyền	`	Low	Trailing	Laxness, breathiness
hỏi	?	Mid-low	Dropping	Tenseness
nặng	.	Low	Dropping	Glottalization or tenseness

Sắc tone

Sac tone in Vietnamese can be divided into two categories. The first one is a high rising tone when its final (coda) does not end up with alphabet letters p, t, c, or ch. Examples are found in the pronunciation of cá, 'fish' , khó 'be difficult', and sáng ' bright'. According to Nguyen and Edmondson's (1997:8) acoustic measurements, sac tone of his informant began at a level of 42 semitones and rose to a value of about 48. Thus he assigns sac tone a value of 35 (rising from 3 to 5) on the Chao's scale-of-five system for transcribing tones. When sac tones do not end up with p, t, c, or ch finals, their shapes are similar to tone 2 in Beijing Mandarin (not Taiwan Mandarin, since tone 2 in TM has become a low falling and then rising tone), such as 麻, 答, 拔. It is also close to the rising part of tone 5 in Taiwanese, but pitch in sac tone is much higher than in Taiwanese tone 5. In addition, sac tone in this category is very similar to Taiwanese tone 9, which occurs in some cases such as the first **âng** in the phrase **âng**-âng-âng (literally means extremely red).

The second category of sac tones ends up with p, t, c, or ch. Examples are found in the pronunciation of sắp, 'forthcoming', tốt 'good', and sách 'books'. Their time duration are relatively shorter than the first category of sac tones. They are abrupt tones with relatively high frequency at the value of 5 on Chao's scale-of-five system. They are considered Entering tonal category from the perspective of Taiwanese speakers. Thus, they are similar to Taiwanese tone 8 , such as 毒 (to̍t), 直(ti̍t) and 逐(ta̍k).

Ngã tone

Nga tone is also high and rising. Its contour is roughly the same as that of sac, but it is accompanied by the rasping voice quality occasioned by tense glottal stricture. In careful speech such syllables are sometimes interrupted completely by a glottal stop or a rapid series of glottal stops (Thompson 1987:40). Examples are found in the pronunciation of sữa 'milk' and cũng 'likewise.' In Nguyen and Edmondson's measurements, nga tone began at the level of 44 semitones and rose to the same top of sac tone. Its trajectory showed a characteristic break in the voicing at about 225 msec (about half of the total duration) into the syllable. In terms of Chiung's (2001b) MOTTA analysis, the angle between falling and rising parts of nga tone is smaller than that of Hoi tone. This tone neither exists in Taiwanese nor in Mandarin. This tone is considered the most difficult one for Taiwanese speakers to learn from. In Vietnam, not all Vietnamese speakers can naturally pronounce nga tone. For example, it is usually pronounced as hoi tone in the southern Vietnam.

Ngang tone

Ngang tone is modal; in contour it is nearly level in non-final syllables not accompanied by heavy stress, although even in these cases it probably trails downward slightly (Thompson 1987:40). Examples are found in the pronunciation of ba 'three' and xe 'vehicle.' Nguyen and Edmondson's measurements coincide with Thompson's description that ngang tone has a slight fall nature from a value of 45 semitones falling to 44 semitones (Nguyen and Edmondson 1997:7). Although ngang tone is phonetically a slight falling, it is phonemically regarded as a level tone with a <u>value of 33</u> on the Chao scale. It is similar to Mandarin tone 1, such as 媽, 搭, 都, and Taiwanese tone 1, such as 君 (kun), 雞(ke), 花(hoe), but with relatively lower pitch.

Huyền tone

Huyen tone is lax, starts quite low and trails downward toward the bottom of the voice range. It is often accompanied by a kind of breathy voicing, reminiscent of a sigh (Thompson 1987:40). Examples are found in the pronunciation of về 'return home' and làng 'village.' Edmondson points out that huyen tone is lower than ngang tone, beginning at 38 semitones and falling to 36 semitones. He assigns huyen tone a Chao scale <u>value of 21</u>. Huyen tone is very close to Taiwanese tone 3, such as 棍(kùn), 庫(khò˙), 豹(pà). It is also similar to tone 3 in Taiwan Mandarin 吻, 滾, 把 or the falling part of tone 3 in Beijing Mandarin.

Hỏi tone

Hoi tone is tense; it starts somewhat higher than huyen and drops rather abruptly. In final syllables, and especially in citation forms, this is followed by a sweeping rise at the end, and for this reason it is often called the 'dipping' tone (Thompson 1987:41). Examples are found in the pronunciation of phải 'must' and ảnh 'photograph.' In Nguyen and Edmondson's (1997:8) measurements, hoi tone began at 42 semitones and fell to 36 semitones only to rise again to about the level of the beginning. Its trajectory could be <u>a value of 212 or 313</u> on the Chao scale. Though hoi tone is usually described as low falling and then rising tone, not all Vietnamese speakers have the rising part. Among Nguyen and Edmondson's six informants, all three Hanoi speakers failed to have the rise, whereas the three non-Hanoi Northerners all had it.

When hoi tone consists of falling and rising contour, it is close to Taiwanese tone 5, such as 群(kûn), 財(châi), 猴(kâu), and similar to Beijing Mandarin tone 3 (馬, 打, 把) or Taiwan Mandarin tone 2 (文, 純, 陳). When hoi tone consists of only the falling part, it is similar to Taiwanese tone 3 (棍 kùn, 厝 chhù, 睏 khùn) or Taiwan Mandarin tone 3 (馬, 打, 把). The development of hoi tone from falling-rising to falling seems to be the same as the change of tone 3 in Mandarin from Beijing (falling-rising) to southern forms, such as Taiwan Mandarin (falling).

Nặng tone

Nang tone in Vietnamese can also be divided into two categories. The first category includes tones when its final (coda) end up with p, t, c, or ch. The second category includes tones in any other cases except category one. The major difference is time duration, in which category one is relatively shorter than category two. Nang tone is also tense; it starts somewhat lower than hoi. With syllables ending in a stop p, t, c, ch it drops only a little more sharply than *huyen* tone, but it is never accompanied by the breathy quality of that tone (Thompson 1987: 41). For example, đẹp 'be beautiful.' Other syllables have the same rasping voice quality as *nga*, drop very sharply and are almost immediately cut off by a strong glottal stop. Examples are found in the pronunciation of mạ 'rice seedling.' According to Nguyen and Edmondson's measurements, nang tone began at almost the identical height of 42 semitones and fell to about 38 semitones. Nang was much shorter than other tones, and it was assigned a tone value of 32, with a tendency to go lower.

When its final (coda) end up with alphabet letters p, t, c, or ch, nang tone is similar to Taiwanese tone 4 (闊 khoah, 骨 kut, 角 kak) or neutral tone in Mandarin Chinese. In all other cases, nang tone is similar to Taiwanese tone 3 or tone 4 depending the tonal duration of speaker's pronunciation.

In summary, contrastive analysis of tonal Systems in Vietnamese, Taiwanese, Taiwan Mandarin and Beijin Mandarin are listed in Table 19.

Table 19. Vietnamese tones in contrast to Taiwanese and Chinese tones

Tones in Vietnamese	ngang	huyền	hỏi	ngã	sắc		nặng	
Tone marks	n/a	`	?	~	´		.	
Numerical tone values	33	21	313	435	35	5	3	3
Tone values in IPA	˧	˨˩	˧˩˧	˦˧˥	˧˥	˥	˧	˧
Notes for Vietnamese	Pitch relatively lower than Taiwanese and Mandarin					With finals **p t c ch**		With finals **p t c ch**
Similar tone in Taiwanese	1	3	5	n/a	9	8	3or4	4
Similar tone in Taiwan Mandarin	1	3	2	n/a	n/a	4*	0**	0
Similar tone in Beijin Mandarin	1	3***	3	n/a	2	4*	0	0

*   It is partially similar to the initial part of the high falling pitch of tone 4 in both Taiwan Mandarin and Beijing Mandarin.

**   0 means neutral tone (輕聲) in Mandarin Chinese.

***   It is similar to the falling part of tone 3 in Beijing Mandarin.

3.2. Written form in Romanized Chu Quoc Ngu

The spelling of current Vietnamese Romanization Chu Quoc Ngu (CQN) can be traced back to its early history of missionaries in the late sixteenth century and the early seventeenth century. Although Alexandre de Rhodes is usually regarded as the person who provided the first systematization of Vietnamese Romanization, it is apparent that the Vietnamese Romanization resulted from collective efforts, with the influences of diverse missionaries of different national origins (Thompson 1987: 54-55; Ly 1996: 5). For example, *gi* [z] is borrowed from Italian spelling (Thompson 1987: 62), *nh* [ɲ] from Portuguese[7], *ph* [f] from ancient Greek (DeFrancis 1977: 58). In some cases, their spelling is not simply influenced by a single language, but could be resulted from multilingual influences. For example, the use of *c, k, q* [k] could be influenced by French, Portuguese, and Italian. In

---

[7] Personal communication with David Silva and Jerold Edmondson.

short, Chu Quoc Ngu possesses the features as described in Table 20, in terms of the Universal Orthography.

Table 20. Vietnamese example of Universal Orthography

		directions			
		R	L	U	D
Morphemes	Stem	-	-	-	-
	Prefix	-	-	-	-
	Infix	-	-	-	-
	Suffix	-	-	-	-
Syllables	Syllables	-	-	-	-
	Initial	-	-	-	-
	Medial	-	-	-	-
	Final	-	-	-	-
Phonemes	Consonants	+	-	-	-
	Vowels	+	-	-	-
Phonetic features		+	-	-	-
Supra-segmental		+	-	-	-
Extra information		-	-	-	-
One-to-one		+	-	-	-
One-to-multiple		-	-	-	-
Multiple-to-one		+	-	-	-
Ambiguity		-	-	-	-

In comparison to Taiwanese Peh-oe-ji, the spelling scheme of CQN is much more complex. The major factors are as follows:

First, CQN requires more diacritics, graphemic sets, and spelling rules because the sound system in Vietnamese is more complicated than in Taiwanese. For example, because Vietnamese has more vowels, additional diacritics < ^ ' v > have to be added to the existing Roman letters to distinguish more vowels.

Second, it resulted from the influences of the multilingual backgrounds of missionaries mentioned above.

The third factor is the influence of language variation. For example, although retroflex /tʂ ʐ ʂ / are not found in standard Hanoi Vietnamese, they are spoken in other forms and are reflected in the spelling of CQN. In the case of /tʂ/, *tr* was chosen to represent the retroflex sound, and *ch* was used to represent its counterpart of non-retroflex. Consequently, the Hanoi speakers may have difficulty in distinguishing the difference between tr and ch. For instance, trồng 'to plant' and chồng 'husband' are homophones in Hanoi but spelled differently.

Fourth, the complexity of CQN was deepened due to the historical change over the past 400 years since its invention. For example, the graphemic sets *d* and *gi* were very likely devised in the early period of the seventeenth century to distinguish [d] and [kj], which gradually merged and became [z] in modern times (Doan 1999:163-164). Because the letter *d* was adopted to represent [d], missionaries had to create additional symbol đ to represent the phoneme /d/, which still exists and has a pre-glottalized quality [ʔd] today.

Fifth, to some extent, the complexity of CQN was due to the limitation of linguistic analysis in the early period of its development. For example, *k* and *q* were adopted to represent the same phoneme /k/ because the sound [k] followed by a glide [w] was regarded as different from that which occurred elsewhere. Consequently, q was chosen to represent [k] followed by a glide [w]. Another example is the short vowel [ɤ̌], which was supposed to be represented with ơ̆ , so it could be consistent with its long vowel counterpart ơ (i.e., /ɤ/). However, it was represented with â, which may lead to confusion between /ɤ̌/ and /a/[8]. In short, despite its complexity and inconsistence, the CQN system overall shows a rather good score for efficiency compared to other systems, as Thompson and Thomas commented.[9]

The consonants, vowels, and tones and their corresponding symbols in CQN are summarized in Table 21, Table 22, and Table 23. For a detailed survey on their correspondence, readers may refer to appendix A of Chiung's dissertation (Chiung 2003).

---

[8] According to Edmondson (personal communication), â is actually [ɐ] not [ɤ̌].
[9] Cited in Hannas (1997:86).

Table 21. Symbols for Vietnamese consonants in the spelling of Chu Quoc Ngu

Consonants	CQN	Conditions	Examples
/t/	t		tôi 'I'
/tʰ/	th		thu 'autumn'
/c/	ch		cho 'give'
/tʂ/	tr	Dialects	trồng 'to plant'
/k/	k	Followed by i, y, e, ê,	kê 'chicken'
	q	Followed by /w/	quả 'fruit'
	c	Elsewhere	cá 'fish'
/ʔ/	unmarked		ăn 'eat'
/b/*	b		ba 'three'
/d/*	đ		đi 'go'
/f/	ph		Pháp 'French'
/s/	x		xa 'far'
/ʂ/	s	Dialects	so 'compare'
/x/	kh		khi 'while'
/h/	h		hỏi 'ask'
/v/	v		về 'go back'
/z/	d	Must be learned	da 'skin'
	gi	Must be learned	gia 'home'
	g	Followed by i	gì 'what'
/ʐ/	r	Dialects	ra 'go out'
/ɣ/	gh	Followed by i, e, ê	ghi 'record'
	g	Elsewhere	gà 'chicken'
/l/	l		là 'is'
/m/	m		mẹ 'mother'
/n/	n		nam 'south'
/ɲ/	nh		nhớ 'miss'
/ŋ/	ngh	Followed by i, e, ê	nghỉ 'rest'
	ng	Elsewhere	ngọc 'jade'

* They are considered /ʔb/ and /ʔd/, respectively (Edmondson, p.c.)

Table 22. Vietnamese vowels in CQN

Vowels	CQN	Conditions	Examples
/i/	i		khi 'when'
	y	Sino-Vietnamese	đồng ý 'agree'
/e/	ê		ghế 'chair'
/ɛ/	e		em 'you'
/ɛ̆/	a	Followed by /ɲ/, /c/	thanh 'sound'
/u/	u		cũ 'old'
/ɯ/	ư		từ 'word'
/o/	ô		cô 'aunt'
/ɤ/	ơ		thơ 'poem'
/ɤ̆/	â		thầy 'see'
/ɔ/	o		co 'to bend'
/ɔ̆/	o	Followed by /ŋ/, /k/	cong 'curved'
/a/	a		ta 'we'
/ă/	ă		ăn 'eat'
	a		tay 'hand'
/i‿e/	iê	Elsewhere	tiên 'fairy'
	yê	Preceded by glottal stop /ʔ/ or glide /w/	yêu 'love' truyện 'story'
	ia	Without glide /w/ and coda	bia 'beer'
	ya	Preceded by glide /w/, and without coda	khuya 'midnight'
/u‿o/	uô	Elsewhere	chuông 'bell'
	ua	Without coda	vua 'king'
/ɯ‿ɤ/	ươ	Elsewhere	được 'able'
	ưa	Without coda	mưa 'rain'

Table 23. Vietnamese tone marks in CQN

Categories	ngang	sắc	huyền	hỏi	ngã	nặng
Tone marks	unmarked	´	`	ʔ	~	.
Tone values	33	35	21	313	435	3
IPA tone value	˧	˧˥	˨˩	˧˩˧	˦˧˥	˨

In CQN system, consonants are represented by one or up to three graphs/letters. For example, /t/ is represented by <t>, /f/ by <ph>, and /ŋ/ by <ngh> or <ng>. All graphs for consonants are made from existing Roman letters, except <đ>. Vowels are represented by one or two graphs/letters with appropriate diacritics < ^ ' >, if necessary. The diacritic <^> represents 'upper' or 'close-mid' vowels, such as <ê> and <ô>; but, occasionally it represents different vowel quality in the only case of <â>, which has a phonetic value [ɤ̆]; <ᵛ> represents 'short' vowels; and < ' > shows 'unrounded' feature.

In general, CQN is spelled according to phonemic principles. That is, phonemes, instead of phones, are represented. But, there are some exceptions. For example, final consonant [c] is represented by <ch> instead of <c>, such as *thich*. In this case, [c] is treated by CQN as a phoneme. In fact, [c] is just an allophone of /k/. The spelling was mislead by a phenomenon of palatalization, where final /k/ become [c] when preceded by front vowels. Another example of palatalization is the case, in which allophone [ɲ] in final position is spelled as <nh>, rather than <ng>.[10]

Although the spelling in CQN may be more complex than Taiwanese Peh-oe-ji, there are predictive rules. Most rules are in accordance with vowel positions. That is, front vs. back, upper vs. lower, and rounded vs. unrounded. For example, initial /k/ is spelled as <k> if followed by from vowels, or <q> followed by the glide /w/, or <c> elsewhere.

Tone marks are added to the nucleus of the syllable after phonemes are spelled out. For polysyllabic words, a space is usually placed between syllables; but, in some cases, mostly in recent foreign loanwords, hyphen <-> takes this job.

---

[10] According to Richard Watson (personal communication), the final nh and ch are historically and phonemically correct. In the whole Mon-Khmer area it is common for final palatals to be realized as alveolars with a preceding palatal onglide. Even though the palatal onglide has weakened in most dialects of Vietnamese, it is still distinct from the historical final /n/ and /t/, which have become velar ng and k in some dialects.

For examples, *Áp-ga-ni-xtan* 'Afghan,' *Ô-xa-ma Bin La-đen* 'Osama Bin Laden.' Occasionally, polysyllabic words are spelled without space or hyphen between syllables, such as *Ucraina* 'Ukraine,' and *photo copy* 'photocopy.' Some Vietnamese scholars attribute the monosyllabic characteristic to the accommodation to the monosyllabic structure in spoken Vietnamese. However, this author would say that this characteristic of monosyllable in CQN is mainly the consequence of influence of Han characters, and only secondly the accommodation to the spoken language.

The monosyllabic feature in CQN has further resulted in some troubles. The major problem is the lack of word division. Many Vietnamese people, even with college degree, cannot easily identify the boundary between words. They even do not have the concept of words and syllables, and simply regard syllables as words. This is the same common phenomenon in Taiwan and China, where "the word is by no means a clear and intuitive notion" by their speakers (Packard 2000:14). This ambiguity of word division can be observed from speakers' contradiction in syntax. For example, 'socialism' in Vietnamese could be spelled xã hội chủ nghĩa or chủ nghĩa xã hội. In the first spelling, it is considered a word of four syllables; and the second spelling is a compound word comprising chủ nghĩa 'doctrine' and xã hội 'social.' Another example is the pair of *Á châu* vs. *châu Á* 'Asia,' in which *Á* means Asia and *châu* means continental. The ambiguity of word boundary also can be observed from the inconsistent use of capitalization for proper nouns. For example, the proper nouns 'Taiwan,' 'Vietnam,' and 'National Language' are all Sino-Vietnamese words, but they are differently capitalized as in Đài Loan, Việt Nam, and Quốc ngữ, respectively. In the case of Quốc ngữ, it is weird to write chữ Quốc ngữ, when chữ 'orthography' is added to refer to National Orthography. In addition, 'The Socialist Republic of Vietnam' could be written as Cộng hòa xã hội chủ nghĩa Việt Nam, Cộng hòa Xã hội chủ nghĩa Việt Nam and Cộng hòa Xã hội Chủ nghĩa Việt Nam.

In short, if spelling reform in CQN is favored, reformers may consider solving the monosyllabic issue as the first priority.

Acknowledgements

This is a revision of chapter four of Wi-vun Chiung's dissertation entitled as *Learning Efficiencies for Different Orthographies: A Comparative Study of Han Characters and Vietnamese Romanization* (2003). University of Texas at Arlington.

References

Ang, Ui-jin. 1985. *The tonal study of Taiwanese* [台灣河佬語聲調研究]. Taipei: Independence Press.

Ang, Ui-jin. 1993a. Introduction to Barclay's supplement to Amoy-English dictionary, and other dictionaries afterward it [巴克禮《廈英大辭典補編》及杜典以後的辭字典簡介]. In *A Collection of Southern Min Classic Dictionaries* [閩南語經典辭書彙編 Vol.4]. Vol.4, pp.10-25. Taipei: Woolin Press.

Ang, Ui-jin. 1993b. Introduction to Douglas' Amoy-English dictionary [杜嘉德《廈英大辭典》簡介]. In *A Collection of Southern Min Classic Dictionaries* [閩南語經典辭書彙編 Vol. 4]. Vol.4, pp.1-9. Taipei: Woolin Press.

Ang, Ui-jin. 1996. *A list of Historical Materials: Language Category* [台灣文獻書目題解: 語言類]. Taipei: NCL-Taiwan.

Campbell, William. 1913. *A Dictionary of the Amoy Vernacular Spoken throughout the Prefectures of Chin-chiu, Chiang-chiu and Formosa* [Ē-mn̂g Im ê Sin Jī-tián]. Tailam: The Taiwan Church Press.

Chao, Yuen Ren. 1968. *A Grammar of Spoken Chinese.* University of California: Berkeley & Los Angeles.

Chen, Matthew. 1987. The syntax of Xiamen tone sandhi. *Phonology Yearbook* 4, pp.109-149.

Cheng, Robert. L. and Cheng, Susie S. 1977. *Phonological Structure and Romanization of Taiwanese Hokkian* [台灣福建話的語音結構及標音法]. Taipei: Student Press.

Chiung, Wi-vun T. 1999. Taiwanese and Taiwan Mandarin tones: tonal drift? Paper presented at The 32nd International Conference on Sino-Tibetan Language & Linguistics, University of Illinois at Urbana-Champaign, October 28-31.

Chiung, Wi-vun T. 2001a. Language attitudes towards written Taiwanese. *Journal of Multilingual & Multicultural Development* 22(6), pp.502-523.

Chiung, Wi-vun T. 2001b. Tone change in Taiwanese: age and geographic factors. *The University of Pennsylvania Working Papers in Linguistics* 8(1), 43-55.

Chiung, Wi-vun T. 2003. *Learning Efficiencies for Different Orthographies: A Comparative Study of Han Characters and Vietnamese Romanization.* PhD dissertation: University of Texas at Arlington.

Chu, Man-ni. 1998. *The tonal system of Taipei Mandarin: cross-dialect comparison.* MA thesis: University of Texas at Arlington.

Dang, Nghiem Van. et al. 2000. *Ethnic Minorities in Vietnam.* Hanoi: The Gioi.

DeFrancis, John. 1996. How efficient is the Chinese writing system? *Visible Language* 30(1), pp.6-44.

Đoàn, Thiện Thuật. 1999. *Vietnamese Phonology* [Ngữ Âm Tiếng Việt]. Hà Nội: NXB Đại học Quốc gia

Fon, Janice. and Wen-Yu Chiang. 1999. What does Chao have to say about tones? a case study of Taiwan Mandarin. *Journal of Chinese Linguistics* 27(1), pp.13-37.

Grimes, Barbara. 2000. *Ethnologue: Language of the World.* (13rd edition). Dallas: SIL International.

Heylen, Ann. 2001. Romanizing Taiwanese: codification and standardization of dictionaries in Southern Min (1837-1923). In Ku Wei-ying and K. De Ridder (eds.). *Preludes to the Development of Authentic Chinese Christianity (19th-20th Centuries)*, pp.135-174. Leuven: F. Verbiest Foundation and Leuven University Press.

Ingulsrud, John E. and Kate Allen. 1999. *Learning to Read in China: Sociolinguistic Perspectives on the Acquisition of Literacy.* Lewiston: The Edwin Mellen Press.

Khou, Kek-tun. 1990. *Introduction to the Taiwanese Language* [台灣語概論]. Taipei: Taiwanese Language Foundation.

Kloter, Henning. 2002. The history of Peh-oe-ji. In proceedings of 2002 Conference on Taiwanese Romanization and its Teaching. National Taitung University.

Lý, Toàn Thắng. 1996. Aspects of Alexandre de Rhodes and Chu Quoc Ngu [Về vai trò của Alexandre de Rhodes đối với sự chế tác và hoàn chỉnh chữ Quốc ngữ]. *Ngôn ngữ* 27(1), pp.1-7.

Nguyen, Dinh Hoa. 1997. *Vietnamese.* John Benjamins.

Nguyen, Khac-Kham. 1971. Influence of old Chinese on the Vietnamese language. *Area and Culture Studies* 21, pp.153-181. Tokyo: Tokyo University of Foreign Studies.

Nguyen, Van Loi and Jerold A. Edmondson. 1997. Tones and voice quality in modern northern Vietnamese: instrumental case studies. *Mon Khmer Studies* 28, pp.1-18.

Ong, Iok-tet. 1993. *Essays on the Taiwanese Language* [台灣話講座]. Taipei: Independence Press.

Packard, Jerome L. 2000. *The Morphology of Chinese.* Cambridge: Cambridge University Press.

Ruhlen, Merritt. 1987. *A Guide to the World's Language.* Volume 1: Classification. London: Edward Arnold.

Thompson, Laurence. 1987. *A Vietnamese Reference Grammar.* Hawaii: University of Hawaii.

Tiuⁿ, Ju-hong. 2001. *Principles of POJ or the Taiwanese Orthography: An Introduction to Its Sound-Symbol Correspondences and Related Issues* [白話字基本論]. Taipei: Crane.

Tseng, Chin-Chin. 1995. *Taiwanese Prosody: An Integrated Analysis of Acoustic and Perceptual Data.* Ph.D. dissertation: University of Hawaii.

Van der Loon, Piet. 1966. The Manila incunabula and early Hokkien studies (part 1). *Asia Major* 12, pp.1-43.

Van der Loon, Piet. 1967. The Manila incunabula and early Hokkien studies (part 2). *Asia Major* 13, pp.95-186.

Weingartner, Fredric F. 1970. *Tones in Taiwanese.* Taipei: Ching Hua Press.

Wenzi Gaige Chubanshe. 1983. *The Design and Application of Hanyu Pinyin* [漢語拼音方案的制定和運用]. Beijin: Wenzi Gaige Chubanshe.

Xu, Chang-an. 1992. *Amoy Colloquial Writing* [廈門話文]. Amoy: Amoy Culture.

Zhou, Youguang. 1987. *A Brief History of World's Alphabets* [世界字母簡史]. Shanghai: Jiaoyu.

5

Learning Efficiencies for Han Characters and Vietnamese Roman Scripts

1. Introduction

Debates on the standardization of national language, and on the use of Han characters (Hanji, Hanzi or Chinese characters) in the Han cultural sphere have been going on for more than a hundred years (Chen 1999; Hannas 1997). The citizenry of Vietnam and Korea eventually shifted from the use of Hanji to phonemic writing of their own, i.e., Romanized *Chữ Quốc Ngữ*[1] in Vietnam, and *Hangul*[2] in Korea. However, writing in Hanji is still the parallel dominant writing system in Taiwan and China though the two places use traditional and simplified characters, respectively (Cheng 1990, 1989; Chiung 2001; Norman 1988; DeFrancis 1950). In Taiwan and China, many people have refused to abandon Hanji because they regard Han characters as the best suited orthography for the Chinese spoken language (DeFrancis 1990). But others have argued that the high number of Han characters constitute a burden on the learner, and may cause further hindrance to national modernization. For example, Chen (1994:367) points out that Han characters are largely "responsible for the country's high illiteracy and low efficiency, and hence an impediment to the process of modernization." Although the controversy about the continued use or abandonment of Hanji has been going on over a century, little comparative research has been done with regard to the learning efficiencies of Hanji and other

---

[1] *Chữ Quốc Ngữ* literally means National Language Orthography. It was derived from missionary orthography in the seventeenth century, and is currently the official Romanized writing system for the Vietnamese language (DeFrancis 1977).

[2] Hangul 한글, the Korean alphabet was originally invented by King Sejong in the 15th century. Hangul is a pure Korean word, thus it does not have corresponding Han characters (Lee 1957). In Taiwan, the Han characters 諺文 are usually used to refer to Hangul.

phonemic writing systems. Lack of true empirical research reveals that the source for people's insistence on maintaining or abandoning Han characters is merely based in their socialization or ideological preference rather than on a scientific study of the alternative orthographies.

In order to address the question of whether or not to abandon Han characters, it is important to evaluate the efficiency of Han writing empirically. While there are several aspects and different approaches with regard to such a study, this paper compares the efficiency of learning to read and write in Hanji versus learning to read and write in alphabetic writing systems, that is, Vietnamese Chu Quoc Ngu (CQN). More specifically, the primary concern of this comparative study is to determine how long it takes for a student to be able develop an ability to read and write textual material of general level[3] written in Han characters and Vietnamese CQN. It is assumed that the more school years needed by students to achieve a certain level of reading and writing capacity, the more difficult the writing system is to master.

2. Writing system and learning efficiency

Traditionally, people regard orthography as either logographic or phonographic writing systems. For example, Han characters are considered logographic or ideographic system, and English alphabets are phonographic or phonetic system according to traditional ideas about writing systems. However, this kind of distinction between logographic and phonographic writing systems is not always accurate and appropriate because neither consists of purely logographic or phonographic symbols in its writing. For instance, 'semi-' and '-er' in English refer to the semantic meaning 'half' and 'agent.' In contrast, none of the characters in the Chinese word '麥當勞' (McDonald) is related to McDonald. The sounds of the characters are simply borrowed to represent the English loanword McDonald.

If Han characters are logographs, the process involved in reading them should be different from phonological or phonetic writings. However, research conducted by Tzeng et al. has pointed out that "the phonological effect in the reading of the Chinese characters is real and its nature seems to be similar to that generated in an alphabetic script" (Tzeng et al. 1992:128). Their research reveals that phonological activation is also involved in the reading process of Han

---

[3] The term "general level" is defined as articles appearing in the selected popular newspapers in this investigation.

characters as that involved in phonetic writing system. In addition, Li (1992:21) has pointed out that 形聲 or the radical-phonetic principle[4], which employ both semantic and phonetic[5] components in the structure of Han character, increased from 27 % (11th century B.C.) to 90 % (12th century A.D.). In other words, most of the existing Han characters contain both semantic and phonographic components and are not exclusively logographic. DeFrancis (1996:40) has pointed out that Han characters are "primarily sound-based and only secondarily semantically oriented." In DeFrancis' opinion, it is just a myth to regard Han characters as logographic. He even asserts that "the inefficiency of the system stems precisely from its clumsy method of sound representation and the added complication of an even more clumsy system of semantic determinatives" (DeFrancis 1996:40).

Regarding the orthographic issues, Gelb (1952) and Smalley (1963) have developed a remarkable classification of the world's writing systems. That is, orthographic systems should be classified based on the sound units they represent. According this norm, orthographies can be grouped into four linguistic levels, i.e. morphemic, syllabic, phonemic, and phonetic writing systems, corresponding to the sound units of morphemes (or words), syllables, phonemes, and phonetic features. Han characters are the best example of morphemic or morphosyllabic[6] writing, because almost every Han character can symbolizes a morpheme or a word and can combine with other characters to form new words. Japanese *Kana* is an example of syllabic writing (syllabary). Examples of phonemic[7] systems are Taiwanese *Peh-oe-ji*, Vietnamese, English, and many other languages using Latin scripts. In phonemic writing, the symbols represent corresponding phonemes[8]. Phonemic or alphabetic[9] writing systems are more widespread than others in the world's existing writing systems. As for phonetic writing, all the detailed features of sound difference are reflected in the transcription. This kind of script is usually

---

[4] For example, the left side or radical of 江(/kang/, river) refers to the semantic meaning "water," and the right side or phonetic 工 represents the sound /kang/.

[5] To be exact, it is a syllabic sound unit.

[6] In terms of DeFrancis (1990), the Han writing system is a form of morphosyllabic writing.

[7] Phonemic writing should be distinguished from phonetic writing. Many people confuse phonemic with phonetic writing, and treat phonemic writing as phonetic writing. In fact, in most cases, what people call phonetic writing is actually a phonemic writing system (Smalley 1963:6).

[8] Whether or not symbols and phonemes have a one-to-one relationship, depends on various languages. In Pėh-ōe-jī, the Taiwanese romanization, each symbol represents only one phoneme in general. In contrast, English has more than one corresponding relationships.

[9] Alphabetic systems here is defined in terms of Smalley's "writing systems based directly upon the individual phonemes of language" (Smalley 1963:6).

the tool of a phonetician who wishes to transcribe spoken language data into written form for linguistic analysis.

Generally speaking, phonemic writing is the most efficient system because it requires the learning of the fewest number of symbols to represent the full range of speech. In contrast, the least efficient is morphemic writing, since in that writing system every morpheme has to be individually learned (Smalley 1963:7). For example, all English lexical items can be expressed by the 26 alphabet letters. In contrast, the number of Hanji learned by elementary students in Taiwan is about 2669 (Chiung 1999:52). Norman (1988:72-73) has pointed out that an ordinary literate Chinese person knows and uses somewhere between 3,000 and 4,000 Han characters. In other words, literacy learners have to learn at least around 3,000 characters to be able to achieve certain levels of literacy in Chinese. Compared to the limited number of letters in English, Chinese writing system has great number of characters to be individually learned. Even if we do not count the number of characters, but the number of components decomposed from the characters, there are still around a thousand of radical and phonetic components need to be learned.

3. Methodology

Because 'efficient' or 'inefficient' will be significant only if we compare Hanji to other writing systems, we need to include other orthographies in the comparison. Theoretically, we should have contrastive groups, such as Hanji groups vs. Roman groups. Subjects in these two groups must have identical backgrounds (e.g. mother tongue, intelligence quotient, educational level, and social class) differing only by having been equally educated in different writing systems, i.e. Hanji in the Hanji groups, and roman script in the Roman groups. However, in practice, it is extremely difficult to find groups that meet these criteria as well as to find volunteers willing to join the experimental groups. Thus, we have to examine the learning efficiency in an indirect way. In this study, Vietnamese CQN was chosen as a contrastive orthography. The main reason choosing Vietnamese are 1) Vietnamese is typologically closer to Mandarin Chinese than other languages using romanized writing systems. 2) Vietnamese used to use Han characters, and it completely shifted to romanization in 1945. Nowadays, romanized CQN is taught through Vietnam's national education system. 3) The researcher has easier access to get subjects and data from Vietnam than other countries.

Students' backgrounds such as Intelligence Quotient (IQ), Educational Quotient (EQ), first language, parents' social-economic class, and school's ranking level may contribute to students' different scores in the comprehension tests. In this study, students are assumed to have the same IQ and EQ except in a few cases, in which some chosen students might turn out to show extreme difficulty in reading and answering (dyslexia etc). In such cases, students' scores would not be included in this study. It is also assumed that students' first language will have only very limited influence since Mandarin has been promoted more than fifty years and much research has shown that language shift from Taiwanese to Mandarin has taken place completely among the young generations (Young 1989; Huang 1993; Chan 1994).

In order to minimize the influence of background on test results, subjects should be chosen from students in the same ranking levels of schools. For example, if elementary students in the Taiwan group are chosen from top ranking elementary schools of the metropolitan area, then high school students should also be chosen from top ranking high schools. In addition, all elementary students in this group should be chosen from the same elementary school, and high school students be chosen from the same high school. The 'same ranking' principle will also apply to the Vietnamese group.

This study consisted of three sets of experiment: reading comprehension tests, dictation tests, and oral reading tests. The subjects included college, high school, and elementary school students. Students' scores were awarded based on the percentage of right answers, ranging from zero to 100. Thus, if a student received a higher score, it indicates that he or she had better proficiency than others. Furthermore, the scores of college students were regarded as an index of maximum proficiency. The learning periods needed for students to reach the maximum proficiency is treated as an index of learning efficiency of students' corresponding orthography. For example, if we find that fifth graders in Taiwan group obtain reading scores statistically equivalent to those students in college, then we conclude that it takes about five years for students in Taiwan to achieve full capacity of reading in Hanji.

The experiments conducted for this study were divided into two periods. The first period experiments were previously conducted in December 2001 and June 2002. A total of 803 students were involved, including students from Taiwan's Au-ang Elementary School (396 students), Tamkang University (57), Vietnam's To Hien Thanh Elementary School (300) and National University (50) in Hanoi. Thereafter, second period experiments were succeed with Taiwanese students only. They were from Chian-hong Junior High School (105) in June 2006, Tainan First Senior High School (76), Tainan Girl's Senior High School (72), Asia High School (62) in May and June 2007, Au-ang Elementary School (187) in December

2007, and National Cheng Kung University (30) in May 2008. During the second period, only dictation tests and oral reading tests were conducted.

3.1. Reading comprehension tests

The main purpose of this experiment is to determine the average number of years needed for literacy learners in Taiwan and Vietnam to be able to comprehend newspaper articles in their own language and orthography, i.e. Taiwan Mandarin (Hanji) and Vietnamese (CQN). Reading texts were prepared in Hanji and Vietnamese based on the orthographic differences. Students in each group were tested with texts in their relevant orthography. That is, Hanji group was tested with texts written in Hanji. Vietnamese group was tested with texts written in Vietnamese CQN. Each reading type consisted of four different soft articles, and each article was followed by five comprehension questions. Reading texts in Hanji group had the same themes as those in Vietnamese, so that the influence of different themes on readers' comprehension tests can be minimized. All these test types had articles of similar length, so as to minimize the potential influence of different lengths, where "length" is defined by number of syllables in texts rather than visual layout of texts.

Subjects were told to complete their test in 30 minutes. Subjects had to turn in their answer sheets even thought they did not finish in time. College students were timed while they were doing the test since they usually completed the test less then 30 minutes.

Students' scores on reading comprehension tests were keyboarded and then analyzed by using statistics software SPSS version 10. The statistical techniques employed in the reading comprehension tests were t-tests, ANOVA (analysis of variance) and post hoc tests. The significance level was set at $\alpha = 0.05$.

3.2. Dictation tests

Although students may be able to comprehend the reading texts, they may not be able to write accurately. Thus, dictation tests were conducted to examine the accuracy of writing in comparison to students' reading comprehension ability. The subjects were divided into groups Taiwan and Vietnam according to their nationality background.

The criteria for dictation tests are the same in both the Taiwan and Vietnam groups. The dictation consisted of two texts: 1) soft article mainly containing frequently used words, and 2) hard article mainly containing less frequently used words. The texts for dictation were first tape-recorded, and later be played to the students. Students were told to listen to the passages and write down what they heard. Subjects in Vietnam group were told to write in CQN. Subjects in Taiwan group were requested to write as many Han characters as they can.

After the students completed their dictation, errors in the dictation tests were marked at a later time for further analysis of the number and kinds of errors made; for example, words or characters left out, missed strokes in the Han characters and misspelled words in Vietnamese. The percentage of Han characters correctly written by a Taiwanese subject was regarded as an index or score to evaluate his/her proficiency in writing Han characters. On the other hand, the percentage of correct segments (including sound segments and suprasegmental tones) received by a Vietnamese subject was regarded as an index or score to evaluate his/her proficiency in writing Vietnamese CQN.

3.3. Oral reading tests

The purpose of the oral reading tests was to examine the accuracy of oral reading with regard to orthography. Oral reading tests were conducted with Vietnamese group in the first experimental period. Taiwanese students were added in the second period.

Subjects were told to read aloud two prepared texts, one of which was considered soft and the other hard. Texts were prepared in Vietnamese CQN for the Vietnamese group, and in Mandarin Chinese for the Taiwanese group. Subjects' oral reading was timed and tape-recorded. Later on, their oral reading was transcribed and keyboarded for further analysis. It was presumed that the more correct segments the subjects have, the more proficiency the subjects have in oral reading skill. So, the correct segments produced by each subject, including sound segments and tonal features, were calculated. The percentage of correct segments was regarded an index or score to evaluate subjects' oral reading skill.

4. Results and discussion

The results of statistics have shown that there is no statistical difference between Hanji and CQN groups with regard to the reading comprehension test. However, CQN group is statistically superior to Hanji group in the aspects of dictation and oral reading tests.

4.1. Reading comprehension tests

The experimental results of each group are presented in Table 1 and Figure 1, in which "Grades" mean the school year of students, "N" is the number of students in the group, "mean" is the average score, and "Sd" shows its standard deviation. The first grade students in Vietnam group were tested again with the same reading texts three months later after their first test. The results of second test were represented by 1.5 grader. In addition, there are only five years in Vietnam's elementary school, so there is no CQN group in the category "grade 6."

Table 1. Scores received by students in each groups

Grades	Groups	N	mean	Sd.
1	Hanji	36	32.64	25.87
	CQN	66	14.09	17.09
	Total	134	21.12	22.63
1.5	CQN	57	24.91	14.59
	Total	57	24.91	14.59
2	Hanji	30	50.00	33.32
	CQN	59	56.02	21.73
	Total	123	46.67	27.58
3	Hanji	30	90.50	12.27
	CQN	58	80.26	19.92
	Total	118	77.71	22.77
4	Hanji	31	96.77	3.77
	CQN	60	87.08	19.32
	Total	124	85.12	20.74
5	Hanji	34	93.38	15.11
	CQN	57	94.91	5.22
	Total	123	86.99	20.41
6	Hanji	39	96.92	5.81
	Total	74	94.53	10.34
college	Hanji	34	96.91	6.28
	CQN	50	92.60	9.27
	Total	107	94.53	8.73
Total	Hanji	234	79.66	30.54
	CQN	407	62.84	35.30
	Total	860	66.89	34.59

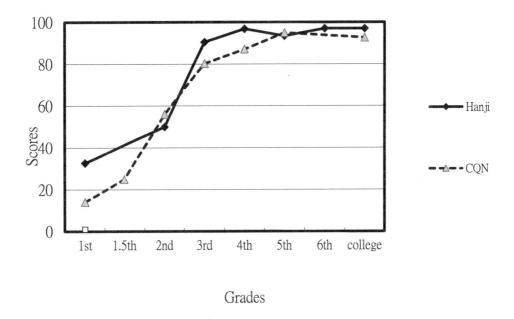

Grades

Figure 1. Scores received by grades in each groups

Statistical analysis was conducted among groups in each grade. Univariate Analysis of Variance (hereafter, UANOVA) statistical technique was employed if there were three groups in comparison; independent samples t-test was applied if there were only two groups. They were conducted by using SPSS 10 with the 5% significance level. The statistical results reveal that gender is not significantly different at the 5% significance level. However, grade level is a significant factor. Findings are as follows:

First, there is no statistically significant difference among the mean scores of students from third grade to college, both in Hanji and CQN groups. This result reveals that orthography is not a significant factor in affecting students' scores on the reading comprehension tests once students are in third grade or higher. Because students in third grade are considered to have the same reading level as collegians, this result implies that Hanji and CQN can all serve as independent writing systems without affecting readers' comprehension.

Second, among the students from the second to the fifth grades, there is no significant difference between the mean scores of Hanji and CQN groups. In this study, although third grade students in Han group have achieved the same score as collegians, it does not necessarily mean that students will have the same achievement when they are encountering texts other than 'soft articles.' Hard articles, in contrast to soft ones, require acquisition of more Han characters. In this situation, it might take more years for the pupils to achieve the same reading level as collegians. Further experiments on this issue are recommended.

The third set of statistical results comes from comparisons among different scripts in the early stage of literacy acquisition, i.e., first and 1.5th grades. To examine these beginners, the pupils were divided into four groups based on their orthographic background. Because pupils in CQN group were tested twice, they are regarded as two groups, i.e., CQN1 and CQN2, for the first and second time tests, respectively. Therefore, we have a total of four groups, Hanji, Bopomo, CQN1, and CQN2.

Statistical result indicates that pupils in Bopomo and Hanji groups have the statistically same mean scores of reading comprehension tests on soft articles. As for the Vietnamese, although the mean score of pupils in CQN1 group is statistically lower than Bopomo and Hanji, they have caught up to the same level three months later in the CQN2 group. Recall that pupils in CQN1 and CQN2 groups were tested in December 2002 and March 2003, respectively; and Hanji and Bopomo groups were tested in January 2002. As for how many pupils and how deeply they have learned scripts in their pre-school days, we have no clues. All these facts indicate that we cannot simply assume pupils in the Hanji, Bopomo, and CQN groups have the same literacy starting point since the time span for the literacy beginners is so sensitive and any tiny increase in the amount of time can improve their orthographic skill greatly. In such a situation, I would suggest that literacy beginners in Hanji, Bopomo, and CQN have overall the same mean scores on reading comprehension tests before the learners are advanced to second grade. Even so, further study of the literacy beginners is needed and recommended to confirm this result.

The most surprising finding here is that the literacy beginners of Hanji are not significantly different from Bopomo and CQN. Under this situation, what does "inefficiency" have to say about Han characters? If the learning of Han characters is time-consuming, how could the first graders in the Hanji group have the statistically same mean scores as other groups? Recall that reading is neither a letter-by-letter nor word-by-word recognition process, but a process of forward and backward saccades (Smith 1994:152). Yang and McConkie's (1999:212) study of thirteen Taiwanese subjects has shown a mean length of three characters in progressive saccades and 2.2 characters in regressive. In other words, not all characters are actually read in the reading of Hanji texts. Therefore, the first graders could retrieve meanings from texts beyond their acquisition of limited number of Han characters. More research is needed to confirm this assumption.

In short, the mean scores of reading comprehension tests among Hanji,

Bopomo, and CQN groups are statistically no different, except subjects in the Bopomo group from the second to fifth grades score significantly lower than subjects in other groups. Since collegian readers among the three scripts show no significant difference with regard to their scores on reading comprehension tests, is there a meaningful difference? The answer is yes. The major difference is the time the subjects spend on reading texts. The reading rates are shown in Table 2, which indicates that reading Han characters is 2.44 times faster than reading Vietnamese CQN among college students.

Table 2. The rates in reading text-based Hanji and CQN by collegians.

	Hanji	CQN
Total characters or syllables	2346	2297
Characters or syllables/per minute	482.72	198.02
Seconds/per character or syllable	0.124	0.303

Why is reading in Hanji faster than in CQN? There are two potential factors: 1) the influence of homophones in CQN, and 2) the influence of physical placement of orthographic symbols. Homophones in Vietnamese CQN are not as well distinguished as those in Chinese characters, so it could reduce the speed in reading CQN. As for the placement of orthographic symbols, the length of sentences in CQN is about twice that of sentences in Hanji when they both are arranged in a linear placement with 14 size fonts in a word processing file. This means that CQN readers have to spend more time with their eye movement searching for words in a wider length. Consequently, the total amount of time spent on reading the prepared CQN texts is higher than Hanji. Whether or not these two factors are significant and which one is more dominant would require further study. This author would suggest applying the same approach in this experiment to other writing systems, particularly the Korean Hangul and English. Experiments in the Korean Hangul should be able to provide helpful information with regard to the relationship between length and reading speed since Korean Hangul is constructed with a monosyllabic shape and its text has roughly the same length as in Han character. On the other hand, experiments in English should be able to clarify the effect of homophones on reading, because English has the same linear structure as CQN, and possesses relatively fewer homophones compared to Vietnamese.

4.2. Dictation tests

Hanji group

There were a total of 729 subjects involved in the Hanji dictation tests. Their descriptive statistics are listed in Table 3 and Table 4, where 'mean' indicates the average number of correct characters students have written, and '%' means the percentage of correct characters in the text. The percentage of correct Han characters is regarded as an index to evaluate students' performance in dictation. 'Maximum/minimum' is the maximum/minimum number of correct characters among the students in a group. For example, the text for soft article (dictation one) consists of 130 characters (excluding punctuation). The male first graders have a mean of 25.24 correct characters, which constitute a percentage of 19.4 (=25.24/130). Among the male first graders, the maximum number of correct characters a student possesses is 57.

Statistical results of UANOVA reveal that gender and grade are significant factors at the 5% significance level. Gender factor is excluded for further analysis since it is not the main concern in this study.

Table 3. Correct Han characters in soft article

Grades	Genders	N	%	mean	Sd.	Max.	Min.
1st graders	male	29	19.4	25.24	15.56	57	1
	female	26	20.2	26.31	15.98	59	2
	Total	55	19.8	25.75	15.62	59	1
2nd graders	male	26	42.1	54.73	26.13	118	6
	female	26	60.8	79.04	25.61	115	19
	Total	52	51.4	66.88	28.41	118	6
3rd graders	male	31	74.6	97.00	32.56	128	4
	female	26	78.1	101.50	35.06	128	13
	Total	57	76.2	99.05	33.49	128	4
4th graders	male	26	89.3	116.15	25.12	130	9
	female	34	93.9	122.09	8.04	130	99
	Total	60	91.9	119.52	17.67	130	9

Grades	Genders	N	%	mean	Sd.	Max.	Min.
5th graders	male	31	89.5	116.35	16.27	129	69
	female	35	93.9	122.03	11.21	130	69
	Total	66	91.8	119.36	14.00	130	69
6th graders	male	46	94.1	122.39	17.10	130	23
	female	26	97.6	126.92	3.32	130	117
	Total	72	95.4	124.03	13.93	130	23
7th graders	male	15	98.5	128.00	2.17	130	124
	female	20	98.4	127.95	2.50	130	122
	Total	35	98.5	128.00	2.31	130	122
8th graders	male	20	98.9	128.60	1.67	130	125
	female	14	98.8	128.43	3.27	130	118
	Total	34	98.9	128.53	2.42	130	118
9th graders	male	14	99.0	128.64	2.98	130	119
	female	21	99.6	129.52	1.12	130	126
	Total	35	99.4	129.17	2.08	130	119
10th graders	male	42	99.7	129.60	0.77	130	127
	female	60	99.5	129.38	1.45	130	123
	Total	102	99.6	129.47	1.22	130	123
11th graders	male	61	98.4	127.89	4.58	130	106
	female	47	99.1	128.77	2.42	130	120
	Total	108	98.7	128.27	3.80	130	106
collegians	male	19	98.6	128.16	3.88	130	119
	female	34	99.2	128.97	1.85	130	121
	Total	53	99.0	128.68	2.74	130	119
Total	male	360	84.2	109.42	42.15	130	1
	female	369	88.3	114.84	38.51	130	2
	Total	729	86.3	112.17	40.19	130	1

Table 4. Correct Han characters in hard article

Grades	Genders	N	%	mean	Sd.	Max.	Min.
1st graders	male	29	8.45	7.52	7.29	39	0
	female	25	7.06	6.28	4.10	16	0
	Total	54	7.80	6.94	6.01	39	0
2nd graders	male	26	17.42	15.50	10.47	46	0
	female	26	21.61	19.23	8.30	34	4
	Total	52	19.52	17.37	9.54	46	0
3rd graders	male	31	34.33	30.55	14.08	57	7
	female	26	40.92	36.42	18.07	66	7
	Total	57	37.34	33.23	16.14	66	7
4th graders	male	26	60.58	53.92	20.54	84	6
	female	34	59.91	53.32	18.59	89	20
	Total	60	60.20	53.58	19.29	89	6
5th graders	male	31	55.24	49.16	20.80	78	10
	female	35	63.37	56.40	15.79	77	22
	Total	66	59.55	53.00	18.53	78	10
6th graders	male	46	68.27	60.76	19.32	86	14
	female	26	75.42	67.12	12.07	83	37
	Total	72	70.85	63.06	17.24	86	14
7th graders	male	15	70.4	62.67	9.12	73	48
	female	20	74.8	66.60	8.92	80	48
	Total	35	72.7	64.69	9.05	80	48
8th graders	male	20	81.2	72.30	17.43	87	2
	female	14	79.8	71.00	8.38	82	52
	Total	34	80.6	71.76	14.25	87	2
9th graders	male	14	88.1	78.43	5.69	86	68
	female	21	87.8	78.14	5.52	87	69
	Total	35	87.9	78.26	5.51	87	68
10th graders	male	42	92.3	82.14	8.24	89	56
	female	60	89.1	79.27	10.41	88	32
	Total	102	90.4	80.45	9.64	89	32
11th graders	male	61	88.8	79.07	14.20	89	0
	female	47	90.8	80.83	8.16	89	55
	Total	108	89.7	79.83	11.93	89	0
collegians	male	19	94.80	84.37	4.49	89	72
	female	35	95.73	85.20	2.62	89	76
	Total	54	95.40	84.91	3.38	89	72
Total	male	360	64.4	57.36	30.05	89	0
	female	369	68.9	61.36	29.22	89	0
	Total	729	66.7	59.38	29.77	89	0

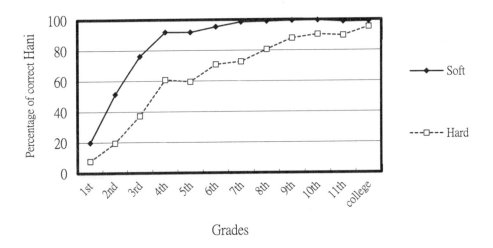

Figure 2. Correct Han characters in soft and hard articles.

To have a better picture, the percentage of correct characters achieved by students in each grade is reflected in Figure 2. For the soft article, the results of UANOVA post hoc tests show that students' percentage of correct characters significantly increases until the fourth grade. Because the results of *post hoc* tests indicate students from fourth grade to college are not statistically significantly different, we may conclude that the beginning learners of Han characters are improving their writing skills over years, and they have achieved the statistically same level as collegians at the stage of fourth grade. In other words, it takes about four years for a learner of Hanji to be able to write soft articles.

As for hard article, it reveals that students' skill in Han writing significantly improves over the years. The most important findings in the results is that the high school students, even in the eleventh grade, have not achieved the same level as collegians. This fact implies that it takes more than eleven years for Hanji learners to be able to write hard articles at the collegian level. Terms "being able to write hard articles" refer only to "being able to handle the required characters in writing hard articles;" it does not mean any other stylistic skills. The results indicate that the number of characters students have learned in elementary school may be enough for soft articles, but it is insufficient for advanced hard articles.

Those errors made by all subjects in writing Han characters were first classified into twelve categories, and the categories were reclassified and reduced by using factor analysis. The results of factor analysis reveal that those twelve error categories may be further regrouped into five or four basic types, as shown in Table 5 and Table 6. The two tables show that "similarity" is the most common error type in both soft and hard articles. Compared to soft article, more phonetic type errors were found in hard article. For example, the percentage of HKI (identical sound, but different meaning) increased from 17.82% to 30.03% in hard article. Also, the percentage of HL (similar sound, but different meaning) increased from 5.76% to 30.41%. In contrast, HLH (similar shape) is decreasing from 34.07% to 13.2%. These findings indicate that phonetic features play a more important role in writing hard articles than in soft articles.

Table 5. Basic error types of Hanji in soft article

Error types	%
Similarity (in sound, meaning, or shape)	78.83
Stroke	10.53
Semantic extension	5.49
Semantic-phonetic principle	4.64
Flip-flop	0.66

Table 6. Basic error types of Hanji in hard article

Error types	%
Phonetic similarity	85.70
Semantic extension	11.29
Semantic-phonetic principle	2.95
Flip-flop	0.08

Vietnamese CQN

There were a total of 349 students involved in the dictation tests. In the CQN writing system, syllables are divided into four sound segments, i.e., onset, glide, nucleus, and coda, plus a suprasegmental feature, i.e., tone. Therefore, the students' scores on dictation are calculated based on the correct sound segments and tonal feature (hereafter, correct segments) they have written. Further, the percentage of correct segments is regarded as the index to show students' performance in writing dictation. For example, the standard text in dictation one consists of 119 syllables, which comprise a total of 308 sound segments and 119 tones. Table 7 shows that male first graders have a mean of 126.36 correct segments out of 427 (= 308 + 119). Its percentage of correct segments is 126.36

divided by 427, equal to 29.59%. Thus this percentage is considered an index to show how well students are handling CQN.

Table 7. Correct segments of CQN in soft article

Grades	Genders	N	%	mean	Sd.	Max.	Min.
1st graders	male	33	29.59	126.36	78.25	309	28
	female	32	39.18	167.31	76.55	349	50
	Total	65	34.31	146.52	79.53	349	28
1.5th graders	male	33	48.53	207.24	58.71	290	68
	female	31	48.77	208.23	54.62	332	80
	Total	64	48.65	207.72	56.32	332	68
2nd graders	male	35	66.50	283.94	63.23	406	118
	female	24	61.06	260.71	74.17	410	117
	Total	59	64.28	274.49	68.25	410	117
3rd graders	male	22	84.98	362.86	70.35	427	179
	female	36	93.17	397.83	53.30	427	211
	Total	58	90.06	384.57	62.14	427	179
4th graders	male	27	97.23	415.19	26.77	427	295
	female	33	96.62	412.58	31.02	427	306
	Total	60	96.90	413.75	28.97	427	295
5th graders	male	28	99.82	426.25	2.24	427	416
	female	29	99.71	425.76	3.33	427	415
	Total	57	99.77	426.00	2.83	427	415
collegians	male	8	99.97	426.88	0.35	427	426
	female	42	99.97	426.88	0.50	427	424
	Total	50	99.97	426.88	0.48	427	424
Total	male	186	69.87	298.33	124.61	427	28
	female	227	78.70	336.03	115.07	427	50
	Total	413	74.72	319.05	120.78	427	28

Table 8. Correct segments of CQN in hard article

Grades	Genders	N	%	mean	Sd.	Max.	Min.
1st graders	male	33	14.07	60.64	29.94	117	8
	female	32	16.98	73.19	27.49	139	29
	Total	65	15.50	66.82	29.22	139	8
1.5th graders	male	33	32.35	139.42	49.41	214	23
	female	30	33.80	145.67	49.52	278	22
	Total	63	33.04	142.40	49.16	278	22
2nd graders	male	35	49.71	214.26	69.44	378	73
	female	24	52.67	227.00	62.48	357	92
	Total	59	50.91	219.44	66.44	378	73
3rd graders	male	22	72.94	314.36	96.27	430	104
	female	36	83.39	359.39	78.58	430	158
	Total	58	79.42	342.31	87.70	430	104
4th graders	male	27	92.73	399.67	54.05	431	195
	female	33	90.36	389.45	43.97	431	274
	Total	60	91.43	394.05	48.60	431	195
5th graders	male	28	93.51	403.04	45.37	431	260
	female	29	96.06	414.00	22.70	431	351
	Total	57	94.81	408.61	35.79	431	260
collegians	male	8	99.83	430.25	1.16	431	428
	female	42	99.89	430.52	1.44	431	422
	Total	50	99.88	430.48	1.39	431	422
Total	male	186	58.05	250.19	144.07	431	8
	female	226	69.85	301.05	140.61	431	22
	Total	412	64.52	278.09	144.26	431	8

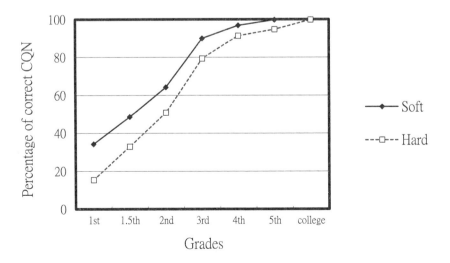

Figure 3. Percentage of correct CQN segments in soft and hard articles.

Statistical results of UANOVA reveal that grade level is a significant factor at the 5% significance level. In soft article, the results (see Figure 3) show that the students statistically improve their skill in writing CQN until the fourth grade, which indicates that it takes about four years for literacy learners of CQN to achieve statistically the same dictation level of Vietnamese collegians. As for hard article, the results show that pupils significantly improve their writing skill in CQN over the years, and have statistically achieved the same level as collegians by the fifth grade. It implies that it takes about five year for CQN learners to be able to write hard articles at the collegian level.

Comparing Chinese characters to Vietnamese CQN, their learners both take about four years to be able to write soft articles. However, Hanji learners have to spend more years than CQN learners in learning to write hard articles. Why are they different in writing hard articles? The major factor is probably that Hanji learners have a large number of Han characters to be learned over a period of years. They must learn new characters in order to read hard articles. On the contrary, CQN learners have very limited number of letters and spelling rules. Once they have acquired the letters and rules, they are able to write down what they heard in any type of articles. This is also the reason why the different percentages between soft and hard articles in writing CQN are not as great as those in writing Han characters.

4.3. Oral reading tests

Hanji group

Oral reading tests were conducted in the second experimental period. Subjects included a total of 187 students from Au-ang elementary school and a total of 30 students from National Cheng Kung University.

Table 9. Correct Han characters in oral reading one (soft)

GRADES	GENDER	N	%	Mean	Sd.	Maximum	Minimum
1st graders	male	15	64.35	83.67	41.78	128	6
	female	16	72.79	94.63	35.54	128	4
	Total	31	68.71	89.32	39.07	128	4
2nd graders	male	17	96.33	125.24	3.39	128	116
	female	15	97.12	126.27	2.38	130	121
	Total	32	96.71	125.72	3.00	130	116

GRADES	GENDER	N	%	Mean	Sd.	Maximum	Minimum
3rd graders	male	16	97.84	127.19	1.55	129	124
	female	15	97.28	126.47	2.42	130	122
	Total	31	97.57	126.84	2.05	129	122
4th graders	male	12	97.95	127.33	1.89	130	123
	female	18	97.65	126.94	2.34	129	120
	Total	30	97.77	127.10	2.18	130	120
5th graders	male	16	97.31	126.50	3.41	130	121
	female	17	96.29	125.18	2.96	130	122
	Total	33	96.78	125.82	3.25	130	121
6th graders	male	15	96.72	125.73	3.28	130	118
	female	15	94.62	123	16.44	130	62
	Total	30	95.68	124.39	11.93	130	62
Total	male	91	91.83	119.31	23.36	130	6
	female	96	92.65	119.98	19.80	130	4
	Total	187	92.23	119.89	20.30	130	4

Table 10. Correct Han characters in oral reading two (hard)

GRADES	GENDER	N	%	Mean	Sd.	Maximum	Minimum
1st graders	male	15	47.27	42.07	23.63	78	5
	female	16	42.81	42.81	25.45	85	2
	Total	31	42.45	42.45	24.59	85	2
2nd graders	male	17	83.41	74.24	9.86	86	49
	female	15	86.89	77.33	7.07	87	63
	Total	32	75.69	75.69	8.80	87	49
3rd graders	male	16	92.84	82.63	4.28	88	71
	female	15	91.91	81.80	2.83	86	77
	Total	31	92.39	82.23	3.68	88	71
4th graders	male	12	94.01	83.67	2.17	87	80
	female	18	93.57	83.28	3.94	88	73
	Total	30	93.75	83.43	3.35	88	73
5th graders	male	16	95.08	84.63	2.29	88	80
	female	17	94.12	83.76	3.56	89	76
	Total	33	94.59	84.18	3.04	89	76
6th graders	male	15	95.66	85.13	3.36	89	75
	female	15	92.73	82.53	12.35	89	37
	Total	30	94.19	83.83	9.14	89	37
Total	male	91	84.58	75.27	18.74	89	5
	female	96	84.66	75.34	19.02	89	2
	Total	187	84.62	75.31	18.86	89	2

Vietnamese group

The subjects for oral reading tests were selected from the same subjects for previous tests. Class A in each grade from first to third was chosen. Only three grades were tested for oral reading because the second and third graders had achieved almost 100% of correct segments, there was no need for further testing for advanced grades. There were a total of 92 pupils involved in the oral reading tests.

Text one for oral reading tests consists of 101 syllables, including 271 sound segments and 101 tones. In other words, there are a total of 372 segments, which are to be calculated toward each subject's score on oral reading. Text two consists of 104 syllables, including 296 sound segments and 104 tones.

The students' number of correct segments and its percentage are summarized in Table 11 and Table 12. The table shows that the first graders on average are able to correctly read 93.82% of the soft article and 87.68% of the hard article. Statistical results of *post hoc* tests under UANOVA reveal that there is no significant difference between second and third graders in reading one and two. It indicates that the second graders have statistically achieved the maximum score on oral reading. Recall that the first graders were tested in December, which is between the third and fourth months of the first school semester. The results of oral reading tests imply that CQN beginners can correctly read about 90% of given articles after about three or four months of learning (40 minutes per period, and 13 periods per week), and then acquire the full oral reading skill a year later. Comparing Han characters to CQN, it is almost impossible for Taiwanese first graders to be able to read 90% of given articles. There is no way for Hanji beginners to be able to read or predict unless they have acquired the characters. This finding reveals that the greatest strength of phonemic writing, such as CQN, is the ease of learning to read aloud.

Table 11. Correct segments of CQN in oral reading one (soft)

GRADES	GENDER	N	%	Mean	Sd.	Maximum	Minimum
1st graders	male	14	94.34	350.93	23.47	371	301
	female	20	93.45	347.65	51.44	372	181
	Total	34	93.82	349.00	41.75	372	181
2nd graders	male	20	98.99	368.25	4.78	372	356
	female	11	98.56	366.64	7.61	372	347
	Total	31	98.84	367.68	5.86	372	347
3rd graders	male	11	97.43	362.45	15.47	372	317
	female	16	99.34	369.56	3.29	372	361
	Total	27	98.57	366.67	10.53	372	317
Total	male	45	97.16	361.44	16.84	372	301
	female	47	96.65	359.55	34.89	372	181
	Total	92	96.90	360.48	27.45	372	181

Table 12. Correct segments of CQN in oral reading two (hard)

GRADES	GENDER	N	%	Mean	Sd.	Maximum	Minimum
1st graders	male	14	87.07	348.29	42.67	393	272
	female	20	88.10	352.40	95.78	400	66
	Total	34	87.68	350.71	77.48	400	66
2nd graders	male	20	97.64	390.55	13.02	400	344
	female	11	97.89	391.55	12.71	400	356
	Total	31	97.73	390.90	12.71	400	344
3rd graders	male	11	98.25	393.00	6.05	400	385
	female	16	98.77	395.06	4.99	400	381
	Total	27	98.56	394.22	5.43	400	381
Total	male	45	94.50	378.00	32.07	400	272
	female	47	94.02	376.09	65.26	400	66
	Total	92	94.26	377.02	51.49	400	66

Subjects' time in reading prepared text was recorded during the tests. The statistical results are described in table 13, which shows that first graders spent an average of 257.59 seconds on oral reading one (soft). It is about five or seven times long as the second and third graders. For comparison with the pupils, thirteen collegians from previous tests were randomly chosen to do timed oral reading. Their results show mean scores of 24.61, and 26.84 seconds for a collegian to complete oral readings one and two, respectively. Comparing collegians and pupils, it indicates that the CQN beginners have to spend more time during their oral reading. Nevertheless, the CQN beginners can reach morn than 90% of accuracy as long as they have sufficient time to do oral reading.

Table 13. Time spent by subjects on oral reading (soft and hard)

Grades	Articles	N	Mean (in sec.)	Sd.	Maximum (in sec.)	Minimum (in sec.)
1	Soft	34	257.59	221.04	1200	55
	Hard	34	398.35	273.31	1200	80
2	Soft	31	47.55	11.84	72	32
	Hard	31	68.16	22.06	125	39
3	Soft	27	38.15	8.18	58	26
	Hard	27	52.70	15.52	98	34
college	Soft	13	24.61	3.04	30	17
	Hard	13	26.84	3.05	32	20

5. Conclusion

Three type of experiments were conducted in this study. The first experiment focused on a study of reading comprehension; the second one focused on a study of accuracy of writing dictation; and the last was a study of oral reading. A total of 985 subjects from Taiwan and 350 subjects from Vietnam were involved in the experiments. Subjects consisted of elementary school, high school and college students.

The statistical results of reading comprehension tests reveal that there was no significant difference between Vietnamese CQN and Taiwanese Hanji group. However, students in CQN group had better scores in dictation and oral reading tests. The results indicate that Han characters are more difficult in writing and oral reading compared with Roman scripts. In contrast, the greatest advantage of Roman scripts or phonemic writing system is that literacy beginners can easily learn to read sentence aloud word by word once they have learned the spelling rules. The second advantage is that literacy learners are easier to write down whatever they heard in dictation.

Acknowledgements

This is a revised English edition of the article 羅馬字 kap 漢字 ê 學習效率 比較：以聽寫 kap 唸讀為測驗項目 originally published in 2009 *Journal of Taiwanese Vernacular,* 1(1), pp.42-61.

References

Chan, Hui-chen. 1994. *Language Shift in Taiwan: Social and Political Determinants.* Ph.D. dissertation: Georgetown University.

Chen, Ping. 1994. Four projected functions of new writing systems for Chinese. *Anthropological Linguistics* 36(3), pp.366-381.

Chen, Ping. 1999. *Modern Chinese: History and Sociolinguistics.* Cambridge: Cambridge University Press.

Cheng, Robert. L. 1989. *Essays on Written Taiwanese* [走向標準化的台灣話文]. Taipei: Independence Press.

Cheng, Robert. L. 1990. *Essays on Taiwan's Sociolinguistic Problems* [演變中的台灣社會語文]. Taipei: Independence Press.

Chiung, Wi-vun T. 1999. *Language Attitudes toward Taibun, the Written Taiwanese.* MA thesis: The University of Texas at Arlington.

Chiung, Wi-vun T. 2001. Missionary scripts: a case study of Taiwanese Peh-oe-ji [白話字，囝 仔人 teh 用 e 文 字?]. *The Taiwan Folkway* 51(4), pp.15-52.

Chiung, Wi-vun T. 2003. *Learning Efficiencies for Different Orthographies: A Comparative Study of Han Characters and Vietnamese Romanization.* Ph.D. dissertation: University of Texas at Arlington.

DeFrancis, John. 1950. *Nationalism and Language Reform in China.* Princeton University Press.

DeFrancis, John. 1977. *Colonialism and Language Policy in Viet Nam.* The Hague.

DeFrancis, John. 1990. *The Chinese Language: Fact and Fantasy.* (Taiwan edition) Honolulu: University of Hawaii Press.

DeFrancis, John. 1996. How efficient is the Chinese writing system? *Visible Language* 30(1), pp.6-44.

Gelb, I. J. 1952. *A Study of Writing.* London: Routledge and Kegan Paul.

Hannas, William. 1997. *Asia's Orthographic Dilemma.* Hawaii: University of Hawaii Press.

Huang, Shuanfan. 1993. *Language, Society, and Ethnic Identity* [語言社會與族群意識]. Taipei: Crane.

Lee, Sang-Beck. 1957. *The Origin of the Korean Alphabet Hangul, According to New Historical Evidence.* Seoul: Tong-Mun Kwan.

Li, Shiao-ting. 1992. *Origin and Evolution of Han Characters* [漢字的起源與演變論叢]. Taipei: Lian-jing.

Norman, Jerry. 1988. *Chinese.* Cambridge: Cambridge University Press.

Smalley, William. et al.1963. *Orthography Studies.* London: United Bible Societies.

Smith, Frank. 1994. *Understanding Reading*. (5th ed.) Hillsdale: Lawrence Erlbaum Associates.

Tzeng, Ovid. et al. 1992. Auto activation of linguistic information in Chinese character recognition. *Advances in Psychology* 94, pp.119-130.

Young, Russell. 1989. *Language Maintenance and Language Shift among the Chinese on Taiwan*. Taipei: Crane.

Zhou, Youguang. 1978. *Introduction to the Reform of Han Characters* [文字改革概論]. Macao: Erya.

6

Impact of Monolingual Policy
on Language and Ethnic Identity:
A Case Study of Taiwan

1. Introduction

Taiwan is a multilingual and multiethnic society. There are more than twenty native languages in Taiwan, including indigenous languages, Hakka, and Tâi-gí Taiwanese (Grimes 1996). Because ethnic identity is not invariant but changes from one occasion to another, it is difficult to clarify the boundary among ethnic groups (Fishman 1999:152). However, in order to provide the readers an overall idea about the ethnicity in Taiwan, subjective classification of the ethnic groups was given in general. There are currently four primary ethnic groups: aborigines (1.7%), Tâi-oân-lâng or Taiwanese (73.3%), Thòi-vân-ngìn or Hakka (12%), and post war Chinese immigrants or Mainlanders (13%) (Huang 1993:21).[1]

In addition to being a multiethnic society, Taiwan has been colonized by several foreign regimes since the seventeenth century. The most recent regimes are Japanese regime (1895-1945) and Chinese ROC[2] regime (1945-). Due to the colonial language policy, the native languages were prohibited in public domain, and Japanese and Mandarin Chinese were adopted as the official languages,

---

[1] The statistical numbers were adopted from Huang, but the name of each ethnic group was renamed by the author of this book.

[2] Republic of China (ROC) was formerly the name of Chinese government, led by Chiang Kai-shek in Mainland China prior to 1949. In 1945, Chiang took over Taiwan and northern Vietnam on behalf of Allied Powers after Japan had surrendered. In 1949, the troops of Chiang were completely defeated by the Chinese Communist Party in Mainland China, so Chiang decided to continue to occupy Taiwan as a base to fight against Chinese communist in order to go back to China. Consequently, Chiang's political regime ROC was thus renewed by in Taiwan and has remained there since 1949.

respectively. In other words, Taiwanese people were not allowed to speak their vernaculars in public. Moreover, they were forced to learn the official language through the national education system. Consequently, most Taiwanese people nowadays are bilingual with their vernacular and official language. Moreover, many researches have revealed that there is a language shift toward Mandarin. Chan's (1994:iii) research shows that "proficiency in *Guoyu* [Mandarin] by the Taiwanese is increasing, while that in Minnanyu [Taiwanese] is decreasing." Young (1989:55) also indicates "there is increased use of Mandarin with succeeding generation." Huang (1993:160) even points out that the indigenous languages in Taiwan are all endangered.

In response to ROC's Chinese language policy, the promoters of Taiwanese have protested against the monolingual policy and have demanded vernacular education in schools since the second half of the 1980s.

This chapter intends to examine the relationships among the three characteristics, ethnic identity, mother tongue, and language ability occurred in the younger generations that grew up under the Mandarin monolingual policy. In other words, for instance, we want to answer whether or not one is more likely to identify herself/himself as ethnic Tâi-oân-lâng if s/he speaks Tâi-gí language; on other hand, is one more likely to be able to speak Tâi-gí language if s/he identifies herself/himself as ethnic Tâi-oân-lâng?

2. Ethnic background

The total area of Taiwan, including the main island and several small islands, is 35,961 square kilometers. The population of Taiwan in 2019 was around twenty three million. Traditionally, people in Taiwan were divided into four ethnic groups: aborigines (1.7%), Tâi-oân-lâng or Taiwanese (73.3%), Thòi-vân-ngìn or Hakka (12%), and post war Chinese immigrants or Mainlanders (13%) (Huang 1993:21) [3]. The Tâi-oân-lâng, Hakka, and Mainlanders are occasionally called Han people and their languages are called Han languages in contrast to the aborigines by Chinese KMT regime. Even though they are called Han people and Han languages, they have different ethnic languages and origins. That is, Taiwanese, Hakka, and Taiwan Mandarin that are not mutually intelligible (DeFrancis 1990:54-57).

In addition to the traditional ethnic groups, international marriages have become more common since the 1990s. In general, about 1/7 of marriage number

---

[3] The statistical numbers were adopted from Huang, but the name of each ethnic group was renamed by the author of this book.

is contributed by the foreign spouses in Taiwan's recent years. According to the statistics of Taiwan's National Immigration Agency, Ministry of Interior, foreign spouses in Taiwan numbered 539.090 by August 2018[4]. These foreign nationals account for 2.28% of Taiwan's total population. Among the foreign spouses, Vietnam is one of the major source countries of foreign spouses.

Some foreign languages such as Japanese and English are also used by Taiwanese people for the purpose of international trade. They were all omitted in my descriptions of ethnicity and languages in Taiwan in this chapter.

2.1. The Taiwanese aborigines

There are several aboriginal tribes who have resided in Taiwan for thousands of years. They belong to Austronesian-Formosan language family. The classification of different tribes varies from scholar to scholar such as G. Taylor, Yoshinori, and Paul Li (1997). It also varies from different policies under different periods of ROC government. By July 2019, the indigenous peoples in Taiwan are recognized as a total of 16 living tribes by the Council of Indigenous People of ROC government. They are Amis, Atayal, Paiwan, Bunun, Tsou, Rukai, Puyuma, Saisiyat, Yami, Thao, Kavalan, Truku, Sakizaya, Sediq, Hla'alua, Kanakanavu.

2.2. The Tâi-oân-lâng people

The *Tâi-oân-lâng* people were the first immigrants in the history of Taiwan. They began to move massively to Taiwan after the Koxinga era in the second half of seventeenth century.

The Tâi-oân-lâng people are also called *Tâi-gí* people, *Hô-ló* people or *Min-nan* people (people of Southern Min) in different occasions by different people (Chiung 2014 & 2015). However, the term 'Tâi-oân-lâng' which is pronounced in its mother tongue with the meaning 'Taiwanese people' is the term frequently used by the Tâi-oân-lâng people. The ethnic language used by Tâi-oân-lâng ethnicity is *Tâi-oân-ōe* or *Tâi-gí*, which is also occasionally called *Hô-ló-ōe*, *Lán-lâng-ōe* or *Bân-lâm-ōe*. Among the varieties, 'Tâi-oân-ōe' and 'Tâi-gí' are the most commonly used ones (Chiung 2015).

The name 'Holo' (or Hoklo in different spellings) may be written in different Han characters and interpreted by different scholars as having different meanings. One assumption is 河洛 (Lim 1991:7-8), which means the plains between the Yellow river and the Lok river (洛水), which are the origins of Holo people. The

---

4 Data provided by Taiwan's National Immigration Agency available at
<https://www.immigration.gov.tw/ct.asp?xItem=1353426&ctNode=29699&mp=1>

second assumption was issued by Ang Ui-jin (1987:148), who asserted that correct Han characters for Holo should be 貉獠. That means Holo people are the descendants of 貉獠, which was one tribe of Oat race (越族) in southeast China. Besides, Khou Kek-tun (1992:10-14) asserted that the widely used term 福佬 is more acceptable. That term means the people of *Hokkian* province. According to *Taiwanese-Japanese Encyclopedic Dictionary* (Ogawa 1931:829), 'Holo' refers to the 'pejorative' name given by the Cantonese to refer to people from Hokkien (Chiung 2015). In addition, missionaries Samuel Wells Williams (1874:ix) and Kennelly (1908:207) both pointed out that 'Hoklo' was the name referring to 'Swataw[5]' (汕頭) people by local Cantonese people.

The Holo people of Taiwan were primarily from *Choan-chiu* (*Quanzhou*) and *Chiang-chiu* (*Zhangzhou*), which are two cities of Hokkian Province in southeast China. According to the census done in 1926, 44.8% of Taiwan's population were from Choan-chiu, 35.2% were from Chiang-chiu, and only 3.1% were from other cities of Hokkian (Khou 1992:28).

Generally speaking, Choan-chiu and Chiang-chiu are two dialects of the Southern Min language. There are some differences between Choan-chiu and Chiang-chiu, such as /koe/ vs. /ke/ to represent the same meaning of word 'chicken.' Although Choan-chiu and Chiang-chiu were originally two different varieties of Southern Min, they gradually merged and became a new 'non-Chiang non-Choan' vernacular after they were carried to Taiwan (Ang 1992:71). Moreover, they were greatly influenced by the languages of the plain tribes, and the Japanese language during Japanese occupation of Taiwan. Today, this new 'non-Chiang non-Choan' language is widely called *Taigi* (Taiwanese).

2.3. The Hakka people

Another immigrant group, aside from the Holo people, are the Hakka. Because Ch'ing dynasty earlier restriction on Hakka migration to Taiwan, Hakka immigrants settled in Taiwan later than Holo people. (Khou 1992:29).

Hakka literally means 'guest' in Chinese. The name was due to their continuing immigrations in the history of the formation of Hakka (Lo 1933; Kiang 1991). *Hakfa* or *Hakkafa* or the recent term *Theukafa* all refer to the ethnic language of Hakka people. There are two main Hakka varieties in Taiwan, that is, *Si-yen* and *Hoi-liuk*. Si-yen means four counties. This was because Si-yen speakers were mainly from Moi (梅縣), Hin-nen (興寧), Chen-phin (鎮平), and Chhong-lok (長樂) counties of the Canton Province of China. Hoi-liuk means

---

[5] Original spelling by S. W. Williams (1874).

Hoi-fong County and Liuk-fong County, because Hoi-liuk speakers were mainly from Hoi-fong (海豐) and Liuk-fong (陸豐) counties of the Canton province. According to the census data in 1926, around 65% of Hakka population were Si-yen speakers, and 35% were Hoi-liuk speakers (Khou 1992). Mainly because Si-yen and Hoi-liuk speakers settled in different places, they did not mix as much as Holo people did, the distinction between Si-yen and Hoi-liuk still exist today.

2.4. The Mainlanders

The third vast immigration to Taiwan was so-called *Goa-seng-lang* (外省人 Mainlanders or people from other provinces) or *Sin-chu-bin* (新住民 New Settlers) or *Bin-hiong-jin/Hoa-hiong-jin* (民鄉人/華鄉人).

In the year 1949, Chiang Kai-shek's army was defeated in China, and then he and his followers moved into Taiwan. Around 1.2 million Mainland Chinese, including soldiers and refugees, came to Taiwan along with Chiang's KMT political regime (Huang 1993:25). Those soldiers and refugees were from all provinces of China where they spoke different languages such as *Cantonese*, *Shanghai*, or *Santong*. Owing to the linguistic diversity and national language policy, most of mainlanders have switched from their first languages to Mandarin Chinese. Therefore, the Mandarin language is generally regarded as the lingua franca among the Mainlanders.

Ong Hu-chhing (1993) pointed out that 54 percent of the Mainlanders still identified themselves as Chinese. Only 7.3% identified themselves as Taiwanese and the rest were neutral. Although most Mainlanders identify themselves as Chinese, some regarded themselves as *Sin-Chu-Bin* (New Settlers) to show their strong identity with Taiwan. It means that they were the recent immigrant Taiwanese instead of Chinese. Moreover, they organized *Goasenglang* Association of Taiwan Independence to promote Taiwan independence in 1992 (GATI 1992).

2.5. Ethnic relations

The ethnic relations in Taiwan are much more complicated than we can describe in this subsection. Gordon (1964) points out that intermarriage is the most difficult stage to achieve between ethnic groups. Therefore, we may use the proportion of intermarriage as an index to examine the current ethnic relations in Taiwan.

In Hu-chhiong Ong's research, he divided his subjects into two groups, i.e. native Taiwanese (本省籍) vs. Mainlanders (外省籍); 9.7% (125/1287) of them are intermarried. He further concluded that "although intermarriage is becoming more popular, the factor of ethnicity still plays a role in choosing one's significant other" (1933:77-85). For more information about ethnic relations in Taiwan, refer to the works such as *Ethnic Relations and National Identity* (Tiunn 1993) and *Ethnicity in Taiwan: Social, historical, and Cultural Perspectives* (Chen 1994).

3. Methodology

The data used for analysis in this study were retrieved from the survey conducted in December 1998 for my previous study on language attitudes (Chiung 2001). The survey was conducted in five undergraduate classes offered at Tamkang University[6] and in an undergraduate class offered at Aletheia University[7] in Taiwan. The subjects included a total of 244 students. Among the students, 157 were female and 87 were male; 138 were from Taipei area and 106 were from other places.

Students' background information was collected based on a self-reported written survey as shown in appendix I. Students' ethnic identity of their own was determined by question 6 on the questionnaire. There were 21 subjects who identified themselves as Mainlanders, 153 as Taigi people, 18 as Hakka people, 2 as Aborigines, and 50 as others.

Students' mother tongue was determined by their response to question 7. There were 58 subjects who considered their own mother tongue to be Mandarin, 152 Taiwanese, 15 Hakfa, 2 as indigenous languages, and 17 as others. The data in this study show that many subjects regarded high ability in a language as the requirement to claim the language as their mother tongue. For example, the subjects who identified themselves as Hakka did not always consider Hakfa their mother tongue when their Hakfa speaking ability is relatively low.

Students' language ability was determined by their answer on question 14. For example, if a rater answered that her/his Hakfa-speaking ability is equal or higher than 3 (based on a 5-points semantic differential scale), then s/he will be assigned a Hakfa-speaking ability. Among the 244 subjects, 30 were Mandarin monolingual, 193 were Mandarin and Taiwanese bilingual, and 19 were Hakfa plus[8]. Two subjects who did not finish answering question 14 were excluded, so there were a total of 242 here. Among the language categories, Mandarin speaking

---

[6] The classes were: Politics, offered by Department of Public Administration; Electronics, offered by Mechanical E.; Modern Japanese language, offered by the Japanese Dept.; Modern literature, offered by the Chinese Dept.; Translation, offered by the English Dept.

[7] The class was Taiwanese language offered by the Taiwanese Dept.

[8] Hakka plus means being able to speak Hakfa plus Taigi or Mandarin.

ability receives a mean of 4.82, Taiwanese 3.39, Hakfa 1.35, and English 2.67. This result reveals that the Hakfa speaking ability of the Taiwanese people is even lower than their English ability.

The non-parametric chi-square (x^2) tests were employed for statistic analysis because ethnic identity, mother tongue, and language ability cannot be measured in units, but are of a yes-or-no type. In addition, because chi-square cannot compare more than two namable characteristics, i.e., we are not able to simultaneously compare ethnic identity, mother tongue, and language, they are arranged into three pairs: Ethnic identity versus mother tongue, ethnic identity versus language ability, and mother tongue versus language ability. The detailed procedure and results of chi-square tests are described and discussed in the next section.

4. Results and discussion

First of all, the relationship between ethnic identity and mother tongue is examined. The 244 subjects were divided into different groups by ethnic background and mother tongue (characteristics). The classifications of ethnicity were Mainlander, Taigi, Hakka, and others. 'Others' here consists of 'indigenous' and any identity other than Mainlander, Taigi and Hakka. Indigenous was not treated as an independent category because there were only two persons who identify themselves as indigenous in the survey. The classifications of mother tongue were Mandarin, Taigi, Hakfa, and others. Finally, each subject was assigned a category, which consists of ethnic identity and mother tongue characteristics.

Table 1 shows the number of each category by ethnic identity and mother tongue characteristics. For instance, among the 244 subjects, 21 identified themselves as Mainlanders; 153 as Taigi people; 18 as Hakka people, and 52 as others; and, among the 21 subjects who identified themselves as Mainlanders, 14 of them regarded Mandarin as their mother tongue; 6 of them regarded Taigi as their mother tongue, etc.

Table 1. Observed number of each category by ethnic identity
and mother tongue characteristics

obs.		Ethnic identity				
		Mainlander	Taigi	Hakka	others	*total*
Mtongue	Mandarin	14	23	4	17	58
	Taigi	6	126	1	19	152
	Hakfa	0	1	12	2	15
	others	1	3	1	14	19
	total	21	153	18	52	244

After all subjects were assigned a category, chi-square tests were conducted. Table 2 shows the expected frequency of each category. It reveals that the observed number is higher than expected frequency in each bold pair of observed and expected frequencies. On the other hand, the observed numbers are smaller than the expected frequency in the pairs other than boldface. For instance, the observed number of the Mainlander-Mandarin category in Table 1 is 14, which is higher than 4.99, the expected frequency of the same category in Table 2. Besides, the observed number, 6, of the Mainlander-Taigi category in Table 1, is smaller than the expected frequency 13.08 in Table 2. Moreover, the chi-square value 199.46 is substantially larger than the critical value 16.92 (degree of freedom is $3*3 = 9$) at the 5% significance level. Although some frequencies in the expected table (Table 2) are less than 5 (usually, greater than 5 in each expected cell is required), it still shows that the chi-square value is larger than the critical value after re-classification, which made all cells greater than 5. The re-classification is Mainlander vs. native Taiwanese (Taigi + Hakka + others), and Mandarin vs. Taiwanese languages (Taigi + Hakfa + others). Therefore, we could reject the null hypothesis, which hypothesizes that there is no association between the two characteristics. In other words, the preliminary conclusion is that ethnic identity and mother tongue are interdependent. That is, if a person identifies Taigi as her/his mother tongue, then s/he is more likely to identify herself/himself as an ethnic Taigi. Or we could say that if a person identifies herself/himself as an ethnic Taigi, then s/he is more likely to accept Taigi as her/his mother tongue. The term 'preliminary conclusion' was used here because we need further evidences to confirm or modify this conclusion. The further evidences and discussion were described in the following paragraphs.

Table 2. Expected frequency of each category by ethnic identity
and mother tongue characteristics

exp.		*Ethnic identity*				
		Mainlander	Taigi	Hakka	others	*total*
Mtongue	Mandarin	4.99	36.37	4.28	12.36	58.00
	Taigi	13.08	95.31	11.21	32.39	152.00
	Hakfa	1.29	9.41	1.11	3.20	15.00
	others	1.64	11.91	1.40	4.05	19.00
	total	21.00	153.00	18.00	52.00	244.00

$$x^2 = 199.46 > 16.92 \ (df=9) \qquad *p < 0.05$$

Although the chi-square test of Table 1 indicates that there is a preliminary interdependent relationship between ethnic identity and mother tongue, there is a contradictory phenomenon deserving our attention. That is, among the 58 Mandarin speakers (in the first row of Table 1), only 24% (14/58) of them identify themselves as Mainlanders. Comparing with Taigi speakers, which consist of 83% (126/152) identifying themselves as Taigi people, or comparing with Hakfa speakers, which consist of 80% (12/15) identifying themselves as Hakka people, it reveals that Mandarin speakers are not highly correlated to the identity of Mainlanders. Therefore, Table 1 was rearranged based on the following classification for further analysis: if a person's ethnic identity coincided with her/his corresponding mother tongue, then s/he was assigned to the ethnic category 'same;' on the other hand, if her/his ethnic identity did not coincide with her/his corresponding mother tongue, s/he was assigned to the ethnic category 'different.' The observed numbers of new arrangement were listed in Table 3. The corresponding expected frequencies were listed in Table 4. Comparing Table 3 with Table 4, the observed values of Taigi, Hakka, and others in the column 'same' are greater than the corresponding expected values. On the other hand, the observed value of Mandarin in the column 'same' is smaller than its expected value. Further, the chi-square value 68.09 is substantially larger than the critical value 7.82 (degree of freedom is 3*1 = 3) at the 5% significance level. The comparisons between Table 3 and Table 4 reveal that Taigi and Hakfa speakers are more likely to coincide with the 'same' ethnic identity, but the Mandarin speakers are more likely to coincide with the 'different' ethnic identity. That is, Taigi/Hakfa speakers are more likely to identify themselves as ethnic Taigi/Hakka people, but Mandarin speakers are not likely to identify themselves as ethnic Mainlanders. Does this finding automatically tell us that Taigi/Hakka people are also more likely to regard Taigi/Hakfa as their mother tongues? No, further analysis is needed to answer the question. Thus, Table 1 was rearranged into Table 5 in the following page.

Table 3. Observed number of ethnic categories "same" and "different" by mother tongues

obs.		*Ethnic id.*		
		same	different	*total*
Mtongue	Mandarin	14	**44**	58
	Taigi	**126**	26	152
	Hakfa	**12**	3	15
	others	**14**	5	19
	total	166	78	244

Table 4. Expected frequency of ethnic categories "same" and "different" by mother tongues

exp.		*Ethnic id*		
		same	different	*total*
Mtongue	Mandarin	39.46	**18.54**	58
	Taigi	**103.41**	48.59	152
	Hakfa	**10.20**	4.80	15
	others	**12.93**	6.07	19
	total	166	78	244

$$x^2=68.09>7.82 \ (df=3) \qquad *p<0.05$$

Table 5 was arranged based on the classification: if a person's mother tongue coincided with her/his corresponding ethnic identity, then s/he was assigned to the mother tongue category 'same;' on the other hand, if her/his mother tongue did not coincide with her/his corresponding ethnic identity, s/he was assigned to the mother tongue category 'different.' The corresponding expected frequencies were listed in Table 6. Comparing Table 5 with Table 6 in the 'same' column, only the observed value of ethnic Taigi greater than its corresponding expected value. The comparisons between Table 5 and Table 6 reveal that only ethnic Taigi people are more likely to coincide with the 'same' mother tongue, but the Mainlanders, Hakka people, and others are more likely to coincide with the 'different' mother tongue. That is to say, Taigi people are more likely to regard Taigi as their mother tongue, but the Mainlanders/Hakka people are not more likely to regard Mandarin/Hakfa as their mother tongue.

Table 5. Observed number of mother tongue categories "same" and "different" by ethnic identities

obs.		*Mtongue*		
		same	different	*total*
Ethnic id.	Mainlander	14	7	21
	Taigi	**126**	27	153
	Hakka	12	**6**	18
	others	14	**38**	52
	total	166	78	244

Table 6. Expected frequency of mother tongue categories "same" and "different" by ethnic identities

exp.		*Mtongue*		
		same	different	*total*
Ethnic id.	Mainlander	14.29	**6.71**	21
	Taigi	**104.09**	48.91	153
	Hakka	12.25	**5.75**	18
	others	35.38	**16.62**	52
	total	166	78	244

$$x^2=54.87>7.82 \text{ (df=3)} \qquad *p<0.05$$

In short, the chi-square tests mentioned above reveal two points: (1) Taigi/Hakfa speaker[9] are more likely to identify themselves as ethnic Taigi/Hakka people, but Mandarin speakers are not more likely to identify themselves as ethnic Mainlanders. (2) Taigi people are more likely to regard Taigi as their mother tongue, but the Mainlanders/Hakka people are not more likely to regard Mandarin/Hakfa as their mother tongue. The relationships between ethnic identity and mother tongue in Taiwan are illustrated in Figure 1. The results in Figure 1 reflect some phenomena in Taiwan: (1) the relationship between mother tongue

---

[9] Here, Taigi/Hakfa spakers are defined as the speakers who identify Taigi/Hakfa as their mother tongue.

of Taigi and ethnic identity of Taigi people is interdependent. (2) Even though a person identifies herself/himself as ethnic Hakka, s/he may not regard Hakfa as her/his mother tongue. The primary factor might be the increasing language shift from Hakfa toward Mandarin. This phenomenon implies that even though a person's mother tongue has shifted, s/he may still maintain her/his original ethnic identity for a while. This phenomenon coincides Edwards' address that "the erosion of an original language – at least in its ordinary, communicative aspects – does not inevitably mean the erosion of identity itself" (Edwards 1985: 48). (3) Mandarin speakers may not identify themselves as Mainlanders. Owing to the Mandarin language policy, Taiwanese people have been taught Mandarin through the national education system since 1945. Consequently, some people may regard Mandarin as their mother tongue. Even so, they may still maintain their original ethnic identity. In this investigation, among the 58 Mandarin speakers, only 14 identify themselves as Mainlanders, the others (i.e., 44) identify themselves as Taigi or Hakka people. We may want to know what factors caused these Mandarin speakers to maintain their original ethnic identity. After tracing the Mandarin speakers' background, it reveals that their parents and grandparents' frequently used languages might play an important role in maintaining their original ethnic identity. For instance, among the 44 Mandarin speakers who did not regard themselves as Mainlanders, 13 reported[10] that their parents both speak Taigi, 20 reported their parents both speak Mandarin (Among the 20 persons, 14 of their grandparents speak Taigi or Hakfa, only 3 of their grandparents speak Mandarin), and the remaining number did not report their answer. On the other hand, among the 14 Mandarin speakers, 10 of them report that their parents both speak Mandarin, and only 1 reports that her parents both speak Taigi.

---

[10] The information of parents and grandparents' frequently used languages is based on question item 13 in the questionnaire. For instance, if a subject reports that the frequency s/he speak Mandarin to her/his father is 3 or higher than 3, then Mandarin was assumed her/his father's frequently used language.

Mother tongue   **Ethnic identity**

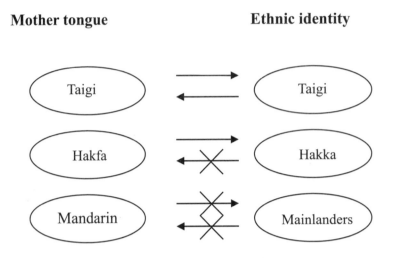

Figure 1. Relationship between ethnic identity and mother tongue in Taiwan.

After doing the chi-square tests for the relationship between ethnic identity and mother tongue, the other two pairs, that is, ethnic identity versus language ability; and mother tongue versus language ability, were also tested and listed in the following paragraphs. Because the procedures of chi-square tests have been described above, only the observed tables and results of the two pairs are briefly mentioned in the following paragraphs. The types of language ability consist of Mandarin-only, bilingual in Mandarin and Taigi, and Hakfa plus (Mandarin-Hakfa or Mandarin-Taigi-Hakfa).

Table 7, Table 8, and Table 9 show the data of ethnic identity versus language ability. Figure 2 illustrates the relationship between ethnic identity and language ability.

Table 7. Observed number of each category by ethnic identity and
language ability characteristics

obs.		**Ethnic id.**				
		Mainlander	Taigi	Hakka	others	*total*
Lang ab.	M-only	**7**	15	2	6	30
	M-Taigi	13	**135**	3	42	193
	Hakfa plus	1	2	**13**	3	19
	total	21	152	18	51	242

Table 8. Observed number of ethnic categories "same" and "different"
by language ability

obs.		**Ethnic id.**		
		same	different	*total*
Lang ab.	M-only	7	**23**	30
	M-Taigi	**135**	58	193
	Hakfa plus	**13**	6	19
	total	155	87	242

$x^2=24.67>5.99$ (df=2)   *p<0.05

Table 9. Observed number of language ability categories "same" and "different"
by ethnic identity

obs.		**Language ab.**		
		same	different	*total*
Ethnic-id	Mainlander	7	**14**	21
	Taigi	**135**	17	152
	Hakka	**13**	5	18
	others	0	**51**	51
	total	155	87	242

$x^2=140.48>7.82$ (df=3)   *p<0.05

Figure 2 indicates (1) Taigi/Hakka people are interdependent with M-Taigi/Hakfa plus. (2) Mainlanders and M-only are not interdependent with each other. Figure 2 reveals that although Mandarin is highly used, people may still maintain their original ethnic identity. This phenomenon corresponds with Lu's (1988: 99) finding "the relationship between ethnic identity and language use in Taiwan was not one of cause-and-effect. Speaking Mandarin may be either due to an instrumental consideration or a conditioned language behavior. They do not have to change their ethnic identity."

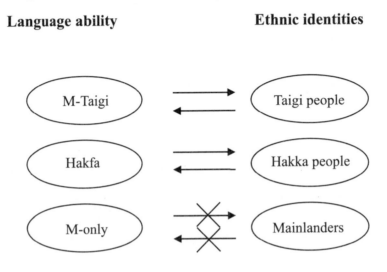

Language ability   **Ethnic identities**

Figure 2. Relationship between ethnic identity and language ability in Taiwan.

Table 10, Table 11 and Table 12 show the data of mother tongue vs. language ability. Figure 3 illustrates the relationship between mother tongue and language ability.

Table 10. Observed number of each category by mother tongue and
language ability characteristics

obs.		*Mother tongue*				
		Mandarin	Taigi	Hakfa	others	*total*
Lang ab.	M-only	**15**	12	0	3	30
	M-Taigi	41	**137**	2	13	193
	Hakfa plus	1	2	**13**	3	19
	total	57	151	15	19	242

Table 11. Observed number of mother tongue categories "same" and "different"
by language ability

obs.		*Mtongue*		
		same	different	*total*
Lang ab.	M-only	15	**15**	30
	M-Taigi	**137**	56	193
	M-Hakfa	**13**	6	19
	total	165	77	242
	$x^2=5.27<5.99$ (df=2)		$p>0.05$	

Table 12. Observed number of language ability categories "same" and "different"
by mother tongue

obs.		*Language ab.*		
		same	different	*total*
Mtongue	Mandarin	15	**42**	57
	Taigi	**137**	14	151
	Hakfa	**13**	2	15
	others	0	**19**	19
	total	165	77	242
	$x^2=124.51>7.82$ (df=3)		*$p<0.05$	

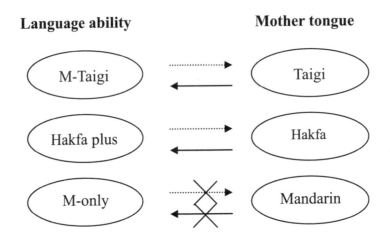

Figure 3. Relationship between mother tongue and language ability in Taiwan.

The dotted line in Figure 3 means that the statistical p value was not substantially smaller than 0.05. The result that language ability does not always correspond to their mother tongue is reasonable because a person may possess the ability of several languages but only recognize one as his/her mother tongue. Figure 3 indicates (1) people with Taigi/Hakfa as a mother tongue are more likely to possess M-Taigi/Hakfa plus ability. (2) People with Mandarin as a mother tongue do not necessarily possess Mandarin-only ability.

In summary, the chi-square tests reveal that only Taigi people show substantially interdependent relationships among the three characteristics, i.e., ethnic identity, mother tongue, and language ability (see Figure 4). Hakka people show partly interdependent relationships among the characteristics as shown in Figure 5. As for Mainlanders, there is no interdependent relationship among the characteristics as shown in Figure 6.

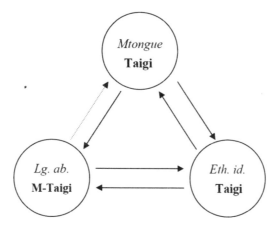

Figure 4. Relationships among Taigi speakers, M-Taigi ability, and Taigi people.

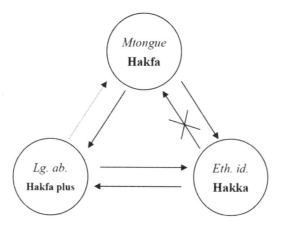

Figure 5. Relationships among Hakfa speakers, Hakfa plus ability, and Hakka people.

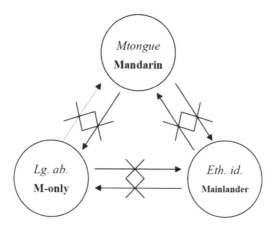

Figure 6. Relationships among Mandarin speakers, M-only ability, and Mainlanders.

5. Conclusion

Much research such as Ross (1979:4) has pointed that the relationship between language and ethnicity is not static, but subject to considerable alternation as the environment around them changes. In this study, the different relationship patterns among the Hakka, Taigi, and Mainlanders categories reveal the effects of monolingual policy on the ecology of languages in Taiwan.

In the Hakka category, the one-way dependent relationship between mother tongue and ethnic identity reveals that people are losing their Hakka mother tongue faster than their Hakka identity. Since the Hakka are a minority compared to the Taigi, the monolingual policy has had a greater impact on the Hakka than the Taigi. On the other hand, the two-way interdependent relationship between language ability and ethnic identity reveals that Hakfa still plays a crucial role in constructing their Hakka identity. The case of Hakka has shown: 1) On one hand, the erosion of one's original ethnic language does not inevitably result in the erosion of ethnic identity itself. 2) On the other hand, the maintenance of one's ethnic language is a contributing factor to the maintenance of one's ethnic identity. These findings imply that the promotion of the Taiwanese language(s) is a plus to foster the identity of Taiwanese, although, people with Taiwanese identity do not necessarily own the ability of speaking the Taiwanese language(s).

As for the Mainlanders category, the interdependent relationships among the Mandarin mother tongue, Mandarin ability, and Mainlanders are not yet well established since Mandarin was introduced as the official language or lingua franca in Taiwan only about 55 years ago. In general, ethnic identity is contextually constructed (Fishman 1999:154). Language may be a primary defining characteristic of a collectivity, while in the meantime, it may play only a modest role (Ross 1979:4). For the Mainlanders, their collective memory of the Chinese civil war and anti-colonialism in the first half of the twentieth century probably plays a more crucial role than Mandarin in constructing their identity of the Mainlanders. For the people other than the Mainlanders, Mandarin is primarily considered a medium of communication rather than a characteristic of ethnicity. Consequently, speakers' ability or mother tongue in Mandarin does not necessary refer to their identity of Mainlanders.

Acknowledgements

This article was originally presented at the International Conference on Language and Identity, Baruch College, City University of New York, Oct. 2-5,

2002. It was originally collected in Wi-vun Chiung 2005. Language, Identity and Decolonization. Tainan: National Cheng Kung University.

I would like to express my appreciation to Dr. John Paolillo, Dr. David Silva, Dr. Jerold Edmondson, Dr. Susan Herring, Super Manuel and Sarah Yao for their insightful discussions and comments on this paper. The author is responsible of any errors and mistakes in this article.

References

Ang, Ui-jin. 1987. *The tonal studies of Taiwanese Holooe*《台灣河洛語聲調研究》. Taipei: Independence Press.

Ang, Ui-jin. 1992. *Taiwan's language problems* 《台灣語言問題》. Taipei: Chian-ui.

Chan, Hui-chen. 1994. *Language shift in Taiwan: social and political determinants.* Ph.D. dissertation, Georgetown University.

Chen, Chung-min., Ying-chang Chuang and Su-min Huang (eds.). 1994. *Ethnicity in Taiwan: social, historical, and cultural perspectives.* Taipei: Institute of Ethnology, Academia Sinica.

Chiung, Wi-vun T. 2001. Language attitudes towards written Taiwanese. *Journal of Multilingual & Multicultural Development* 22(6), pp.502-523.

Chiung, Wi-vun T. 2014. *Let's speak Taiwanese and write in Taiwanese* 《喙講台語・手寫台文》. Tainan: Asian Atsiu International.

Chiung, Wi-vun T. 2015 "Taiwanese or Southern Min? on the controversy of ethnolinguistic names in Taiwan," *Journal of Taiwanese Vernacular*, 7(1), pp.54-87.

DeFrancis, John. 1990. *The Chinese language: fact and fantasy.* Taipei: Crane.

Edwards, John. 1985. *Language, society, and identity.* NY: Basil Blackwell.

Fishman, Joshua A. (ed). 1999. *Handbook of language and ethnic identity.* NY: Oxford University Press.

GATI. 1992. *Mainlanders' love of Taiwan* 《外省人台灣心》. Taipei: Chian-ui.

Huang, Shuanfan. 1993. *Language, society, and ethnic identity*《語言社會與族群意識》. Taipei: Crane.

Khou, Kek-tun. 1992. *An introduction to the Taiwanese language*《台灣語概論》. Kaoshiung: First Press.

Kiang, Clyde. 1991. *The Hakka search for a homeland.* Allegheny Press.

Li, Paul J. K. 1997a. *A history and interaction of the Plain Tribes in Taiwan* 《台灣平埔族的歷史與互動》. Taipei: Formosa Folkways.

Li, Paul J. K. 1997b. *The tribes and their migrations of Austronesian in Taiwan* 《台灣南島民族的族群與遷徙》. Taipei: Formosa Folkways.

Lim, Chai-hok. 1991. *Min-nan people* 《閩南人》. Taipei: San-min Bookstore.

Lo, Hsiang-lin. 1933. *An introduction to the study of the Hakkas in its ethnic, historical, and cultural aspects* 《客家研究導論》. (Taiwan edition 1992) Taipei: SMC Publishing Inc.

Lu, Li-Jung. 1988. *A study of language attitudes, language use and ethnic identity in Taiwan.* M.A. Thesis: Fu-jen Catholic University.

Ong, Hu-chhiong. 1993. The nature of assimilation between Taiwanese and Mainlanders 《省籍融合的本質》. In Bou-kui Tiunn (ed.), *Ethnic relations and national identity*, 53-100. Taipei: Iap-kiong.

Ross, Jeffrey A. 1979. Language and the mobilization of ethnic identity. In Howard Giles and Saint-Jacques Bernard (eds.) *Language and Ethnic Relations.* NY: Pergamon Press.

Su, Beng. 1980. *Taiwan's 400 Year History* 《台灣人四百年史》. San Jose: Paradise Culture Associates.

Tiunn, Bou-kui. 1993. *Ethnic relations and national identity* 《族群關係與國家認同》. Taipei: Iap-kiong.

Tsuchida, Shigeru. 1991. *Linguistic materials of the Formosan sinicized populations I: Siraya and Basai.* Tokyo: University of Tokyo.

Young, Russell. 1989. *Language maintenance and language shift among the Chinese on Taiwan.* Taipei: Crane.

APPENDIX I: QUESTIONNAIRE

1. Sex ☐Female ☐Male
2. Age _ _
3. Major ☐Taiwanese ☐English ☐Chinese ☐Public Administration ☐Mechanical E. ☐ others
   _____
4. What class are you in, as you complete this survey?_____
5. In which city have you lived the longest amount _____
6. What 's your ethnic identity ?

   5 Mainlander (New settler) 4 Taigi (Southern Min) 3 Hakka 2 Aborigines 1 uncertain

7. What do you feel your "mother tongue" is?

   5 Mandarin 4 Taiwanese 3 Hakka 2 Aboriginal language 1 uncertain

8. In which language do you speak most fluently?

   5 Mandarin 4 Taiwanese 3 Hakka 2 Aboriginal language 1 uncertain

9. What is the language you learned before attending elementary school ?

   5 Mandarin 4 Taiwanese 3 Hakka 2 Aboriginal language 1 uncertain

10. What is the language you use most often?

   5 Mandarin 4 Taiwanese 3 Hakka 2 Aboriginal language 1 uncertain

11. What is the language your father uses most often?

   5 Mandarin 4 Taiwanese 3 Hakka 2 Aboriginal language 1 uncertain

12. What is the language your mother uses most often?

   5 Mandarin 4 Taiwanese 3 Hakka 2 Aboriginal language 1 uncertain

13. Please indicate the frequency of each language you use when you talk with these persons.
    (leave it blank if you don't understand that language)

    Frequency scale 5 always 4 often 3 sometimes 2 seldom 1 almost never

	Grand-p.		parents		Siblings		Friends		Significant other
	G.pa	G.ma	Pa.	Ma.	Bro.	Sis.	male	female	
Mandarin									
Taiwanese									
Hakka									
others									

14. What degree do you feel your listening and speaking ability of these languages might be?

Listening

Mandarin   5 native 4 no problem 3 so so 2 a little 1 zero

Taiwanese   5 native 4 no problem 3 so so 2 a little 1 zero

Hakka   5 native 4 no problem 3 so so 2 a little 1 zero

English   5 native 4 no problem 3 so so 2 a little 1 zero

Speaking

Mandarin   5 native 4 no problem 3 so so 2 a little 1 zero

Taiwanese   5 native 4 no problem 3 so so 2 a little 1 zero

Hakka   5 native 4 no problem 3 so so 2 a little 1 zero

English   5 native 4 no problem 3 so so 2 a little 1 zero

7

Romanization and language planning in Taiwan prior to 2000

1. Introduction

Although Taiwan is currently a Hanji (Han characters)-dominated society, romanization once was the unique and first writing system used in Taiwan. This system of romanization was introduced by the Dutch missionaries in the first half of the seventeenth century. Thereafter, Han characters were imposed to Taiwan by the Sinitic Koxinga regime in the second half of the seventeenth century. As the number of Han immigrants from China dramatically increased, Han characters gradually became the dominant writing system in Taiwan. At present, only Han characters and modern standard Chinese are taught in Taiwan's national education system. In contrast, romanization is excluded from school education.

This chapter intends to provide readers an overall introduction to the history and current development of romanization in Taiwan from the perspectives of literacy and sociolinguistics. In this chapter, the socio-political background of Taiwan is described first, followed by an introduction to each romanization era, and ending with a conclusion on the future of romanized writing in Taiwan.

2. Socio-political background

Taiwan is a multilingual and multiethnic society. There are more than twenty native languages in Taiwan, including indigenous languages, Hakka, and Taigi Taiwanese (Grime 1996). Generally speaking, there are currently four primary ethnic groups: indigenous (1.7%), Hakka (12%), Tâi-gí (73.3%), and Mainlanders[1] (13%) (Huang 1993:21).

---

[1] Mainly the immigrants came to Taiwan with the Chiang Kai-shek's KMT regime around 1945.

In addition to being a multiethnic society, Taiwan has been colonized by several foreign regimes since the seventeenth century. In 1624 the Dutch occupied Taiwan and established the first alien regime in Taiwan. Roman script was then introduced to Taiwan by the Dutch. In 1661 *Koxinga*, a remnant force of the former Chinese *Ming* Empire, failed to restore the Ming Empire against the new *Qing* Empire, and therefore he retreated to Taiwan. Koxinga expelled the Dutch and established a sinitic regime in Taiwan as a base for retaking the Mainland. Confucianism and civil service examination were thus imposed to Taiwan since Koxinga's regime until the early twentieth century. The Koxinga regime was later annexed by the Chinese Qing Empire (1683). Two centuries later, the sovereignty of Taiwan was transferred from China to Japan as a consequence of the Sino-Japanese war in 1895. At the end of World War II, Japanese forces surrendered to the Allied Forces. *Chiang Kai-shek*, the leader of the Chinese Nationalist (KMT[2] or *Kuomintang*) took over Taiwan on behalf of the Allied Powers under General Order No.1 of September 2, 1945 (Peng, 1995:60-61). Simultaneously, Chiang Kai-shek was fighting against the Chinese Communist Party in Mainland China. In 1949, Chiang's troops were completely defeated and then pursued by the Chinese Communists. At that time, Taiwan's national status was supposed to be dealt with by a peace treaty among the fighting nations. However, because of Chiang's defeat in China, Chiang decided to occupy Taiwan as a base and from there he would fight back to the Mainland (Kerr 1992; Ong 1993; Peng 1995; Su 1980). Consequently, Chiang's political regime Republic of China[3] (R.O.C) was renewed in Taiwan and has remained there since 1949. The relationship between language, orthography and political status was shown in Table 1.

---

[2] KMT was the ruling party in Taiwan since 1945 until 2000, in which year *Chen Shui-bian*, the presidential candidate of opposition party Democratic Progressive Party was elected the new president. Thereafter, KMT retrieved regime again in 2008.

[3] Republic of China was formerly the official name of the Chinese government (1912-1949) in China, but was replaced by the People's Republic of China (P.R.C) in 1949.

Table 1. Relation between language, orthography and political status in Taiwan

Period	Political status	Spoken Languages	Writing Systems**
-1624	Indigenous society	Aboriginal	Tribal totem
1624-1661	Dutch colonialism	Aboriginal/Taiwanese*	Sinkang Classical Han
1661-1683	Koxinga colonialism	Aboriginal/Taiwanese	Classical Han Sinkang
1683-1895	Qing colonialism	Aboriginal/Taiwanese	Classical Han Koa-a-chheh Peh-oe-ji Sinkang
1895-1945	Japanese colonialism	Aboriginal/Taiwanese/Japanese	Japanese Classical Han Colloquial Han (in Taiwanese) Colloquial Han (in Mandarin) Peh-oe-ji Kana-Taiwanese
1945-present	R.O.C colonialism	Aboriginal/Taiwanese/Mandarin	Chinese (Mandarin) Taiwanese Aboriginal

* Taiwanese means Hakka-Taiwanese and Taigi-Taiwanese in this table.
** The order of listed writing systems in each cell of this column do not indicate the year of occurrences. The first listed orthography refers to the official written language adopted by its relevant governor.

National Language Policy[4] or monolingual policy was adopted both during the Japanese and KMT occupations of Taiwan. In the case of KMT's monolingual policy, the Taiwanese people are not allowed to speak their vernaculars in public. Moreover, they are forced to learn Mandarin Chinese and to identify themselves as Chinese through the national education system (Cheng 1996; Tiuⁿ 1996). As Hsiau (1997:307) has pointed out, "the usage of Mandarin as a national language becomes a testimony of the Chineseness of the KMT state;" that is, the Chinese KMT regime is trying to convert the Taiwanese into Chinese through Mandarin monolingualism. Consequently, research such as Chan (1994) and Young (1988) has revealed that a language shift toward Mandarin is in progress. Huang

---

[4] For details, see Huang 1993.

(1993:160) goes so far as to suggest that the indigenous languages of Taiwan are all endangered.

3. Romanization prior to 1945

Romanization in Taiwan prior to 1945 can be divided into two eras. The first era of romanization is *Sinkang* writing, which was mainly devised for the indigenous languages, and occurred in the first half of the seventeenth century during the Dutch occupation of Taiwan, and ended up in the early nineteenth century. The second romanization is *Peh-oe-ji* writing. It was devised for Taigi and Hakka Taiwanese languages, and it has existed in Taiwan since the second half of nineteenth century.

3.1. Sinkang Romanization (1624-early nineteenth century)

Sinkang writing was the first romanization and the first writing system in the history of Taiwan. It was devised by Dutch missionaries and employed mainly to the writing of Siraya, an indigenous language in southwest plain of Taiwan. Sinkang romanization[5] was not well documented until the discovery of so-called *Sinkang Bunsu* or Sinkang manuscripts in the nineteenth century.

Conversion to Christianity as well as exploiting resources were important purposes for the Dutch during their occupation of Taiwan. As Campbell described it, "during that period they [i.e., Dutch] not only carried on a profitable trade, but made successful efforts in educating and Christianising the natives; one missionary alone having established a number of schools and received over five thousand adults into the membership of the Reformed Church" (Campbell 1903:vii). The natives around Sinkang[6] were first taught Christianity through the learning of the romanization of Sinkang dialect. There were some textbooks and testaments written in romanized Sinkang, such as the The Gospel of St. Matthew in Formosan Sinkang Dialect and Dutch (*Het Heylige Euangelium Matthei en Jonannis Ofte Hagnau Ka D'llig Matiktik, Ka na Sasoulat ti Mattheus, ti Johannes appa. Overgefet inde Formosaansche tale, voor de Inwoonders van Soulang, Mattau, Sinckan, Bacloan, Tavokan, en Tevorang.*), which was translated and

---

[5] Although romanized writing in indigenous language had been mentioned in earlier historical materials such as *Chulo Koanchi* (Topographical and Historical Description of Chulo 1717), and *E-tamsui-sia Kiagi* (A Glossary of the Lower Tamsui Dialect 1763), romanization in Sinkang was not well known until the discovery of Sinkang manuscripts.

[6] Sinkang, originally spelled in *Sinkan*, was the place opposite to the *Tayouan* where the Dutch had settled in 1624. The present location is *Sin-chhi* of *Tainan* county.

published by Daniel Gravius in 1661 (Campbell 1996; Lai 1990:121-123).

After Koxinga drove the Dutch out from Taiwan, the roman scripts were still used by those plain tribes for some period. There were several manuscripts found after those native languages disappeared. Those manuscripts were written either in language(s) of native aborigines or they were bilingual texts with romanization and Han characters. Most of the manuscripts were either sale contracts, mortgage bonds, or leases (Naojiro 1933:IV). Because most of those manuscripts were found in Sinkang areas and were written in Sinkang language, they were named Sinkang Manuscripts by scholars, or *Hoan-a-khe* (the contract of barbarians) by the public (Lai 1990:125-127).

There are 141 examples of Sinkang Manuscripts discovered to date, the earliest manuscript dated 1683, and the most recent one dated 1813. In other words, those indigenous people continued to use the romanization for over a century-and-a-half after the Dutch had left Taiwan (Naojiro 1933:XV).

3.2. Peh-oe-ji Romanization (1865-present)

If Sinkang writing represents the first foreign missionary activities in Taiwan, then the development of *Peh-oe-ji* [7] reveals the comeback of missionary influences after the Dutch withdrawal from Taiwan.

More and more missionaries came to preach in China in the seventeenth century, even though there were several restrictions on foreign missionaries under the Qing Empire. The restrictions on foreign missionaries were continued until the Treaty of *Tientsin* was signed between Qing Empire and foreign countries in 1860. Taiwan, at that time, was under the control of Qing Empire, therefore, foreign missionaries were allowed after that treaty. Consequently, the first mission after the Dutch, settled in *Taioan-hu* [8] by missionary James L. Maxwell and his assistants in 1865 (Hsu 1995:6-8; Lai 1990:277-280).

Before missionaries arrived in Taiwan, there were already several missionary activities in southeast China. They had started developing romanization of some languages such as Southern Min and Hakka. For instance, the first textbook for learning the romanization of the Amoy [9] dialect, *Tngoe Hoan Ji Chho Hak* (Amoy Spelling Book) was published by John Van Nest Talmage in 1852 in Amoy. That romanization scheme was called Poe-oe-ji in Taiwan. It means the script of

---

[7] For details about Peh-oe-ji, see Cheng 1977 and Chiung 2000b.

[8] Present *Tailam* city.

[9] Amoy was a dialect of Southern Min, and was regarded as mixed *Chiang-chiu* and *Choan-chiu* dialects. The Amoy dialect was usually chosen by missionaries as a standard for Southern Min.

vernacular speech in contrast to the complicated Han characters of *wenyen*.

Peh-oe-ji was originally devised and promoted by missionaries for religious purposes. Consequently, most of its applications and publications are related to church activities. Those applications and publications of Peh-oe-ji since the nineteenth century can be summarized into the following six categories: 1) textbooks, 2) dictionaries, 3) translation of the Bible, catechisms, and religious tracts, 4) newspaper, 5) private note-taking or writing letters, and 6) other publications, such as physiology, math, and novels.

Missionaries' linguistic efforts on the romanization are reflected in various romanized dictionaries. Medhurst's *A Dictionary of the Hok-keen Dialect of the Chinese Language* published in 1837 is considered the first existing romanized dictionary of Lan-lang-oe (Southern Min) compiled by western missionary (Ang 1996:197-259). Douglas' *Chinese-English Dictionary of the Vernacular or Spoken Language of Amoy* of 1873 is regarded as the remarkable dictionary of influence on the orthography of Peh-oe-ji (Ang 1993:1-9). After Douglas' dictionary, most romanized dictionaries and publications followed his orthography without or with just minor changes. Generally speaking, missionaries' linguistic efforts on Lan-lang-oe and Peh-oe-ji have reached a remarkable achievement since Douglas's dictionary (Ang 1993:5). William Campbell's dictionary *E-mng-im Sin Ji-tian* (*A Dictionary of the Amoy Vernacular Spoken throughout the Prefectures of Chin-chiu, Chiang-chiu and Formosa* 1913), which was the first Peh-oe-ji dictionary published in Taiwan, is the most widespread romanized dictionary in Taiwan. This dictionary has been published in fourteen editions by 1987 (Ang 1996; Lai 1990).

The first New Testament in romanized Amoy, *Lan e Kiu-chu Ia-so Ki-tok e Sin-iok* was published in 1873, and the first Old Testament *Ku-iok e Seng Keng* in 1884. The wide use of Poe-oe-ji in Taiwan was promoted by the missionary Reverend Thomas Barclay while he published monthly newspaper *Tai-oan-husia^n Kau-hoe-po* [10] (Taiwan Prefectural City Church News) in July 1885. In addition to publications related to Christianity, there were some other publications written in Peh-oe-ji, such as *Pit Soan e Chho Hak* (Fundamental Mathematics) by *Ui-lim Ge* in 1897, *Lai Goa Kho Khan-ho-hak* (The Principles and Practice of Nursing) by G. Gushue-Taylor in 1917, the novel *Chhut Si-Soa^n* (Line between Life and Death) by *Khe-phoan Te^n* in 1926, and the collection of commentaries

---

[10] Taiwan Prefectural City Church News has changed its title several times, and the recent title is *Taioan Kau-hoe Kong-po* (Taiwan Church News). It was published in Peh-oe-ji until 1970, and thereafter it switched to Mandarin Chinese (Lai 1990:17-19).

Chap-hang Koan-kian (Opinions on Ten Issues) by *Poe-hoe Chhoa* in 1925.

Usually, the religious believers apply Peh-oe-ji writing to their daily life after they acquire the skill of romanization. For example, they may use Peh-oe-ji as a skill of note taking or writing letters to their daughters or sons or friends in addition to reading the Bible. Peh-oe-ji was widely used among the church[11] people in Taiwan prior to 1970s[12]. Among its users, women were the majority. Most of those women did not command any literacy except Peh-oe-ji. Today, there are still a few among the elder generations especially women who read only Peh-oe-ji.

Although Peh-oe-ji was originally devised for religious purposes, it is no longer limited to religious applications after the contemporary *Taibun*[13] movement was raised in the late 1980s. Peh-oe-ji has been adopted by many Taibun promoters as one of the romanized writing systems to write Taiwanese. For example, famous Taibun periodicals such as *Taioanji, Tai-bun Thong-sin* and *Taibun Bong-Po* adopt Peh-oe-ji as the romanization for writing Taiwanese. In addition, there were recently a series of novels translated from world literatures into Peh-oe-ji in a planned way by the members of *5% Tai-ek Ke-oe*[14] (5% Project of Translation in Taiwanese) since 1996.

In short, the Peh-oe-ji was the ground of romanization of modern Taiwanese colloquial writing. Even though there were several different schemes of romanization for writing Taiwanese, many of them were derived from Peh-oe-ji[15]. Peh-oe-ji and its derivatives are the most widely used romanization even nowadays.

For readers' better understanding of Peh-oe-ji, how Peh-oe-ji works in the *E-mng-im Sin Ji-tian* is demonstrated below. The symbols for representing the

---

[11] Especially the Presbyterian Church in Taiwan.

[12] *Taioan Kau-hoe Kong-po* (Taiwan Church News), which was originally published in Peh-oe-ji, switched to Mandarin Chinese in 1970. I use this year as an indicator to the change of Peh-oe-ji circulation.

[13] Taibun literally means Taiwanese literature or Taiwanese writing. It refers to the orthography issue in the Taiwanese language movement since 1980s. For details of the modern movement of written Taiwanese, see Chiung (1999:33-49).

[14] In November of 1995, some Taiwanese youths who were concerned about the writing of Taiwanese decided to deal with the Taiwanese modernization and loanwords through translation from foreign language into Taiwanese. The organization 5% Project of Translation in Taiwanese was then established on February 24, 1996. Its members have to contribute 5% of their income every month to the 5% fund. The first volume includes 7 books. They are Lear Ong, Kui-a Be-chhia, Mi-hun-chhiuⁿ e Kui-a, Hoa-hak-phin e Hian-ki, Thiⁿ-kng Cheng e Loan-ai Ko·-su, Pu-ho·-lang e Lek-su, and Opera Lai e Mo·-sin-a, published by Tai-leh press in November 1996.

[15] For more information about different romanized schemes, see Iuⁿ 1999.

consonants, vowels, and tones[16] in Taiwanese are given in Table 2, Table 3 and Table 4. Generally speaking, there is a one-to-one relationship between orthographic symbols and phonemes as shown in Table 2 and Table 3. The only exception is the pair of *ch* and *ts* that both refer to the phoneme /ts/. The different usages between /ts/ and /ch/ are based on vowel position. That is, /ts/ preceding back vowels such as *tso*, and /ch/ preceding front vowels such as *chi*. For nasal sounds, a superscript n is added to indicate nasalization, such as in the example of *ti*ⁿ (sweet). After phonemes are represented, tone marks are imposed to the nuclei of syllables and a hyphen is added between syllables, such as **ō·-kóe-khiau** (Taiwanese taro cake). Because Taiwanese is a tone language with rich tone sandhi, there can be several ways to represent tones. In the design of Peh-oe-ji, the base tone or underlying tone of each syllable is chosen and represented by its tone mark. For example, the word Taiwanese taro cake must be represented by its underlying form **ō·-kóe-khiau** rather than surface form **ò·-koe-khiau** (this is the form in actual pronunciation).

Table 2. Symbols for Taiwanese consonants in the spelling of Peh-oe-ji

Consonants	Peh-oe-ji	Conditions	Examples
/p/	p		pí 'compare'
/pʰ/	ph	initial only	phoe 'letter'
/t/	t		tê 'tea'
/tʰ/	th	initial only	thâi 'to kill'
/k/	k		ka 'add'
/kʰ/	kh	initial only	kha 'foot'
/b/	b	initial only	bûn 'literature'
/g/	g	initial only	gí 'language'
/h/	h		hí 'glad'
/s/	s	initial only	sì 'four'
/ts/	ch	before i, e	chi 'of'
	ts	eleswhere	tsa 'investigate'
/tsʰ/	chh	initial only	chha 'differ'
/dz/	j	initial only	jit 'sun'
/l/	l	initial only	lí 'you'
/m/	m		mī 'noodle'
/n/	n		ni 'milk'
/ŋ/	ng		âng 'red'

---

[16] Originally, there were 8 tones in Taiwanese. But, nowadays tone 6 has merged with tone 2.

Table 3. Symbols for Taiwanese vowels in the spelling of Peh-oe-ji

Vowels	Peh-oe-ji	Conditions	Examples
/i/	i		ti 'pig'
/e/	e	Elsewhere	tê 'tea'
	ia	Followed by n or t	tiān 'electric' kiat 'to form'
/a/	a		ta 'dry'
/u/	u		tú 'meet'
/ə/	o		to 'knife'
/o/	o·	Elsewhere	o· 'black'
	o	Followed by finals, except /ʔ/	tong 'east' kok 'state'

Table 4. Inventory of tone marks in the orthography of Peh-oe-ji

Categories	君 [kun˥] gentle	滾 [kunˈ] boil	棍 [kunˋ] stick	骨 [kut·l] bone	裙 [kun˩] skirt	-	近 [kun˩] near	滑 [kutˈl] glide
Numerical categories	1	2	3	4	5	6	7	8
Tone marks in Peh-oe-ji	unmarked	´	`	unmarked	^		-	˙
Peh-oe-ji samples	kun	kún	kùn	kut	kûn		kūn	ku̍t
Numerical tone values	44	53	31	3	12		22	8
IPA tone values	˥	˧˥	˥˩	˙	˨˩		˨˦	˙˥

4. Romanization from 1945 to 2000

Romanization after 1945 can be categorized into romanized Chinese and romanized Taiwanese in terms of the language the romanization is used for. The development of Chinese romanization can be traced back to the KMT's language planning in China in the first half of the twentieth century. Generally speaking, Chinese romanization is not considered by the KMT as an independent writing system, but rather as a set of phonetic symbols for transcribing Han characters.

As for the Taiwanese romanization, it is intentionally ignored (once forbidden) by the KMT regime, but it is the main concern of the promoters of the Taibun movement. For Taibun promoters, romanization is regarded as an independent orthography and thus is currently adopted as one of the proposals for writing Taiwanese.

4.1. Romanization for Mandarin Chinese

In the late nineteenth century and the early twentieth century, the language issues with which the Chinese government and the general public were concerned with were: 1) the unification of pronunciation (of Han characters) and the formation of a national language, and 2) the transition of written language from classical Han (*wenyen*) to colloquial writing (*baihua*).[17]

Mandarin was eventually chosen as the national language and the standard pronunciation for reading Han characters. At that time, neither domestically created phonetic symbols nor western roman scripts were considered independent orthographies, but auxiliary tools for learning the national language (DeFrancis 1950:221-236; Norman 1988:257-263). *Jhuyin Zimu* or Phonetic Alphabet, a set of symbols derived from radicals of Han characters was devised and proposed by the Committee on Unification of Pronunciation (*Duyin Tongyihue*) in 1913 and later officially adopted by the Chinese government in 1918 as a tool for learning the correct pronunciation of the national language. It was revised slightly in 1928 and renamed *Jhuyin Fuhao*[18] or Phonetic Symbols (henceforth NPS1) in 1930. This scheme was used in China until 1958 when *Hanyu Pinyin* (henceforth HP) was promulgated. Jhuyin Fuhao was brought to Taiwan by the KMT in 1945 and it has been taught through Taiwan's national education system and has been in continuous use since then.

The first romanized phonetic scheme proposed and recognized by the Chinese government was the *Guoyu Luomazi* or National Language Romanization, which was approved in 1928 (Chen 1999:182). Although Guoyu Luomazi was approved by the government, in reality it was not promoted for practical use. It was even less widely used in comparison to another romanized

---

[17] For details, see Chen 1999; DeFrancis 1950; Gao 1992; Jhou 1978; Norman 1988; Png 1965; Tsao 1999.

[18] The purpose of using Jhuyin Fuhao 'sound-annotating symbols' is to "dispel any faint hope that they were to be used as bona fide writing systems" (Chen 1999:189). This scheme was later called *Guoyu jhuyin fuhao di yi shih* or National Phonetic Symbols, 1st Scheme in Taiwan (henceforth NPS1).

scheme *Latinxua sin wenz*[19] (Norman 1988:259). Guoyu Luomazi was later brought together with Jhuyin Fuhao to Taiwan by the KMT during the Chiang Kai-shek occupation of Taiwan. The Guoyu Luomazi scheme was later revised and renamed *Guoyu jhuyin fuhao di er shih*[20] or National Phonetic Symbols, 2nd Scheme (henceforth NPS2) and promulgated by Taiwan's Ministry of Education (MOE) in 1986.

Although both NPS1 and NPS2 were officially promulgated by the KMT regime in Taiwan, only NPS1 is taught in schools and is actually used as an auxiliary tool for learning to pronounce Mandarin. In contrast, NPS2 is excluded from school curriculum and is simply used to transliterate Chinese names into other languages (Chen 1999:189). As a matter of fact, not only NPS2 but also other traditional romanized schemes devised by foreigners, such as Wade-Giles and Postal schemes are used for Mandarin transliteration[21]. Moreover, the majority of Taiwanese people who are not educated in the romanized schemes, simply adapt the English K.K. phonetic symbols[22] to transliterate as they see fit (Yu 1999). Consequently, the transliteration in romanization is in a serious chaotic situation. For example, 曹 may be transliterated *tsao, tsau, ts'ao, ts'au, chao, chau, chhao, chhau, c'ao, c'au,* and so on.

As a result of this chaos, much attention was paid to transliteration issues, with the government trying to unify the romanized schemes in the late 1990s. In April 1999, a national conference on transliteration schemes was held by the MOE, focusing on the review of the four existing romanized schemes, i.e. Wade-Giles, NPS2, HP, and *Tongyong Pinyin* (TYP)[23]. In July of the same year, the Executive Yuan (*Heng-cheng-i*[n]; similar to the cabinet in western countries) announced that HP would be adopted as the standardization for future transliteration. However, this announcement soon aroused opposition and protests against the HP system in August (Chiang, Luo, Tiu[n], Yu 2000). Consequently, the final decision on a transliteration scheme was intentionally left until after the presidential election in

---

[19] Latinxua sin wenz was first published in 1929 and employed among the 10,000 Chinese living in the USSR. It was considered an autonomous writing system and later introduced to China. This scheme was very popular especially in the Northwestern part of China where were under the control of the Chinese Communist Party at that time (Chen 1999:184-186).

[20] Guoyu Luomazi was renamed National Phonetic Symbols 2nd Scheme, to distinguish it from the 1st scheme of Jhuyin Fuhao.

[21] Even for the government, different departments and different counties may use different romanized schemes.

[22] In Taiwan, the K.K. phonetic symbols are taught in schools serving as instructions of pronunciations in learning English.

[23] For more discussion on these schemes, see Cheng 2000; Tsao 1999.

March 2000. However, the result of the 2000 presidential election fell short of the KMT's expectation. The pro-Taiwanese Independence Democratic Progressive Party (DPP) won the election and the KMT lost power for the first time since 1945 after ruling Taiwan for fifty-five years.

Since the 2000 presidential election, the Mandarin transliteration issue has remained unresolved and it has even brought more heated controversy and conflict between the new government and the pro-Chinese opposition parties, i.e. KMT, People First Party (*Cinmindang*), and New Party (*Sindang*). On September 16 of that year, the Mandarin Promotion Council (*Guoyu Tuesing Ueyuanhoe*) under the MOE of the new government approved the TYP for Mandarin transliteration. In October that too soon aroused criticism and protests from the opposition parties. *Ma Yingjiu*, the KMT mayor of Taipei started a boycott against the new government on the pinyin issue. He criticized the TYP saying that it is not an international standard for Mandarin Chinese; it would create an obstacle for Taiwan to achieve globalization. He further asserted that Hanyu Pinyin would have to be adopted to achieve this objective (Jhongshih 2000; Jhongyangse 2000; Mingrihbao 2000).

This 'pinyin controversy,' or dispute over mandarin transliteration schemes has been generally considered the biggest crisis to the new government aside from the 'anti-nuclear power plant' event[24]. In fact, the current pinyin controversy is probably the most widely broadcasted dispute over the issues of transliteration that has ever occurred in Taiwan. One may be curious as to why a linguistic issue could result in such an ire and political crisis. There are two contributing factors: 1) the different national identity possessed by different parties, 2) the ruling DPP is a minority party in the Legislative Yuan (*Lip-hoat-i*[n]; similar to congress).

The conflicts between TYP and HP fundamentally resulted from different perspectives of national identity rather than different linguistic designs. From the point of view of Chinese nationalism, it is important to avoid contributing to pro-Taiwanese Independence activities. During the old days while the pro-unification KMT was a ruling party, there was no doubt or problem to using the Guoyu Luomazi with regard to the nationalism issue. However, the pro-unification opinion has been decreasing since the late 1980s when the native political movement started flourishing (Chiung 1999:8-11). Moreover, the pro-Taiwanese Independence DPP became the ruling party after the 2000 presidential election.

---

[24] The 4th nuclear power plant in Taiwan was approved and under construction in the 1990s during the period of KMT government. After the DPP became the ruling party, the new government stopped its construction. Consequently, it aroused protests and boycott from the opposition parties, which proposed to unseat the new president Chen Shui-bian.

Under this strong pro-Taiwanese independence atmosphere, using a transliteration scheme different from China was considered an attempt of the new government to move toward Taiwanese independence[25]. Although Mayer Ma criticized the TYP scheme of not being an internationally recognized system, what he really implied was that TYP was distinct from the 'Chinese PRC standard.'[26] What really concerned Ma was that TYP would lead to a further estrangement between Taiwan and China (Kang 2000; Te 2000).

Although the DPP won the 2000 presidential election, the new government could do little until the next election of legislative representatives in the end of 2001. The fact that the KMT still has the majority in the Legislative Yuan has inflated the pinyin controversy. To some extent, what mostly interested the KMT were fronts to boycott the new government rather than to arrive at a finding on a transliteration scheme. In this case, to unseat the new president was probably the first priority, and the adoption of the HP was simply the second. For example, those who accused the new government of not adopting the HP did not accuse the KMT of promulgating the NPS2.

In order to better understand the pinyin controversy, the history and differences between TYP and HP, are briefly described in the following. TYP (Tongyong Pinyin), literally means general or common transliteration scheme. TYP was proposed and devised by a research fellow at Academia Sinica, *Yu Buocyuan* and his associates in the late 1990s. The fundamental purpose of this new design was to find the maximum transferability between the Hanyu Pinyin scheme and Taiwanese vernacular scheme. In other words, Yu tried to devise a transliteration scheme, which could be used for both Mandarin and Taiwanese languages without lethal conflicts in learning. There were two proposals for TYP, i.e. TYP1 (*Kah-sek*) and TYP2 (*It-sek*) (Cheng 2000; Yu 2000). In the scheme of TYP1, the letter p represents [p] in IPA; however, in TYP2, the letter p represents [pʰ], and b represents [p]. TYP2 was the scheme involved in the pinyin controversy. Generally speaking, TYP2 is considered to be the revised version of Hanyu Pinyin, with minor change such as the initial symbols q, x, and zh (see Table 5). It was estimated that there were around 15% differences between transliterations using TYP2 and HP (Chiang and Huang 2000).

[25] For example, in a press conference on November 29, 2000 the *Guotaiban* (Office for Taiwan Affairs) of the PRC claimed that someone was trying to promote Taiwanese independence in the areas of culture and education through using a different transliteration scheme from Hanyu pinyin.
[26] For example, if Ma really was concerned about the international standardization and globalization, he should also abandon the Jhuyin Fuhao, which is used in Taiwan only.

HP (Hanyu Pinyin) literally means transliteration scheme for Han language (to be exactly, only for Mandarin). HP was designed during the mid-1950s in China and officially promulgated in 1958 by the government of the People's Republic of China. HP is currently considered the only legal transliteration scheme in China for the transcription of modern standard Chinese (Wenzi 1983). It was also adopted by the International Standardization Organization in 1982 as the standard form for transcribing Chinese words (Chen 1999:187). Although the original design of HP was on the ground of autonomous orthography, it has been continuously claimed by the Chinese government that HP is intended for learners as an aid in learning standard Chinese (Chen, 1999:188-189; Hannas, 1997:24-25; Norman 1988:263; Wenzi 1983:6-21). In fact, not only HP, but also other phonemic writing schemes, such as Guoyu Luomazi and Jhuyin Fuhao have always been prevented from serving as independent writing systems. From the point of view of Chinese nationalism, Han characters embody the function of linguistic uniformity. In contrast, alphabetic writing would result in linguistic polycentrism and further be harmful to national unity (DeFrancis 1950:221-236; Norman 1988:263). Apparently, national and political unity is considered to have priority over literacy by the Chinese government.

Table 5. Mandarin consonants represented by IPA, HP, TYP, and Jhuyin Fuhao

IPA

p ph m f t th n l k kh h tɕ tɕh ɕ tʂ tʂh ʂ ɻ ts tsh s

Hanyu Pinyin 漢語拼音

b p m f d t n l g k h j q x zh ch sh r z c s

Tongyong Pinyin 通用拼音

b p m f d t n l g k h ji ci si jh ch sh r z c s

Jhuyin Fuhao 注音符號

ㄅ ㄆ ㄇ ㄈ ㄉ ㄊ ㄋ ㄌ ㄍ ㄎ ㄏ ㄐ ㄑ ㄒ ㄓ ㄔ ㄕ ㄖ ㄗ ㄘ ㄙ

4.2. Romanization for Taiwanese

At present, because spoken Taiwanese is not well standardized, there are correspondingly many proposals for writing Taiwanese. Those proposals may be generally divided into two groups based on their scripts: Han character script[27]

---

[27] This is the traditional way to write Taiwanese in classical style, as Hancha in classical Korean prior to the invention of Hangul. There are several problems encountered when writing

and non-Han character script. Non-Han character may be further divided into two subtypes: A new alphabet, such as *Ganbun* (Hangul-like[28] scheme) designed by Ang Ui-jin, or a ready-made alphabet, which makes use of the present roman letters or Jhuyin Fuhao to write Taiwanese. To better understand the development of non-Han schemes, the number of each category is listed in Table 6 based on the 64 collections by Iu[n] (1999).

Table 6. Number of each category of non-Han schemes

	Roman script	Revised Jhuyin Fuhao	Revised Kana	Hangul-like	Total
-1895	1	0	0	0	1
1985-1945	4	0	2	0	6
1945-1987	15	3	0	1	19
1987-	30	6	0	2	38
Total	50	9	2	3	64

Owing to the wide use of the personal computer and electronic networks in Taiwan since the 1990s, most orthographic designs, that need extra technical support other than regular Mandarin Chinese software could not survive. Therefore, the majority of recent Taiwanese writing schemes were either in Han characters-only, roman script-only or mixed scripts with roman and Han[29]. At present, there are mainly three competing romanized schemes in relation to the Taiwanese language, i.e. Peh-oe-ji, TLPA, and TYP. Among the romanization proposals, Peh-oe-ji is definitely regarded as an independent orthography rather than just a transliteration scheme (Cheng 1999; Chiung 2000b). However, so far there is no common agreement of whether TLPA and TYP would be treated as writing systems or simply transliteration schemes.[30]

Peh-oe-ji is the traditional romanization for writing Taiwanese (Taigi and Hakka) as introduced in the previous section. Prior to the Taibun movement in the 1980s, Peh-oe-ji was the only romanized scheme in practical use for writing

---

colloquial speech by using Han characters. For more details in relation to this issue, see Chiung (1999:50-51) and Chiung (1998).

[28] *Ganbun* is a Hangul-like system, which takes its idea from the design of Korean Hangul.

[29] Roman and Han mixed scheme was proposed mainly to solve the problem that some native Taiwanese words do not have appropriate Han characters (Cheng 1990, 1989). To some extent, it is like the mixture style of Korean Hancha plus Hangul or Japanese Kanji plus Kana. For more discussion on these three Taiwanese schemes, see Chiung 1999 and Tiu[n] 1998.

[30] For comparisons and contrasts between Peh-oe-ji and TLPA, see Cheng 1999 and Khou 1999.

Taiwanese. Compared to other romanized schemes, Peh-oe-ji is still the romanization with the richest inventory of written work, including dictionaries, textbooks, literature works, and other publications in many areas (Iu[n] 1999).

TLPA or Taiwanese Language Phonetic Alphabet was proposed in the early 1990's by the Association of Taiwanese Languages[31]. The major motivation for the TLPA designers to modify Peh-oe-ji is to overcome inconvenience in typing some special symbols of Peh-oe-ji in modern computer network. TLPA has been revised several times, and the latest version was finalized in 1997. In January 1998, the MOE announced that TLPA would be adopted as the official romanized scheme for Hakka and Taigi Taiwanese. The hasty decision adopting TLPA immediately aroused fierce opposition from Peh-oe-ji users and Taibun-promoting groups[32]. Based on the petition proposed by the Taibun groups against TLPA, we can summarize three factors initiating the controversy. First, the MOE's procedure for determining the romanized scheme for Taiwanese was considered insufficiently detailed. Taibun groups object, moreover, that TLPA was approved without negotiations with the public in advance. The protestors even considered the whole event a strategy of the MOE to polarize Taibun groups. Second, the TLPA was simply a theoretical design and had never seen practical use. However, Peh-oe-ji has been used since the nineteenth century, and thus it has a long history of literacy convention. Third, Peh-oe-ji is definitely orthography rather than a set of transliteration symbols. However, the designers of TLPA have never clarified whether or not TLPA is intended to be a writing system[33]. The ambiguity of orthographic status of the TLPA can not conform to the expectation of the protestors.

Briefly speaking, the major differences between Peh-oe-ji and TLPA are phonetic symbols, tone marks and spelling rules. For the phonetic symbols, there are three differences. That is, *ch* and *chh* in Peh-oe-ji were modifid and became *c* and *ch* in TLPA; back vowel *oʻ* was represented by *oo* in TLPA; and superscript *n* was replaced with regular letters *nn*, such as in the case of *tinn* (sweet). In TLPA, tones were represented by Arabic numerals. For example, tai5 (platform) represents 5th tone. As for the spelling, some conventional spellings such as *eng*, *ek*, *oa*, and *oe* were spelled as *ing*, *ik*, *ua*, and *ue*.

---

[31] Association of Taiwanese Languages (*Tai-oan Gi-bun Hak-hoe*) was established in 1991.

[32] For example, see Ngou 1998, Lu 1998, Te[n] 1998, and the "Petition against the MOE's adoption of TLPA" (March 14, 1998).

[33] For example, in the design of TLPA, Taiwanese tones are represented by Arabic numerals, such as *hun5* (cloud) representing the fifth tone. People criticized that numerals should not be used in an orthography.

5. The Future of Romanization in Taiwan

Although any romanization is much more efficient[34] than Han characters, romanizations are currently not widely accepted by people in Taiwan[35]. Writing in roman script is regarded as the low language in digraphia[36]. There are several reasons for this phenomenon:

First, people's preference for Han characters is caused by their internalized socialization. Because Han characters have been adopted as the official orthography for two thousand years, being able to master Han characters well is the mark of a scholar in the Han cultural areas. Writing in scripts other than Han characters may be regarded as childish writing (Chiung 2000b). For example, when *Tai-oan-hu-sia^n Kau-hoe-po*, the first Taiwanese newspaper in romanization, was published in 1885, the editor and publisher Rev. Thomas Barclay exhorted readers of the newspaper not to "look down at Peh-pe-ji; do not regard it as childish writing" (Barclay 1885).

Second, misunderstanding of the nature and function of Han characters has enforced people's preference for Han characters. Many people believe that Han characters are ideally suited for all members of the Han language family, which includes Taigi and Hakka Taiwanese. They believe that Taiwanese can not be expressed well without Han characters because Han characters are logographs and each character expresses a distinctive semantic function. In addition, many people believe Lian Heng's (1987) claim that "there are no Taiwanese words which do not have corresponding characters." However, DeFrancis (1996:40) has pointed out that Han characters are "primarily sound-based and only secondarily semantically oriented." In DeFrancis' opinion, it is a myth to regard Han characters as logographic (DeFrancis 1990). He even concludes that "the inefficiency of the system stems precisely from its clumsy method of sound representation and the added complication of an even more clumsy system of semantic determinatives" (DeFrancis 1996:40). If Han characters are logographs, the process involved in reading them should be different from phonological or phonetic writings. However, research conducted by Tzeng et al. has pointed out

---

[34] Regarding the efficiency issues, refers to Chiung 2000b; DeFrancis 1996, 1990.

[35] For more details about the public's attitudes toward Han characters and romanization, see Chiung 1999.

[36] Digraphia, which parallels to Ferguson's (1959) idea of diglossia, has been defined by Dale (1980:5) as "the use of two (or more) writing systems for representing a single language," or by DeFrancis (1984:59) as "the use of two or more different systems of writing the same language." For discussion on the digraphia in Taiwan, refer to Chiung, 2001 and Tiu^n, 1998.

that "the phonological effect in the reading of the Chinese characters is real and its nature seems to be similar to that generated in an alphabetic script" (Tzeng, Hung, Tzeng 1992:128). Their research reveals that the reading process of Han characters is similar to that for phonetic writing. In short, there is no sufficient evidence to support the view that the Han characters are logographs.

The third reason that romanization is not widespread in Taiwan is because of political factors. Symbolically, writing in Han characters was regarded as a symbol of Chinese culture by Taiwan's ruling Chinese KMT regime. Writing in scripts other than Han characters was forbidden because it was perceived as a challenge to Chinese culture and Chinese nationalism. For example, the romanized New Testament *Sin Iok* was once seized in 1975 because writing in roman script was regarded as a challenge to the orthodox status of Han characters (Li 1996).

Usually, many factors are involved in the choice and shift of orthography. From the perspective of social demand, most people in current Taiwan have already attained the reading and writing skills in Han characters to a certain level. It seems not easy for them to abandon their literacy conventions and shift to a completely new orthography. However, for the younger generation who are at the threshold of literacy, a new orthography may be attractive to them if it is much easier to learn to read and write. If education in romanized writing could be included in schools and taught to the beginners, romanization could quickly be a competing orthography to Han writing.

From the perspective of politics, political transitions usually affect the language situation (Si 1996). In the case of Taiwan, the current ambiguous national status and diversity of national identity reflect people's uncertain determinations on the issues of written Taiwanese. On the other hand, people's uncertain determinations on the Taibun issues also reflect the political controversy on national issues of Taiwan. My research (Chiung 1999) on the attitudes of Taiwanese college students toward written Taiwanese reveals that national identity is one of the most significant factors that affect students' attitudes toward Taiwanese writing. It is true that national identity played an important role in the orthographic transition of Vietnam, where romanization eventually replaced Han characters and became the official orthography (Chiung 2000a; DeFrancis 1977). Will this replacement happen to the case of Taiwan? Whether or not roman script will replace Han characters and Taiwanese replace Chinese depends on people's orthographic demands and their attitudes toward written Taiwanese. Moreover, people's national identity will play a crucial role in the transition. From my point of view, Han characters, at least, will retain their dominant status until the

Taiwanese people are released from their ambiguity in regard to national identity.

6. Conclusion

For Mandarin Chinese, it is apparent that roman script will not be adopted as a writing system in the foreseeable future. As for the Taiwanese languages, there is no significant sign so far that romanization such as the existing Peh-oe-ji will spread or be promoted to a national status. There are three crucial landmarks in regard to whether or not Taiwanese romanization will move toward official orthography and be widely used. First, whether or not romanization will be included in school curriculum. No matter whether romanization is taught as a transliteration scheme or as orthography, it is the important first step for the promotion of romanized writing since most Taiwanese people are 'illiterate' in romanization. The second crucial landmark is the attitude of the new DPP government towards roman script and Han characters, and the political stability of the new government if it decides to promote romanization. The third one is the common agreement on romanization among the Taiwanese language promoters. For a long while, the disagreement on romanized scheme has only added to the chaos about the romanization question and shaken the promotion of written Taiwanese. The agreement can thus improve the promotion of romanization.

Acknowledgements

This is an updated revision of the article with same title originally published in 2001 *The Linguistic Association of Korea Journal* 9(1), pp.15-43.

For the Romanization development after 2000, readers may refer to Wi-vun Chiung 2018. Languages under colonization: the Taiwanese language movement. Paper collected in Bruce Jacobs; Peter Kang (eds.). *Changing Taiwanese Identities*. New York: Routledge.

References

Ang, Ui-jin. 1993. Introduction to Douglas' Amoy-English dictionary [To·-ka-tek E-eng Tai-su-tian Kankai]. In *A Collection of Southern Min Classic Dictionaries* [*Ban-lam-gi Keng-tian Su-su Hui-pian*]. 4, pp.1-9. Taipei: Woolin Press.

Ang, Ui-jin. 1996. *A List of Historical Materials: Language Category* [Tai-oan Bun-hian Su-bok Te-kai : Gi-gian-lui]. Taipei: NCL-Taiwan.

Barclay, Thomas. 1885. *Taiwan Prefectural City Church News* [Tai-oan-hu-sia[n] Kau-hoe-po]. No.1.

Campbell, William. 1992. *Formosa Under the Dutch.* (originally published in 1903). Taipei: SMC Publishing Inc.

Campbell, William. 1996. *The Gospel of St. Matthew in Formosan (Sinkang Dialect) With Corresponding Versions in Dutch and English Edited From Gravius's Edition of 1661.* (originally published in 1888). Taipei: SMC Publishing Inc.

Chan, Hui-chen. 1994. *Language Shift in Taiwan: Social and Political Determinants.* Ph.D. dissertation: Georgetown University.

Chen, Ping. 1996. Modern written Chinese, dialects, and regional identity. *Language Problems and Language Planning* 20(3), pp.223-43.

Chen, Ping. 1999. *Modern Chinese: History and Sociolinguistics.* Cambridge: Cambridge University Press.

Cheng, Robert L. 1989. *Essays on Written Taiwanese* [Kia[n] Hiong Phiau-chun-hoa e Tai-oan-oe-bun]. Taipei: Independence Press.

Cheng, Robert L. 1990. *Essays on Taiwan's Sociolinguistic Problems* [Ian-pian tiong e Tai-oan Sia-hoe Gi-bun]. Taipei: Independence Press.

Cheng, Robert L. 1996. Democracy and language policy [Bin-chu-hoa Cheng-ti Bok-phiau kap Gi-gian Cheng-chhek]. In Si (1996), pp.21-50.

Cheng, Robert L. 1999. The transferability between Peh-oe-ji and other romanized schemes [Tai-gi Lo-ma-ji Su-bin-gi kap Tai-oan Sia-khu lai Phiau-im He-thong e Kiong-thong Seng-keh]. In proceedings of the Conference on the Rebirth and Reconstruction of the Taiwanese Languages, pp.46-61.

Cheng, Robert L. 2000. A review of the four transliteration schemes in terms of learners of English and Taiwanese vernacular [Chiam-tui Eng-bun Hak-sip Su-iau ham Tai-oan Bo-gi Tek-seng Pheng 4 Tho Hoa-gi Phin-im Thong-iong-seng]. Paper presented at the Conference on Transliteration Scheme for Han Characters, held by the Linguistics Institute, Academia Sinica, Taiwan.

Cheng, Robert. L. and Cheng, Susie S. 1977. *Phonological Structure and Romanization of Taiwanese Hokkian* [Tai-oan Hok-kian-oe e Gi-im Kiat-kau kap Phiau-im-hoat]. Taipei: Student Press.

Chiang, Wen-yu and Shuanfan Huang. 2000. Using TYP can get connection to the world easier than HP [Thong-iong Phin-im Li i i Se-kai Chiap-kui]. Taiwan Tribune, no. 1856.

Chiang, Wen-yu, Jhao-jin Luo, Hak-khiam Tiu[n] and Buocyun Yu. 2000. On the issue of transliteration scheme: a balance of globalization and localization [Lun Tai-oan Phin-im : Kok-che-seng kap Chu-the-seng Peng-heng Koan-tiam]. Paper presented at the Conference on Transliteration Scheme for Han Characters, held by the Linguistics Institute, Academia Sinica, Taiwan.

Chiung, Wi-vun T. 1998. The influence of Han characters on Taiwanese people's linguistic perception [Han-ji tui Tai-oan-lang e Gi-gian Gin-ti e Eng-hiong]. Paper presented at the 4th Annual North America Taiwan Studies Conference, University of Texas at Austin. < http://uibun.twl.ncku.edu.tw/chuliau/lunsoat/ginti.htm>

Chiung, Wi-vun T. 1999. *Language Attitudes toward Taibun, the Written Taiwanese.* MA thesis: The University of Texas at Arlington. < http://ebook.de-han.org/attitude/>

Chiung, Wi-vun T. 2000a. Language, literacy, and nationalism: a comparative study of Vietnam and Taiwan. Paper presented at the 5th International Symposium on Languages & Linguistics: Pan-Asiatic Linguistics, Vietnam National University, TPHCM, Vietnam. <http://uibun.twl.ncku.edu.tw/chuliau/lunsoat/english/pan-asiatic/abstract.htm>

Chiung, Wi-vun T. 2000b. Peh-oe-ji: a childish writing? Paper presented at the 6th Annual North American Taiwan Studies Conference, Harvard University. <http://uibun.twl.ncku.edu.tw/chuliau/lunsoat/english/pehoeji.html>

Chiung, Wi-vun T. 2001. Digraphia with and without biliteracy: a case study of Taiwan. Paper presented at the Graduate Student Conference on East Asia, Columbia University. <http://uibun.twl.ncku.edu.tw/download/index.htm>

Dale, Ian R.H. 1980. Digraphia. *International Journal of the Sociology of Language* 26, pp.5-13.

DeFrancis, John. 1950. *Nationalism and Language Reform in China.* Princeton University Press.

DeFrancis, John. 1977. *Colonialism and Language Policy in Viet Nam.* The Hague. DeFrancis,

John. 1984. Digraphia. *Word* 35(1), pp.59-66.

DeFrancis, John. 1990. *The Chinese Language: Fact and Fantasy.* (Taiwan edition). Honolulu: University of Hawaii Press.

DeFrancis, John. 1996. How efficient is the Chinese writing system? *Visible Language* 30(1), pp.6-44.

Ferguson, Charles. 1959. Diglossia. *Word* 15, pp.325-40.

Gao, Tianru. 1992. *Theory and Practice of the Modern Language Planning in China* [Jhongguo Siandai Yuian Jihua de Lilun yu Shihjian]. University of Fudan Press, China.

Grimes, Barbara. 1996. *Ethnologue: Language of the World.* (12th edition). Dallas: Summer Institute of Linguistics.

Hannas, William. C. 1997. *Asia's Orthographic Dilemma.* University of Hawaii Press.

Hsiau, A-chin. 1997. Language ideology in Taiwan: the KMT's language policy, the Tai-yu language movement, and ethnic politics. *Journal of Multilingual and Multicultural Development* 18(4), pp.302-315.

Hsu, Chian Hsin. (eds.). 1995. *A Centennial History of The Presbyterian Church of Formosa* (Tai-oan Ki-tok Tiuⁿ-lo Kau-hoe Pah-ni-su). (3rd edition). Tailam: Presbyterian Church of Formosa Centenary Publications Committee.

Huang, Shuanfan. 1993. *Language, Society, and Ethnic Identity* [Gi-gian Sia-hoe i Chok-kun I-sek]. Taipei: Crane.

Iuⁿ, Un-gian and Hak-khiam Tiuⁿ. 1999. A review of the non-Han alphabetic schemes for Taigi

Taiwanese [Tai-oan Ho-lo-oe hui-Han-ji Phin-im Hu-ho e Hoe-kou kap Hun-sek]. In proceedings of the Conference on the Rebirth and Reconstruction of the Taiwanese Languages, pp.62-76.

Jhongshih. 2000. Taipei is against the MOE in regard to the transliteration scheme [Jhongwen Yiyin Sithong Beishih Maosang Jiauyubu]. China Times.com, October 8.

Jhongyangse. 2000a. Taipei has opposite views on the transliteration issue [Jhongwen Engyi Beishih yu Jhongyang Bu Tong Diau]. Central News, October 5.

Jhongyangse. 2000b. Taipei will not adopt TYP [Caiyong Tongyong Pinyin Beishihfu BuYi]. Central News, October 7.

Jhou, Yiuguang. 1978. *Introduction to the Reform of Han Characters* [Hanzi Gaige Gailun]. Macao: Erya.

Kang, Tong-eng. 2000. Anti-Taiwanization is real, but globalization is a lying [Hoan-pun-thou-hoa si Chin-e, Kok-che-hoa si Ke-e]. Taiwan Daily News, October 12.

Kerr, George H. 1992. *Formosa Betrayed* [*Pi Chhut-be e Tai-oan*]. (Taiwan edition). Taipei: Chian-ui Press.

Khou, Tiong-bo. 1999. The importance of romanization and national orthography for the Taiwanese languages [Iu Tai-gi-bun Kok-ka Gi-gian-hoa Lun Lo-ma Phin-im e Tiong-iau]. In proceedings of the Conference on the Rebirth and Reconstruction of the Taiwanese Languages, pp.154-163.

Lai, Young-hsiang. 1990. *Topics on Taiwan Church History* [*Kau-hoe Su-oe*]. Vol. 1. Tailam: Jin-kong Press.

Li, Khin-hoann. 1996. Language policy and Taiwanese independence [Gigian Cheng-chhek kap Taioan Toklip]. In Si (1996), pp.113-134. Taipei: Chian-ui.

Lian, Heng. 1987. *Taiwanese Etymology* [*Tai-oan Gi-tian*]. (originally published in 1957). Taipei: Chin-fong.

Lu, Heng-chhiong. 1998. Only 5% of the Peh-oe-ji revised? essay on the MOE's TLPA [Jhen de jhih Gai lo 5% ma: Tan Jiauyubu Taiyu Yinbiau de Gonggau]. Taiwan Church News. No. 2412.

Mingrihbao. 2000. Ma Yingjiu emphasized on the importance to get connection to the world [Ma Yingjiu Ciangdiau Jhongwen Yiyin Sitong iau yu Shihjie Jiegue]. Tomorrow News, October 13.

Naojiro Murakami, B. 1933. *Sinkan Manuscripts*. Taipei: Taihoku Imperial University.

Ngou, Siu-le. 1998. Some thoughts on the adoption of the TLPA [Tui Kau-iok-pou Pan-teng Tai-oan Gi-gian Im-phiau e Khoa[n]-hoat]. Taiwan Church News. No. 2412.

Norman, Jerry. 1988. *Chinese.* NY: Cambridge University Press.

Ong, Iok-tek. 1993. *Taiwan: A Depressed History* [Tai-oan: Khou-bun e Lek-su]. Taipei: Independence Press.

Peng, Ming-min. and Yuzin Chiautong Ng. 1995. *The Legal Status of Taiwan* [*Tai-oan chai Kok-che-hoat siong e Te-ui*]. Taipei: Taiwan Interminds.

Phe[n]. 1998. Petition on the adoption of the TLPA [Khong-gi Kau-iok-pou Phian-bin Kong-pou Tai-oan Gi-gian Im-phiau e Put-tong Chhok-si Lian-su-su]. <http://ws.twl.ncku.edu.tw/>

Png, Su-tok. 1965. History of the National Language Movement in China in the past 50 years [Wushihnian lai Jhongguo Guoyu Yundongshih]. Taipei: Mandarin Daily News Press.

Si, Cheng-hong. 1996. The relationship between language and politics [Gi-gian e Cheng-ti Koan-lian-seng]. In Si (1996), pp.53-80.

Si, Cheng-hong. (eds.). 1996. *Linguistic Politics and Policy* [Gi-gian Cheng-ti kap Cheng-chhek]. Taipei: Chian-ui.

Su, Beng. 1980. *Four Hundred Years of Taiwanese History* [*Tai-oan-lang 400 Ni Su*]. California: Paradise Culture Associates.

Taiwan Pinyin Info Online < http://pinyin.info/>

Te, Cheng-tek. 2000. Re-thinking the adoption of the Hanyu pinyin [Hanyu Pinyin de Shangcyue]. Liberty News, October 15.

Te[n], Iong. 1998. The MOE's TLPA is controversial [Kau-iok-pou Tai-oan Gi-gian Im-phiau Cheng-gi Che]. Taiwan Church News. No. 2411

Tiu,[n] Lu-hong. 1996. An analysis on the Taiwan's current language policy [Tai-oan Hian-heng Gi-gian Cheng-chhek Tong-ki e Hun-sek]. In Si (1996), pp.85-106.

Tiu[n] Hak-khiam. 1998. Writing in two scripts: a case study of digraphia in Taiwanese. *Written Language and Literacy* 1(2), pp.225-47.

Tsao, Feng-fu. 1999. The language planning situation in Taiwan. *Journal of Multilingual and Multicultural Development* 20 (4&5), pp.328-75.

Tzeng, Ovid, Daisy Hung & Angela Tzeng. 1992. Auto activation of linguistic information in Chinese character recognition. *Advances in Psychology* 94, pp.119-30.

United news. 2000. PRC Office for Taiwan Affairs: the across parties team is playing with words [Jhonggong Guotaiban: Kuadangpai Siaozu Gongshih Wenzih Iousi]. United News, November 30.

Wenzi Gaige. 1983. *The design and application of the Hanyu pinyin* [Hanyu Pinyin Fangan de Jhihding he Yingyong]. Orthographic Reform Press.

Young, Russell. 1988. Language Maintenance and Language Shift in Taiwan. *Journal of Multilingual and Multicultural Development* 9(4), pp.323-38.

Yu, Buocyun, Wenfang Fan, and Ovid Tzeng. 1999. An analysis of the design and policy on Chinese transliteration [Jhongwen Yiyin de Yanjiu yu Jhengce Jhihding Fensi].

Yu, Buocyuan et al. 2000. On the TYP1 and TYP2 [Lun Kah-lui ham It-lui Phin-im: Kah It Siong-thong Koan-tiam]. Paper presented at the Conference on Transliteration Scheme for Han Characters, held by the Linguistics Institute, Academia Sinica, Taiwan.

8

Pėh-ōe-jī as
Intangible Cultural Heritage of Taiwan

1. Introduction

In May 2013, the Festival on Taiwanese Romanization was held in Tainan to celebrate the centennial anniversary of William Campbell's Taiwanese Dictionary, which was published in Romanized *Pėh-ōe-jī*[1] (白話字). Peh-oe-ji literally means 'the scripts of vernacular speech', in contrast to the complicated Han characters of classical Han writing. It was introduced into Taiwan by Western missionaries in the second half of the nineteenth century (Lai 1990; Chiung 1999; Klöter 2005:89; Chang 2015). Therefore, it is usually called "Church Roman Scripts." Although Pėh-ōe-jī was originally devised for religious purposes, it is no longer limited to religious applications after the contemporary *Tâi-bûn* movement rose in the late 1980s. Peh-oe-ji has been adopted by many Tai-bun promoters as the Romanized writing system to write Taiwanese. Therefore, it is also called "*Tâi-oân-jī*" or Taiwanese Scripts by the promoters.

Although Taiwan is currently a Hanji (Han characters)-dominated society, once Romanization was the unique and first writing system used by the populace in Taiwan. Romanization in Taiwan prior to 1945 can be divided into two eras. The first era of Romanization is *Sinkang* writing, and the second Romanization is Pėh-ōe-jī writing. Sinkang scripts were a Romanized system for writing the vernacular of the indigenous *Siraya* tribes during the Dutch occupation (1624-1661) of Taiwan in the seventeenth century. Nowadays, the language of Siraya has become nearly extinct and only a very limited number of researchers could read the manuscripts written in Sinkang. Thereafter, the classical Han writing was

---

[1] For details about the sound system and spellings in Pėh-ōe-jī, see Chiung 2003 and Cheng 1977.

adopted as an official language, and *Koa-á-chheh* (歌仔冊) was treated as the popular writing for the public during the *Koxinga* (鄭成功 1661-1683) and the *Qing* Empire (清 1683-1895) occupations. In the second half of the nineteenth century, another Romanized system, Pèh-ōe-jī, was devised by missionaries to write Taiwanese. It plays important roles in three aspects: 1) cultural enlightenment, 2) education for all people and 3) literary creation in colloquial Taiwanese. Although Pèh-ōe-jī was originally devised for religious purposes, it is no longer limited to religious applications, especially after the contemporary Tâi-bûn (Written Taiwanese) movement rose since the late 1980s. Pèh-ōe-jī has been adopted by many Tâi-bûn promoters to write Taiwanese either in either Roman-only or a hybrid Han-Lo styles. In short, Pèh-ōe-jī is not only the foundation of Romanization of modern Taiwanese colloquial writing, but is also the intangible cultural heritage of Taiwan.

2. Sociolinguistic settings in Taiwan

Taiwan is a multilingual and multiethnic society with a total of 23 million in population in 2013. Generally speaking, there are four primary ethnic groups: indigenous (1.7%), *Thòi-vân-ngìn* or Hakka (12%), *Tâi-oân-lâng* or Taiwanese[2] (73.3%), and post war Chinese immigrants (13%) (Huang 1993:21). The mother tongue of the *Tâi-oân-lâng* people is called Tâi-gí (台語), the Taiwanese language in Taiwan. It is also occasionally called *Hô-ló-ōe*, *Lán-lâng-ōe* or *Bân-lâm-ōe* (Southern Min[3])

Although Taiwanese was originally brought from Southern Hokkien in China to Taiwan, it is not exactly the same as Southern Min of today. For example, although Choan-chiu and Chiang-chiu were originally two major varieties of Southern Min, they gradually merged and became a new "non-Chiang non-Choan" (不漳不泉) vernacular after they were brought to Taiwan (Iwasaki 1913; Ong 1957:3-5, 1987:18-23; Ang1992a, 1992b:71)[4]. Moreover, they were greatly influenced by the languages of indigenous plain tribes, and particularly by the Japanese language during the Japanese ruling period (Ong 1957:44-45). For instance, 'tá-káu' (former name of Kaohsiung city), 'Tâi-oân' (current name of

---

[2] Huang adopted the term Southern Min instead of *Tâi-oân-lâng*.

[3] 'Min' is the abbreviation of Hokkien province in China. In addition, it is a pejorative name with the meaning 'barbarians with snake origin,' according to Chinese classical dictionaries. Therefore, this term is not widely accepted by Taiwanese people (Chiung 2015).

[4] There are some differences between Choan-chiu and Chiang-chiu, such as /koe/ vs. /ke/ to represent the same meaning of word 'chicken.'

Taiwan), 'má-se' (drunken) and 'Báng-kah' (a place name in Taipei) are cognates from Formosan Austronesian languages. In addition, 'chù-bûn' (ちゅうもん to order), 'sú-sih' (すし Japanese sushi), 'se-bí-loh' (セビロ a suit), 'ò-bah' (オーバーan overcoat) are loanwords in Taiwanese coined from Japanese. In short, this new "non-Chiang non-Choan" language has been widely called 'Tâi-gí' or 'Tâi-oân-ōe,' which all mean the 'Taiwanese language' by the Taiwanese people since the early twentieth century (Chiung 2015:62).

Taiwanese could be written in different orthographies. Currently, there are three major writing systems: 1) Roman-only, or exclusive use of Roman scripts, 2) Han characters only, which means exclusive use of Hanji; and 3) Han-Lo 'Hanji with Roman script,' which means a combination of Hanji with Roman scripts (Cheng 1990:219-237; Ong 1993a; Tiuⁿ 1998:230-241; Chiung 2001; Klöter 2005).

Thòi-vân-ngìn and Tâi-oân-lâng are the so-called sinicized Han people. In fact, many of them are descendants of intermarriage between sinitic immigrants and local Formosan Austronesians during the *Koxinga* and *Qing* periods (Brown 2004:149). Mainlanders were the soldiers, dependents, and refugees who moved to Taiwan from China around the 1940s with Chiang Kai-shek's political regime ROC. Mandarin Chinese is the lingua franca among the Mainlanders. Although Thòi-vân-ngìn, Tâi-oân-lâng, and Mainlanders were all immigrants originally from China, they have different national identities. Research conducted by Ông (1993) and Corcuff (2004) have revealed that most of the Tâi-oân-lâng and Thòi-vân-ngìn people identify themselves as Taiwanese. However, more than half of the Mainlanders still identified themselves as Chinese (Chiung 2007a:110).

At the end of World War II, Chiang Kai-shek, the leader of the Chinese Nationalists (KMT) took over China (excluding Manchuria), Taiwan, and French Indo-China north of 16° north latitude on behalf of the Allied Powers under General Order No.1 of September 2, 1945 (Hodgkin 1981:288; Peng and Ng 1995:60-61; Chiung 2007:110-111, 2008). In accordance with this order, Chiang sent troops to Taiwan and Vietnam. After Japanese forces were disarmed, Chiang was requested by Ho Chi Minh and French power to withdraw his troops from Vietnam in 1946. However, Chiang's troops remained in Taiwan even though the well-known February 28 Revolution occurred in 1947 (Kerr 1992; Su 1980:749-801; Ong 1993b:157-162). Simultaneously, Chiang Kai-shek was fighting against the Chinese Communist Party in Mainland China.

In 1949, Chiang's troops were completely defeated and then pursued by the Chinese Communists. At that time, Taiwan's national status was supposed to be dealt with by a peace treaty among the nations at war. That is the Treaty of Peace with Japan signed by 48 nations at a later time in San Francisco in September 1951. However, because of Chiang's defeat in China, Chiang decided to occupy Taiwan as a base and from there he would fight to recover the Mainland (Kerr 1992; Ong 1993b; Peng and Ng 1995; Su 1980). Consequently, Chiang's political regime Republic of China (ROC) was renewed in Taiwan and has remained there since 1949.

Chiang claimed that Taiwan was a province of China, and ROC was the only legitimate government of China even though the People's Republîc of China (PRC) was established in Beijing by the Chinese Communist Party (CCP) in October 1949. Due to Chiang's control of Taiwan, his mortal enemy, the communist leader Mao Zedong, also claimed that Taiwan was a part of PRC. In fact, both KMT and CCP used to support Taiwan to become an independent state from the Japanese during the 1920s and 1930s (Siau 1981). Nevertheless, the current relation between Taiwan and China remains a political issue to solve. From the perspective of the people in Taiwan, many public opinion polls done lately have shown that the majority of the Taiwanese people are more likely to support Taiwanese independence. For example, the polls conducted by Taiwan Thinktank in July 2014 revealed that 82.9% of the subjects agreed that Taiwan and China are two countries independent from each other.[5]

Monolingual Mandarin Chinese policy was adopted during ROC's occupation of Taiwan (Huang 1993; Heylen 2005). Taiwanese people were forced to learn Mandarin Chinese and to identify themselves as Chinese through the national education system (Cheng 1996; Tiuⁿ 1996; Hsiau 1997:307). Consequently, research has revealed that a language shift toward Mandarin is in progress (Lu 1988:73; Young 1989:55; Chan 1994:iii). In response to ROC's Chinese language policy, the promoters of Taiwanese have protested against the monolingual policy and have demanded vernacular education in schools. This is the so-called 'Tâi-bûn Ūn-tōng' or 'Taiwanese language movement' that has substantially grown since the second half of the 1980s (Hsiau 1997; Erbaugh 1995; Li 1999; Lim 1996; Chiung 1999, 2007; Klöter 2005).

3. From missionary scripts to Taiwanese scripts

The origin of Pėh-ōe-jī could be traced back to the achievements of cooperation between Western missionaries and ethnic Chinese (Tñg-lâng) in Southeast Asia. In the 18th and 19th centuries, the Qing Empire adopted hostile

---

[5] Press release available at Taiwan Thinktank<http://www.taiwanthinktank.org>

policies toward Western missionaries. Therefore, Southeast Asia was usually chosen by missionaries as the base prior to their missionary activities in China, people such as Robert Morrison (1782-1834) and Walter Henry Medhurst (1796-1857) of the London Missionary Society.

In 1817, Medhurst arrived in Malacca (Lai 1990; Ang 1993d). He taught at the Anglo-Chinese College and was in charge of the printing business. At a later time, he also preached in several areas such as Penang, Singapore, Batavia (present-day Jakarta) and Shanghai. During the period in Batavia, he compiled *A Dictionary of the Hok-kёёn Dialect of the Chinese Language* and later it was published in Macao in 1837. This dictionary is considered the first existing Romanized dictionary of Lán-lâng-ōe (Southern Hokkien) compiled by western missionary (Ang 1993d, 1993e) [6]. The role of Medhurst's dictionary for Lán-lâng-ōe is somewhat similar to Alexandre de Rhodes's dictionary for Vietnamese.

Once the Pėh-ōe-jī laid the foundation in Southeast Asia, it further spread to Hokkien and Taiwan. In 1864, James L. Maxwell (1836-1921) of the Presbyterian Church of England came to Taiwan for the first time. Thereafter, he founded the first Presbyterian church in Tainan in 1865. When he was in Tainan, he found that the indigenous Siraya tribes used to use Romanized Sinkang scripts for more than a hundred years even though the Dutch had left Taiwan. It convinced him that Romanization was helpful to Bible reading for the Taiwanese people. Therefore, Pėh-ōe-jī, which once was acquired by Maxwell, was introduced to Taiwan. In addition to Maxwell, missionaries such as Rev. George Leslie Mackay (1844-1901), Rev. William Campbell (1841-1921), and Rev. Thomas Barclay (1849-1935) made contributions to the promotion of Pėh-ōe-jī in Taiwan. Due to the many contributions of missionaries and Taiwan's different social backgrounds from China, Taiwan eventually has become the society where Pėh-ōe-jī is more flourishing than in Southeast Asia or Hokkien. At present, Taiwan possesses the greatest number of users and plentiful cultural products of Pėh-ōe-jī in the Pėh-ōe-jī cultural sphere (Chiung 2012, 2013a). For example, the Pėh-ōe-jī bibles and hymnals used by people in Hokkienese/Chinese churches in Malaysia were mainly printed by the Taiwan Church Press.

Generally speaking, Pėh-ōe-jī made important impact in three significant aspects: 1) cultural enlightenment, 2) education for all people and 3) literary creation in colloquial Taiwanese (Chiung 2013b:111, Chiung 2011:ix).

Those applications and publications of Pėh-ōe-jī since the nineteenth century

---

[6] It was also reported that the earliest development of Pėh-ōe-jī was contributed by the Spanish missionaries of Mania in the early 17th century (Klöter 2002 & 2004; Tiuⁿ 2015).

can be summarized in the following six categories: 1) textbooks, 2) dictionaries, 3) religious literature, including the translation of the Bible, catechisms, and religious tracts, 4) newspapers, 5) private note-taking or letters, and 6) other publications, such as physiology, math, and novels (Chiung 2005:36, 2012).[7]

Missionaries' linguistic efforts on the Romanization are reflected in various Romanized dictionaries. In addition to the publication of Walter H. Medhurst's *A Dictionary of the Hok-kёen Dialect of the Chinese Language*, there are several remarkable dictionaries compiled by missionaries.

Carstairs Douglas's *Chinese-English Dictionary of the Vernacular or Spoken Language of Amoy* of 1873 is regarded as an influential dictionary on the orthography of Pėh-ōe-jī[8]. After Douglas's dictionary, most Romanized dictionaries and publications followed his orthography with little or no changes (Ang 1993b:1-9, 1993a). George L. Mackay's *Chinese Romanized Dictionary of the Formosan Vernacular*, which was considered the first dictionary to focus on the vernacular spoken in Taiwan, was completed in 1874 and printed in Shangha in 1891i. William Campbell's dictionary *Ē-mn̂g Im Sin Jī-tián* or *A Dictionary of the Amoy Vernacular Spoken Throughout the Prefectures of Chin-chiu, Chiang-chiu and Formosa,* first published in 1913, was the first Pėh-ōe-jī dictionary published in Taiwan[9]. It is the most widely used Romanized dictionary in Taiwan (Lai 1990; Ang 1996). This dictionary has been reprinted and renamed as *Kam Uî-lîm Tâi-gú Jī-tián* or *William Campbell's Taiwanese Dictionary* since 2009.

Generally speaking, missionaries' dictionaries were using the Amoy vernacular as the criteria by the early twentieth century. Thereafter, the vernacular spoken in Taiwan gradually became the criteria. For example, *The Amoy-English Dictionary* and *English-Amoy Dictionary,* published by The Maryknoll Language Service Center in Taichung in 1976 and 1979, are two such dictionaries. Their vocabularies and pronunciation systems are mainly based on the local Taichung vernacular even thought 'Amoy' was named. The publisher had to use 'Amoy' rather than 'Taiwanese' due to the factor that Taiwan was under ROC's martial law from 1949 to 1987. At a later time, they were republished as *Taiwanese-English Dictionary* in 2001 and *English-Taiwanese Dictionary* in 2013, respectively.[10]

---

[7] Some publications may be available at the website of Memory of the Written Taiwanese, which was initiated by Iûn Ún-giân. This site is located at <http://ip194097.ntcu.edu.tw/Memory/TGB>

[8] This dictionary was scanned and available at < http://ip194097.ntcu.edu.tw/memory/TGB>

[9] This dictionary was digitized and available at<http://taigi.fhl.net/dick>

[10] This dictionaries is available at <http://www.taiwanesedictionary.org>

In addition to dictionaries, the Bible is regarded as an important medium for the standardization of written Taiwanese. There were two major contributors to the completion of the Taiwanese Romanized Bible: Dr. James L. Maxwell and Rev. Thomas Barclay. Dr. Maxwell was the first medical missionary to Taiwan in 1865. Under his supervision, *Lán ê Kiù-chú Ia-so Ki-tok ê Sin-iok*, the first Romanized *Taiwanese New Testament* was published in 1873, and *Kū-iok ê Sèng Keng*, the *Taiwanese Old Testament,* was published in 1884. They were both printed in the UK (Lai 1990). Their revised editions were completed by Rev. Barclay. The revised New Testament was published in 1916. Later, the Revised Old Testament along with the revised New Testament were collected together and published in 1933. The 1933 Barclay edition of the Bible is the most widespread Romanized Bible in Taiwan (Niu 2013). In short, the Taiwanese Bible of Barclay and Maxwell plays the same role as Martin Luther's translation of the Bible from Latin into the German vernacular.

Amoy vernacular was regarded as the criteria for compiling the Bible by both Maxwell and Barclay. Thereafter, all editions of the Bible were translated in the Taiwanese vernacular. For example, the *Ko-Tân edition of Colloquial Taiwanese New Testament*[11], which was mainly translated based on the vernacular spoken in the central Taiwan areas, was completed by the Maryknoll Society in 1972 (Niu 2005; Lim 2005). This Bible is also called 'Âng-phôe Sèng-keng' or 'Red Cover Bible' because of the color of its front cover. It was expected to fulfill the needs of modern Taiwanese speakers. Unfortunately, it was seized by the ROC regime in 1975. It was later transcribed into Han-Lo version by Lîm Chùn-iòk and published by the Taiwan Church Press in 2005.[12]

Several revised or newly translated editions of the Bible in Taiwanese were published again after the martial law was lifted in Taiwan. During this period, the Taiwanese Bibles were published in three ways: 1) Roman-only, 2) Han-only, and 3) Han-Lo hybrid. For example, *Hiān-tāi Tâi-gú Sin-iok Sèng-keng*, or The Today's Taiwanese New Testament, which was translated directly from Greek into Romanized Taiwanese based mainly on northern Taiwanese varieties, was published by the Bible Society in Taiwan in 2008 (Li 2010:74-75)[13]. It was later published again in the Han-Lo version in 2013 (Tiuⁿ 2014:16-17). Recently, *Choân-bîn Tâi-gí Sèng-keng* or The Common Taiwanese Bible, which was revised

---

[11] *Ko-Tân Tâi-oân Pèh-ōe Sèng-keng Èk-pún* 高陳台灣白話聖經譯本.

[12] Its original texts are available at <http://taigi.fhl.net/list.html>, and sound archives are available at <http://bible.fhl.net/new/audio_hb.php?version=6>

[13] The Bible was copyrighted in 2007 and published in 2008. For the comparisons of different editions of Taiwanese Bible, readers may refer to Niu (2005) or Iuⁿ (2013).

from the 1933 Barclay's edition and transcribed into southern Taiwanese accents, was completed in 2013. It contains three versions: 1) Roman-only, 2) Han-Lo, and 3) Han-Lo plus Ruby functions[14]. The Roman-only and Han-Lo editions were officially published in 2015. In addition to Roman-only and Han-Lo editions, Taiwanese Bible in Han characters "台語漢字本聖經" was published in 1996 for the first time. This Hanji edition was merely transcribed from Barclay's edition into Han characters.

In addition to dictionaries and the Bible, newspapers and other publications are also important in the promotion and standardization of written Taiwanese. The first modern newspaper *Tâi-oân-hú-siân Kàu-hōe-pò* (*Taiwan Prefectural City Church News*) was published monthly by Rev. Barclay in July 1885 (Tiun 2005; Tan 2007). This newspaper was published in Pėh-ōe-jī until March 1969. Thereafter, it was shifted to Mandarin Chinese under the political pressure from ROC.

In order to print Taiwanese Roman scripts, which contain some distinctive features and tone marks, a state-of-the-art printing machine was imported. The first printing machine in Taiwan was donated by Dr. James L. Maxwell in 1880. It was transported from Scotland to Taiwan in 1881. This printer was operated for printing Taiwan Prefectural City Church News and other publications in Pėh-ōe-jī. This printer was in operation from May 1885 until the 1960s. After the printer was imported, the first publishing house in Taiwan, known as Chū-tin-tông or Sin-lâu Bookstore, was established in Tainan by Rev. Barclay in 1884. It was later called the Taiwan Church Press. [15]

Although *Taiwan Prefectural City Church News* was a religion-oriented newspaper, it also contained a variety of articles, such as those on aspects of literature, history, culture and science (Ng 2000; Chiung 2011; Si 2015). For example, a short story entitled as "Jit-pún ê koài-sū" (an oddity in Japan) and a travel note "Pak-káng Má ê sin-bûn" (news on the goddess Pak-kang Ma) were published in 1886.[16]

In addition to newspapers, there were some other publications, such as *Pit Soàn ê Chhơ Hak* (Fundamental Mathematics) by *Ûi-lîm Gê* in 1897, *Lāi Gōa Kho Khàn-hō·hak* (The Principles and Practice of Nursing) by G. Gushue-Taylor

---

[14] Three versions of Common Taiwanese Bible are available at <http://taigi.fhl.net/list.html>

[15] It was originally located nearby library of Tainan Theological College and Seminary and the current Sin-lâu Street in Tainan. Nowadays, Taiwan Church Press located in Youth Road was built in 1983 with donation from German church.

[16] Articles in this newspaper were digitized and researchable at <http://210.240.194.97/nmtl/dadwt/pbk.asp>

in 1917, the novel *Chhut Sí-Sòaⁿ* (Line between Life and Death) by *Khe-phoàn Tēⁿ* in 1926, and the collection of commentaries *Chàp-hāng Koán-kiàn* (Opinions on Ten Issues) by *Pôe-hóe Chhòa* in 1925.[17]

Due to the successful promotion of written Taiwanese in the second half of nineteenth century, it had contributed to the emergence of Taiwanese new literature, which was written in accordance with the Taiwanese colloquial vernacular rather than traditional classical Han writing (Chiung 2005:35). Comparing to the May Fourth New Culture Movement of 1919 in China, Taiwanese people had experienced colloquial writing decades earlier than the Chinese people. This is one of the reasons why the development of modern literature in Taiwan is quite different from that in China.

Usually, the religious believers apply Pėh-ōe-jī writing to their daily life after they acquire the skill of Romanization. For example, they may use Pėh-ōe-jī as a skill of note taking or writing letters to their children or friends in addition to reading the Bible. Pėh-ōe-jī was widely used among the church people in Taiwan prior to the 1970s (Chiung 2012, 2013a). Among its users, women were the majority. Most of these women did not command any other form of literacy except Pėh-ōe-jī. Even today, there are still a few among the older generations, especially women, who read only Pėh-ōe-jī (Chiung 2012, 2013a).

Why did Pėh-ōe-jī declined severely in the 1970s? It is the consequence of the ROC colonialism. Because of the Nationalist leader Chiang kai-shek's defeat in China, Chiang decided to occupy Taiwan as a base from which to fight back and reclaim the Mainland. Consequently, Chiang's political regime Republic of China (R.O.C) resurrected in Taiwan and has remained since 1949. The ROC government adopted the Monolingual Mandarin Chinese policy forcing the people to learn Mandarin Chinese and to identify themselves as Chinese by using the national education system as a propagandistic tool. In consequence, language use shift toward Mandarin.

Although Pėh-ōe-jī was originally devised for religious purposes, it is no longer limited to religious applications after the contemporary Tâi-bûn movement rose in the late 1980s (Chiung 1999:42, 2005:40). Pėh-ōe-jī has been adopted by many Taiwanese promoters to write Taiwanese either in Roman-only or Han-Lo styles. For example, famous Taiwanese periodicals such as *Tôi-oân-jī (Taiwanese Scripts)*, *Tâi-bûn Thong-sìn (TBTS Newsletter)*, *Tâi-bûn Bóng Pò (Bong Newspaper)*, and *Hái-ang (Whale of Taiwanese Literature)* all adopt Pėh-ōe-jī as

---

[17] Some photos of these publications are available at
<http://www.de-han.org/pehoeji/ exhibits/index.htm>

the Romanization for writing Taiwanese. Moreover, academic Journal, such as *Journal of Taiwanese Vernacular* accepts Pėh-ōe-jī as an official writing. In addition, professional organizations such as Tâi-oân Lô-má-jī Hiåp-hōe (Taiwanese Romanization Association) was organized in August 2001 for the promotion of writing in fully Romanized Taiwanese [18] . Tâi-bûn Pit-hōe (Taiwanese Pen), the literary society of Taiwanese writers for the promotion of literary creations in Taiwanese vernacular, was established in 2009. The Center for Taiwanese Languages Testing at National Cheng Kung University was established in 2010[19]. In addition, professional conferences on Pėh-ōe-jī entitled "International Conference on Taiwanese Romanization" have been organized every two years since 2002. They all recognized Pėh-ōe-jī as the official orthography for Taiwanese.

In short, the Pėh-ōe-jī was the foundation of the Romanization of modern Taiwanese colloquial writing. Even though there were several different schemes of Romanization for writing Taiwanese, many of them were derived from Pėh-ōe-jī[20]. Pėh-ōe-jī and its derivatives are the most widely used Romanization even today.

4. Linguistic evaluation of the Pėh-ōe-jī

Smalley (1963:34-52) has proposed five criteria of an adequate writing system. We may examine the Pėh-ōe-jī writing system based on Smalley's criteria listed as follows: (in order of importance)

1. Maximum motivation for the learner, acceptance by its society, and controlling groups such as the government.
2. Maximum representation of speech.
3. Maximum ease of learning.
4. Maximum transfer.
5. Maximum ease of reproduction.

All the strengths and weaknesses of Pėh-ōe-jī come from its nature of phonemic writing. In terms of efficiency, the ease of learning to read and write Pėh-ōe-jī becomes a higher motivation than Hanji for its learners. In the former agricultural society, most people were peasants who labored in the fields all day long, and they had little interest in learning complicated Han characters. In

---

[18] TLH's official website at <http://www.tlh.org.tw/>
[19] CTLT's official website at < http://ctlt.twl.ncku.edu.tw/>For more information on the development of General Taiwanese Proficiency Test, please refer to Chiung (2011).
[20] For more information about different Romanized schemes, see Iûn 1999.

contrast to Han characters, the ease of learning Pèh-ōe-jī provides those farmers a good opportunity to acquire literacy. This is one of the reasons why there are a certain amount of people who do not command any abilities in Han characters besides Pèh-ōe-jī (Chiung 2012, 2013a). Although Pèh-ōe-jī has maximum motivation for individual learners, it may not have the same motivation for the Han dominated society and government. Chiung's (1999, 2001) empirical studies of 244 college students' attitudes toward various contemporary Taibun writing schemes have revealed the fact that Mandarin and Hanji educated college students tend to favor Han characters more than Roman scripts. As for the attitudes of the Chinese KMT government, Pèh-ōe-jī was not only excluded from the national education system, but was also restricted in its daily use. For instance, the romanized *Sin Iok* (New Testament) was once seized by KMT in 1975, because Hanji was considered the only national orthography, and romanization was regarded as a challenge to KMT's Chinese nationalism.

To have a maximum representation of speech usually requires a good linguistic analysis on the language before devising its orthography. Campbell's "*Ē-mn̂g Im Sin Jī-tián*" of 1913 has shown the achievement of missionaries' linguistic knowledge on Amoy or Taiwanese (Chiung 2003:109, 2013b). Campbell's choice of symbols for representing Taiwanese consonants and vowels are listed in Tables 1, 2, 3 and 4 based on their articulation manners and places. Tone marks are listed in Table 5. In Campbell's dictionary, he uses a total of 24 symbols to represent 23 Taiwanese phonemes (i.e. consonants and vowels), and those symbols consist of only 17 roman letters. Campbell's analysis and choice of symbols are pretty accurate and efficient at certain levels in terms of modern linguistics. For example, he primarily assigns a single letter (except /ch/) to a phoneme. The letters he assigned to sound segments are very close to the IPA system (International Phonetic Alphabet), which is adopted by many contemporary linguists for transcribing linguistic data. If it is difficult to avoid having two letters representing a phoneme, he tries to make the symbol easy and have rules to follow up. For example, 'h' indicates 'aspiration' when it is attached to p, t, k, or ch, and it represent glottal stop when it occurs in the final position of a syllable. Other than these two situations, 'h' refers to a glottal fricative sound.

Table 1. Symbols for Taiwanese consonants in Péh-ōe-jī.

		bi-labial	alveolar	velar
		-asp/+asp	-asp/+asp	-asp/+asp
voiceless	stop	p/ph	t / th	k/kh
voiced	stop	b		g
voiceless	C. fricative			h
voiceless	G. fricative		s	
voiceless	affricate		ch/chh	
voiced	affricate		j	
voiced	lateral		l	
voiced	nasal	m	n	ŋ

Table 2. Symbols for Taiwanese consonants in Péh-ōe-jī.

POJ	IPA	Conditions	Examples
b	/b/		bûn 'literary'
p	/p/		pí 'compare'
ph	/pʰ/		phoe 'letter'
l	[d]	Elsewhere	lí 'you'
	[l]	Followed by a	lâi 'come'
t	/t/		tê 'tea'
th	/tʰ/		thâi 'kill'
g	/g/		gí 'language'
k	/k/		ka 'plus'
kh	/kʰ/		kha 'foot'
h	[h]	Initial only	hí 'happy'
	[ʔ]	Coda only	ah 'duck'
s	/s/		sì 'four'
ch	/ts/		chi 'of'
chh	/tsʰ/		chha 'bad'
j	/dz/		jit 'sun'
m	[m]		mī 'noodles'
	[m̩]	Syllabic	m̄ 'no'
n	/n/		ni 'milk'
ng	[ŋ]		âng 'red'
	[ŋ̩]	Syllabic	n̂g 'yellow'

Table 3. Symbols for Taiwanese vowels in Pe̍h-ōe-jī

	front	central	back
high	i		u
mid	e	o	o·
low		a	

Table 4. Symbols for Taiwanese vowels in Pe̍h-ōe-jī

POJ	IPA	Conditions	examples
a	/a/		ta 'dry'
i	/i/		ti 'pig'
u	/u/		tú 'meet'
e	/e/		tê 'tea'
o·	/o/		o· 'black'
o	/ə/	Elsewhere	to 'knife' koh 'more'
	/o/	With any coda except h ([ʔ])	tong 'East' kok 'state'

Table 5. Tonal categories in Taiwanese

Categories	君 [kun] gentle	滾 [kun] boil	棍 [kun] Stick	骨 [kut] bone	裙 [kun] skirt	-	近 [kun] near	滑 [kut] glide
Numerical categories	1	2	3	4	5	6	7	8
Tone marks in Pe̍h-ōe-jī	unmarked	´	`	unmarked	∧		-	'
Pe̍h-ōe-jī samples	kun	kún	kùn	kut	kûn		kūn	ku̍t
Numerical tone values	44	53	31	3	12 or 213*		22	8
IPA tone values	⌐	⌐	⌐	·	⌐		⌐	'

*There are two varieties in Taiwanese tone 5: a low-rising tone with tone values 12, and a falling-rising tone with tone value 213 or 313. The younger generation are more likely to possess the falling-rising feature.

Overall, Campbell's choice of phonemic symbols is pretty good. The only controversial part is the alveolar voiceless affricate sounds. What Campbell distinguishes between 'ch' and 'ts' is actually 'phonetic' rather than 'phonemic' differences. In his orthography, 'ch' occurs if followed by a front vowel, and 'ts' occurs in any other situation. It is clear that 'ch' and 'ts' are in a complementary distribution. That is to say, he could choose either 'ch' or 'ts' to represent the phonetically different but phonemically identical segments.

In addition to the choice of phonemic symbols, the spelling in Campbell's dictionary is also pretty simple. His fundamental principle of spelling is to do phonemic transcriptions of spoken language. That is, to write down what you hear phonemically. His second principle is to treat Pe̍h-ōe-jī as an independent orthography once the spelling of words are confirmed, instead of a supplementary phonetic tool to the learning of Han characters. In Campbell's opinion, the spelling of the romanized Bible (1873) was considered the official orthography of Pe̍h-ōe-jī. Therefore, as Campbell described in the preface of his dictionary, "none of the current words whose spelling differ from that of the standard were taken in." He made efforts to maintain that existing Pe̍h-ōe-jī orthography. The issue of the spelling of Pe̍h-ōe-jī is still controversial among some of its users today. For example, people have tried to replace the existing forms such as 'ian,' 'oa,' and 'eng,' with 'en,' 'ua,' and 'ing.'

The spelling rules of Pe̍h-ōe-jī are pretty easy. In general, there is a one-to-one relationship between orthographic symbols and phonemes. After phonemes are represented, tone marks are imposed to the nuclei of syllables and a hyphen '-' is added between syllables, such as **ō-kóe-khiau** (芋粿曲 Taiwanese cake). Because Taiwanese is a tone language with rich tone sandhi, there can be several ways to represent tones. In the design of Pe̍h-ōe-jī, the base tone or underlying tone of each syllable is chosen and represented by its tone mark. For example, 'Taiwanese cake' must be represented by its underlying form **ō-kóe-khiau** rather than surface form **ò·-koe-khiau** (this is the form in actual pronunciation).

Although romanized Pe̍h-ōe-jī has the strengths of maximum representation and efficiency, many people suspect its capacity of being used as an independent orthography because they thought that romanization is too deficient to differentiate homophones. Such questions on the romanization of Asian languages have been raised for a long time since the nineteenth century in the Hanji cultural sphere (cf. DeFrancis 1990; Hannas 1997; Chen 1999). As matter of fact, romanization can differentiate homophonous morphemes as well as Han characters. It just depends on how the spelling of the romanization is devised in order to make semantic distinctions. For example, in English, see and sea are spelled in different ways to refer to different things with the identical pronunciation. To, too, and two is another example from English. As for Taiwanese, for example, *Kho-kun* (科根) is proposed by *Kheng-Chiu Tan* as a system to write Taiwanese. Basically, Tan defines 60 categories with 60 simple symbols to refer to different semantic categories of words. He adds a symbol to each romanized Taiwanese word, so readers can distinguish the different meaning from the same pronunciation of the words. Although adding rules or affixes to spelling may increase the capacity of differentiating homophones, it can also increase the degree of difficulty in spelling, and thus reduce the efficiency and ease of learning the romanization. To what extent these methods will be applied to a Romanized writing just depends on how the designers evaluate their costs and benefits.

Maximum of transfer is another virtue of Pėh-ōe-jī. Since Pėh-ōe-jī consists of roman letters, and roman script is the most widespread orthography (Zhou 1997:3) among the world's writing systems, Pėh-ōe-jī users will have a more knowledgeable approach to the orthographies of other Romanized languages such as English.

From the perspective of the reproduction of orthography, reproducing Romanized Pėh-ōe-jī is even easier and more efficient than Han characters (recalling that there are a total of 47,035 characters in the *Kangxi* Dictionary). Compared to the small amount of roman letters and diacritic marks in the Pėh-ōe-jī writing, Han characters are much more difficult to be reproduced such as in typographic composition (DeFrancis 1996:19-21). In the information age, although personal computers can easily reproduce Han characters, dealing with Han characters still involves more troubles than dealing with roman scripts, such as compatibility, OCR, and machine translation.

5. Conclusion

In 2003, The Convention for the Safeguarding of Intangible Cultural Heritage[21] was passed by the UNESCO General Conference. The definition of "intangible cultural heritage" was defined in article 1 of the convention, as follows:

The "intangible cultural heritage" means the practices, representations, expressions, knowledge, skills – as well as the instruments, objects, artifacts and cultural spaces associated therewith – that communities, groups and, in some

---

[21] The texts of convention are available at
<http://unesdoc.unesco.org/images/0013/001325/132540e.pdf>

cases, individuals recognize as part of their cultural heritage. This intangible cultural heritage, transmitted from generation to generation, is constantly recreated by communities and groups in response to their environment, their interaction with nature and their history, and provides them with a sense of identity and continuity, thus promoting respect for cultural diversity and human creativity.

The "intangible cultural heritage", was further manifested in article 1 in the following domains:

(a) oral traditions and expressions, including language as a vehicle of the intangible cultural heritage;

(b) performing arts;

(c) social practices, rituals and festive events;

(d) knowledge and practices concerning nature and the universe;

(e) traditional craftsmanship.

In accordance with the definition of The Convention for the Safeguarding of Intangible Cultural Heritage, Pe̍h-ōe-jī and the Taiwanese language are definitely qualified as intangible cultural heritage in Taiwan.

Today, there are twenty three million of populations in Taiwan. About 80% of them speak Taiwanese. However, the Taiwanese people are forced by the Chinese ROC government to be educated in Chinese rather than in Taiwanese. In accordance with the spirits of Universal Declaration of Linguistic Rights (1996), Convention for the Safeguarding of the Intangible Cultural Heritage (2003) and the Universal Declaration on Cultural Diversity (2001), Taiwanese language and Pe̍h-ōe-jī are not only the intangible cultural heritage for the Taiwanese people, but also for all human beings!

Acknowledgements

This is an updated revision of the article with same title originally published in Wi-vun CHIUNG 2016. *The Odyssey of Taiwanese Scripts*. Tainan: Taiwanese Romanization Association & National Museum of Taiwan Literature.

References

Ang, Ui-jin. 1992a. 台語文學與台語文字 [*Taiwanese Literature and Taiwanese Orthography*]. Taipei: Chian-ui.

Ang, Ui-jin. 1992b. 台灣語言問題 [*Taiwan's Language Problems*]. Taipei: Chian-ui.

Ang, Ui-jin. 1993a. 巴克禮《廈英大辭典補編》及杜典以後的辭字典簡介[Introduction to Barclay's supplement to Amoy-English dictionary, and other dictionaries afterward it]. In 閩南語經典辭書彙編 no.4 [*A Collection of Southern Min Classic Dictionaries*]. Vol.4, pp.10-25. Taipei: Woolin Press.

Ang, Ui-jin. 1993b. 杜嘉德《廈英大辭典》簡介[Introduction to Douglas' Amoy-English dictionary]. In 閩南語經典辭書彙編 no.4 [*A Collection of Southern Min Classic Dictionaries*]. Vol.4, pp.1-9. Taipei: Woolin Press.

Ang, Ui-jin. 1993c. 日據時代的辭書編纂[The compiling of dictionaries in Japanese occupied era]. In 閩南語經典辭書彙編 no.7 [*A Collection of Southern Min Classic Dictionaries*]. Vol.7, pp.1-26. Taipei: Woolin Press.

Ang, Ui-jin. 1993d.麥都思傳[Medhurst]. In 閩南語經典辭書彙編 no.3 [*A Collection of Southern Min Classic Dictionaries*].Vol.3, pp.9-41. Taipei: Woolin Press.

Ang, Ui-jin. 1993e.麥都思福建方言字典的價值[The value of Medhurst's Hokkien dictionary]. In 閩南語經典辭書彙編 no.3 [*A Collection of Southern Min Classic Dictionaries*]. Vol.3, 43-75. Taipei: Woolin Press.

Ang, Ui-jin. 1996. 台灣文獻書目題解:語言類 [*A list of Historical Materials: Language Category*]. Taipei: NCL-Taiwan.

Chan, Hui-chen. 1994. *Language Shift in Taiwan: Social and Political Determinants*. Ph.D. dissertation: Georgetown University.

Chang, Der-Ling. 2015. History of Taiwanese Roman Scripts POJ. *Journal of Taiwanese Vernacular* 7(2), pp. 4-29.

Chen, Ping. 1999. *Modern Chinese: History and Sociolinguistics*. Cambridge: Cambridge University Press.

Cheng, Robert L. 1990. 演變中的台灣社會語文 [*Essays on Taiwan's Sociolinguistic Problems*]. Taipei: Chu-lip.

Cheng, Robert L. 1996. 民主化政治目標與語言政策 [Democracy and language policy]. In Si, Cheng-hong. (ed), pp.21-50.

Cheng, Robert. L. and Cheng, Susie S. 1977. 台灣福建話的語音結構及標音法 [*Phonological Structure and Romanization of Taiwanese Hokkien*]. Taipei: Student Press.

Chiung, Wi-vun Taiffalo. 1999. *Language Attitudes toward Taibun, the Written Taiwanese*. MA thesis: The University of Texas at Arlington.

Chiung, Wi-vun Taiffalo. 2001. Language attitudes toward written Taiwanese. *Journal of Multilingual and Multicultural Development* 22(6), pp.502-523.

Chiung, Wi-vun Taiffalo. 2003. *Learning Efficiencies for Different Orthographies: A Comparative Study of Han Characters and Vietnamese Romanization*. PhD dissertation: The University of Texas at Arlington.

Chiung, Wi-vun Taiffalo. 2005. 語言認同與去殖民 [*Language, Identity and Decolonization*].

Tainan: National Cheng Kung University.

Chiung, Wi-vun Taiffalo. 2007a. Language, literacy, and nationalism: Taiwan's orthographic transition from the perspective of Han Sphere. *Journal of Multilingual and Multicultural Development* 28(2), pp.102-116.

Chiung, Wi-vun Taiffalo. 2007b. *Language, Literature, and Reimagined Taiwanese Nation*. Tainan: National Cheng Kung University.

Chiung, Wi-vun Taiffalo. 2011. *Tâi-gí Pe̍h-ōe-jī Bûn-ha̍k Soán-chip* [*Collection of Literary Works in Romanized Taiwanese*] Vol.1 of 5. Tainan: National Museum of Taiwan Literature.

Chiung, Wi-vun Taiffalo. 2012. 教會羅馬字調查研究計畫期末報告書 [*Final Report of the Project on Church Roman Scripts*]. Tainan: Tainan Municipal Administration of Cultural Heritage.

Chiung, Wi-vun Taiffalo. 2013a. A survey of Romanized Taiwanese Pe̍h-ōe-jī users and usages in Taiwan's church. *Journal of Taiwanese Vernacular* 5(1), pp.74-97.

Chiung, Wi-vun Taiffalo. 2013b. Missionary scripts in Vietnam and Taiwan. *Journal of Taiwanese Vernacular* 5(2), pp.94-123.

Chiung, Wi-vun Taiffalo. 2015 "Taiwanese or Southern Min? on the controversy of ethnolinguistic names in Taiwan," *Journal of Taiwanese Vernacular*, 7(1), pp.54-87.

Corcuff, Stephane. 2004. Fong He Rih Ruan: Taiwan Wayshenren yu Guojia Rentong de Jhuanbian [Changing Identities of the Mainlanders in Taiwan]. Taipei: Unsin.

DeFrancis, John. 1990. *The Chinese Language: Fact and Fantasy.* (Taiwan edition) Honolulu: University of Hawaii Press.

DeFrancis, John. 1996. How efficient is the Chinese writing system? *Visible Language* 30(1), pp.6-44.

Erbaugh, Mary. 1995. Southern Chinese dialects as a medium for reconciliation within Greater China. *Language in Society* 24, pp.79-94.

Hannas, William. C. 1997. *Asia's Orthographic Dilemma.* University of Hawaii Press.

Heylen, Ann. 2005. The legacy of literacy practices in colonial Taiwan. Japanese-Taiwanese-Chinese: language interaction and identity formation. *Journal of Multilingual & Multicultural Development* 26(6), pp.496-511.

Hodgkin, Thomas. 1981. *Vietnam: The Revolutionary Path.* London: The Macmillan Press Ltd.

Hsiau, A-chin. 1997. Language ideology in Taiwan: the KMT's language policy, the Tai-y language movement, and ethnic politics. *Journal of Multilingual and Multicultural Development* 18(4), pp.302-315.

Huang, Shuan Fan. 1993. 語言社會與族群意識 [*Language, Society, and Ethnic Identity*]. Taipei: Crane.

Iun, Un-gian. 2013. 台語語詞使用分析研究——以三本台語新約聖經做例 [Analysis of Taiwanese word usage: Using three Taiwanese New Testaments as examples]. *Journal of Taiwanese Vernacular* 6(1), pp.4-20.

Iwasaki, Keitarō [岩崎敬太郎]. 1913. 新撰日臺言語集 [*New Japanese-Taiwanese Conversions*]. Taipei: New Japanese-Taiwanese Conversions Publisher.

Kerr, George. H. 1992. 被出賣的台灣 [*Formosa Betrayed*]. (Chinese edition). Taipei: Chian-ui.

Klöter, Henning. 2005. *Written Taiwanese*. Wiesbaden: Otto Harrassowitz Verlag.

Lai, Young-hsiang. 1990. 教會史話 [*Topics on Taiwan Church History*]. Vol. 1. Tainan: Jin-kong Press.

Li, Heng-chhiong. (eds.). 1999. *Collection of Essays on Taigi Literature Movement* [台語文學運動論文集]. Taipei: Chian-ui.

Li, Lam-heng. 2010. 現代台灣基督徒 tiòh 讀《現代台語聖經》 [Modern Christians should read the Modern Taiwanese New Testament]. *New Messenger Magazine* no.119, pp.74-75.

Lim, Chun-iok. 2005. 台灣文化資產(一)—白話字紅皮聖經 [Taiwanese cultural heritage: the Taiwanese Red Cover Bible]. Tâi-gí Sìn-bōng-ài Bāng-chām at <http://taigi.fhl.net/classic/classic3.html>

Lim, Iong-bin. 1996. 台語文學運動史論 [*Essay on the Taigi Literature Movement*]. Taipei: Chian-ui.

Lu, Li-Jung. 1988. *A Study of Language Attitudes, Language Use and Ethnic Identity in Taiwan*. M.A. Thesis: Fu-jen Catholic University.

Ng, Ka-hui. 2000. *Literary works in the Pèh-ōe-jī Materials*. MA thesis: National University of Tainan.

Niu, Siok-hui. 2005. 當上帝開口說台語：台語新約聖經三種版本的比較 [While the God Speaks in Taiwanese: Comparisions and Contrasts of Three Taiwanese New Testaments]. Tainan: Jin-kong.

Niu, Siok-hui. 2013. 《聖經》「巴克禮譯本」對台灣社會 kap 語言 ê 貢獻 [The contribution of the "Amoy Romanized Bible" to the Taiwan society and language]. *Journal of Taiwanese Vernacular* 5(2), pp.76-93.

Ong Iok-tek. 1957. 台灣語常用語彙 [*The Basic Vocabulary of the Formosan Dialect*]. (Japanese edition). Tokyo: Eiwa Language Institution.

Ong Iok-tek. 1987. 台灣語音の歷史的研究 [*Historical Phonology of the Taiwanese Language*]. (Japanese edition). Tokyo: First Bookstore.

Ong Iok-tek. 1993a. 台灣話講座 [*Essay on the Taiwanese Language*]. Taipei: Independence Press.

Ong, Iok-tek. 1993b. 台灣:苦悶的歷史 [*Taiwan: A Depressed History*]. (Taiwan edition). Taipei: Independence Press.

Ông, Hú-chhiong. 1993. 省籍融合的本質 [The nature of assimilation between Taiwanese and Mainlanders]. In M. K. Chang (ed.) 族群關係與國家認同 [*Ethnic Relations and National Identity*]. pp. 53-100. Taipei: Iap-kiong.

Peng, M. M. and Ng, Y. C. 1995. 台灣在國際法上的地位 [*The Legal Status of Taiwan*]. Taipei: Taiwan Interminds Publishing Inc.

Si, Chun-chiu. 2015a. 台語作家著作目錄 [*Inventory of Taiwanese Writers' Literary Works*]. Tainan: National Museum of Taiwan Literature.

Si, Chun-chiu. 2015b. 台語文學發展年表 [*Timeline of Taiwanese Literature*]. Tainan: National Museum of Taiwan Literature.

Siau, Him-gi. 1981. 國共長期倡導台灣獨立的史實 [Historical facts on Chinese KMT and Communists' supports for Taiwanese independence]. *Taiwanese Independence Monthly*

No.110-112. Web resource at < http://www.wufi.org.tw/國共長期倡導台灣獨立的史實（上）> (2014/07/20)

Smalley, William. et al.1963. *Orthography Studies.* London: United Bible Societies.

Su, Beng. 1980. 台灣人四百年史 [*Taiwan's 400 Year History*]. (Chinese edition). San Jose: Paradise Culture Associates.

Tan, Bo͘-chin. 2007. 漢字之外：《台灣府城教會報》kap 台語白話字文獻中 ê 文明觀 [Beyond Han Characters: Viewpoints on Civilization Revealed from the Taiwan Prefectural City Church News and Other Taiwanese Pe̍h-ōe-jī Materials]. Tainan: Jin-kong.

Tiuⁿ, Chong-liong. 2014. 全然為台灣的聖經譯本 [The Bible for the Taiwanese]. *Lusoan Magazine* 410, pp.16-17.

Tiuⁿ, Hak-khiam. 1998. Writing in two scripts: a case study of digraphia in Taiwanese. *Written Language and Literacy* 1(2), pp.225-47.

Tiuⁿ, Ju-hong. 1996. 台灣現行語言政策動機的分析 [An analysis on the Taiwan's current language policy]. In Si, Cheng-hong. (ed.), pp.85-106.

Tiuⁿ, Ju-hong. 2015. 一寡有 400 kúi-chha̍p 年歷史 ê 台語白話字拼寫法 [A manuscripts written in Romanized Peh-oe-ji in the early seventeenth century]. *Journal of Taiwanese Vernacular* 7(2), pp.108-110.

Young, Russell. 1989. *Language Maintenance and Language Shift among the Chinese on Taiwan.* Taipei: Crane.

Zhou, Youguang. 1987. 世界字母簡史 [*A Brief History of World's Alphabets*]. Shanghai: Jiaoyu.

9

Taiwanese or Southern Min?
On the Controversy of Ethnolinguistic Names
in Taiwan

1. Introduction

Taiwan is a multilingual and multiethnic society. Traditionally, the people are divided into four primary ethnic groups: the indigenous (around 1.7% of Taiwan's population), Tâi-oân-lâng or Taiwanese (73.3%), Thòi-vân-ngìn or Hakka (12%) and post war Chinese immigrants[1] (13%) (Huang 1993:21). In addition, as international marriages have become more and more common in the globalization era, and Taiwan being no exception, foreign spouses in Taiwan numbered 539,090 as of August 2018, according to the statistics of Taiwan's National Immigration Agency, Ministry of Interior[2]. These foreign nationals account for 2.28% of Taiwan's total population.[3]

The speakers of Tâi-gí (台語 Taiwanese language) are traditionally and commonly called Tâi-oân-lâng (台灣人), literally 'the Taiwanese people.' Occasionally, they are called Hō-ló-lâng (or Hô-ló, Hok-ló, in different spellings) or Bân-lâm-lâng (閩南人 Southern Min people) by other ethnic groups. The language Tâi-gí is also occasionally called Hō-ló-ōe (福佬話) or Bân-lâm-ōe (閩南話 Southern Min language) in different contexts. Although the term 'Tâi-gí' has been used for more than one hundred years in society in Taiwan, it has not always

---

[1] Mainly the immigrants came to Taiwan with the Chiang Kai-shek's KMT regime after 1945.
[2] Data provided by Taiwan's National Immigration Agency available at
<https://www.immigration.gov.tw/ct.asp?xItem=1353426&ctNode=29699&mp=1>
[3] By September of year 2018, the amount of Taiwan's total population is 23,577,488 according to Taiwan's recent updated statistics of the Department of Household Registration of MOI, available at < https://www.ris.gov.tw/app/portal/346 >

been politically and officially approved by the government of Republic of China on Taiwan (ROC, thereafter). On the contrary, 'Southern Min' is officially adopted by the ROC to refer to Taiwanese.

'Min' comes from the abbreviation of Hokkien (福建) province of China. In addition, it is a pejorative name with the meaning 'barbarians with snake origin,' according to the famous Chinese classical dictionaries *Shuō Wén Jiě Zì* (說文解字 *Interpretation of Chinese Characters*) by Xǔ Shèn (許慎) and *Shuō Wén Jiě Zì Zhù* (說文解字注) by Duàn Yù Cái (段玉裁).

Because the Ma Ying-jeou regime of ROC still considers itself a Chinese regime rather than a native Taiwanese regime, Ma insists on using the term 'Southern Min' in order to make a connection to China. For example, the term 'Southern Min' was officially adopted in the "2008 Grade 1-9 Curriculum Guidelines" (97 年九年一貫課程綱要) by the ROC's Ministry of Education (thereafter MOE) in July 15, 2009. In response to MOE's discriminatory labeling for Taiwanese speaking people, around 40 Taiwanese organizations formed an alliance called 'Alliance against the Discrimination Term on Southern Min' (「反對閩南語歧視稱呼」正名聯盟) and demonstrated against MOE in July 29, 2009.

Another case occurred in 2013. Five Chinese KMT members of the Committee on Education and Culture of the ROC Legislative Yuan, Tēⁿ Thian-châi (鄭天財), Lí Tông-hô (李桐豪), Khóng Bûn-kiat (孔文吉), Chiúⁿ Nái-sin (蔣乃辛) and Tân Siok-hūi (陳淑慧), proposed to cut 10% of the promotional budget for exhibition for the National Museum of Taiwan Literature. Their major claim was that the term 'Taiwanese literature' (台語文學) was adopted in the exhibition entitled "Exhibition on Vernacular Literature in Native Languages of Taiwan." They demanded that the term 'Taiwanese' be replaced by Southern Min or Hō-ló-ōe.

The purpose of this paper is to survey the controversy over the term 'Tâi-gí' from the perspective of sociolinguistics and political science. Some historical background and current developments are surveyed. Solutions are also provided for readers' considerations.

2. The historical context of migration, indigenization and ethnic relations

Generally speaking, Taiwan was an indigenous society before Dutch occupation (1624-1661) in the early seventeenth century. There was only tribal awareness and no awareness of being "Taiwanese" at that time.

The aboriginal tribes, which belong to the Austronesian-Formosan language family, have been living in Taiwan for over a thousand years (cf. Lewis 2009). The classification of different tribes varies from scholar to scholar. Up to July 2014, the existing indigenous people are officially recognized as sixteen ethnic groups by the government of R.O.C. on Taiwan. Their ethnic names also vary from past to present. For example, 'Sėk-hoan' (熟番; 'cooked savages' or 'sinicized barbarians') or 'Chheⁿ-hoan' (生番; 'raw savages' or 'rude barbarians') were frequently used during the Chinese feudal period. Those pejorative names were later replaced by 'Takasago' (タカサゴ高砂族 [4]) during the Japanese rule. 'Takasago' was further replaced by 'Shānbāo' (山胞 mountain compatriots) by the Chinese ROC regime. The current official name 'Yuánzhùmín' (原住民 indigenous peoples) was not approved by the ROC until 1994.

The first half of the seventeenth century saw the fall of the Ming Empire (1368-1644) in China. The Qing Empire was then eventually established in China by the Manchurians. There were several remnant forces after the last Ming emperor was killed. The remnant forces spread out to different areas, such as Taiwan, Vietnam and other Southeast Asian areas. They tried to resist the military attacks of the Qing with the slogan "opposing Qing to restore Ming." This situation lasted for several decades after the fall of Ming.

Koxinga (國姓爺 or 鄭成功), leader of one of the remnants, brought 25,000 soldiers to Taiwan and drove away the Dutch, who were the colonizers of Taiwan at that time. The Koxinga Regime was then shortly established in Taiwan from 1662 to 1683 (Su 1980:102; Ong 1993b:56). The Koxinga regime was later defeated by the Qing armies. Consequently, Taiwan became the colony of Qing Empire from 1883 to 1895.

Among the soldiers of Koxinga, they mainly came from southern Hokkien and partly from eastern Canton (廣東). The language spoken by the people from southern Hokkien is the so-called 'Southern Min.' In fact, 'Southern Min' was not even a common term by its speakers at that time. A local prefecture or county name where the speaker lived was usually used by its speaker to refer to her/his vernacular. For example, the terms, such as Chiang-chiu (漳州), Choan-chiu (泉州), Amoy (廈門), and Formosan, were widely employed in dictionaries compiled by missionaries in the nineteenth and early twentieth centuries (see appendix I). The term 'Southern Min' was not even common until ROC's promotion of it in Taiwan after World War II.

The languages used by the people from northeastern and eastern Canton are

---

[4] A cognate name derived from an indigenous tribe in Kaohsiung.

Hakka (客家) and Tio-chiu (or spelled Teochew 潮州). Hakka means 'outsiders' or 'guests,' which was the name given by other neighboring ethnic groups during their continual immigrations in the history of the formation of Hakka (Lo 1933). In addition to Hakka, there are some other terms used to refer to Hakka in different areas and social contexts. For example, Hakka is also called Ngái or Hẹ in Vietnam. Nowadays, 'Hakka' is the official name approved by governments both in ROC and People's Republic of China (PRC). In addition to Hakka, the terms 'Thòi-vân-ngìn' or 'Theù-kâ-ngìn' or 'Ngìn' or 'Ngài' were recently coined to refer to 'Hakka people in Taiwan.'

Due to Qing's restrictions on migration, Hakka and Tio-chiu people are less numerous than the Hokkien during the process of migration to Taiwan. For example, right after Qing defeated Koxinga regime in 1683, the Qing announced such restrictions as "people who lived in Tio-chiu and Hui-chiu (Fuichiu 惠州) were not allowed to move to Taiwan, because those places were suspected of being the bases for pirates." Such restrictions on Hakka were continued until 1760 (Su 1980:129).

After the restrictions on migration were completely lifted by the Qing emperor, more and more Hokkien and Hakka people moved to Taiwan. Conflicts among the Hokkien, Hakka and aborigines frequently occurred in regard to disputes such as land and natural resources (Ong 1993b:84-87). As a result, some pejorative terms were coined by each ethnic group to refer to other groups. For example, 'hoan-á' (番仔 'barbarians' or 'savages') was used to refer to indigenous people by the Hokkien and Hakka; 'pailang' (白浪 or 歹人), which means 'bad guys' was coined by indigenous people in return to refer to the Hokkien and Hakka. 'Kheh-hiaⁿ-kong' (客兄公), which literally means 'Hakka adulterer' was used by Hokkien to refer to male Hakka speakers. In return, 'Hok-lo-ma' (福佬嫲 Hok-lo concubine) was created by Hakka to refer to the female Hokkien speakers.

The number of immigrants increased and soon became higher than the number of the indigenous people. The majority of the early immigrants who moved to Taiwan were male. Many of them intermarried with local indigenous women. The indigenous tribes that mainly resided in the western plain areas were more likely to come into contact with immigrants than tribes living in the mountains. They either were conquered by immigrants or intermarried with them (Su 1980).

There is an old Taiwanese saying reflecting this history of intermarriage: "ū Tn̂g-soaⁿ-kong, bô Tn̂g-soaⁿ-má" (有唐山公, 無唐山媽). Tn̂g-soaⁿ was the old-fashioned term widely used by these immigrants to refer to their homeland in

China. The saying literally means, "We have got a Mainland Grandpa, but no Mainland Grandma" (Kan 1995:152-162). Moreover, recent DNA studies by Doctor Lin Marie (2010) have revealed that the gene of Taiwanese people are much closer to People in Vietnam and Southeast Asia than those in China. It shows that although only 1.7% of the Taiwanese population are currently "pure" aborigines, as a matter of fact, most of the current Taiwanese population are partly descended from aboriginal stock (Brown 2004:149; Lin 2010). This phonomenoun is similiar to those cases such as Ming Huong people in Vietnam, and Baba Nyonya in Singapore and Malaysia.

In the early period of migration, most of those immigrants only intended to live in Taiwan provisionally, and they identified themselves with their original clans in southeast China (Tan 1994:140-141). However, during the course of indigenization, they moved from an immigrant society to a native society in the nineteenth century (Tan 1994:92). That means that the immigrants began to settle down and to distinguish themselves from the people who lived in China. For example, there was an old Taiwanese saying, "Tn̂g-soaⁿ-kheh, tùi-pòaⁿ soeh" (唐山客,對半說). Literally, it means that "you should discount the words of the guests from China." It advised that you should not believe the Chinese too much while you are doing business with them. This old saying also reveals that the indigenized immigrants had considered themselves as 'masters' rather than 'guests' in Taiwan, where they have been living for several generations. In short, the late nineteenth century saw the origin of a proto-Taiwanese nation, according to historian Su Beng (Su 1992:196-200).

In 1895, Taiwan and the Pescadore islands were transferred by the Qing emperor to Japanese emperor as a consequence of the Treaty of Shimonoseki, which ended the first Sino-Japanese War. The Japanese colonization (1895-1945) of Taiwan was the historical turning point in Taiwan in the transition from traditional Chinese feudal society to a modern capitalist society (Su 1992:205-215). Owing to modernization and capitalization during the Japanese rule, the earlier proto-Taiwanese identity advanced to Taiwanese nationhood (Su 1992:220). Those immigrant identities, once connected to the homeland of their ancestors such as 'Chiang-chiu people' and 'Choan-chiu people,' began to be replaced by a developing sense of being a 'Taiwanese people' in contrast to being a Japanese people. Thereafter, 'Taiwanese language' and 'Taiwanese people' were widely used by the people all over Taiwan.

The strong Taiwanese identity during the Japanese era could be well illustrated by the formation of political organizations, such as Sin Bîn Hoe (新民會 New People Association), established in 1920. Its organization guidelines mentioned: "To promote political reforms in Taiwan in order to improve the happiness of the Taiwanese people" (Ong 1988:44-49). Moreover, the declarations (1925) of the Tokyo Association of Taiwanese Academic Studies (東京台灣學術研究會), which was organized by some overseas Taiwanese students in Tokyo, included: (Ong 1988:91-92)

"To support the liberation of Taiwan!" (支持台灣的解放運動)

"To obtain the freedom to speak Taiwanese!" (獲得使用台灣話的自由)

"Taiwan independence forever and ever!" (台灣獨立萬歲)

In addition to the identity transition from seeing themselves as immigrants to seeing themselves as native Taiwanese, the linguistic genres of vernacular spoken by the immigrants also changed. For example, although Choan-chiu and Chiang-chiu were originally two major different varieties of Southern Min, they gradually merged and became a new "non-Chiang non-Choan" (不漳不泉) vernacular after they were brought to Taiwan (Iwasaki1913; Ong 1957:3-5, 1987:18-23; Ang1992a, 1992b:71) [5]. Moreover, they were greatly influenced by the languages of indigenous plain tribes, and particularly the Japanese language during the Japanese ruling period (Ong 1957:44-45). For instance, 'tá-káu' (former name of Kaohsiung city), 'Tâi-oân' (current name of Taiwan), 'má-se' (drunken) and 'Báng-kah' (a place name in Taipei) are cognates from Formosan Austronesian languages. In addition, 'chù-bûn' (ちゅうもん to order), 'sú-sih' (すし Japanese sushi),'se-bí-loh' (セビロ a suit), 'ò-bah' (オーバーan overcoat) are loanwords in Taiwanese coined from Japanese. In short, this new "non-Chiang non-Choan" language has been widely called 'Tâi-gí' or 'Tâi-oân-ōe,' which all mean the 'Taiwanese language' by the Taiwanese people since the early twentieth century.

3. Dictionaries, Bibles and literary works in Taiwanese

The Taiwanese language could be written in different orthographies. Currently, there are three major writing systems: 1) Roman-only, or exclusive use of Roman scripts, 2) Han characters only, which means exclusive use of Hanji, and 3) Han-Lo 'Hanji with Roman script,' which means a combination of Hanji with Roman scripts (Cheng 1990:219-237; Ong 1993a; Tiuⁿ 1998:230-241; Chiung 2001; Klöter 2005).

The Roman scheme for writing Taiwanese was mainly developed and

---

[5] There are some differences between Choan-chiu and Chiang-chiu, such as /koe/ vs. /ke/ to represent the same meaning of word 'chicken.'

contributed by Western missionaries in the nineteenth to early twentieth century (Klöter 2005:89). Called Pėh-ōe-jī, which means the scripts of vernacular speech in contrast to the complicated classical Han writing, it was introduced in Taiwan in the second half of the nineteenth century[6]. It is currently also called 'Tâi-oân-jī' or Taiwanese scripts. It made important impact in three significant aspects: 1) cultural enlightenment, 2) education for all people, and 3) literary creation in colloquial Taiwanese (Chiung 2011:ix, Chiung 2013b:111).

Those applications and publications of Pėh-ōe-jī since the nineteenth century can be summarized in the following six categories: 1) textbooks, 2) dictionaries, 3) religious literature, include in the translation of the Bible, catechisms, and religious tracts, 4) newspapers, 5) private note-taking or letters, and 6) other publications, such as physiology, math, and novels (Chiung 2005:36, 2012).[7]

Carstairs Douglas's *Chinese-English Dictionary of the Vernacular or Spoken Language of Amoy* of 1873 is regarded as an influential dictionary on the orthography of Pėh-ōe-jī [8]. After Douglas's dictionary, most Romanized dictionaries and publications followed his orthography with little or no changes (Ang 1993b:1-9, 1993a). George L. Macky's *Chinese Romanized Dictionary of the Formosan Vernacular*, which was considered the first dictionary to focus on vernacular spoken in Taiwan, was completed in 1874 and printed in 1891 in Shanghai. William Campbell's dictionary *Ē-mn̂g Im Sin Jī-tián* or *A Dictionary of the Amoy Vernacular Spoken Throughout the Prefectures of Chin-chiu, Chiang-chiu and Formosa,* firstly published in 1913 was the first Pėh-ōe-jī dictionary published in Taiwan[9]. It is the most widely used Romanized dictionary in Taiwan (Lai 1990; Ang 1996). This dictionary has been reprinted and renamed as *Kam Uî-lîm Tâi-gú Jī-tián* or *William Campbell's Taiwanese Dictionary* since 2009.

Generally speaking, missionaries' dictionaries were using Amoy vernacular as the criteria by the early twentieth century. Thereafter, the vernacular spoken in Taiwan gradually became the criteria. For example, *The Amoy-English Dictionary* and *English-Amoy Dictionary,* published by The Maryknoll Language Service Center in Taichung in 1976 and 1979, are two such dictionaries. Their vocabularies and pronunciation systems are mainly based on the local Taichung

---

[6] It was reported that the earliest development of Pėh-ōe-jī was contributed by the Spanish missionaries of Mania in the early 17th century (Klöter 2002 & 2004).

[7] Some publications may be available at the website of Memory of the Written Taiwanese, which was initiated by Iûⁿ Ún-giân. This site is located at <http://ip194097.ntcu.edu.tw/Memory/TGB>

[8] This dictionary was scanned and available at <http://ip194097.ntcu.edu.tw/memory/TGB>

[9] This dictionary was digitized and available at<http://taigi.fhl.net/dick>

vernacular even thought 'Amoy' was named. The publisher had to use 'Amoy' rather than 'Taiwanese' was due to the factor that Taiwan under R.O.C.'s martial law from 1949 to 1987. At a later time, they were republished as *Taiwanese-English Dictionary* in 2001 and *English-Taiwanese Dictionary* in 2013, respectively.[10]

In addition to missionaries' efforts, the Taiwan Governor-General's Office also published several dictionaries during the period of Japanese rule (Ang 1993c). For example, we have the *Japanese-Taiwanese Encyclopedic Dictionary* in 1907 and *Taiwanese-Japanese Encyclopedic Dictionary* in 1931 and 1932. Vocabularies based on Taiwanese were collected in those dictionaries and they were written in Hanji with revised Japanese Kana.[11]

Dictionaries compiled by individuals were mainly published after 1945 (see Appendix I). These could be divided into two periods: 1) the martial law period before 1987, and 2) after the martial law. Many more dictionaries were published after the martial law was lifted. In addition, the term 'Taiwanese' was adopted by almost all dictionary publishers, except the one published by R.O.C.'s National Translation and Compilation Center in 2001. In this case, 'Southern Min' was adopted to fit the political ideology of R.O.C.. On the contrary, dictionaries published during martial law period were much more limited in number. Moreover, more than half of them had to politically compromise with R.O.C. and use the name 'Southern Min.'

In addition to dictionaries, the Bible is regarded as an important medium for the standardization of written Taiwanese. There were two major contributors to the completion of the Taiwanese Romanized Bible: Dr. James L. Maxwell and Rev. Thomas Barclay. Dr. Maxwell was the first medical missionary to Taiwan in 1865. Under his supervision, *Lán ê Kiù-chúIa-so Ki-tok ê Sin-iok*, the first Romanized *Taiwanese New Testament* was published in 1873, and *Kū-iok ê SèngKeng*, the *Taiwanese Old Testament,* was published in 1884. They were both printed in the UK (Lai 1990). Their revised editions were completed by Rev. Barclay. The revised New Testament was published in 1916. Later, the Revised Old Testament along with the revised New Testament were collected together and published in 1933. The 1933 Barclay edition of the Bible is the most widespread Romanized Bible in Taiwan (Niu 2013). In short, the Taiwanese Bible of Barclay and Maxwell plays the same role as Martin Luther's translation of the Bible from

---

[10] These dictionaries are available at <http://www.taiwanesedictionary.org>

[11] *Taiwanese-Japanese Encyclopedic Dictionary* was digitized and supplemented with modern Taiwanese translations in Han-Roman style, available at <http://taigi.fhl.net/dict>

Latin into the German vernacular.

Amoy vernacular was regarded as the criteria for compiling the Bible by both Maxwell and Barclay. Thereafter, all editions of the Bible were translated in Taiwanese vernacular. For example, the *Ko-Tân edition of Colloquial Taiwanese New Testament*[12], which was mainly translated based on the vernacular spoken in the central Taiwan areas, was completed by the Maryknoll Society in 1972 (Niu 2005; Lim 2005). This Bible is also called 'Âng-phôe Sèng-keng' or 'Red Cover Bible' because of the color of its front cover. It was expected to fulfill the needs of modern Taiwanese speakers. Unfortunately, it was seized by the R.O.C. regime in 1975. It was later transcribed into Han-Lo version by Lîm Chùn-iòk and published by the Taiwan Church Press in 2005.[13]

Several revised or newly translated editions of the Bible in Taiwanese were published again after the martial law was lifted in Taiwan. During this period, the Taiwanese Bibles were published in three ways:1) Roman-only, 2) Han-only, and 3) Han-Lo hybrid. For example, *Hiān-tāi Tâi-gú Sin-iok Sèng-keng*, or The Today's Taiwanese New Testament, which was translated directly from Greek into Romanized Taiwanese mainly based on northern Taiwanese varieties, was published by the Bible Society in Taiwan in 2008 (Li 2010:74-75) [14]. It was later published again in the Han-Lo version in 2013 (Tiuⁿ 2014:16-17). Recently, *Choân-bîn Tâi-gí Sèng-keng* or The Common Taiwanese Bible, which was revised from 1933 Barclay's edition and transcribed into southern Taiwanese accents, was completed in 2013. It contains three versions:1) Roman-only, 2) Han-Lo, and 3) Han-Lo plus Ruby functions[15]. They are expected to be published in recent years. In addition to Roman-only and Han-Lo editions, Taiwanese Bible in Han characters "台語漢字本聖經" was published in 1996 for the first time. This Hanji edition was merely transcribed from Barclay's edition into Han characters.

In addition to dictionaries and the Bible, newspapers and other publications are also important in the promotion and standardization of written Taiwanese. The first modern newspaper *Tâi-oân-hú-siâⁿ Kàu-hōe-pò* (*Taiwan Prefectural City Church News*) was published monthly by Rev. Barclay in July 1885 (Tiuⁿ 2005; Tan 2007). This newspaper was published in Pèh-ōe-jī until March 1969. Thereafter, it was shifted to Mandarin Chinese under ROC's political pressure.

---

[12] Ko-Tân Tâi-oân Pèh-ōe Sèng-keng Èk-pún 高陳台灣白話聖經譯本.

[13] Its original texts are available at <http://taigi.fhl.net/list.html>, and sound archives are available at <http://bible.fhl.net/new/audio_hb.php?version=6>

[14] The Bible was copyrighted in 2007 and published in 2008. For the comparisons of different editions of Taiwanese Bible, readers may refer to Niu (2005) or Iuⁿ (2013).

[15] Three versions of Common Taiwanese Bible are available at <http://taigi.fhl.net/list.html>

In order to print Taiwanese Roman scripts, which contain some distinctive features and tone marks, a state-of-the-art printing machine was imported from Scotland in 1881.This printer was in operation from 1885 until 1960s. After the printer was imported, the first publishing house in Taiwan, known as Chū-tin-tông or Sin-lâu Bookstore, was established in Tainan by Rev. Barclay in 1884. It was later called Taiwan Church Press.

Although *Taiwan Prefectural City Church News* was a religious oriented newspaper, it also contained a variety of articles, such as aspects of literature, history, culture and science (Ng 2000; Chiung 2011). For example, a short story entitled as "Jit-pún ê koài-sū" (an oddity in Japan) and a travel note "Pak-káng Má ê sin-bûn"(news on the goddess Pak-kang Ma) were published in 1886.[16]

In addition to newspapers, there were some other publications, such as *Pit Soàn ê Chho͘ Hak* (Fundamental Mathematics) by *Ûi-lîm Gê* in 1897, *Lāi Gōa Kho Khàn-hō͘-hak* (The Principles and Practice of Nursing) by G. Gushue-Taylor in 1917, the novel *Chhut Sí-Sòaⁿ* (Line between Life and Death) by *Khe-phoàn Tēⁿ* in 1926, and the collection of commentaries *Chap-hāng Koán-kiàn* (Opinions on Ten Issues) by *Pôe-hóe Chhòa* in 1925.[17]

Due to the successful promotion of written Taiwanese in the second half of nineteenth century, it had contributed to the emergence of Taiwanese new literature, which was written in accordance with the Taiwanese colloquial vernacular rather than traditional classical Han writing (Chiung 2005:35). Comparing to the May Fourth New Culture Movement of 1919 in China, Taiwanese people had experienced colloquial writing decades earlier than the Chinese people. This is one of the reasons why the development of modern literature in Taiwan is quite different from China.

4. People's resistance to ROC's Chinese policy

Usually, the religious believers apply Peh-ōe-jī writing to their daily life after they acquire the skill of Romanization. For example, they may use Peh-ōe-jī as a tool for note taking or writing letters to their daughters, sons, or friends in addition to reading the Bible. Peh-ōe-jī was widely used among the church people in Taiwan prior to 1970s (Chiung 2012, 2013a). Among its users, women were the majority. Most of those women did not command any literacy except Peh-ōe-jī.

---

[16] Articles in this newspaper were digitized and researchable at
  <http://210.240.194.97/nmtl/dadwt/pbk.asp >
[17] Some photos of these publications are available at
  <http://www.de-han.org/pehoeji/exhibits/index.htm>

Today, there are still a few among the elder generations, especially women, who read only Pe̍h-ōe-jī.

Why did Pe̍h-ōe-jī declined severely in the 1970s? It is the consequence of the R.O.C. colonialism. From the political perspective of R.O.C., Mandarin Chinese in traditional Chinese characters was considered the only orthodox language. The Bible in Romanized Taiwanese was definitely regarded as a challenge to the Chinese regime, which is considered a foreign regime by many Taiwanese.

At the end of World War II, Chiang Kai-shek, the leader of the Chinese Nationalist (KMT) took over China (excluding Manchuria), Taiwan, and French Indo-China north of 16° north latitude on behalf of the Allied Powers under General Order No.1 of September 2, 1945 (Hodgkin 1981:288; Peng and Ng 1995:60-61; Chiung 2007:110-111, 2008). In accordance with this order, Chiang sent troops to Taiwan and Vietnam. After Japanese forces were disarmed, Chiang was requested by Ho Chi Minh and French power to withdraw his troops from Vietnam in 1946. However, Chiang's troops remained in Taiwan even though the well-known February 28 Revolution occurred in 1947 (Kerr 1992; Su 1980:749-801; Ong 1993b:157-162). Simultaneously, Chiang Kai-shek was fighting against the Chinese Communist Party in Mainland China.

In 1949, Chiang's troops were completely defeated and then pursued by the Chinese Communists. At that time, Taiwan's national status was supposed to be dealt with by a peace treaty among the nations at war. That is Treaty of Peace with Japan signed by 48 nations at a later time in San Francisco in September 1951. However, because of Chiang's defeat in China, Chiang decided to occupy Taiwan as a base and from there he would fight to recover the Mainland (Kerr 1992; Ong 1993b; Peng and Ng 1995; Su 1980). Consequently, Chiang's political regime Republic of China (R.O.C.) was renewed in Taiwan and has remained there since 1949.

Chiang claimed that Taiwan was a province of China, and R.O.C. was the only legitimate government of China even though the People's Republic of China (PRC) was established in Beijing by the Chinese Communist Party (CCP) in October 1949. Due to Chiang's control of Taiwan, his mortal enemy, the communist leader Mao Zedong, also claimed that Taiwan was a part of PRC. In fact, both KMT and CCP used to support Taiwan to become an independent state from the Japanese during the 1920s and 1930s (Siau 1981). Nevertheless, the current relation between Taiwan and China remains a political issue to solve. From the perspective of people in Taiwan, many public opinion polls done lately have shown that the majority of Taiwanese people are more likely to support

Taiwanese independence. For example, the polls conducted by Taiwan Thinktank in July 2014 revealed that 82.9% of the subjects agreed that Taiwan and China are two countries independent from each other.[18]

Monolingual Mandarin Chinese policy was adopted during R.O.C.'s occupation of Taiwan (Huang 1993; Heylen 2005). Taiwanese people were forced to learn Mandarin Chinese and to identify themselves as Chinese through the national education system (Cheng 1996; Tiuⁿ 1996; Hsiau 1997:307). Consequently, research has revealed that a language shift toward Mandarin is in progress (Lu 1988:73; Young 1989:55; Chan 1994:iii). In response to R.O.C.'s Chinese language policy, the promoters of Taiwanese have protested against the monolingual policy and have demanded vernacular education in schools. This is the so-called 'Tâi-bûn Ūn-tōng' or 'Taiwanese language movement' that has substantially grown since the second half of the 1980s (Hsiau 1997; Erbaugh 1995; Li 1999; Lim 1996; Chiung 1999, 2007; Klöter 2005).

Although Péh-ōe-jī was originally devised for religious purposes, it is no longer limited to religious applications after the contemporary Tâi-bûn movement was raised in the late 1980s (Chiung 1999:42, 2005:40). Péh-ōe-jī has been adopted by many Taiwanese promoters to write Taiwanese either in Roman-only or Han-Lo styles. For example, famous Taiwanese periodicals such as *Tôi-oân-jī (Taiwanese Scripts), Tâi-bûn Thong-sìn (TBTS Newsletter), Tâi-bûn Bóng Pò (Bong Newspaper)*, and *Hái-ang (Whale of Taiwanese Literature)* all adopt Péh-ōe-jī as the Romanization for writing Taiwanese. Moreover, academic Journal, such as *Journal of Taiwanese Vernacular* accepts Péh-ōe-jī as official writing. In addition, professional organizations such as Tâi-oân Lô-má-jī Hiáp-hōe (Taiwanese Romanization Association) was organized in August 2001 for the promotion of writing in fully Romanized Taiwanese [19]. Tâi-bûn Pit-hōe (Taiwanese Pen), the literary society of Taiwanese writers for the promotion of literary creations in Taiwanese vernacular was established in 2009. The Center for Taiwanese Languages Testing at National Cheng Kung University was established in 2010[20]. They all recognized Péh-ōe-jī as the official orthography for Taiwanese.

Under the pressure of the Taiwanese language movement, the ruling KMT regime had no choice but to open up some possibilities for vernacular education. Eventually, the president Lee Teng-hui, who is a native of Taiwan, approved the compromised proposal that elementary schools be allowed to have vernacular

---

[18] Press release available at Taiwan Thinktank <http://www.taiwanthinktank.org/>
[19] TLH's official website at <http://www.tlh.org.tw/>
[20] CTLT's official website at < http://ctlt.twl.ncku.edu.tw/>For more information on the development of General Taiwanese Proficiency Test, please refer to Chiung (2010a).

education starting in fall semester 2001. Prior to implementation of the vernacular education proposal, KMT lost its regime during the 2000 presidential election for the first time in Taiwan. Chen Shui-bian was elected president. Consequently, the Democratic Progressive Party (DPP) became the ruling party until 2008 when the KMT retrieved regime again.

This vernacular education proposal was thus conducted by the ruling DPP. A class called 'pún-thó͘ gí-giân'(native languages), with a period of 40 minutes per week, is required in all elementary schools from fall semester 2001. Schools may choose the vernacular languages to teach in accordance with the demands of their students. In the vernacular education, course titles were officially named 'Taiwan Southern Min Language,' 'Taiwan Hakka Language' and 'Formosan Austronesian languages' to refer to the languages taught in class. In addition to elementary schools, universities were encouraged to establish new departments of Taiwanese languages and literatures or relevant studies. About twenty some such departments or graduate institutes were therefore established by 2008. The National Museum of Taiwan Literature was also officially established in Tainan in 2003.

While people were feeling hopeful and confident about mother tongue education, Ma Ying-jeou, from the KMT, won the presidential election in 2008. Once KMT became the ruling party again, all native policies regarding Taiwanese languages and culture adopted by the DDP were gradually changed. For example, the budget for Taiwanese proficiency test was cut by KMT legislators in February 2009[21]. Also, 'Taiwan' was withdrawn by MOE from 'Taiwan Southern Min' of the "Grade 1-9 Curriculum Guidelines" in 2009. Moreover, private publishers such as King-an were later forced to replace 'Taiwanese' with 'Southern Min' on the title of Taiwanese textbooks for elementary students[22]. The major excuse of the MOE officials and KMT legislators was that the term 'Taiwanese' would mislead people into thinking that Hakka and indigenous Formosan languages were excluded from the list of native languages in Taiwan. It sounded like that they were calling for racial equality. In fact, they were oppressing the Taiwanese speaking people's growing awareness of their own identity and sowing seeds of discord among ethnic groups in Taiwan.

---

[21] Petition and press release are available at <http://www.tlh.org.tw/liansu.htm> Relevant news reports, available at <http://www.peopo.org/news/29178>,
<http://www.youtube.com/watch?v=pz1b6dWrpuE>, and
<http://news.ltn.com.tw/news/politics/paper/283646>

[22] The press releases against the policy are available at
<http://ungian.pixnet.net/blog/post/28744136>and <http://taigi.fhl.net/News/News41.html>

Because Ma Ying-jeou was regarded as a pro-China president by the Taiwanese people, these actions hostile toward Taiwanese were considered Ma's step toward de-Taiwanization (去台灣化). In response to MOE's racial discrimination against Taiwanese speaking people, around 40 Taiwanese organizations immediately formed an alliance called "Alliance against the Discrimination Term on Southern Min" (ADTSM) and protested against the MOE[23]. The organizations include Taiwanese Romanization Association, Haiang Taiwanese Association, Taiwan South Society, Taiwan Hakka Society, etc (Chiung 2010b).

The major arguments by the ADTSM are summarized, as follows:

First of all, 'Southern Min' contains the Chinese character 閩 'Min', which is an offensive and pejorative word. It means 'savages' or 'barbarians' according to Chinese classical dictionaries *Shuō Wén Jiě Zì* (說文解字) by Xǔ Shèn (許慎) and *Shuō Wén Jiě Zì Zhù* (說文解字注) by Duàn Yù Cái (段玉裁). It was the term used by the officials in northern China, where was the political center of ancient China. Although the term 'Min' have been used for a thousand years to refer to Hokkien, it does not mean that it is still appropriate today. In the Universal Declaration of Human Rights of UN of 1948 it was stated that all human beings are born free and equal in dignity and rights. How can we use such a pejorative and insulting term to refer to a modern people?

Secondly, 'Taiwanese' is the traditional term which has been used for more than one hundred years in society in Taiwan. It is used not only by the Taiwanese people, but also by the Chinese people in Taiwan. For example, Lian Heng (連橫), grandfather of KMT's former chairperson Lian Chian (連戰), published a book entitled as *Etymology of Taiwanese Language* (台灣語典) in 1933. In addition, a book entitled as *Taiwanese Dialect Symbols* (台語方音符號) was published by the Provincial Council for National Language Promotion in 1955. Also, *Taiwanese Conversions in Phonetic Symbols* (注音台語會話) was published by the Ministry of National Defense in 1958. They all used the term *Taiwanese* in these books. The term was not replaced by 'Southern Min' until the 1960s when the KMT tried to strengthen their assimilation policy. That is, force

---

[23] The videos on the protest are viewable with keyword '送蛇到教育部' (sent snakes to MOE) on Youtube, or at <http://www.youtube.com/watch?v=GdkkAobYkFQ>, <http://www.youtube.com/watch?v=yuWDOQqBIV4>, <http://www.youtube.com/watch?v=9D0EGCC4zHM> Their relevant news reports are available at <http://hongtintgb.pixnet.net/blog/post/277018-090729「反對閩南語歧視稱呼」新聞連結 2> and <https://groups.yahoo.com/neo/groups/nihonnokoe/conversations/messages/1555>

the Taiwanese people to identify themselves as Chinese rather than as Taiwanese.

To give readers a better idea of how different names are preferred and used in Taiwan, search results using Google Taiwan, dated on July 23, 2014, of different names (in Han characters) are provided in Table 1. It reveals that 台灣話 or Taiwanese Language was the most popular one with 20.6 million items found on Google. It was even higher than Chinese except Beijinghua in number. 台語 or Taiwanese was the second largest in number. 閩南語 or Southern Min is the fourth one and accounted only 1.1 million. This shows that Taiwanese language is the most favored name by the Taiwanese people.

Table 1. Searching results of different names by Google Taiwan (2014/7/23)

Names	台灣話 (Taiwanese1)	台語 (Taiwanese2)	鶴佬話 (Ho-lo1)	閩南語 (Southern Min)	河洛話 (Ho-lo2)	福佬話 (Ho-lo3)
Results	20,600,000	3,420,000	2,180,000	1,100,000	978,000	432,000

Name	北京話 (Beijinghua)	國語 (National Language)	華語 (Huayu)	漢語 (Hanyu)	普通話 (Putonghua)	中國話 (Zhongquahua)
Results	32,900,000	6,650,000	4,500,000	4,140,000	1,790,000	1,410,000

Thirdly, 'Taiwanese' is simply a proper noun rather than an abbreviation of "languages in Taiwan." ADTSM pointed out that Hakka, Formosan Austronesian languages and Taiwanese are all native languages in Taiwan. It does not necessarily mean that Taiwanese is the only native language in Taiwan as MOE officials and KMT legislators faulted. If their logic was correct, National Taiwan University (NTU) should be the first one to be renamed since there are around 160 universities in Taiwan. Why is NTU the only one using 'Taiwan'? In addition, aboriginal people such as 'Seedig' and 'Tao' should both be renamed because the terms all mean 'people' in their languages. How can they use the name 'people' since they are not the only people in Taiwan!?

Fourthly, there are also Hakka people living in the so-called 'Southern Min' areas, such as Chiau-an (詔安) and Lam-cheng (南靖) in southern Hokkien, China. In MOE officials' logic, the term 'Southern Min' should not be used either!

Fifthly, the so-called Southern Min language is not limited to the southern Hokkien areas, but is also spoken in the eastern part of Canton, especially in the areas of Tio Soaⁿ (潮汕) and Hai Liok Hong (海陸豐). Following the officials' logic, the term 'Southern Min' would exclude the speakers in eastern Canton.

The sixth reason is that, in practice, none of the Taiwanese promoters asserted that Hakka and Formosan Austronesian languages are not languages of Taiwan. For example, in the case of the National Museum of Taiwan Literature, Taiwanese as well as Hakka and Formosan Austronesian languages were all included in the Exhibition on Vernacular Literature in Native Languages of Taiwan. How could we say Taiwanese promoters were narrow-minded?

Seventhly, the right to use one's own name in one's own language is an important issue recognized by international organizations. For example, in the Universal Declaration of Linguistic Rights of 1996 is found the statement that "all language communities have the right to preserve and use their own system of proper names in all spheres and on all occasions," in article 31; and "all language communities have the right to refer to themselves by the name used in their own language. Any translation into other languages must avoid ambiguous or pejorative denominations", in article 33. The term 'Taiwanese' has been widely used for more than a hundred years in Taiwan. Therefore, R.O.C. regime should respect it.

5. Solutions and conclusion

A name referring to an ethnic group could be given by members of the group themselves, or by neighboring ethnic groups. In the past, the reference was more frequently given by other people. It would be acceptable if the name is a neutral term without any discriminatory intent. For example, the term 'Tâi-oân' was originally given by new settlers to refer to the tiny area of An-pêng, where the indigenous Siraya tribe resided (Ong 1993b:17). Later on it was expanded to refer to the whole territory of Taiwan, and the suffix 'lâng' (people) was added as 'Tâi-oân-lâng' to refer to the Taiwanese.

On the contrary, the ethnic name is neither appropriate nor acceptable if it contains pejorative denominations, such as 'hoan-á' and 'Min' as mentioned above. In this case, it is best to respect the way members of an ethnic group use "to refer to themselves by the name used in their own language" as declared in the Universal Declaration of Linguistic Rights.

In the case of 'Southern Min,' it is definitely not appropriate to be used any more since it contains a pejorative meaning. I propose that 'Lán-lâng-ōe' (咱人話) be used to refer to all language varieties spoken in southern Hokkien, eastern Canton, Taiwan, Malaysia, Singapore, Philippine, Vietnam, Thailand and other places, which were formerly considered as 'Southern Min' speaking areas. 'Lán-lâng' literally means 'our people' or 'we as human beings,' referring to the ethnic name. A suffix 'ōe' (language) is added as 'Lán-lâng-ōe' to refer to its language.

Actually, the term 'Lán-lâng-ōe'is not a brand new one but has been used by 'Hokkien' speakers in Philippine for a long time.

While 'Lán-lâng-ōe' is assigned to refer to the language family, particular local terms can also be given to its varieties in particular areas, as long as their speakers agree with the practice. For example, 'Tâi-gí'or 'Tâi-oân-ōe' (Taiwanese) is given to specify the varieties spoken in Taiwan, and 'Pin-siâⁿ-ōe' or 'Pinang-ōe'refer to the varieties spoken in Penang, Malaysia. Further, 'Tâi-gí-lâng' is given as an ethnic name to the speakers of Tâi-gí, and 'Pin-siâⁿ-lâng' to the speakers of Pin-siâⁿ-ōe.

Someone may suggest that 'Hô-ló,''Hō-ló' or 'Hok-ló' be used instead of Taiwanese. However, they cannot represent the characteristics of Taiwan. 'Hô-ló,''Hō-ló' and 'Hok-ló' are merely spellings of varieties spoken in different areas. In Taiwan, they were not widely and commonly known until the 1990s when the language revival movement became a hot issue. It was usually the name used by Hakka people to refer to Taiwanese speaking people. For those Taiwanese speakers who do not live near Hakka communities, they might have never heard this word. For example, the famous Taiwanese linguist Ông Iòk-tek (1924-1985), who was born in Tainan, had never heard of 'Hô-ló' until he went to university in Taipei in the 1940s (Ong 2002:185).

'Hô-ló' may be written in different Han characters and different scholars have interpreted as having different etymological meanings. However, there is no consensus yet. One assumption was 河洛 (Lim 1991:7-8), which means the plains between the Yellow River and the Lok River (洛水) in China. It was said that Hô-ló people were originally from these areas. The second assumption, raised by Ang Ui-jin (1987:148), asserted that the Han characters should be 貉獠, which was one tribe of the Hundred Yue (越族) in southeast China. Thirdly, Kho˙Kek-tun (1992:10-14) asserted that it might be 福佬, which means the people from Hokkien province.

According to *Taiwanese-Japanese Encyclopedic Dictionary* (Ogawa 1931:829), 'Hô-ló' and 福佬 were recorded and it means the 'pejorative' name given by the Cantonese to refer to people from Hokkien. In addition, missionaries Samuel Wells Williams (1874:ix) and Kennelly (1908:207) both pointed out that 'Hoklo' was the name referring to 'Swataw[24]' (汕頭) people by local Cantonese people. The name was later written in different varieties of Han characters, such as 學老,福猪, or 福佬. In Canton, in addition to Cantonese, there are also Hakka and the so-called 'Southern Min' speakers. Teochew (潮州) and Swataw speakers

---

[24] Original spelling by S. W. Williams (1874).

mainly reside in eastern part of Canton. They were traditionally considered as a branch of 'Southern Min' because they were descended from Chiang-chiu, Hokkien (Ong 1987:13-15).

All the facts have shown that Hakka people used to assign the name 'Hoklo' to 'Hokkien descendants in Canton.' Once the Hakka immigrated to Taiwan, they kept using the name to refer to Taiwanese speakers who were mainly descended from Hokkien. However, the population of Hakka accounts for only 12%, and they are limited to certain areas. Therefore, the name 'Hoklo' is not widely known by the Taiwanese speakers except those who have frequent contacts with Hakka.

In short, 'Taiwanese' is probably the best ethnolinguistic name to refer to the language spoken by Tâi-gí speakers in Taiwan. Further, 'Southern Min' should be replaced by 'Lán-lâng-ōe' from a broader perspective to refer to all speech varieties spoken in China, Taiwan, and Southeast Asian countries.

Acknowledgements

This paper was originally presented at the 16th North America Taiwan Studies Conference, June 18-20, 2010, UC Berkeley, USA. It was revised and published as the title "Taiwanese or Southern Min? on the controversy of ethnolinguistic names in Taiwan," Journal of Taiwanese Vernacular, 7(1), 54-87, in 2015. I am thankful for the comments and suggestions provided by the discussants and reviewers.

References

Ang, Ui-jin. 1987. 台灣河洛語聲調研究 [*The Tonal Studies of Taiwanese Ho-looe*]. Taipei: Independence Press.

Ang, Ui-jin. 1992a. 台語文學與台語文字 [*Taiwanese Literature and Taiwanese Orthography*]. Taipei: Chian-ui.

Ang, Ui-jin. 1992b. 台灣語言問題 [*Taiwan's Language Problems*]. Taipei: Chian-ui.

Ang, Ui-jin. 1993a. 巴克禮《廈英大辭典補編》及杜典以後的辭字典簡介 [Introduction to Barclay's supplement to Amoy-English dictionary, and other dictionaries afterward it]. In 閩南語經典辭書彙編 no.4 [*A Collection of Southern Min Classic Dictionaries*]. Vol.4, pp.10-25. Taipei: Woolin Press.

Ang, Ui-jin. 1993b. 杜嘉德《廈英大辭典》簡介 [Introduction to Douglas' Amoy-English dictionary]. In 閩南語經典辭書彙編 no.4 [*A Collection of Southern Min Classic Dictionaries*]. Vol.4, pp.1-9. Taipei: Woolin Press.

Ang, Ui-jin. 1993c. 日據時代的辭書編纂 [The compiling of dictionaries in Japanese occupied era]. In 閩南語經典辭書彙編 no.7 [*A Collection of Southern Min Classic Dictionaries*]. Vol.7, pp.1-26. Taipei: Woolin Press.

Ang, Ui-jin. 1996. 台灣文獻書目題解:語言類 [*A list of Historical Materials: Language Category*]. Taipei: NCL-Taiwan.

Brown, Melissa J. 2004. *Is Taiwan Chinese? The Impact of Culture, Power, and Migration on Changing Identities.* Berkeley: University of California Press.

Chan, Hui-chen. 1994. *Language Shift in Taiwan: Social and Political Determinants.* Ph.D. dissertation: Georgetown University.

Cheng, Robert L. 1990. 演變中的台灣社會語文 [*Essays on Taiwan's Sociolinguistic Problems*]. Taipei: Chu-lip.

Cheng, Robert L. 1996. 民主化政治目標與語言政策 [Democracy and language policy]. In Si, Cheng-hong. (ed), pp.21-50.

Chiung, Wi-vun Taiffalo. 1999. *Language Attitudes toward Taibun, the Written Taiwanese.* MA thesis: The University of Texas at Arlington.

Chiung, Wi-vun Taiffalo. 2001. Language attitudes toward written Taiwanese. *Journal of Multilingual and Multicultural Development* 22(6), pp.502-523.

Chiung, Wi-vun Taiffalo. 2005. 語言認同與去殖民 [*Language, Identity and Decolonization*]. Tainan: National Cheng Kung University.

Chiung, Wi-vun Taiffalo. 2007 Language, literacy, and nationalism: Taiwan's orthographic transition from the perspective of Han sphere. *Journal of Multilingual and Multicultural Development* 28(2), pp.102-116.

Chiung, Wi-vun Taiffalo. 2008. 1945 年蔣介石軍隊代表聯軍同時佔領台灣 kap 北越 [Taiwan and northern Vietnam were occupied by Chiang's troops in 1945]. *The Taiwan Fokways* 58(3), pp.9-15.

Chiung, Wi-vun Taiffalo. 2010a. Development of the Taiwanese Proficiency Test. *Journal of Taiwanese Vernacular* 2(2), pp.82-103.

Chiung, Wi-vun Taiffalo. 2010b. Politics and Ethnicity Names: A Case Study on Southern Min

People in Taiwan. 16th North America Taiwan Studies Conference, June 18-20, UC Berkeley.

Chiung, Wi-vun Taiffalo. 2011. *Tâi-gí Pe̍h-ōe-jī Bûn-ha̍k Soán-chip* [*Collection of Literary Works in Romanized Taiwanese*] Vol.1 of 5. Tainan: National Museum of Taiwan Literature.

Chiung, Wi-vun Taiffalo. 2012. 教會羅馬字調查研究計畫期末報告書 [*Final Report of the Project on Church Roman Scripts*]. Tainan: Tainan Municipal Administration of Cultural Heritage.

Chiung, Wi-vun Taiffalo. 2013a. A survey of Romanized Taiwanese Peh-oe-ji users and usages in Taiwan's church. *Journal of Taiwanese Vernacular* 5(1), pp.74-97.

Chiung, Wi-vun Taiffalo. 2013b. Missionary scripts in Vietnam and Taiwan. *Journal of Taiwanese Vernacular* 5(2), pp.94-123.

Erbaugh, Mary. 1995. Southern Chinese dialects as a medium for reconciliation within Greater China. *Language in Society* 24, pp.79-94.

Heylen, Ann. 2005. The legacy of literacy practices in colonial Taiwan. Japanese-Taiwanese-Chinese: language interaction and identity formation. *Journal of Multilingual & Multicultural Development* 26(6), pp.496-511.

Hodgkin, Thomas. 1981. *Vietnam: The Revolutionary Path*. London: The Macmillan Press Ltd.

Hsiau, A-chin. 1997. Language ideology in Taiwan: the KMT's language policy, the Tai-y language movement, and ethnic politics. *Journal of Multilingual and Multicultural Development* 18(4), pp.302-315.

Huang, Shuan Fan. 1993. 語言社會與族群意識 [*Language, Society, and Ethnic Identity*]. Taipei: Crane.

Iuⁿ, Un-gian. 2013. 台語語詞使用分析研究——以三本台語新約聖經做例 [Analysis of Taiwanese word usage: using three Taiwanese New Testaments as examples]. *Journal of Taiwanese Vernacular* 6(1), pp.4-20.

Iwasaki, Keitarō [岩崎敬太郎]. 1913. 新撰日臺言語集 [*New Japanese-Taiwanese Conversions*]. Taipei: New Japanese-Taiwanese Conversions Publisher.

Kan, Keng-jin. 1995. 台灣開發與族群 [*Cultivation and Ethnic Groups in Taiwan*]. Taipei: Chian-ui Press.

Kennelly, M. 1908. *Comprehensive geography of the Chinese Empire and dependencies*. Shanghai: T'usewei Press.

Kerr, George. H. 1992. 被出賣的台灣 [*Formosa Betrayed*]. (Chinese edition). Taipei: Chian-ui.

Kho͘, Kek-tun. 1992. 台灣語概論 [*An Introduction to Taiwanese language*]. Kaoshiung: First Press.

Klöter, Henning. 2002. The history of Peh-oe-ji. Paper presented at the 2002 International Conference on Taiwanese Romanization. Taitung: National Taitung Teachers College.

Klöter, Henning. 2004. Early Spanish romanization systems for Southern Min. Paper presented at the International Conference on Taiwanese Romanization. Tainan: National Cheng Kung University & National Museum of Taiwanese Literature.

Klöter, Henning. 2005. *Written Taiwanese*. Wiesbaden: Otto Harrassowitz Verlag.

Lai, Young-hsiang. 1990. 教會史話 [*Topics on Taiwan Church History*]. Vol. 1. Tainan: Jin-kong Press.

Lewis, Paul M. 2009. *Ethnologue: Languages of the World*. (16th edition). Dallas: SIL International. Online version available at <http://www.ethnologue.com/>

Li, Heng-chhiong. (eds.). 1999. *Collection of Essays on Taigi Literature Movement* [台語文學運動論文集]. Taipei: Chian-ui.

Li, Khin-hoann. 1996. 語言政策及台灣獨立 [Language policy and Taiwan independence]. In Si, Cheng-hong. (ed.), pp.113-134. Taipei: Chian-ui.

Li, Lam-heng. 2010. 現代台灣基督徒 tio̍h 讀《現代台語聖經》[Modern Christians should read the Modern Taiwanese New Testament]. *New Messenger Magazine* no.119, pp.74-75.

Lim, Chai-hok. 1991. 閩南人 [*Min-nan People*]. Taipei: San-min Bookstore.

Lim, Chun-iok. 2005. 台灣文化資產(一)—白話字紅皮聖經 [Taiwanese cultural heritage: the Taiwanese Red Cover Bible]. Tâi-gí Sìn-bōng-ài Bāng-chām at <http://taigi.fhl.net/classic/classic3.html>

Lim, Chun-iok. 2013. 人人愛讀 ê《全民台語聖經》[Ererybody's Common Taiwanese Bible]. *New Messanger Magazine* no.137, pp. 74-75.

Lim, Iong-bin. 1996. 台語文學運動史論 [*Essay on the Taigi Literature Movement*]. Taipei: Chian-ui.

Lin, Marie. 2010. 我們流著不同的血液：台灣各族群身世之謎 [*We Are Not of the Same Blood: Myth of the Ethnic Groups in Taiwan*]. Taipei: Chian-ui.

Lo, Hsiang-lin. 1933. 客家研究導論 [*An Introduction to the Study of the Hakkas in Its Ethnic, Historical, and Cultural Aspects*]. (Taiwan edition 1992). Taipei: SMC Publishing Inc.

Lu, Li-Jung. 1988. *A Study of Language Attitudes, Language Use and Ethnic Identity in Taiwan*. M.A. Thesis: Fu-jen Catholic University.

Ng, Ka-hui. 2000. *Literary works in the Peh-oe-ji Materials*. MA thesis: National University of Tainan.

Niu, Siok-hui. 2005. 當上帝開口說台語：台語新約聖經三種版本的比較 [*While the God Speaks in Taiwanese: Comparisions and Contrasts of Three Taiwanese New Testaments*]. Tainan: Jin-kong.

Niu, Siok-hui. 2013. 《聖經》「巴克禮譯本」對台灣社會 kap 語言 ê 貢獻 [The contribution of the "Amoy Romanized Bible" to the Taiwan society and language]. *Journal of Taiwanese Vernacular* 5(2), pp.76-93.

Ogawa, Naoyoshi [小川尚義]. 1931. 臺日大辭典(上) [*Taiwanese-Japanese Encyclopedic Dictionary*]. Taipei: Taiwan Governor-General's Office.

Ong Iok-tek. 1957. 台湾語常用語彙 [*The Basic Vocabulary of the Formosan Dialect*]. (Japanese edition). Tokyo: Eiwa Language Institution.

Ong Iok-tek. 1987. 台湾語音の歴史的研究 [*Historical Phonology of the Taiwanese Language*]. (Japanese edition). Tokyo: First Bookstore.

Ong Iok-tek. 1993a. 台灣話講座 [*Essay on the Taiwanese Language*]. Taipei: Independence Press.

Ong, Iok-tek. 1993b. 台灣:苦悶的歷史 [*Taiwan: A Depressed History*]. (Taiwan edition). Taipei: Independence Press.

Ong, Iok-tek. 2002. 落入漢字的陷阱：「福佬」、「河洛」的語源之爭[Do not be trapped by

Han characters: on the controversy of Hoklo and Holo]. In 王育德全集 2：台灣語研究卷 [*Collection of Ong Iok-tek's Works (2)*], pp.185-207. Taipei: Chian-ui.

Ong, Si-long. 1988. 台灣社會運動史 [*A History of Taiwanese Social Movement*]. Taipei: Tiu-hiong Press.

Peng, M. M. and Ng, Y. C. 1995. 台灣在國際法上的地位 [*The Legal Status of Taiwan*]. Taipei: Taiwan Interminds Publishing Inc.

Si, Cheng-hong. (ed.). 1996. 語言政治與政策 [*Linguistic Politics and Policy*]. Taipei: Chian-ui.

Siau, Him-gi. 1981. 國共長期倡導台灣獨立的史實 [Historical facts on Chinese KMT and Communists' supports for Taiwanese independence]. *Taiwanese Independence Monthly* no.110-112. Web resource at < http://www.wufi.org.tw/國共長期倡導台灣獨立的史實（上）/> (2014/07/20)

Su, Beng. 1980. 台灣人四百年史 [*Taiwan's 400 Year History*]. (Chinese edition). San Jose: Paradise Culture Associates.

Su, Beng. 1992. 民族形成與台灣民族 [*The Forming of a Nation and the Taiwanese Nation*]. Published by the author.

Tan, Bo-chin. 2007. 漢字之外：《台灣府城教會報》kap 台語白話字文獻中 ê 文明觀 [*Beyond Han Characters: Viewpoints on Civilization Revealed from the Taiwan Prefectural City Church News and Other Taiwanese Peh-oe-ji Materials*]. Tainan: Jin-kong.

Tan, Ki-lam. 1994. 台灣的傳統中國社會 [*The Traditional Chinese Society of Taiwan*]. (2nd edition). Taipei: Un-sin Press.

Tiuⁿ, Biau-koan. 2005. 開啟心眼：《台灣府城教會報》與長老教會的基督徒教育 [*Open Your Minds: Christian education of the Taiwan Prefectural City Church News and the Presbyterian Church in Taiwan*].Tainan: Jin-kong.

Tiuⁿ, Chong-liong. 2014. 全然為台灣的聖經譯本 [The Bible for the Taiwanese]. *Lusoan Magazine* no.410, pp.16-17.

Tiuⁿ, Hak-khiam. 1998. Writing in two scripts: a case study of digraphia in Taiwanese. *Written Language and Literacy* 1(2), pp.225-47.

Tiuⁿ, Ju-hong. 1996. 台灣現行語言政策動機的分析 [An analysis on the Taiwan's current language policy]. In Si, Cheng-hong. (ed.), pp.85-106.

Young, Russell. 1989. *Language Maintenance and Language Shift among the Chinese on Taiwan*. Taipei: Crane.

Appendix I: Dictionaries relevant to Taiwanese.

Year published	Titles	Editors	LG written	Given names	Places	publishers
1837	Dictionary of the Hok-keen Dialect of the Chinese Languages, According to the Reading and Colloquial Idioms (福建方言字典)	W. H. Medhurst (麥都思)	閩南語、英語	福建話	澳門	Honorable East India Company (英國東印度公司)
1838	A vocabulary of the Hok-keen Dialect as spoken in the county of Tsheang-tshew (漳州語彙)	S. Dyer	漳州話、英語	福建漳州話	Malacca	Anglo-Chinese College Press
1853	Anglo-Chinese Manual with Romanized Colloquial in the Amoy Dialect (翻譯英華廈腔語彙)	Elihu Doty (羅啻)	廈門話、英語	廈門話	廣州	S. Wells Williams
1866	A Vocabulary of the Hokkien Dialect, as Spoken at Amoy and Singapore	J.A. Winn	閩南語、英語	福建話	新加坡	
1873	Chinese-English Dictionary of the Vernacular or Spoken Language of Amoy (廈英大辭典)	Carstairs Douglas (杜嘉德)	廈門話、英語	廈門話	倫敦	Missionary of the Presbyterian Church in England
1874	A Syllabic Dictionary of the Chinese Language; Arranged According to the Wu-Fang Yuen Yin, with the Pronunciations of Peking, Canton, Amoy, and Shanghai (漢英韻府)	S.W. Williams (衛三畏)	北京話、廣東話、廈門話、上海話	廈門話	上海	上海長老教會
1882	Chineesch-Hollandsh Voordenbook van het Emoi Dialect (廈荷辭典)	J.J.C Franken & C.F.M. de Grijs	廈門話、荷蘭話	廈門話	Bata-via	Landsdrukkerij
1882-1890	Nederlandsch-Chineesch Woorden Book Met de Transcriptie der Chineesche Karaters in het Tsiang-tsiu Dialect (荷華文語類參)	Gustave. Schlegel	漳州話、荷蘭話	漳州話	荷蘭 Leiden	E.J.Brill
1883	English and Chinese Dictionary of the Amoy Dialect (英廈辭典)	John Macgowan	英語、廈門話	廈門話	倫敦	Fruber & Co
1874 完成 1891 出版	Chinese Romanized Dictionary of the Formosan Vernacular (中西字典)	George L. Makay (馬偕)	廈門話、英語	Formosan	上海	台北耶穌聖教會
1894	Ē-mn̂g-im ê jī-tián (廈門音 ê 字典)	John Talmange (打馬字)	廈門話	廈門話	廈門	鼓浪嶼萃經堂
1898	日臺小字典	上田萬年、小川尚義	台語、日語	台灣語	台北	總督府
1900	Diccinario Tonico Sino-Espanol, Del Dialecto de Emoy, Chiang-chiu, Choan-chiu Formosa	R.P.Fr. Ramon Colomer	閩南語、西班牙語	Formosa	廈門	鼓浪嶼萃經堂

1904	日臺新辭典	杉房之助	台語、日語	台灣語	台北	日本物產合資會社
1907	日臺大辭典	小川尚義	台語、日語	台灣語	台北	總督府
1908	日臺小辭典	小川尚義	台語、日語	台灣語	東京	大日本圖書株式會社
1913	廈門音新字典 (A Dictionary of the Amoy Vernacular Spoken Throughout the Prefectures of Chin-chiu Chiang-chiu and Formosa (Taiwan))	William Campbell (甘為霖)	閩南語、英語	Formosa	台南	台灣教會公報社
1923	Supplement to Dictionary of the Vernecular or Spoken Language of Amoy (廈英大辭典補編)	Thomas Barclay (巴克禮)	閩南語、英語	廈門話	上海	台南長老教會
1931	臺日新辭書	東方孝義	台語、日語	台灣語	台北	總督府
1931-1932	臺日大辭典(上)(下)	小川尚義	台語、日語	台灣語	台北	總督府
1932	臺日小辭典	小川尚義	台語、日語	台灣語	台北	總督府
1938	新訂日臺大辭典(上)	小川尚義	台語、日語	台灣語	台北	總督府
1946	國臺音萬字典	二樹庵、詹鎮卿	華語、台語	臺語	嘉義	蘭記
1954	增補彙音寶鑑	沈富進	台語	台語	斗六	文藝學社
1957	臺灣語常用語彙	王育德	台語、日語	台灣語	東京	永和語學社
1957	台灣語典	連橫	台語、文言	台灣語	台北	中華叢書編審委員會
1969	閩南語國語對照常用辭典	蔡培火	閩南語、華語	閩南語	台北	正中
1970	漢英台灣方言辭典	陳嘉德	台語、英語	台灣方言	臺北	南天
1971	A Dictionary of Southern Min	Bernard L.M. Embree	台語、英語	閩南語		
1976	中國閩南語英語字典 (Amoy-English Dictionary)	The Maryknoll Language Service Center	台語、英語	閩南語	台中	The Maryknoll Language Service Center
1979	英廈辭典(English-Amoy Dictionary)	The Maryknoll Language Service Center	英語、台語	閩南語	台中	The Maryknoll Language Service Center
1980	臺語辭典	徐金松	台語	臺語	台北	南天
1981	現代閩南語辭典	村上嘉英	閩南語、日語	閩南語	日本	天理大學
1984	普通話閩南方言詞典	黃典誠 etc	普通話、閩南語	閩南語	廈門	廈門大學
1986	綜合閩南方言基本字典	吳守禮	閩南語、華語	閩南語	台北	文史哲
1986	台灣禮俗語典	洪惟仁	台語、	台語、	台北	自立

			華語	閩南語、鶴佬語		
1991	簡明台語字典	林央敏	台語	台語	台北	前衛
1991	台灣話大詞典	陳修	台語、華語	台灣話	台北	遠流
1992	台語大字典	魏南安	台語、華語	台語	台北	自立晚報
1991	國台音彙音寶典	陳成福	華語、台語	台語	台南	西北
1992	常用漢字臺語詞典	許極燉	台語	臺語	台北	自立晚報
1992	台灣漢語辭典	許成章	臺語、華語	漢語	台北	自立晚報
1992	國台雙語辭典	楊青矗	台語、華語	台語	台北	敦理
1994	分類臺語小辭典	胡鑫麟	台語	臺語	台北	自立晚報
1994	實用臺語小字典	胡鑫麟	台語	臺語	台北	自立晚報
1995	蘭記臺語字典	二樹庵、詹鎮卿	華語、台語	臺語	嘉義	蘭記
1996	實用華語臺語對照典	邱文錫、陳憲國	華語、台語	臺語	台北	樟樹
1997	台語語彙辭典	楊青矗	台語、華語	台語	台北	敦理
1997	台灣俗諺語典	陳主顯	台語、華語	台語	台北	前衛
1998	台華字典	陳慶洲、陳宇勳	台語、華語	台語	台北	陳慶洲
1998	福全台諺語典	徐福全	台語、華語	台語	台北	徐福全
1998	常用漢字台語詞典	許極燉	台語、華語	台語	台北	前衛
1999	實用臺灣諺語典	陳憲國、邱文錫	台語、華語	台語	台北	樟樹
2000	台語字彙	王王辰	台語、華語	台語	台北	萬人
2000	國臺對照活用辭典	吳守禮	華語、台語	台語	台北	遠流
2001	台灣閩南語辭典	國立編譯館	閩南語、華語	台灣閩南語	台北	五南
2001	台語俗語辭典	楊青矗	台語、華語	台語	台北	敦理
2001	Taiwanese-English Dictionary	The Maryknoll Language Service Center	台語、華語、英語	台語	台中	The Maryknoll Language Service Center
2002	新編華台語對照典	邱文錫、陳憲國	華語、台語	台語	台北	樟樹
2002	普實台華詞典	邱豔菱、莊勝雄	台語、華語	台語	台中	台灣語文研究社
2002	台灣彙音字典	謝達鈿	台語、華語	台語	台中	謝達鈿
2003	台語實用字典	董峰政	台語	台語	台南	百合文化
2003	通用台語字典	吳崑松	台語、	台語	台北	南天

			華語			
2004	新編台日大辭典	王順隆	台語、日語	台語	台北	王順隆
2004	國語台語對比辭典	陳成福	華語、台語	台語	台南	建利書局
2005	台語音外來語辭典	張光裕	台語、華語	台語	台中	雙語
2005	國語臺語綜合字典	陳成福	華語、台語	台語	台南	大正書局
2007	東方台湾語辞典	村上嘉英	台語、日語	台湾語	東京	東方書店
2007	重編新訂日台大辭典上卷	王順隆	日語、台語	台語	台北	王順隆
2007	高階標準臺語字典	陳冠學	台語、華語	台語	台北	前衛
2009	甘為霖台語字典 Kam Uî-lîm Tâi-gú Jī-tián (William Campbell's Taiwanese Dictionary)	William Campbell (甘為霖)	台語、閩南語、英語	台語	台南	台灣教會公報社
2009	台語白話小詞典	張裕宏	台語、華語	台語	台南	亞細亞國際傳播社
2009	福爾摩莎語言文化詞典	張宏宇	台語、華語、英語	台語	台北	文鶴
2011	全民台語認證語詞分級寶典	蔣為文	台語、華語	台語	台南	亞細亞國際傳播社
2011	實用台語詞典	盧廣誠	台語、華語	台語	台北	文水藝文
2012	精解台語漢字詞典	王華南	台語、華語	台語	台北	文水藝文
2013	English- Taiwanese Dictionary	The Maryknoll Language Service Center	英語、台語、華語	台語	台中	The Maryknoll Language Service Center

*This inventory was updated by Wi-vu Taiffalo Chiung with some references from Ang (1996) (2014/7/27 updated).

Major Han characters with English translation:

福建話 Hokkien language

閩南話 Southern Min

漳州 Chiang-chiu

泉州 Choan-chiu

廈門 Amoy

台語/臺語/台湾語/台灣話 Taiwanese

華語 Mandarin Chinese

鶴佬 Ho-lo, Hoklo

英語 English

日語 Japanese

10

Language Attitudes
toward Written Taiwanese

1. Introduction

Digraphia, as parallel to Ferguson's (1959) idea of diglossia, has been defined by Dale (1980:5) as "the use of two (or more) writing systems for representing a single language," or by DeFrancis (1984:59) as "the use of two or more different systems of writing the same language." This is currently the situation in Taiwan, where the Taiwanese language is written in several different ways.

Cheng (1990:219-237) and Tiu[n] (1998:230-241) have pointed out that there are currently three main writing systems for writing Taiwanese. They are: (1) Han character only, which means exclusive use of Hanji, (2) Han-Lo 'Hanji with Roman script,' which means a combination of Hanji with Roman script, and (3) Roman-only, or 'exclusive use of Roman script.' Therefore, the situation of writing in Taiwanese is clearly a case of digraphia. That is, Taiwanese speakers speak in Taiwanese, but write in Hanji, Roman script, or a mixture of Hanji and Roman.

Taiwan is a multilingual and multiethnic society. There are more than twenty native languages in Taiwan, including Hakfa, Taiwanese[1], and indigenous languages (Grimes, 1996). In addition, Taiwan has been colonized by several foreign regimes since the seventeenth century. The most recent of these are the

---

[1] Taiwanese is also called Taigi (台語), Tai-yu, Holooe, Southern Min, or Min-nan. The broad definition of Taiwanese languages include all the indigenous languages, Hakfa, and Taigi. Occasionally, Taiwanese refers to Taigi only.

Japanese regime (1895-1945) and the Chinese KMT[2] regime (1945-2000[3]). According to colonial language policies (Li 1996), the native languages were prohibited in the public domain, and Japanese and Mandarin Chinese were adopted as the only official languages in each colonial period. As a consequence, the native languages in Taiwan are today declining.

Whether vernacular speech eventually will completely shift to Mandarin or be maintained depends largely on language attitudes. In other words, people's language attitudes play an important role in Taiwan's language future. However, research on language attitudes in Taiwan is rather scanty. Most research, such as Lu (1988), Feifel (1994), and Wang (1995), focus on spoken Taiwanese, not on written Taiwanese.

The purpose of the present study is to examine readers' responses toward different writing systems of *Taibun* (台文) or written Taiwanese. The subjects of this investigation were 244 students of Tamkang University and Tamsui College in Taiwan. Seven reading samples with different writing systems were prepared and subjects were asked to evaluate the characteristics of each sample. The main research questions are: 1) Does a rater evaluate each of the reading samples differently? If so, what factors influence a rater's judgment? 2) Do the raters' own characteristics, such as gender, residence, academic major, national identity and language ability, have effects on their evaluations? In other words, what particular groups of people tend to accept written Taiwanese, and what writing systems do they prefer?

---

[2] KMT or the Chinese Nationalist Party, was formerly a political party in Mainland China prior to 1949. In 1945 KMT took over Taiwan on behalf of Allied Powers after Japan had surrendered. In 1949, the troops of the KMT were completely defeated by the Chinese Communist Party in Mainland China, so the KMT decided to continue to occupy Taiwan as a base to fight against Chinese communist in order to go back to China. Lee Teng-hui, the former KMT chair and Taiwan's president (1988-2000) revealed in 1994 that "the KMT is also a foreign regime. It is necessary to reform it to become a KMT of the Taiwanese" during an interview with a Japanese writer Shiba Ryotaro (The *Independence Weekly Post* 1994:issue 258). Thus, the KMT was considered a foreign regime in this paper.

[3] KMT has been the alien ruling party since 1945 until 2000, in which year the presidential candidate Shui-bian Chen of Democratic Progressive Party, the native opposition party, was elected as the new president of Taiwan.

2. Background

There are currently four primary ethnic groups in Taiwan: indigenous (1.7%), Hakka[4] (12%), Taigi[5] (73.3%), and Mainlanders[6] (13%) (Huang, 1993:21). Due to the Chinese KMT's monolingual policy, the Taiwanese people are not allowed to speak their vernaculars in public. Moreover, they are forced to learn Mandarin Chinese and to identify themselves as Chinese through the national education system. As Hsiau (1997:307) has pointed out, "the usage of Mandarin as a national language becomes a testimony of the Chineseness of the KMT state;" that is, the Chinese KMT regime is trying to convert the Taiwanese into Chinese through Mandarin monolingualism. Consequently, most Taiwanese people are bilingual with their vernacular and the official language. Moreover, research such as Chan (1994) and Young (1989) has revealed that a language shift toward Mandarin is in progress. Huang (1993:160) goes so far as to suggest that the indigenous languages of Taiwan are all endangered.

Owing to the monolingual policy, the decline of vernacular languages in Taiwan has in recent years become increasingly pronounced and apparent. In response, people in Taiwan have protested against the monolingual policy, and have demanded bilingual education in schools[7]. This is the so-called Taiwanese language movement (*Taigibun Untong*) that has arisen since the second half of the 1980s (Hsiau 1997; Erbaugh 1995; Huang 1993). There are two core issues for the Taiwanese language movement. First, the movement wishes to promote spoken Taiwanese in order to maintain people's vernacular speech. Second, the movement aims to promote and standardize written Taiwanese in order to develop Taiwanese (vernacular) literature. Because written Taiwanese is not well

---

[4] Hakka is the name of the ethnic group; Hakfa or Hakka refer to the mother tongue of people of Hakka ethnicity.

[5] Tai-gi-lang (台語人) or Tai-oan-lang (台灣人) is the name of the ethnic group; Taigi refers to the mother tongue of Tai-gi-lang ethnicity.

[6] Mainlanders refer to the immigrants who came to Taiwan with the KMT in the 1940s. Mandarin is regarded as the mother tongue or lingua franca among Mainlanders.

[7] There are several organizations devoted to the vernacular education and standardization of written Taiwanese, such as *Tai-Bun Thong-Sin-Sia* (Taiwanese Writing Forum), *Tai-bun Bong-po-sia* (Taiwanese Language Magazine), *Tai-oan Gi-bun Hak-hoe* (Association of Taiwanese Languages), *Tai-gi-sia* (Taiwanese Language Society), *Hak-seng Tai-oan Gi-bun Chhiok-chin-hoe* (Students Taiwanese Promotion Association), *Tai-gi-bun Thui-tian Hiap-hoe* (Taiwanese Development Association). They claim the right to use Taiwanese in public places and in the mass media, as well as the right for younger generations to participate in vernacular education. In addition, they advocate writing in Taiwanese languages. They hold workshops and Taigi camps, and they have issued several periodicals such as *Tai-Bun Thong-Sin*, *Tai-bun Bong-po*, *Ia-cheng*, and *Ga-dang*.

standardized and not taught through the national education system, Taiwanese speakers have to write in Modern Written Chinese (MWC) instead of Written Taiwanese (WT). In other words, the written language of the Taiwanese people is separated from their daily colloquial speech; people speak in Taiwanese, but write in MWC. Although more than a hundred orthographies have been proposed by different persons enthusiastic for the standardization of Taibun, most of the designs have probably been accepted and used only by their own designers. Moreover, many of the designs were never applied to practical Taibun writing after they were devised.

These orthographic designs may be divided into two groups based on their graphic construction: Han character script and non-Han character script. Non-Han characters may be further subdivided into two types: New phonetic script, such as *Ganbun* designed by Ui-jin Ang, or ready-made phonetic script, which makes use of the present Roman alphabets or *Bopomo* (ㄅㄆㄇ) to write Taibun. Even if designers use the identical Roman alphabets, they may have different spelling systems, such as *Peh-oe-ji*, *Dai-im*, TLPA, *PS daibuun* and *Kho-kun*.

Because of the wide use of the personal computer and electronic networks in Taiwan since the 1990s, most orthographic designs, which require extra technical support other than regular Mandarin software, are unable to survive. Therefore, the majority of recent Taiwanese writing systems are either in Han characters, Roman alphabet or a mixed system combing Roman and Han.

Taiwanese writing in Hanji-only can be regarded as the High language in digraphia, which is often employed in official situations such as in government documents[8], the imperial examination system (prior to the 20th century), and traditional temples. Han characters have been used in Han cultural areas such as Taiwan, Japan, Korea, Vietnam and China for more than two thousand years. Writing in Hanji can be divided into two styles based on its historical background: First, there is the so-called "*wenyen*" or classical Han writing prior to the 20th century. This old writing style was not based on colloquial speech, but in a specific classical writing style. Second, there is the "*baihua*" or contemporary vernacular writing in the 20th century. Because writing in classical Han was very difficult to learn and comprehend, the issue of writing in colloquial speech was raised at the end of the 19th century, and became widely accepted by the public in the 20th century (cf. Chen 1996, 1994, 1993; DeFrancis 1990; Norman 1988; Tsao 1999).

Although colloquial writing has been available for a century in the Han

---

[8] Prior to the Japanese regime (1895-1945), government documents were written in classical Han writing.

cultural areas, some languages, such as Taiwanese and Cantonese which are not recognized by their governments as official languages, do not fare very well in their colloquial writing. Writing in Taiwanese or Cantonese is neither widespread nor standardized. Moreover, under the situation of nonstandardization, the usage of Han characters may vary from user to user. That is to say, different writers could choose different characters to represent the same word. For example, some Taiwanese lexical items cannot be expressed well in Han characters. According to Cheng (1989: 332), approximately 5% of the Taiwanese morphemes have no appropriate Han characters, and they account for as much as 15% of the total number of characters in a written Taiwanese text. Those 15% purely Taiwanese words are most likely to be written in different Han characters by different writers. Han-Roman mixed writing is proposed by some promoters to solve this problem. That is, Roman script should be adopted for the lexical items which do not have appropriate Han characters, and Han characters should be used elsewhere.

Taiwanese writing in Roman script can be regarded as the Low language in digraphia. The traditional Romanization for Taiwanese is the so-called "*Peh-oe-ji*," which was developed by missionaries in the second half of the 19th century (Chiung 2000, 2001; Tiuⁿ 2001). Peh-oe-ji is used mostly by church people, especially those who were not educated in Japanese or Mandarin Chinese. Peh-oe-ji is often employed in church worship, private letters, and note taking among the people who do not know Han characters.

The main reason for using Romanization is because of its economy and learnability compared to Han characters, which may require several years to learn to read and write. For instance, a total of 47,035 different Han characters were collected in the *Kangxi* Dictionary (1716). However, an ordinary literate Chinese person knows and uses somewhere between 3,000 and 4,000 Han characters (Norman 1988:72-73). An elementary school student in Taiwan may know around 2,669 characters[9] after sixth grade. As Chen has pointed out, the use of traditional Han characters is "to a large extent responsible for the country's high illiteracy and low efficiency, and hence an impediment to the process of modernization" (Chen 1994:367).

However, although Romanization is much more efficient than Han characters, Romanization is not widely accepted by people in Taiwan. Writing in Roman script is regarded as the Low language in digraphia. There are several

---

[9] According to the latest (1995) elementary textbooks compiled by the National Institute for Compilation and Translation, the number of Han characters learned by students at each grade is 328 for first grade, 479 for second grade, 455 for third grade, 529 for fourth grade, 493 for fifth grade, and 385 for sixth grade.

reasons for this phenomenon:

First, people's preference for Han characters is caused by their internalized socialization. Because Han characters have been adopted as the official orthography for two thousand years, being able to master Han characters well is a symbol of scholarship in the Han cultural areas. Writing in scripts other than Han characters may be regarded as childish writing. For example, when *Tai-oan-hu-sia^n Kau-hoe-po*, the first Taiwanese newspaper in Romanization, was published in 1885, the editor and publisher Rev. Thomas Barclay exhorted readers of the newspaper not to "look down at Peh-pe-ji; do not regard it as a childish writing" (Barclay 1885).

Second, misunderstanding of the nature and function of Han characters has enforced people's preference for Han characters. Many people believe that Han characters are ideally suited for the Han language family, which includes the Taiwanese language; they believe that Taiwanese cannot be expressed well without Han characters because Han characters are logographs and each character expresses a distinctive semantic function. In addition, many people believe Lian Heng's (1987) claim that "there are no Taiwanese words which do not have corresponding characters." However, DeFrancis (1996:40) has pointed out that Han characters are "primarily sound-based and only secondarily semantically oriented." In DeFrancis' opinion, it is a myth to regard Han characters as logographic. He even concludes that "the inefficiency of the system stems precisely from its clumsy method of sound representation and the added complication of an even more clumsy system of semantic determinatives" (DeFrancis 1996:40). If Han characters are logographs, the process involved in reading them should be different from phonological or phonetic writings. However, research conducted by Tzeng et al. has pointed out that "the phonological effect in the reading of the Chinese characters is real and its nature seems to be similar to that generated in an alphabetic script" (Tzeng et al. 1992:128). Their research reveals that the reading process of Han characters is similar to that for phonetic writing. In short, there is no evidence to support the view that the Han characters are logographs.

The third reason that Peh-oe-ji is not widespread in Taiwan is because of political factors. Symbolically, Han characters are regarded as a symbol of Chinese culture by Taiwan's ruling Chinese KMT regime. Writing in scripts other than Han characters is forbidden because it is perceived as a challenge to Chinese culture and Chinese nationalism. For example, the Romanized New Testament "*Sin Iok*" was once seized in 1975 because the Romanization Peh-oe-ji was regarded as a challenge to the orthodox status of Han characters.

Since writing in Taiwanese is currently in a chaotic situation, what are readers' reactions to different Taiwanese orthographies? Do they prefer a particular orthography? And what are their attitudes toward Taiwanese writing in general? The investigation described below attempts to answer these questions.

3. Methodology

The matched-guise technique, which was first developed by Lambert (Lambert et al. 1960, 1975; Lambert 1967) and his associates, is often adopted for research in language attitudes toward spoken language. However, research in attitudes toward written language vs. spoken language is quite different. Thus, Lambert's matched-guise technique was modified here in order to meet the needs of research on written Taiwanese.

The modified matched-guise for the present research was conducted as follows: seven reading samples (or writing samples) written in different orthographies of *Taibun* were prepared and the subjects were told to rate each reading on six characteristic scales such as interesting, expressive and friendly (see Appendix B). The ratings were based on semantic differential scales, ranging from the lowest 1 to the highest 7. For example, with respect to the characteristic "interesting," 1 means very boring, 4 means neutral, and 7 means very interesting.

The reading samples were adopted from published articles, and they were revised in orthography to varying degrees to fit our survey needs. The texts of all the reading samples were written in the same narrative style, talking about traditional life in the countryside of Taiwan. The purpose of choosing reading samples that are written in the same style is to minimize the influence of contents on readers. Accordingly, it is assumed that different contents do not substantially affect readers' evaluations. The scores of the reading samples as rated by readers could thus be assumed to reflect the readers' responses to different orthographies. The score is treated as a "reading index" which shows a reader's degree of favor toward a particular reading sample (i.e., toward a particular orthography).

In addition to the modified matched-guise, readers' backgrounds were collected through a questionnaire design. Additional self-reported information including political leanings, national identity, mother tongue, and language ability were also requested. The principal goals were to examine how readers' backgrounds may affect their evaluations on reading samples, and to further formulate an equation for predicting scores of reading samples rated by different subjects. This equation is called the Taibun equation; it predicts and indicates readers' degrees of acceptance of various orthographic designs.

3.1. Selection of reading samples

In this research design, there are seven reading samples, named A, B, C, D, E, F, and G (see Appendix A). All were written in Taiwanese (Taigi) except for reading D which was in Hakfa and reading G which was intermediate between Taiwanese and Mandarin. The following are brief descriptions of the different orthographies used:

(1) Han Characters Only: this was used in readings C and G. Reading C was entirely written in colloquial Taiwanese. However, reading G was intermediate between Taiwanese and Mandarin. The style of G is quite similar to the writing style of so-called *Hiong-thou Bun-hak* (Home Village Literature), used since the 1970s. (2) Roman Script Only: Reading B was completely written in *Peh-oe-ji*, the traditional Taiwanese Romanization. (3) Mixed Han and Roman writing: This is used in readings A, D (in Hakfa), and F. Reading A used more Roman script than D and F did. Generally speaking, the spelling of Roman scripts here is the same as Peh-oe-ji, but without tone marks. (4) Han with *bo-po-mo*: Reading E was written in Han characters with bo-po-mo, the National Phonetic Symbols, a special phonetic system used for learning Mandarin in Taiwan.

In order to gain a better understanding of the reading samples, we may analyze the seven readings according to six distinctive features based on orthography and language used in the texts: Han characters, Roman script, Bopomo, Mandarin Chinese, Hakka, and the Ratio of Han to Roman script, as shown in table 1.

The properties of the distinctive features are binary, either "+," which means "yes," or "-," meaning "no." Each reading sample can be analyzed as consisting of six features; the combinations of features differ from reading to reading.

The Han feature refers to whether or not Han characters are employed in the writings. The Roman and Bopomo features indicate whether or not Roman script and Bopomo phonetic symbols are employed in the writing. If Han and Roman are both used (Mixed style) in readings, we need another distinctive feature, the ratio of words in Han characters to words in Roman script, to distinguish between the two mixed writings. The Ratio feature is described as "+" if the proportion of Han characters in the text is greater than half. On the other hand, the Ratio feature is described as "-" if the proportion of Han is less than half. In the reading samples, the proportions of Han characters in readings A and B are less than 50%, so A and B are described as [-Ratio], and the others are [+Ratio].

The Mandarin feature indicates whether or not a reading was written with a grammar and lexicon close to Mandarin Chinese. The Hakka feature indicates whether a reading was written in Hakka or not.

3.2. Selection of raters

The subjects in my survey were limited to the college students from *Tamkang* University and *Tamsui* Oxford University College[10], both of which are located in *Tamsui*, a college town half an hour away from Taipei by bus.

A total of 244 students participated in my survey, 157 female and 87 male. 138 are from Taipei, and 106 are from other places. Because college major was hypothesized to be a factor that could influence readers' evaluations on Taibun writing, the subjects were primarily chosen based on their majors. Most of the subjects were from Tamkang University, and their majors were: Public Administration (46 students), Mechanical Engineering (34), Japanese (21), Chinese (52), English (37), and others (14). Owing to the fact that there is no Taiwanese department at Tamkang University, the students (40) of the Taiwanese Literature Department at Tamsui College[11] were chosen.

3.3. Procedure for conducting the research

The survey was conducted in December of 1998. Several classes offered by the departments were borrowed to conduct the survey. In the classes, students were told to evaluate the reading samples based on their first impressions. During the survey, they were not allowed to discuss the questions with each other. Their answers were directly marked on the questionnaire sheets. The purpose of the study, and the languages used in the readings, were not revealed until the students had all handed in their questionnaire sheets. The classes did not take a break until all students had finished the survey.

3.4. Data analysis

Several statistical techniques were employed to analyze the research results. They are the t-test, ANOVA (analysis of variance), post hoc comparison, factor analysis, chi-square test, and regression analysis. The significance level was set at 5% to reject the null hypothesis. The software programs adopted for managing the data and conducting statistical analyses were Microsoft Excel 97 and SPSS 8.0.

---

[10] It was renamed Aletheia University in August 1999.

[11] Up to now (1999), Tamsui College is still the only school in Taiwan that offers a Taiwanese major.

4. Results and discussion

4.1. Evaluations of the six characteristic scales

Raters rated six characteristic scales for each reading sample. Because we need to use these six characteristic scales as criteria to measure raters' preferences for each reading, it would be better if we could reduce these six scales to fewer categories. To do so, factor analysis was employed using SPSS. The analysis reveals that only one component was extracted from the six scales, and that component accounts for 78.31% of the total variance. This means that we may conclude that there is only one primary factor among the six characteristic scales. In other words, we may employ the combined mean value of the six characteristic scales as an index of a rater on a particular reading sample, instead of using all six individual characteristic values, yielding seven indexes for each rater, one for each reading sample A, B, C, D, E, F, and G. If a rater has an index 5 on reading A, and an index 3 on reading B, it means that the rater evaluates reading A higher than reading B. This index will be called the "reading index." The notion of "reading index" will be used for further comparisons throughout the research.

4.2. Different readings show different scores

The results of the one-way ANOVA, reveal that there are significant differences among the seven reading samples at the 5% significance level. In order to specify which pairs of readings are significantly different, paired t-tests were conducted using SPSS. The results show that all pairs (except E-F) are significantly different at the 5% significance level (see Table 1 for the mean score received by each reading sample, ordered from lowest to highest). In other words, we may treat reading E and F as if they have the same rating, while all other readings differ significantly from each other. (The results of post-hoc comparisons presented in the following section also reveal that raters evaluated the readings as being significantly different).

Table 1. Mean score received by each reading sample

mean	2.11	3.61	4.42	4.98	5.07	5.28	6.02
	B	A	D	E	F	C	G
Han	-	+	+	+	+	+	+
Roman	+	+	+	-	+	-	-
Bopomo	-	-	-	+	-	-	-
Mandarin	-	-	-	-	-	-	+
Hakka	-	-	+	-	-	-	-
Ratio	-	-	+	+	+	+	+

Based on the statistical results, we can determine the influence of each distinctive feature on the reading. First of all, a reading categorized as [+Han] is evaluated higher than a reading that is [-Han]. For example, there is only one different feature between reading A and B, that is, the Han feature. Given that the evaluations of A and B are significantly different, we may assume that the difference of rating between A and B is affected by the Han feature. Since A has a higher rating than B does, we can conclude further that a reading with [+Han] will be evaluated higher than the other. Second, a reading that is [+Roman] is evaluated lower than a reading that is [-Roman]. A reading that is [+Bopomo] is rated lower than a reading with [-Bopomo]. A reading that is [+Mandarin] is evaluated higher than a reading that is [-Mandarin]. A reading that is [+Hakka] is evaluated lower than a reading with [-Hakka]. Finally, a reading that is [+Ratio] is evaluated higher than a reading that is [-Ratio].

The findings mentioned above are the "surface" factors that may affect raters' evaluations of the seven reading samples. We may go further to see whether or not there are any "underlying" factors. The statistical technique Factor Analysis was conducted using SPSS. Two factors were extracted from the reading samples after Varimax rotation (Table 2).

Table 2. Factor loadings on reading samples after rotation

	Factor	
	1	2
G	0.86	-0.12
F	0.78	0.15
C	0.75	0.25
E	0.75	0.16
D	0.54	0.53
B	-0.13	0.88
A	0.34	0.70

Rotated Factor Matrix

Based on the rotated factor matrix, factor 1 covers readings G, F, C, E, and D. This means that if a rater gives a high/low rating to reading G, then s/he will probably also give high/low ratings to readings F, C, E, and D. Because of the fact that readings G, F, C, E, and D were written either partly or entirely in Han characters, and they were given higher ratings than B and A, we may assume that Han characters, which make a reading more "readable" for the Han character-educated subjects, play an important role in factor 1. On the other hand, factor 2 covers readings B and A, which were written with a high proportion of Roman script. We may say that Romanization plays an important role in factor 2. Because most of the subjects were not skilled in Taiwanese Romanization, the use of a high proportion of Roman words made the readings "unreadable" to the subjects. Therefore, B and A got lower ratings than G, F, C, E, and D. The term "readable" means that an orthography which is more recognizable and familiar to a reader will enable the reader to understand the text more easily and clearly than another orthography.

It seems that whether or not a writing system is readable to a particular reader has a great deal of influence on her/his attitude toward the reading. That is, if a particular orthography is more readable to a reader, then s/he is more likely to give a high rating to the reading. We may further assume that there is only one underlying factor based on the findings of factor 1 and factor 2. That is to say, people will give higher ratings to those writing systems which are more "readable" to them. In other words, the ratings of readings are based on the degree of readability to a particular person. Based on this assumption of the underlying factor, we may examine those surface factors mentioned earlier to see whether or not they coincide with the underlying factor.

The surface factors reveal that the [+Han], [+Mandarin] and [+Ratio] features will cause a reading sample to be evaluated higher than [-Han], [-Mandarin] and [-Ratio]. These findings are not surprising. In Taiwan, Mandarin Chinese and Han characters have been taught through the national education system since the occupation of the KMT regime in 1945. Therefore, all the subjects in this experiment, who are under age 30, are more familiar with Mandarin and with Han characters. Because readers are skilled in Mandarin and Han characters, [+Mandarin] and [+Han] features, which made the texts more "readable" to them, were rated higher than the others. Therefore, the surface factors Han, Mandarin, and Ratio coincide with the hypothetical underlying factor. On the other hand, because most of the subjects are not Hakfa speakers (only 19 among the 244 subjects are able to speak Hakfa), the [+Hakka] feature will reduce the ratings of readings. We are more confident of this assumption after comparing the mean scores between Hakka and non-Hakka speakers of reading D (in Hakfa). Table 3 is the result of the unpaired t-test; it reveals that the mean scores of Hakka speakers and non-Hakka speakers are significantly different at the 5% significance level. This means that the [+Hakka] feature will raise the rating of a reading if the readers are able to speak Hakfa. In other words, their Hakfa-speaking ability made them give high scores to reading D (The fact that language ability can affect readers' evaluations is further confirmed in later section).

Table 3. T-test between Hakka and non-Hakka on reading D

	no.	mean	sd.
Hakka	19	5.35	0.80
non-Hakka	225	4.34	1.03

t=5.17   1 tailed p=0.00 < 0.05

As for the Roman feature, even though English is taught to students as a second language from high school on, it does not mean that students are skilled in Taiwanese Romanization. Therefore, the [+Roman] feature, which makes texts more "unreadable," will reduce the rating of a reading if the readers are not familiar with Romanization.

Regarding the Bopomo feature, although every student is taught Bopomo as a supplementary tool while learning Mandarin, Bopomo is not suitable for representing the Taiwanese languages. In fact, Bopomo becomes a barrier and reduces reading efficiency. Therefore, [+Bopomo] feature can reduce the rating of a reading.

The results reveal that readers showed positive attitudes overall toward Taibun (regardless of different orthographies), with a mean score of 5.15 ((C+D+E+F+G)/5) or 4.50 ((A+B+C+D+E+F+G)/7). In addition, the survey reveals that people will give higher ratings to those orthographies that are more "readable" to them. Therefore, we may conclude that the different ratings of the seven reading samples are the reflection of their readability to the 244 subjects, who represent Mandarin and Han character-educated college students. Furthermore, we may assume that the acceptability of Taibun, written Taiwanese, is represented by its readability. (Readability is usually affected by various factors, such as language and orthography abilities.) We are then able to predict which particular systems will be accepted by particular persons. According to the results above, reading G is the most acceptable to the readers. However, the content of G is the least Taiwanese (i.e., the language used is closer to Mandarin than Taiwanese). On the other hand, B has the lowest rating, and is the least acceptable. But the content of B is the most Taiwanese. This result indicates that even though an orthography may be well designed to represent a language, the orthography will not necessarily be accepted more than others. In other words, the users' orthographic backgrounds and social context may play important roles in choosing a new orthography.

4.3. Raters' evaluations on writers' backgrounds

Questions 7 to 12 on each reading sample test subjects' reaction to the writer of a particular reading. It was assumed that a particular person will favor a particular writing system. Therefore, the subjects' impressions of the authors reflect their impressions of the corresponding writing systems. In other words, through questions 7 to 12, we can learn readers' expectations concerning the backgrounds of Taibun writers. In the study, the subjects were told to judge the authors' age, gender, political leaning, religion, opinion on national status, and the languages the authors are writing in. The statistical results reveal that readers had little idea regarding the writers' backgrounds. However, if readers associated writers with particular expectations, Taibun writers were mostly regarded as male, with native political leanings, native religions, and native identity.

Subjects were asked their impressions of the authors' age in question 7. The average percentage of subjects on Taibun writer's age category reveals that readers do not associate the Taibun writer with a particular age category.

Subjects were asked their impressions of the authors' gender in question 8. Most subjects (i.e., 19% + 43% = 62%) did not assign the authors a particular gender. However, if they did assign a gender, most of them associated the author with male (31%), and fewer with female (7%). The results reveal that readers' association with writers' gender is close to the fact that all the reading were written by males.

In question 9, the subjects' judgments on the authors' political leanings were elicited. The political parties listed on the answer sheet were the KMT, the Democratic Progressive Party (DPP), the Chinese New Party (CNP), the Green Party Taiwan (GPT), and the Taiwan Independence Party (TAIP). Most of the 244 subjects did not associate the authors with particular parties (i.e., 63%). The remaining subjects associated the authors mostly with the DPP (24%), a few with the KMT (8%), the TAIP (3%), the CNP (2%), and the GPT (1%). It seems predictable that more people would associate Taibun writers with DPP, the first native opposition party of influence during the KMT era in Taiwan. Although TAIP[12] and GPT[13] also represent native Taiwanese parties, the fact that they have been recently formed (both in 1996) and are still not well recognized by the public may reduce their likelihood of being associated with the Taibun writers. On the other hand, the well-known third major party CNP was not associated with Taibun writers. Its low association with Taibun coincides with the expectation of people in Taiwan that CNP represents Chinese nationalism rather than Taiwanese nationalism.

On question 10, the subjects' judgments on the authors' religion were evaluated. The religions listed on the answer sheet were Buddhism, Taoism, Christianity and Catholicism[14]. Most of the subjects (71%) did not associate the authors with any religion. The rest of the subjects associated the authors mostly either with Buddhism (10%) or Taoism (11%). Christianity and Catholicism only received 7%. The proportion seems reasonable because most Taiwanese believe in the traditional Buddhism and Taoism.

In the experiment, reading B was written in pure *Peh-oe-ji*, the traditional Romanized Taiwanese writing system that was developed by western missionaries. In the case of reading B, more subjects associated the writer with foreign religions (Christianity 11%, Catholicism 8%) than traditional religions (Buddhism 2%, Taoism 3%). We may interpret that this is because Buddhism and Taoism are usually regarded as symbols of Han culture, whereas Christianity and

---

[12] The percentage of votes received by TAIP in the national legislative election of 1998 was 1.45%. Other major parties were: KMT 46.43%, DPP 29.56%, and CNP 7.06%.

[13] The percentage of votes received by GPT in the national assembly election of 1996 was 2.97%.

[14] Although Catholicism is a form of Christianity, they were listed separately because they are regarded as two different religions by the majority of Taiwanese people.

Catholicism are considered to be western, associated with the cultures where Roman scripts were invented.

Question 11 tested subjects' judgments on authors' national identity, that is, whether the authors tend to want to unify with the People's Republic of China, be independent, or maintain Taiwan's current national status. Over half of the 244 subjects (63%) did not associate Taibun writers with any national identity. The rest of the subjects associated the Taibun writers mostly with independence (20%) and maintenance of current status (13%), while only 4% of the subjects associated the writers with unification. In other words, if readers believe there is a connection between a Taibun writer and national identity, then most of them will associate Taibun writers with independence and current status rather than unification. This also coincides with the result mentioned above, that some people connect Taibun writers with Taiwanese political parties (DPP, TAIP, and GPT, total 28%) rather than with the Chinese party CNP (2%). This suggests that people will consider Taibun to be representative of Taiwanese if they believe there is a connection between writing and national identity.

Finally, question 12 tested the subjects' understanding of the languages the authors were expressing. The purpose was to see whether or not the reader realized that a particular article was written in Taiwanese, when the reader faced the article without any advance hint of the language. The results reveal that more than half (72%) of the subjects were able to tell the languages the authors were using in each reading sample, except for B and D.

It is reasonable that most of the subjects (83%) were not able to recognize that reading B was written in Taiwanese. The main reason is because most Taiwanese people are not skilled in Romanization; it may even be said that they do not know there is a Taiwanese Romanization. Fully 21% of subjects considered reading B as either in French or Spanish, higher than the 17% percentage considering B to be in Taiwanese. That suggests that Taiwanese people associate Roman script with foreign languages. According to the survey on religions described before, people may also associate Roman script with foreign religions. In other words, we could say that Roman script is considered by some people to be representative of foreign cultures, and thus associated with foreign languages and foreign religions.

Reading D was written in Hakfa rather than Taigi-Taiwanese. The statistical results reveal that 48% of the subjects still considered reading D as Taigi writing. Only 30% (i.e., 73 persons) of the subjects were aware that D was written in Hakfa. We may be curious about which subjects are potentially able to tell Hakfa writing from Taigi writing. Table 4 indicates that 68% (i.e., 13/19) of Hakfa speakers[15] were aware of the Hakfa writing; on the other hand, only 27% of non-Hakfa speakers were aware of this Hakfa writing. A Chi-square test on Table 4 also reveals that the chi-square value 12.65 (after Yates's correction) is substantially larger than the critical value 3.84 (1 degree of freedom) at the 5% significance level. That is to say, Hakfa speakers are really more able to tell Hakfa writing from Taigi, compared with non-Hakfa speakers. The comprehension of Hakfa language led Hakfa speakers to be aware of Hakfa writing. In other words, language ability is an important factor determining whether a person can recognize the language of a particular writing or not. (The fact that language ability can affect readers' evaluations is further confirmed in section 4.4). Suppose that there are some Taigi and Hakfa articles in a newspaper or magazine. Most Hakfa speakers might be able to make the distinctions among Hakfa, Taigi, and Mandarin. In contrast, most Taigi speakers might only be able to distinguish Taigi from Mandarin. This is because most Hakfa speakers are able to speak Hakfa, Taigi, and Mandarin. However, Taigi speakers are typically only able to speak Taigi and Mandarin. For instance, based on the 244 subjects, 53% (10/19) of Hakfa speakers possess ability in Hakfa, Taigi, and Mandarin. Only 5% (10/203) of Taigi speakers possess the same ability.

Table 4. Classification of subjects for speakers and awareness

(observed)	aware	not aware	*total*
Hakfa speaker	13	6	19
non-Hakfa speaker	60	165	225
total	73	171	244

12.65>3.84 (df=1; after Yates's correction); p<0.05

4.4. Effects of raters' backgrounds on their evaluations

In previous sections, I examined the evaluations of all raters regardless of background. In this section, I consider whether or not raters' backgrounds may

---

[15] The definitions of Hakfa speakers and Taigi speakers in this section are defined by subjects' language ability only, and do not necessary correlate to their mother tongue or ethnicity. For example, the classification of a Hakfa speaker here was based on subjects' self-report on background questions. The subject was treated as a Hakfa speaker if s/he answered her/his Hakfa speaking ability was equal to or higher than 3, based on a five-point semantic differential scale.

affect their evaluations on the reading samples. In other words, do the raters' own characteristics, such as gender, residence, major, age, mother tongue, language ability, national identity, and assertions on Taiwan's national status, have an effect on their evaluations? In order to answer this question, Tukey's Honest Significant Difference (HSD) tests of General Linear Model (GLM) were conducted using the SPSS program. However, some assumed factors, such as gender and residence, consist of only two groups (i.e., female vs. male; Taipei vs. non-Taipei). Because the post hoc comparisons require more than two groups in a factor, the gender and residence factors were examined with linear regression, a statistical technique adopted for calculating the Taibun equation in the survey.

Before we determine the significant factors, we need to assume some possible factors so that we can examine whether or not the factors are significant. The assumed factors here are: (1) gender, (2) place of residence, (3) major, (4) age, (5) ethnic identity, (6) mother tongue, (7) language ability, (8) political leanings, (9) national identity, and (10) assertion on Taiwan's national status. The statistical results reveal that gender, age[16], ethnic identity, and political leanings are not significant factors, but the others are significant. The significant factors are described as follows:

(1) Place of residence: Among the subjects, 138 were from Taipei and 106 from other places. The result of regression reveals that there is significant difference between subjects from Taipei and non-Taipei; people from places other than Taipei give higher evaluations to the reading samples than people from Taipei.

(2) Major: There are significant differences among the three groups of major, that is, Taiwanese and English vs. Chinese, Japanese, and Public Administration vs. Mechanical Engineering (groups' evaluations are in descending order).

(3) Mother tongue: The classification of readers' mother tongue was based on readers' self-report on the mother tongue question. There were 152 subjects considering their own mother tongue to be Taiwanese, 15 Hakfa, 58 Mandarin, and 19 others. Those whose mother tongues are native Taiwanese languages (i.e., Taiwanese and Hakfa) evaluate the readings significantly higher than speakers of non-native Taiwanese languages.

(4) Language ability: The classification of readers' language ability was based on readers' self-report on the language ability question. For example, if a

---

[16] In this investigation, all the subjects were college students. This fact reveals that we have limited age range in this survey. Age might be a significant factor if we have a wider age range of subjects. Further research needs to be conducted to see whether or not age is a significant factor.

reader answered that her/his Hakfa speaking ability is equal to or higher than 3 (based on a 5-point semantic differential scale), then s/he was assigned a Hakfa speaking ability. Among the 244 subjects, 30 were Mandarin monolingual and the others were bilingual or multilingual. The results show that Mandarin-only speakers evaluate the readings significantly lower than non-Mandarin-only speakers.

(5) National identity: The classification was based on readers' self-reports to the identity questions. Among the 244 subjects, 48 persons belong to the Taiwanese-only type, 130 to the Taiwanese-Chinese type, 2 to the Chinese-only type, and 64 to the others. The Taiwanese-only and Taiwanese-Chinese were grouped together as a category Taiwanese, and Chinese-only and others were grouped together as a category non-Taiwanese. The results reveal that Taiwanese rate the readings significantly higher than non-Taiwanese.

(6) Assertion on Taiwan's national status: This classification was based on readers' self-reports to the assertion questions. After calculation, there were 67 persons for independence (TI), 102 for maintaining the current status (MT), 14 for unification with China (UNI), and 61 for others. There is a significant difference between Taiwan independence supporters and non-TI supporters (i.e. MT, UNI, and others). The independence group evaluates the readings significantly higher than the non-TI group.

4.5. The Taibun equation for predicting reading scores

After we have examined the influences of orthographic designs and readers' backgrounds, a Taibun equation which can predict a reader's mean score on a particular reading can be formulated based on the significant factors. In order to formulate the Taibun equation, a linear regression was employed using the SPSS software program. All the independent variables were encoded in dummy coding, that is, either as "1," which means "yes", or as "0," which means "no." For example, the residence variable Taipei was encoded in "1," and non-Taipei was encoded in "0."

There are two types of independent variables in the regression analysis. All variables mentioned here are significant. The first type consists of reading samples A, B, C, D, EF, and G. They were treated as 6 independent variables, and encoded in dummy coding. "EF" means that the original E and F were combined, since Tukey's HSD reveals that there is no significant difference between them. The results of Tukey's HSD reveal that all reading samples (after E and F were combined) are significantly different from each other.

The second type of independent variable consists of the significant background factors. The factors were treated as seven independent variables. They are: (1) Taipei as a residence, (2) major in Taiwanese or English, (3) major in Mechanical Engineering, (4) native Taiwanese languages (i.e., Taiwanese or Hakfa) as mother tongues, (5) monolingual in Mandarin, (6) Taiwanese identity (i.e., Taiwanese-only, or Taiwanese-Chinese), and (7) assertion of Taiwanese independence. The variables were all encoded in dummy coding.

After the independent variables were decided, the scores already evaluated by the 244 subjects were treated as a dependent variable Y (Y is observed; Y' is predicted) in order to calculate the constant and coefficients. In other words, the data of the 244 subjects were treated as a model to formulate the prediction equation. Table 5 is part of the SPSS output from a linear regression analysis. Reading sample EF was excluded from Table 5 as a criterion to compare with other reading samples. Table 5 reveals that all coefficients of the independent variables are significantly different at the 1% level.

Table 5. SPSS output (coefficients) from a linear regression analysis of the equation data

Model		Unstandardized Coefficients		Standardized Coefficients		
		B	Std. Error	Beta	t	Sig.
1.00	(Constant)	4.78	0.08		62.17	0.000
	A	-1.41	0.07	-0.32	-19.68	0.000
	B	-2.92	0.07	-0.67	-40.66	0.000
	C	0.25	0.07	0.06	3.51	0.000
	D	-0.61	0.07	-0.14	-8.51	0.000
	G	1.00	0.07	0.23	13.91	0.000
	Taipei	-0.13	0.05	-0.04	-2.95	0.003
	TB-EN	0.18	0.05	0.06	3.67	0.000
	ME	-0.23	0.07	-0.05	-3.46	0.001
	NTL	0.23	0.05	0.07	4.58	0.000
	M-only	-0.34	0.07	-0.07	-4.82	0.000
	T-id	0.15	0.05	0.04	2.96	0.003
	TI	0.15	0.05	0.05	3.30	0.001

Based on the results of Table 5, we could formulate our Taibun equation as follows:

$Y' = 4.78 - 1.41$ (A) $- 2.92$ (B) $+ 0.25$ (C) $- 0.61$ (D) $+ 0.00$ (EF) $+ 1.00$ (G)$- 0.13$ (Taipei) $+ 0.18$ (TB-EN) $- 0.23$ (ME) $+ 0.23$ (NTL) $- 0.34$ (M-only) $+ 0.15$ (T-id) $+ 0.15$ (TI)

Key: A, B, C, D, EF, G refer to the reading sample

Taipei: Taipei as a residence

TB-EN: major in Taiwanese or English

ME: major in Mechanical Engineering

NTL: native Taiwanese languages (i.e., Taiwanese or Hakfa) as mother tongues

M-only: monolingual in Mandarin

T-id: Taiwanese identity (i.e., Taiwanese-only, or Taiwanese-Chinese)

TI: assertion of Taiwanese independence

All the independent variables must be encoded either 1 (yes) or 0 (no) when applied to the Taibun equation. The value of Y' is between the highest 7 and the lowest 1, based on a seven-point semantic differential scale.

The following illustrates how the Taibun equation can apply to predict reading scores. Suppose we want to predict John's score on reading sample A (so, fill out A with "1" and B, C, D, EF, G with "0"). The background information on John is: living in *Kaohsiung* (non-Taipei, so fill out the Taipei variable with "0"); major in English (fill out TB-EN with "1," and ME with "0"); Hakfa as his mother tongue (fill out NTL with "1"); with speaking capability in Hakfa, Taiwanese, and Mandarin (fill out M-only with "0"); with an identity of Taiwanese-only (fill out T-id with "1"); and with an assertion of Taiwanese independence (fill out TI with "1"). Therefore, John's predicted score on reading sample A will be 4.08 (on a scale of 1-7) as follows:

$Y' = 4.78 - 1.41$ (1) $- 2.92$ (0) $+ 0.25$ (0) $- 0.61$ (0) $+ 0.00$ (0) $+ 1.00$ (0)

-0.13 (0) $+ 0.18$ (1) $- 0.23$ (0) $+ 0.23$ (1) $- 0.34$ (0)

$+ 0.15$ (1) $+ 0.15$ (1)

$= 4.78 - 1.41 + 0.18 + 0.23 + 0.15 + 0.15$

$= 4.08$

5. Implications

There are three fundamental Taibun writing schemes currently at issue for written Taiwanese. They are Han character-only, Han-Roman mixed, and Roman script-only. The results of the present investigation reveal that the college students surveyed have positive attitudes toward Taibun overall (regardless of orthography). As for which orthography is preferred, the results reveal that the college students tend to prefer Han-only over Han-Roman and Roman-only. These results reflect the preferences of the Mandarin and Han character-educated college students with regard to written Taiwanese. Since all students in Taiwan have been taught Mandarin and Han characters through the national education system since 1945, these findings imply the potential difficulty of promoting Roman script in a Han character dominated society.

Many factors are generally involved in the choice and shift of orthography. From the perspective of social demand, the increasing use of spoken and written Mandarin by Taiwanese people has reduced the demand for a new orthography. People may not feel the necessity of learning a new orthographic tool, since they have already acquired writing skill in modern standard Chinese. Even so, the readers' positive attitudes toward Taibun indicate that it is still possible for Taibun to be accepted in addition to the existing Mandarin writing.

Thus, what findings of the survey may contribute to the promotion of Taibun? According to the results of the survey, seven factors could affect readers' evaluations of Taibun. They are orthographic design, place of residence, major, mother tongue, language ability, national identity, and national status. Since place of residence and academic major are not controllable factors (because there always will be people living in different places and with different majors), a Taibun promoter may concentrate attention on the other factors, which can be divided into three domains:

(1) Orthographic domain, which refers to the designs of orthography. Even good orthographic designs are not absolutely guaranteed to be accepted by the public. Conversely, the acceptance of orthographies by people does not necessarily mean that the orthographies were well designed. In this survey, although Roman script was rated lower than Han characters, the economy and easy learnability of Roman script make Romanization still worth consideration. The fact that most of the current Taibun publications are in the Han-Roman mixed scheme instead of Han-only points out that readers may tend to prefer Roman script after they are skilled in Taiwanese Romanization. If the current *Bopomo,* which is taught through the national education system in Taiwan, could be replaced by Romanization, the circumstance of using Romanization would thus most likely increase the possibility of promoting Romanized Taibun. Over time, the Roman script might come into competition with Han characters, or even replace Han characters if Romanization were taught together with Han characters at the time students enter elementary school.

(2) Language domain, which includes the factors of mother tongue and language ability. The survey reveals that people who are able to speak native Taiwanese languages are more likely to give higher ratings to Taibun. This fact points out that the promotion of Taibun should focus on the particular groups who frequently use or are able to use Taiwanese or Hakfa. Moreover, Taibun should be promoted to the Taiwanese public as soon as possible, before people shift entirely to become monolingual in Mandarin Chinese.

(3) Political domain, which covers the factors of national identity and national status. Political transitions can affect the language situation, such as in the case of Vietnam (DeFrancis, 1977). In the case of Taiwan, the current ambiguous national status and diversity of national identities mirror people's uncertain determinations on the issue of written Taiwanese. At the same time, people's uncertain determinations on the Taibun issue also reflect the political controversy on national issues of Taiwan. Since Taiwan has been released from the rule of the Chinese KMT in the 2000 presidential election, in which the candidate Shui-bian Chen of the Taiwanese opposition party DDP was elected to form a new government. The language attitude of the new government will play an important role on current language issues in Taiwan.

6. Conclusion

The statistical results of this research reveal that the readers' (244 students from *Tamsui* and *Tamkang* Universities) overall attitudes toward written Taiwanese are positive. Further, the results reveal that the readers evaluated the prepared seven reading samples as significantly different (except E vs. F), in a ranking that reflects the preferences of the Mandarin and Han-character educated college students with regard to the orthographies of written Taiwanese. Thus Roman script and *Bopomo* used in Taibun texts received more negative evaluations by the 244 readers; Han characters received the most positive evaluations. The survey indicates that readers will give higher ratings to those orthographies which are more "readable" to them, where readability is determined by readers' language and orthography abilities.

In addition to the orthography factor, the backgrounds of the readers also affect their evaluations. The results of the investigations reveal six factors which can affect readers' evaluations: place of residence (Taipei vs. non-Taipei), academic major (Taiwanese and English vs. Mechanical Engineering vs. Chinese, Japanese, and Public Administration), mother tongue (Taiwanese vs. non-Taiwanese), language ability (Taiwanese vs. non-Taiwanese, or non-Mandarin-only vs. Mandarin-only), the individual's evaluation of her/his national identity (Taiwanese vs. non-Taiwanese), and assertions on Taiwan's preferred national status (independence vs. non-independence). Three factors which do not appear to affect readers' evaluations are gender, age, and political leanings.

In short, whether or not Taibun will be accepted and successfully promoted to a national status depends on people's orthography demands and their attitudes toward written Taiwanese. Moreover, their language ability and national identity also will play an important role while they are making the determinations. The present investigation implies that although Taiwanese people may not have strong demands for a new orthography, their positive attitudes toward written Taiwanese make the promotion of Taibun writing possible. In addition, particular groups, such as those who are able to speak Taiwanese, and those who identify themselves as Taiwanese, have higher preference for Taibun writing. These groups may be treated as priority targets in the promotion of written Taiwanese.

Acknowledgements

This is an updated revision of the article with same title originally published in 2001 *Journal of Multilingual and Multicultural Development*, 22(6), 502-523.

References

Barclay, T. 1885. *Taiwan Prefectural City Church News* [Tai-oan-hu-sia^n Kau-hoe-po]. No.1.

Chan, H. C. 1994. *Language Shift in Taiwan: Social and Political Determinants*. Ph.D. dissertation: Georgetown University.

Chen, P. 1993. Modern written Chinese in development. *Language in Society* 22, pp.505-37.

Chen, P. 1994. Four projected functions of new writing systems for Chinese. *Anthropological Linguistics* 36(3), pp.366-81.

Chen, P. 1996. Modern written Chinese, dialects, and regional identity. *Language Problems and Language Planning* 20(3), pp.223-43.

Cheng, R. L. 1989. *Essays on Written Taiwanese* [Chau Hiong Phiauchunhoa e Taioan Gibun]. Taipei: Chu-lip.

Cheng, R. L. 1989. Taiwanese morphemes in search of Chinese characters. In *Essays on Written Taiwanese* [Chau Hiong Phiauchunhoa e Taioan Gibun]. Taipei: Chu-lip.

Cheng, R. L. 1990. *Essays on Taiwan's Sociolinguistic Problems* [Ianpian-tiong e Taioan Siahoe Gibun]. Taipei: Chu-lip.

Chiung, W. T. 2000. Peh-oe-ji: childish writing? Paper presented at the 6th Annual North American Taiwan Studies Conference, June 16-19, Harvard University.

Chiung, W. T. 2001. Romanization and language planning in Taiwan. *The Linguistic Association of Korea Journal* 9(1), pp.15-43.

Dale, I. R. H. 1980. Digraphia. *International Journal of the Sociology of Language* 26, pp.5-13.

DeFrancis, J. 1977. *Colonialism and Language Policy in Viet Nam*. The Hague.

DeFrancis, J. 1984. Digraphia. *Word* 35(1), pp.59-66.

DeFrancis, J. 1990. *The Chinese Language: Fact and Fantasy*. (Taiwan edition) Honolulu: University of Hawaii Press.

DeFrancis, J. 1996. How efficient is the Chinese writing system? *Visible Language* 30(1), pp.6-44.

Erbaugh, M. 1995. Southern Chinese dialects as a medium for reconciliation within Greater China. *Language in Society* 24, pp.79-94.

Feifel, K. 1994. *Language Attitudes in Taiwan*. Taipei: Crane.

Ferguson, C. 1959. Diglossia. *Word* 15, pp.325-40.

Grimes, B. 1996. *Ethnologue* (13th edition) (ed.). Dallas: Summer Institute of Lingustics.

Hsiau, A. 1997. Language ideology in Taiwan: the KMT's language policy, the Tai-yu language movement, and ethnic politics. *Journal of Multilingual and Multicultural Development* 18(4), pp.302-315.

Huang, S. F. 1993. *Language, Society, and Ethnic Identity* [Gigian Siahoe kap Chokkun Isek]. Taipei: Crane.

Lambert, W. et al. 1960. Evaluative reactions to spoken language. *Journal of Abnormal and Social Psychology* 60, pp.44-51.

Lambert, W. et al. 1975. Language attitudes in a French-American community. *International Journal of Sociology of Language* 4, pp.127-52.

Lambert, W. E. 1967. A social psychology of bilingualism. *Journal of Social Issues* 23(2), pp.91-109.

Li, K. H. 1996. Language policy and Taiwanese independence [Gigian Cheng-chhek kap Taioan Toklip]. In *Taiwanese Collegian* [Taioan Hakseng] 18, pp.14-22

Lian, H. 1987. Taiwanese Etymology [Taioan Gitian]. Originally published in 1957. Taipei: Chin-fong.

Lu, L. J. 1988. *A Study of Language Attitudes, Language Use and Ethnic Identity in Taiwan*. M.A. Thesis. Fu-jen Catholic University.

Norman, J. 1988. *Chinese*. NY: Cambridge University Press.

Tiuⁿ, H. K. 1998. Writing in two scripts: a case study of digraphia in Taiwanese. *Written Language and Literacy* 1(2), pp.225-47.

Tiuⁿ, J. H. 2001. *Principles of POJ or the Taiwanese Orthography: An Introduction to Its Sound-Symbol Correspondences ans Related Issues* [Peh-oe-ji Ki-pun-lun]. Taipei: Crane.

Tsao, F. F. 1999. The language planning situation in Taiwan. *Journal of Multilingual and Multicultural Development* 20 (4&5), pp.328-75.

Tzeng, O. et al. 1992. Auto activation of linguistic information in Chinese character recognition. *Advances in Psychology* 94, pp.119-30.

Wang, C. M. 1995. *A Study of Gender and Language Attitudes of Adolescents in Taiwan*. MA thesis: The University of Texas at Arlington.

Young, R. 1988. Language Maintenance and Language Shift in Taiwan. *Journal of Multilingual and Multicultural Development* 9(4), pp.323-38.

Appendix A

Samples of Taibun Readings

Reading A

Se-han 的 si-chun, kui 家伙仔 kah 阿公阿媽 toa 做伙;he 是半 chng-kha 的所在,因為若講草地,離車頭 koh 近近 a nia,騎車 to 免 5 分鐘 leh。He 是 hit 種古早式的<u>厝瓦厝</u>,...

Reading B

Hit-sî mā kài chhù-bī, iû-kî nā tńg tiȯh chhit-goȯh sî-á, taȯk-àm nā siūⁿ-tiȯh ài khiâ kàu kū-chhù tō ē khí ke-bó-phôe, put-sî tō ài kiò hiaⁿ-ko kap góa ...

Reading C

佇讀小學仔儘前,全家伙仔攏是蹛咧茲,茲阮攏給號做「舊厝」(因為這是相對於以後的新厝)。雖然佇我幼稚園讀煞迄冬,父母因為嗳做生理的關係,...

Reading D

過年炊粄麼還 chhin 記得,過年定著做甜粄 lau 菜頭粄。甜粄炊好以後硬硬,放幾隻月 mo 問題。愛食時正切來冷食,多少像 tu 美國,切 *cheese* 共樣。麼有拿來煎,...

Reading E

阿爸阿母搬來新厝了就開米店做生意。ㄅㄧㄚ ㄅㄧㄚ有人問我阮厝ㄅㄝ創啥物?我若講ㄅㄝ賣米,人ㄌㆲㄥ ㄍㄧㆤ ㄙ阮ㄅㄠ開米絞,ㄍㄚ ㄅㄧ有ㄅㄝ ㆤ米ㄅㄝ,...

Reading F

有機質肥料 kap 化學肥料到底有啥物無工? Ti chia, 做一個簡單 e 介紹。講到有機肥料, 咱就想著「有機農業、永續性有機農業」, 這個道理真簡單, 咱將作物 e 果實收成,...

Reading G

阿媽養的雞仔、鴨仔都是正港的土雞、番鴨。日時就放它們去四界跑,暗時才趕進去雞稠。有時雞母若要生卵,都會跑去牛車頂、或是柴間仔裡面,找一個好位,...

Appendix B

Translations of Reading Questions

1. How do you feel about this reading?

7	6	5	4	3	2	1
friendly						unfriendly

2. What percentage of this reading do you understand?

7	6	5	4	3	2	1
100%						0%

3. Do you feel this reading is easy to read?

7	6	5	4	3	2	1
easy						difficult

4. Do you feel you like this reading?

7	6	5	4	3	2	1
like it						dislike it

2. What percentage of this reading do you understand?

7	6	5	4	3	2	1
100%						0%

5. What's your feeling about the writing style in this reading.

7	6	5	4	3	2	1
interesting						boring

6. Do you think this kind of writing expresses author's idea very well?

7	6	5	4	3	2	1
well						bad

7. How old would you think the author is?

7	6	5	4	3	2	1
over 60	50-59	40-49	30-39	20-29	10-19	Not related

8. What gender do you think the author might be?

4 male	3 female	2 either	1 uncertain

9. What political parties do you feel the author might support?

7	6	5	4	3	2	1
KMT	DPP	CNP	GPT	TAIP	not related	uncertain

10. What religion do you feel the author might be?

7 Buddhism 6 Taoism 5 Christianity 4 Catholicity 3 others 2 not related 1 uncertain

11. What do you think is the author's opinion on national status?

5 unification   4 independence   3 maintain status   2 not related   1 uncertain

12. What language do you feel the author might be trying to express in this reading?

7 Mandarin 6 Taiwanese 5 Hakka 4 indigenes 3 Japanese 2 French or Spanish 1 uncertain

11

Development of the Taiwanese Proficiency Test

1. Introduction

Taiwan is a multilingual and multi-ethnic society. Traditionally, it is divided into four primary ethnic groups. Because nation-wide linguistic census has not been conducted in recent decades, no accurate ethnolinguistic demographics are available. However, according to frequently cited data, the speakers of each ethnic group were estimated as follows: indigenous (1.7%), Hakka (12%), Taigi or Taiwanese (73.3%), and Mainlanders [1] (13%) (Huang 1993:21). International marriages have become more common in the globalization era and Taiwan is no exception. According to the statistics of Taiwan's Ministry of Interior (2009), there were a total of 414,699 foreign spouses in Taiwan by January 2009. They are the fifth ethnic group in Taiwan.

In addition to being a multi-ethnic society, Taiwan has been colonized by several foreign regimes since the seventeenth century. Two centuries later, the sovereignty of Taiwan was transferred from China to Japan in 1895 as a consequence of the Sino-Japanese War. At the end of the World War II, Japanese forces surrendered to the Allied Forces. *Chiang Kai-shek*, the leader of the Chinese Nationalist (KMT[2] or *Kuomintang*) took over Taiwan on behalf of the Allied Powers under General Order No.1 of September 2, 1945 (Peng 1995:60-61). At the time, Chiang Kai-shek was fighting against the Chinese Communist Party in Mainland China. In 1949, Chiang's troops were completely defeated and then pursued by the Chinese Communists. At that time, Taiwan's national status was supposed to be dealt with by a peace treaty among the fighting nations.

---

[1] Mainly the immigrants came to Taiwan with the Chiang Kai-shek's KMT regime around 1945.
[2] KMT was the ruling party in Taiwan since 1945 until 2000, in which year *Chen Shui-bian*, the presidential candidate of opposition party Democratic Progressive Party was elected the new president. Thereafter, the KMT won the presidential election again in 2008, and has become the ruling party again since 2008.

However, because of Chiang's defeat in China, Chiang decided to occupy Taiwan as a base from which he would fight back and retake Mainland China (Kerr 1992; Ong 1993; Peng 1995; Su 1980). Consequently, Chiang's political regime the Republic of China (R.O.C) was relocated and resurrected in Taiwan and has remained there since 1949.

The National Language Policy[3], or monolingual policy, was adopted both during the Japanese and the KMT occupations of Taiwan. In the case of the KMT's monolingual policy, the Taiwanese people were not allowed to speak their vernaculars in school and in public. Moreover, they were forced to learn Mandarin Chinese and to identify themselves as Chinese through the national education system (Cheng 1996; Tiuⁿ 1996). As Hsiau (1997:307) has pointed out, "the usage of Mandarin as a national language becomes a testimony of the Chineseness of the KMT state." Consequently, researches such as Chan (1994) and Young (1988) have revealed that a language shift toward Mandarin is in progress. Huang (1993:160) goes so far as to suggest that the indigenous languages of Taiwan are all endangered.

Mother tongue education was not implemented nation-wide until 2001, the year after the KMT lost the presidential election for the first time in Taiwan. Since then, all elementary school classes are required to have a class called "local language", lasting 40 minutes, once a week in school. The schools may choose which local language to teach in accordance with the demands of the students. In order to ensure that all local language teachers have certain level of local language proficiency, proficiency tests in local languages had been planned and administered. Three language tests were prepared. The indigenous languages test has been planned and executed by the Council of Indigenous Peoples, Executive Yuan, since 2001. The Hakka language test was prepared by the Council for Hakka Affairs, Executive Yuan, and the first official test was conducted in 2005. As for Tai-gi or the Taiwanese language, since there is no special council for Tai-gi speakers, the task for Taiwanese proficiency test was taken over by the National Languages Committee (NLC) of the-Ministry of Education (MOE).

2. Historical background of Taiwanese language testing

Although mother tongue education has been officially included in elementary schools starting from the 2001 academic year, there was no Taiwanese proficiency test held in preparation for classroom teaching. Because most

---

[3] For details, see Huang 1993.

elementary teachers were neither fluent in spoken Taiwanese nor educated in written Taiwanese as a consequence of monolingual policy, they were facing problems in teaching Taiwanese. To overcome this predicament, several proposals were put forward. Among the proposals, a teaching assistant policy was adopted. That is, a teaching assistant who does not have a teaching certificate but has a good knowledge of the Taiwanese language will be in charge of language teaching along with the classroom teacher. To find linguistically qualified assistants, a hastily-held proficiency test in Taiwanese took place nationally in March of 2002. The persons who passed the test had to take a 36-hour training course before he or she can teach in the classroom. Because the test was given in a rush, no preliminary tests were conducted. In other words, neither reliability nor validity was analyzed. After that, Taiwan's Ministry of Education (MOE) gave authority to local governments to hold language tests in local languages. As a result, some local governments, such as Tainan county, Tainan city and Kaohsiung city, held their versions of the Taiwanese proficiency tests. However, due the limited budgets and professional resources, the tests were not well planned and conducted. The criteria of proficiency varied from county to county.

A professional Taiwanese test was not well planned until 2006, when the General Taiwanese Proficiency Test League (GTPTL) was founded. GTPTL was first convened at Tainan Theological College and Seminary on December 4, 2005. The league consisted of academic institutions and Taiwanese language associations, such as Tainan Theological College and Seminary, Department of Taiwanese Literature of National Cheng Kung University, Department of Taiwanese Languages of Chung Shan Medical University, and Taiwanese Romanization Association (Teng 2006). After several months of preparations, the first preliminary test was conducted with a total of 253 subjects on September 23, 2006. Its statistical results were presented at the first conference on Taiwanese proficiency test held by Tainan Theological College and Seminary on December 2, 2006 (Chiung 2006). Thereafter, a second pilot test was arranged with a total of 66 subjects on April 2007. An official Taiwanese proficiency test was proposed by the GTPTL to be conducted in 2008. However, the test was postponed because major members of GTPTL were commissioned by the Ministry of Education to work on a research project to develop a new national level test in Taiwanese.

It turned out that while the GTPTL was working on the Taiwanese test, the National Languages Committee (NLC) of the MOE decided to develop a Taiwanese test, too. Its first meeting on the planning of the test was convened on April 19, 2007, and finally an Operating Guideline for Language Proficiency Test in Taiwanese Southern Min was promulgated on November 21, 2007. According to the resolution of the meetings, the Common European Framework of Reference for Languages: Learning, Teaching, Assessment (Thereafter, CEF) was adopted as a guideline for the proposed Taiwanese test. Preliminary tests were scheduled for 2008 and an official nationwide test in 2009.

In accordance with the results of public biddings, National Cheng Kung University was in charge of the research project for 2008, and National Taiwan Normal University was in charge of the administrative affairs of executing the test in 2009. The members of GTPTL became the major constituents of the research team. During the research periods, two preliminary tests were conducted on August 23 and November 29, 2008, respectively. Each test contained 500 subjects. Although the preliminary tests were done well and the official test was expected to be conducted in August 2009, the budget for administrative affairs was suddenly deleted by the KMT legislators in early January 2009. Consequently, the official nation-wide test that was originally scheduled to take place in 2009 was also forced to be terminated. In response, more than twenty grassroots organizations protested against the KMT legislators on February 27, 2009 [4]. Under the pressure of grassroots organizations, the MOE promised to subsidize local governments as a remedy for the test. In other words, Taiwanese tests will be conducted by counties/cities, rather than the central government. According to the meeting convened by MOE's Department of Elementary Education on May 26, 2009, there were 13 counties/cities willing to hold the Taiwanese test. All the counties/cities agreed to appoint the research team of National Cheng Kung University (NCKU) as the planner to carry out the test. The first official test was co-organized by Tainan City, Tainan County, Chiayi City, Chiayi County, and Pingung County. It was scheduled for November 14, 2009, and 793 test-takers were registered. [5]

3. Formats of the current Taiwanese proficiency test

The Taiwanese Proficiency Test (TPT) described in this paper was designed by the Center for Taiwanese Languages Testing (CTLT), National Cheng Kung University. The initial purpose for developing TPT was to measure Taiwanese language proficiency of elementary school teachers and language teaching assistants to ensure that they fulfill the requirement of minimal language ability. Later it was expanded to college students majoring in Taiwanese and to all

---

[4] For more information on the demonstration, visit <http://www.TLH.org.tw>
[5] For details on the test, visit <http://ctlt.twl.ncku.edu.tw>

members of the public (adults only). The current format, which was adjusted and revised based on 4 preliminary tests, was carried out for the first official test in November 2009. Table 1 presents the format of the current Taiwanese proficiency test designed by the CTLT.

Table 1. Format of the Taiwanese Proficiency Test by CTLT

Sections	Time	Scores	

Reading
(a) Vocabulary and grammar (36 questions)
    Vocabulary (24 questions)
    Grammar (12 questions)
(b) Reading comprehension (24 questions)
	70 mins.	(a) 108	(b) 72

		subtotal: 180	
Listening (a) Conversations (24 questions) (b) Talks and lectures (16 questions)	40 mins.	(a) 72	(b) 48
		subtotal: 120	
Dictation Word dictation in Ban-lo Pheng-im (40 words)	20 mins.	80	
Speaking Using picture prompts for storytelling (2 questions) Oral readings (2 questions) Oral expressions (2 questions)	30 mins.	20 for each subtotal: 120	
Total	160 mins.	500	

Generally speaking, norm-referenced and criterion-referenced tests are the major approaches in language testing (McNamara 2000:62). Criterion-referenced measurement was adopted by the CTLT for the TPT. The major reasons are as follows: 1) The TPT was initially designed for examining Taiwanese teacher's Taiwanese language proficiency level. The criteria for language levels were set in advance. The purpose of the TPT is to locate teachers' standardized language level in accordance with the criteria, rather than finding a teacher's relative level among all the teachers. 2) The number of test-takers was not expected to be high.

The TPT consists of 4 sections: reading, listening, dictation, and speaking tests. The total score is 500 points. The TPT divides Taiwanese language proficiency into 6 levels in accordance with the CEF criteria, that is, A1, A2, B1, B2, C1, and C2. Test items of an individual TPT test comprise all six language levels. In other words, a test-taker does not have to take six tests, from the most basic to the most advanced level to locate his/her level. Instead, a test-taker needs to take only one test and s/he will be assigned a language proficiency level depending on the score s/he gets, as shown in Table 9. The main reasons for not creating tests in different proficiency levels are: 1) the budget and resources for the TPT are not sufficient to hold 6 individual tests of different language levels in a year. It can only hold tests once or twice a year under the current conditions. 2) The test needs to be done as quickly and efficiently as possible to find out the Taiwanese teachers' language ability. It is an economic way to include all test-takers of different language levels in one test.

The first issue that needed to be solved was the selection of a Taiwanese writing system that will be used consistently throughout the test. Taiwanese writing systems are either in Han characters, Roman alphabet or a mixed system combining the two systems. Currently, the dominant writing system is called Han-lo, or literarily Han characters plus Roman scripts. However, different users may have different opinions on choosing the Han characters or the Romanization schemes (Chiung 2001). To standardize Romanization, Ban-lo Pheng-im (閩羅拼音), a Romanization scheme for Taiwanese, was promulgated by the MOE in October 14, 2006. Han characters with traditional Peh-oe-ji and MOE's Ban-lo Pheng-im are adopted by the CTLT for tests.

The TPT reading tests are divided into two parts: a) vocabulary and grammar and b) reading comprehensions. Readings are arranged in Han-lo style. There are a total of 60 multiple-choice questions. Each question has 4 answer choices, and only one choice is correct. A test-taker will get 3 points if s/he gets a correct answer. In contrast, s/he will be deducted 1 point if s/he gets a wrong answer. No point will be added or deducted if s/he does not answer the questions. The test items of vocabulary and grammar comprise A1, A2, B1, B2, C1, and C2 levels. As for the reading comprehension questions, they comprise B1, B2, C1, and C2 levels.

The listening tests are divided into two parts too: a) conversations and b) talks and lectures. There are a total of 40 multiple-choice questions. The calculation of the score is the same as for the reading test. Conversations refer to dialogues between two or more people. They comprise A1, A2, B1, B2, C1, and

C2 levels. Talks and lectures refer to individual talks and lectures on some topics (such as weather reports, storytelling, class lectures, and professional speeches). They are expected to be at intermediate and higher levels, so they comprise B1, B2, C1, and C2 levels.

Instead of writing tests, dictation tests in Ban-lo Pheng-im are arranged specifically for the Taiwanese language. The major reasons are: 1) written Taiwanese is currently neither widespread nor standardized. There are several ways to write in Taiwanese. To avoid arguments over the writing criteria, it is better to exclude composition. 2) Ban-lo Pheng-im is taught in Taiwanese classes. Besides, Ban-lo Pheng-im is a fundamental tool to the writing of Taiwanese.

There are 40 Taiwanese words in the dictation tests. The words consist of all consonants, simple vowels, and tones in Taiwanese. They are all tape recorded in advance. Test-takers are asked to write down what they hear in Ban-lo Pheng-im. Each word is repeated three times, and then 3 seconds are left for writing. Scores are calculated in accordance with the percentage of correct phonemes and tonemes the test-taker perceives. For example, assuming that there are a total of 350 phonemes and tonemes in the word list. A test-taker will get 68.6 points ($=80\times(300/350)$) if s/he get 300 correct phonemes and tonemes.

The speaking tests consist of 3 parts: a) Using picture prompts for storytelling, b) oral readings, and c) oral expressions. There are 2 types of storytelling. The first type is a single picture with some concrete objects. The test-taker is told to describe the contents in simple words. This type of storytelling is classified as an A1 level question. The second type of storytelling comprises 4 pictures in series. Test-takers have to give a short talk in simple ways on the pictures. This type is classified as an A2 level question. For each question in both types, test-takers have 30 seconds to prepare and 1 minute to record.

For oral readings, there are 2 prepared paragraphs (B1 and B2 levels). Each paragraph is written in Han-lo style and about 300 words long. Test-takers are told to read the paragraphs aloud as fluently as they can. They have 30 seconds to prepare and 2 minutes to record.

As for oral expressions, there are 2 prepared questions (C1 and C2 levels) requesting the test-taker's opinions and ideas on some issues. Test-takers have to express their opinions and ideas fluently. They have 1 minute to prepare and 2 minutes to record.

4. Statistic results of preliminary tests

There were several preliminary tests, and the latest test was held in

November 29, 2008. In the latest test, a total of 462 volunteers were registered and their actual attendance was 82.3% (380). They were divided into 3 groups and were tested in Tainan, Taichung, and Taipei, respectively. The backgrounds and scores of the subjects are as follows:

Table 2. Background of preliminary test volunteers (n = 462)

Occupation	Number	Percentage
Elementary school teachers	125	27.1%
Teaching assistants in elementary schools	151	32.7%
General publics	69	14.9%
Professional in Taiwanese	14	3.0%
Students	75	16.2%
Others	28	6.1%
Total	462	100%

Table 3. Mean scores of the preliminary test-takers (n = 380)

Sections	N*	Means	Max.	s.d.
Reading	378	109.25	180	24.81
(a) Vocabulary and grammar	378	69.50	108	16.55
(b) Reading comprehension	378	39.75	72	12.71
Listening	380	79.29	120	17.89
(a) Conversations	380	52.29	72	11.15
(b) Talks and lectures	380	27.01	48	9.45
Dictation	380	54.30	80	23.27
Speaking	365	82.89	120	18.80
(a) Picture telling	365	30.25	40	6.45
(b) Oral readings	365	25.00	40	7.59
(c) Oral expressions	365	27.64	40	7.43
Total	363	327.99	500	61.30

* N is the actual number completed for each section.

As mentioned earlier, the TPT is a criterion-reference test (CRT). Therefore, CRT statistical approach should be employed for the TPT. However, the subjects for the preliminary tests were not from the same group. In addition, there was no course given to the subjects to distinguish pre-test and post-test scores. Consequently, norm-referenced (NRT) statistic approach was adopted for the researchers' reference. Readers should be cautious of the statistical differences between CRT and NRT.[6]

The reliability of test was calculated according to Cronbach's α. The results show that internal consistency of the reading section is 0.827, and listening section is 0.771. The overall Cronbach's α for both reading and listening tests is 0.873. These figures show that the items in the TPT listening and reading tests were highly reliable and consistent.

Item facility (IF), also called item difficulty, was calculated according the following formulas:

IF = Ncorrect / Ntotal

Ncorrect = number of subjects who answered correctly

Ntotal = number of subjects taking the test

A P value was further calculated and adapted as an item facility index based on the following formulas:

P = (IFupper + IFlower)/2

IFupper = item facility for the upper group (1/3 of the total) on the whole test

IFlower = item facility for the lower group (1/3 of the total) on the whole test

In addition to P value, Δ value was also calculated in accordance with Fan's item analysis table for readers' reference (Fan 1952).

As for the item discrimination (ID) index, it was calculated by subtracting the IF for the lower group from the IF for the upper group as follows (Brown and Hudson 2002:116-118):

ID = IFupper − IFlower

Item facility and discrimination statistics are listed in Table 4, Table 5 and Table 6. Values in Table 4 were calculated for both reading and listening tests for readers' overall view of the TPT. For the p value, the smaller the value the more difficult it is. As for the Δ value, the higher the value the more difficult it is. So, it is expected that the p value should decrease and the Δ value should increase, from A1 to C2. However, the results showed some exceptions. For example, in Table 4, the p value of B2 is unexpectedly higher than B1. Nevertheless, if we

---

[6] For the differences, readers may refer to Brown and Hudson (2002).

reduce the levels to only three, the p value will decrease from A to C. The results reveal some possibilities: 1) the test items in the preliminary test were good enough to distinguish three rather than six levels, or 2) it was the results of statistical errors since the average number of test items in each level was only sixteen. The statistical results might be improved if the number of test items was increased. Further investigation is needed to find the answer.

Item discrimination (ID) index and difference index [7] (DI) are usually calculated for norm-referenced tests and criterion-referenced tests, respectively (Brown at al., 2002). In Table 4, the ID values range from 0.16 to 0.30, with an average of 0.22. The reason for not having a high ID could be that the Taiwanese language ability of the preliminary test volunteers was rather even. According to my observation, only persons who possess a sufficient level of ability in Taiwanese were willing to take the test. Although the ID values are not considered high, it does not mean that the test items were invalid. If we regard the upper group (1/3 of the total) as mastery-level speakers, and the lower group (1/3 of the total) as non-mastery-level speakers, the DI value could be the same as ID value. If so, most ID values of Table 4 are higher than 0.20, which are considered acceptable.

Table 4. Item facility and discrimination statistics
on both reading and listening tests

Levels	Item facility index		Item discrimination index
	P	Δ	ID
C2	0.48	13.21	0.26
C1	0.63	11.63	0.30
B2	0.80	9.63	0.26
B1	0.74	10.49	0.22
A2	0.92	7.35	0.13
A1	0.89	8.06	0.16

---

[7] The difference index is calculated by subtracting the proportion of the non-mastery group answering the item correctly from the proportion of the mastery group answering the item correctly (Brown et al. 2002:120). Difference index of 0.20 and above is considered acceptable (Brown et al. 2002:122).

Table 5. Item facility and discrimination statistics on reading tests

Levels	Item facility index		Item discrimination index
	P	Δ	ID
C2	0.47	13.32	0.30
C1	0.64	11.59	0.30
B2	0.77	10.09	0.33
B1	0.67	11.19	0.25
A2	0.91	7.75	0.17
A1	0.88	8.26	0.17

Table 6. Item facility and discrimination statistics on listening tests

Levels	Item facility index		Item discrimination index
	P	Δ	ID
C2	0.50	13.03	0.19
C1	0.63	11.71	0.30
B2	0.86	8.73	0.15
B1	0.84	9.04	0.17
A2	0.93	6.88	0.08
A1	0.90	7.85	0.15

In the design of TPT, test-takers take test once and they are assigned a language level according to their scores. Therefore, it is necessary to investigate the relation between scores and language levels. The relation was calculated by our team members by running ordinal logistic regression based on the testing results of sampled test-takers (Chang, Tu and Chang 2009).

For this analysis, data were taken from 160 sampled test-takers, who were included in the 462 volunteers and participated in the preliminary test. Prior to the preliminary test, the sampled test-takers were interviewed by five researchers of the research team and assigned language levels in accordance with the CEF criteria. It would be much better if we could interview all 462 volunteers. However, due to the project's time limitation, only 160 were interviewed. The sampled test-takers play an important role in running the ordinal logistic regression. We need to use the scores of test-takers to double check whether or not the test items are valid for differentiating language levels.

The number of these sampled test-takers who are at different proficiency levels is listed in Table 7. Their mean scores are listed in Table 8 and figured in Figure 1. Figure 1 shows our expectation that the scores in all sections significantly increase from A1 to C2. Among the four sections, the listening has the feature of low slope. After rechecking the testing procedure and test-takers' background, we found the potential factors as follows: In the listening test, the test-takers were told to listen to the recorded passage and then mark their answers on a computer formatted answer sheet with a B2 pencil. No extra writing paper of the answer choices was provided. It was not an easy job for the elderly test-takers to complete the listening test in such conditions[8]. We further checked their scores and found that the older test-takers were more likely to have lower listening scores than reading scores. In contrast, the collegian test-takers who are familiar with testing skills are more likely to have better listening scores. To solve this problem, an extra sheet of writing paper for working out answer choices was provided and the test-takers were allowed to make any notes on it in the first official test in November 2009.

Table 7. Sampled test-takers of different levels

levels	C2	C1	B2	B1	A2	A1	Total
N	8	23	38	39	20	32	160*

* The actual number attended and completed the test is 130

Table 8. Mean scores of sampled test-takers

Levels		Reading	Listening	Dictation	Speaking	Total
C2	mean	148.60	102.40	76.18	101.20	428.38
	s.d.	9.53	3.58	2.70	6.53	13.56
C1	mean	136.81	92.76	71.00	97.95	398.53
	s.d.	8.42	13.62	9.10	9.92	18.89
B2	mean	121.18	79.89	67.39	91.68	360.14
	s.d.	7.96	14.81	11.60	12.80	18.92
B1	mean	105.56	76.22	51.17	80.82	313.77
	s.d.	14.03	21.67	21.93	15.44	26.84
A2	mean	84.37	72.70	41.34	67.11	265.51
	s.d.	20.57	18.90	21.41	17.65	34.38
A1	mean	71.29	64	23.08	41.43	199.79
	s.d.	21.87	12.82	16.81	13.88	43.57
Total	mean	107.05	78.56	53.53	79.30	318.45
	s.d.	27.04	19.30	23.15	22.29	69.58

---

[8] Among the test-takers, their age ranges from 77 to 10, and the average age is 42.

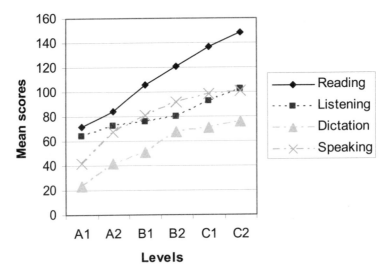

Figure 1. Mean scores of sampled test-takers.

The probabilities of the sampled test-takers' language levels were calculated according to their scores by using ordinal logistic regression as shown in Figure 2. For example, the node of the two left-most curves is 220. If a sampled test-taker receives a grade less than 220, s/he is more likely to be regarded as A1 level. In contrast, if s/he receives a score between 220 and 290 (the node between the second and third curve), s/he is more likely to be A2 level.

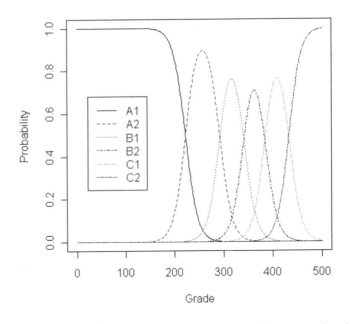

Figure 2. Probability of sampled test-takers' language levels.

According to the results of ordinal logistic regression, the nodes between the curves are 220, 290, 340, 380, and 430, respectively. They are treated as the boundary scores between different language levels, as shown in Table 9.

As for the minimum scores of A1, the range (70=290-220) between A2 and A1 is treated as the range between A1 and zero levels. Therefore, the minimum scores of A1 is 150 (=220-70).

Table 9. Contrasts between scores and language levels

Levels	Scores
C2 Mastery	$430 < scores \leqq 500$
C1 Effective Operational Proficiency	$380 < scores \leqq 430$
B2 Vantage	$340 < scores \leqq 380$
B1 Threshold	$290 < scores \leqq 340$
A2 Waystage	$220 < scores \leqq 290$
A1 Breakthrough	$150 < scores \leqq 220$

The accuracy of rating scale of language levels on scores was calculated and obtained 0.68 (=(9+18+21+22+15+3)/130), as shown in Table 10. The number of sampled test-takers of different language levels assigned in advance by the researchers was listed in the column "total." The row "total" is the forecasted number of different language levels according to the scores after test of sampled test-takers. For example, in the column of A1, 4 subjects who were evaluated as A2 level before test, were forecasted to be in the A1 level according to their scores after test. In the same column, 9 subjects were graded as A1 both before and after test. The results reveal that TPT's judgment on subjects' language levels reach a

0.68 accuracy, which is much higher than the probability 0.17 (=1/6) by guessing.

Table 10. Cross table of assigned and forecasted language levels

assigned	Forecasted levels by actual scores						total
	A1	A2	B1	B2	C1	C2	
C2	0	0	0	0	2	3	5
C1	0	0	0	6	15	0	21
B2	0	0	4	22	2	0	28
B1	0	8	21	3	0	0	32
A2	4	18	8	0	0	0	30
A1	9	5	0	0	0	0	14
total	13	31	33	31	19	3	130

In the TPT, a test-taker will be assigned a language level only if s/he completed all four sections of the tests. When the same scoring scheme was applied to all the subjects who participated in the preliminary test in November 2008, the results reveal that 46.32% of the subjects received level B2 or higher (see Table 11). This result meets the expectation as B2 is the recommended level by CTLT as the minimum Taiwanese ability requirement for teaching Taiwanese in elementary schools.

Table 11. Levels obtained by all subjects

Levels	N	%	Accumulated %
C2	6	1.58	1.58
C1	62	16.32	17.90
B2	108	28.42	46.32
B1	98	25.79	72.11
A2	73	19.21	91.32
A1	26	6.84	98.16
Less than A1	7	1.84	100
total	380	100	

5. Conclusion

The Taiwanese Proficiency Test (TPT) is a newly developed language testing scheme for educational purpose. In the test, test-takers are assigned a language level according to the scores they receive. The relation between the language levels and scores is calculated based on the statistical results of 160 sampled test-takers by using ordinal logistic regression. Its accuracy for predicting test-takers' language levels reaches as high as 0.68. The accuracy may not be perfect. However, it probably is the best under time and resource constraints. The first official TPT was held by the CTLT with a total of 793 test-takers on November 14, 2009. In addition, more trial tests are proposed to be conducted later. Accuracy is expected to improve gradually with the employment of official and trial tests in the near future. Hopefully, the TPT will benefit to the teaching of Taiwanese language, and it will further empower the revival of Taiwanese.

Acknowledgments

This paper is a result of research project (period: 2008.4.17-2009.4.16) sponsored by the National Languages Committee of Taiwan's Ministry of Education. As the coordinator of the project, I am indebted to all participants who were involved in the research project. The TPT would not come true without their contributions. This is an updated revision of the article with same title originally published in 2010 Journal of Taiwanese Vernacular 2(2), 82-103.

References

Brown, James D. and Hudson, Thom. 2002. *Criterion-referenced language testing.* Cambridge: Cambridge University Press.

Chan, Hui-Chen. 1994. *Language shift in Taiwan: social and political determinants.* Ph.D. dissertation: Georgetown University.

Chang, L. C., Tu, Y. H., and Chang, S. M. 2009. 統計方法於試題研發之應用 [Statistic Approaches for the Taiwanese Proficiency Test]. Proceedings of the Second Conference on Taiwanese Proficiency Test (March). Tainan, Taiwan: National Cheng Kung University.

Cheng, Robert L. 1996. 民主化政治目標 kap 語言政策 [Democracy and language policy]. In C. H. Si, pp.21-50.

Chiung, Wi-vun T. 2001. Language attitudes toward written Taiwanese. *Journal of Multilingual and Multicultural Development*, 22(6), pp.502-523.

Chiung, Wi-vun T. 2006. 全民台檢第一擺試考結果統計分析 [Statistical analysis of the first GTPT preliminary test]. Proceedings of the First Conference on Taiwanese Proficiency Test (December). Tainan, Taiwan: Tainan Theological College and Seminary.

Fan, C. T. 1952. *Item analysis table.* Princeton: Educational Testing Service.

Hsiau, A-chin. 1997. Language ideology in Taiwan: the KMT's language policy, the Tai-yu language movement, and ethnic politics. *Journal of Multilingual and Multicultural Development* 18(4), pp.302-315.

Huang, Shuan F. 1993. 語言社會與族群意識 [*Language, Society, and Ethnic Identity*]. Taipei: Crane.

Kerr, George H. 1992. 被出賣的台灣 [*Formosa Betrayed*]. Taipei: Chian-ui Press.

McNamara, Tim. 2000. *Language testing*. Oxford: Oxford University Press.

Ong, Iok-tek. 1993. 台灣苦悶的歷史 [*Taiwan: a depressed history*]. Taipei: Independence Press.

Peng, Ming M. and Ng, Yuzin C. 1995. 台灣在國際法上的地位 [*The legal status of Taiwan*]. Taipei: Taiwan Interminds Publishing Inc.

Si, Cheng-hong. (ed.). 1996. 語言政治與政策 [*Linguistic politics and policy*]. Taipei: Chian-ui.

Su, Beng. 1980. 台灣四百年史 [*Taiwan's 400 year history*]. San Jose: Paradise Culture Associates.

Teng, Hong-tin, Tan, Le-kun., Goo, Jin-sek., Lim, Ju-khai., Ho, Sin-han., and Chiung, Wi-vun. 2006. 全民台語能力檢定測驗規劃 ê 現況 [A survey on current General Taiwanese Proficiency Test]. Proceedings of the First Conference on Taiwanese Proficiency Test (December, pp.53-63). Tainan, Taiwan: Tainan Theological College and Seminary.

Tiuⁿ, Juhong. 1996. 台灣現行語言政策動機 ê 分析 [An analysis on the Taiwan's current language policy]. In Cheng-hong Si, pp. 85-106.

Young, Russell. 1988. Language maintenance and language shift in Taiwan. *Journal of Multilingual and Multicultural Development* 9(4), pp.323-338.

INDEX

About the Author

The author Wi-vun Taiffalo Chiung (a.k.a. Tưởng Vi Văn in Vietnamese, Chiúⁿ Ûi-bûn in Taiwanese, and 蔣為文 in Han characters) obtained his Ph.D degree in linguistics from the University of Texas at Arlington. He is professor of linguistics in the Department of Taiwanese Literature at the National Cheng Kung University in Taiwan. He is also the director of Center for Vietnamese Studies at NCKU. His major research languages include Taiwanese and Vietnamese. His research fields are sociolinguistics and applied linguistics. Currently, he is interested in the relevant studies of language and orthography reforms in Hanji cultural areas, including Taiwan, Vietnam, Korea, Japan, and China.

Về tác giả

Tác giả Wi-vun Taiffalo Chiung (tên tiếng Việt: Tưởng Vi Văn) là tiến sĩ Ngôn ngữ học tại Đại học Texas-Arlington Mỹ. Hiện nay là Giáo sư Khoa Văn học Đài Loan, và giám đốc Trung tâm Nghiên cứu Việt Nam, Đại học Quốc gia Thành Công, Đài Loan. Ông chuyên nghiên cứu, so sánh đối chiếu giữa tiếng Đài và tiếng Việt.